Critical praise for Susanna Kaysen

"Susanna Kaysen possesses a lyrical wryness that splendidly evokes . . . all the scents and unnamed sadnesses that lay claim to memory and give us reason to go on."
　　　　　　　　　—Boston Globe

"Kaysen's strong point is her language—lyrical, precise, and at times self-mocking, the language of someone for whom words must be an end in themselves. The sensibility is poetic, descriptions bordering on the virtuoso."

　　　　　　—Village Voice

"Luminous."
　　　　　—San Francisco Chronicle

Asa, as I Knew Him

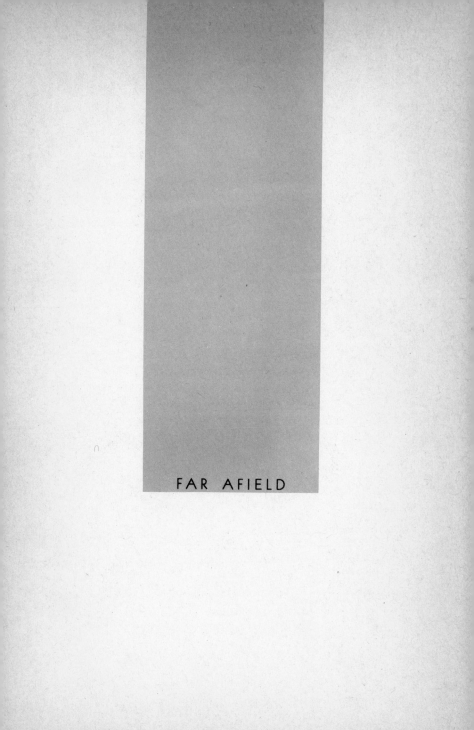

FAR AFIELD

FAR AFIELD

Susanna Kaysen

VINTAGE CONTEMPORARIES
VINTAGE BOOKS
A DIVISION OF RANDOM HOUSE, INC.
NEW YORK

I am grateful to the MacDowell Colony, Inc., and the
Artists Foundation of Massachusetts for their generosity,
and to Jay Wylie for starting me on this long journey.

A VINTAGE CONTEMPORARIES ORIGINAL, OCTOBER 1990
FIRST EDITION

Copyright © 1990 by Susanna Kaysen
Map copyright © 1990 by Maura Fadden Rosenthal

Library of Congress Cataloging-in-Publication Data
Kaysen, Susanna, 1948–
Far afield / Susanna Kaysen.—1st ed.
p.   cm.—(A Vintage contemporaries original)
ISBN 0-394-75822-6
I. Title.
PS3561.A893F37 1990   89-21538
813′.54—dc20   CIP

Book design by Maura Fadden Rosenthal

Manufactured in the United States of America
10 9 8 7 6 5 4 3 2 1

For Annette and Carl

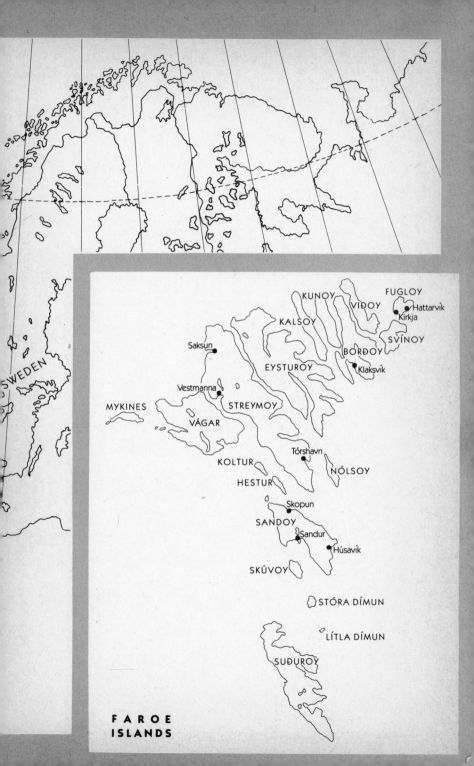

SWEDEN

KUNOY
FUGLOY
VIĐOY
KALSOY
Hattarvík
Kirkja
Saksun
SVÍNOY
EYSTUROY
BORĐOY
Klaksvík
Vestmanna
MYKINES
STREYMOY
VÁGAR
KOLTUR
Tórshavn
NÓLSOY
HESTUR
Skopun
SANDOY
Sandur
Húsavík
SKÚVOY
STÓRA DÍMUN
LÍTLA DÍMUN
SUĐUROY

**FAROE
ISLANDS**

CONTENTS

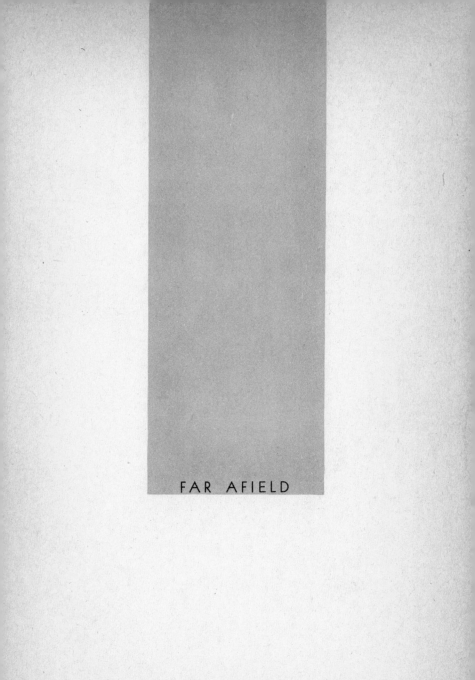

FAR AFIELD

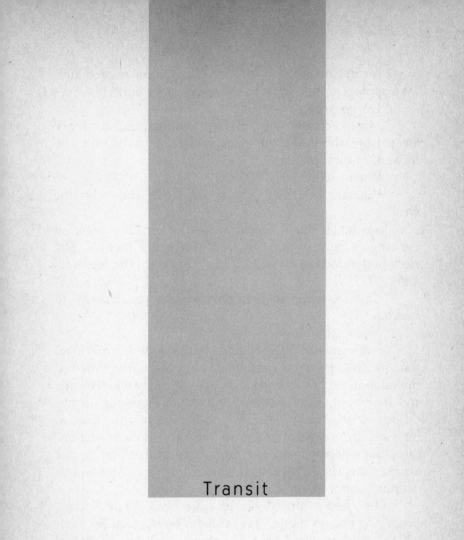

Transit

Jonathan was in the Reykjavík Airport with his passport and travelers' checks in his jacket pocket, his Icelandair ticket with baggage claim checks attached in his shirt pocket, and no baggage at all.

"It's in Copenhagen, sir," the ticket clerk assured him. "We apologize, but in fact it happens quite normally."

"Do you *know* it's there?"

"Most certainly it is." When Jonathan did not move away from the desk, the clerk said, "You wish it to be forwarded to your hotel?"

"When will it arrive?"

"Within a few days. Yes, certainly. By the end of the week."

Jonathan's shirt, which smelled of airplane, took on the tang of fresh sweat at this. "It won't do," he said. The clerk pretended not to understand. "I'm only staying over-night."

"You are going to London? We can also forward to London."

"No, to the Faroes."

In the months before his departure from Cambridge, Jonathan had grown accustomed to the glaze that followed this announcement and had learned to be ready with latitude and longitude, brief history, population statistics, justifi-cations—particularly these, which had been worn thin, to his ears, in conversations with the professors of the an-thropology department. He did not expect that here, in the closest thing the archipelago had to a neighbor. And he was definitely unprepared for derision.

The clerk widened his ice-blue eyes. "The Faroes! People do not go there." He issued a strange smile. "You are an ornithologist?" Jonathan shook his head. "There is nothing there," said the clerk. To prove his point he turned his back on Jonathan.

"But you will forward there?" Jonathan noticed he was taking on the clerk's lilting cadence. "Will you?"

"There is only one plane a week."

"No, there are two." This information had cost Jon-athan forty dollars in transatlantic phone calls, and he was proud of it.

But Scandinavians do not like to be contradicted. "The next plane is on the following Tuesday," the clerk said. "We can forward on that."

It was Wednesday. His plane to the Faroes left Thursday afternoon from this airport; he had a ticket inside his passport. "Well, do that," he said. "Forward on the plane next week." He wrote his hotel in block letters on a paper from the spiral-bound notebook kept at the ready in his jacket pocket. "Here. The Seaman's Home, in Tórshavn. Jonathan Brand."

"You should consider changing your reservation to the Hafnia."

"Oh, Christ," said Jonathan.

"Pardon?"

"Nothing. Where do I get the bus into town?"

The clerk leaned over his desk and pointed to the left. Then he said, "Excuse me, sir, but how long are you planning to stay in the Faroes, in the event that your luggage arrives after the following Tuesday and we cannot forward until the week succeeding?"

"Don't worry." Jonathan had the small pleasure of turning his back on the clerk. Over his shoulder he said, "I'll be there for a year."

In the bus he stayed awake only long enough to determine that Iceland looked like the moon, or maybe Mars. The terrain—he couldn't call it earth because it seemed to be lava—was red and rippled as if frozen in mid-flow. Deposited at his hotel, he trudged down a clean bare corridor to a clean bare room where a white eiderdown puff occupied his bed. Jonathan got underneath it and slept for twelve hours.

He woke shortly before midnight, hungry and hot. A sulfurous atmosphere pervaded the room, along with a weak but insistent streetlight. Was someone banging on the door? He sat up to sort all this out. None of it was as it seemed: the banging and the sulfur were both emanations of the radiator. Sulfur springs, he remembered, provided heat to Iceland. He put his hand on the white iron and got a burn and a bang for a reprimand. As for the streetlight, it was everybody's favorite northern fantasy, the midnight sun. A tired-looking item, it perched above a corrugated tin roof across the street, pale pink, flat, smaller than a moon.

Food, he decided—although he also wanted, with equal fervor, a shower, clean clothes, darkness, and the rustling of leaves at night in warm, moist Cambridge.

Nobody was at the front desk. A teenager was sleeping in a chair beside the hotel entrance, though, so Jonathan approached him and coughed. He didn't wake. "Ahem," said Jonathan. "Hey." He touched the boy's arm.

"*Rrrrn*," said the boy. Then he said some irritated things in Icelandic, which Jonathan hadn't learned because it had been difficult enough to learn Faroese. But the gist was clear.

"Food." Jonathan pointed to his mouth. "Hungry." He tried the Faroese word for hungry, and the boy laughed.

"No, no, no," he said. "English? You English?" Then: "No eating now here."

"But I must."

"I brother he fishing in Liverpool."

Jonathan nodded. "Bread," he said, chewing his finger. He ran through his entire repertoire of food in Faroese: potatoes, soup, cheese, fish, and meat. Fruit and vegetables were not available there.

"I Lars. I brother he fishing in Newfoundland."

"You said Liverpool."

"I Lars."

"Johan." This was Jonathan's first opportunity to use his new name.

"Johan." Lars put out his clean Icelandic hand. "Be." He indicated the floor a few times with his forefinger, and Jonathan decided he was being told to wait. Lars went away, behind the front desk. For the few minutes he was gone,

Jonathan stared out the hotel's glass door at the lurid light on the street. The shadows of the buildings were long and faint, like the light of the sun. A group of boys about Lars's age tumbled into view around a corner, drunk, silent with concentration on staying upright, all with their eyes closed. They were wearing Nike running shoes. Jonathan thought of the stories he'd heard around the anthropology department of Bushmen in Bermuda shorts, Sarawak chieftains with transistors pressed to their bone-bedecked ears; Nikes on white men were less jarring, maybe, but still he felt cheated.

Lars came back with his hands full: a beer, half a loaf of bread, a hunk of cheese, a pyramidal cardboard container. He shook this last in front of Jonathan's nose and said, "Excellent."

"*Hvat?*" What? But why ask, as the answer would be incomprehensible. It was.

"*Skyr.*" Lars summoned from his depths an English equivalent: "Yaaoort." He tugged rhythmically on an invisible object. Jonathan's mouth was full of saliva. He grabbed the bread. Lars held on to the beer and resumed his seat by the door.

Jonathan alternated bites of bread with bites of cheese. He didn't understand how to open the "excellent" container, so left it alone. Lars gurgled his beer slowly. The sunlight changed color, taking on a twilight blueness that comforted Jonathan because it reminded him of the earth, whereas the true midnight sun had been extraterrestrial in aspect. Lars opened the container for him by revealing a little hole hidden under a tab near one of the points. It was yogurt—a delicate, sweet yogurt as different from American yogurt as the Icelandic sun was from the sun that shone on Boston. Jonathan leaned against the wall drinking yogurt, entirely happy.

"Thank you, Lars," he said, and repeated "*Manga tak*," which was perceived as the native language in Iceland, Denmark, Sweden, Norway, and the Faroes. "I'm going to sleep now."

"No sleep," said Lars, smiling and shaking his head.

Too tired to argue or pursue it—was this a warning, an order, a prediction?—Jonathan went off down the corridor and got back under his puff.

It was a prediction, and accurate. The problem was the sun. Jonathan had reset his watch when he landed in Iceland, while waiting for his baggage to arrive, so one-thirty in the morning was correct. Nine-thirty at night in the U.S.A. The sun, now a normal sunlike yellow, had nothing to do with either of these times. And there were no curtains. Unbelievable, unbelievable. Jonathan shook his head and poked in drawers for a blanket to drape over the window, but no, there was no need for a blanket because of the eiderdown, which was much too hot to get under, what with the sun and the sulfurous energy of the unstoppable radiator—he was ready to cry. He sat on the bed and cried. He cried for his lost baggage, his mind, which he would also lose if he didn't get more sleep, and his home, which already was but a speck across the ocean and whose balmy, tree-lined, predictable shore he would not see again for a year.

When he woke up, it was dark. His watch, resting on the pillow next to him, said ten-thirty. The room was gray and cool, the radiator quiet. His head was clear. He sat up in bed, wrapped in the puff, and made a list in his notebook.

Shirt, pants, socks. A sweater? He made his way to the window, somewhat hampered by his wrapping. The day was chilled by a mist that had put out the sun. A sweater would be wise. There were many sweaters in his suitcase. And his vitamins, his paprika, his framed photograph of the pine woods on Mount Desert, which he'd taken along as a savage would bundle up his wooden ancestors when setting out on a journey. And his Mallory, his late Dickens, his thermal underwear, his dehydrated vegetable soup: everything he'd considered necessary for a year in the bush.

You can get through a week, he said to himself. But the idea had been that he could not, that these things were essential to life. If this turned out not to be true, perhaps they would never show up, knowing themselves to be extraneous. Do not anthropomorphize, Jonathan told himself. He loved to tell himself this (it was an order he needed to give often), because the next thought, that he was the anthropomorphizing anthropologist, inevitably followed and made him laugh.

However, he didn't laugh. He added *sweater* to his list and put himself into the shower, which smelled exactly like Hell. Fragrant with brimstone, swatting at his thighs with a tiny towel, he scribbled *soap, shampoo, toothbrush* on his list.

Two hours later, congratulating himself on his intelligence in adding a small bag to his purchases, Jonathan stood at the untended front desk of the hotel listing to the left with his bundles and hoping for Lars. He did this for five minutes before he noticed a bell near the ledger. He was about to ring it when a woman who looked to be Lars's mother came out from behind a chintz curtain.

"Please?" she said.

"Good day," said Jonathan, to gain time and to explore her English.

"Is it you the American who is traveling to the Faroes?"

"I am." News traveled faster than he did, apparently. He had told only the ticket clerk at the airport.

"Please. The weather. You will not go today."

Language difficulties again obscured the mood of this sentence: was he being threatened, informed, or pleaded with? Rain had started while he'd been shopping, but rain didn't deter planes in America. "I don't understand," he said.

"Please. My husband speaks better." She went behind

the curtain and was replaced shortly by Lars in thirty years, or herself as a man.

He was a man to inspire confidence. The blondness, the icy eyes, the chiseled features that on a woman or a boy were eerie and a little blank, on this man combined to create an ideal type. Miles of sea and years of horizons were in his eyes, untold yards of nets had passed through his hands, and every wind on earth had burnished his skin to a fine gold hue. Carved in wood, he could have been the figure-head on the first ship of the Viking fleet; in bronze, the statue in the city square.

"You can't go today, lad," he said. He sounded exactly like Paul McCartney. "You see, they haven't any radar, and it's a rough landing there, rough winds over there, so you'll have to wait till it lifts up. The weather." He gestured at the ceiling. "It'll lift, in a day or two."

"No radar," said Jonathan, but more to keep him talking than to comment.

"You'd do better on a boat," he conceded. "Do you like the sea?" He looked Jonathan up and down. "There's many as can't be on it."

"Oh, I like it," said Jonathan. He thought of the ferry out to the Cranberry Isles, with the black-backed gulls screaming at the cormorants, the comforting chug of the engine in the effervescence of July waves.

"Well, now, I could find you a boat."

"I have my plane ticket." Jonathan felt courage ebbing. After all, the Faroes lay hundreds of miles away over empty, open Atlantic. "How will I know, though, when I can leave?"

"I'll tell you." The hotelkeeper smiled, which brought brown wrinkles to his gilded face.

And how, Jonathan wondered, would he know? And what was he to do with himself in the meantime? He'd seen all of Reykjavík in his shopping spree; he couldn't imagine occupying himself there for two days. Some of this must have shown in his face, because the modern Viking put a large hand on his arm and said, "Come into the dining room and have some lunch, lad. There'll be the time to make your plans after you eat."

As Jonathan followed his host into the dining room, he wondered how to make him stay and talk; his voice was soothing, and Jonathan felt the lack of company. But was it proper for a guest to invite a hotelkeeper to lunch? And who would pay? The etiquette of this situation would have been daunting in America; here it was impenetrable. Jonathan resigned himself to ordering something awful out of ignorance and eating it alone. But the Viking drew up a chair for himself and spoke quickly to Lars, who had come to the table to take their order. Seeing them together, Jonathan was sure they were father and son.

"Herring in brine, herring in cream, herring with salt only. Salt cod—you may not like this. White bread for you. Americans eat only white bread, isn't it so? Russian salad"—this was a bowl of chopped carrots and potatoes, swimming in what looked like mayonnaise—"soup of cod. Here's a sausage from the butcher next door, *skyr*—you had that last night, excellent—and here's some jam, lingonberry, very nice, from Sweden."

Under his host's benevolent ice gaze, Jonathan tried everything. Most of it was palatable, though the salt cod was indeed not to his liking: tough, more like an old piece of rope than food. The herrings in their various dressings were wonderful. He alternated between bread with herring and bread with jam, moistening himself with cod soup now and then. There was nothing to drink. Toward the end of the meal Lars carried two cups of tea, black as night in America, to the table.

And through all this the innkeeper talked.

"I shipped out of Liverpool fifteen years. That's where I learned your language. We went all the way round the Cape of Good Hope, but I spent most of my life in these

waters. The fishing's best here, in the north. Up by Spitzbergen it's fine. Up there's it's sun all the time. You'd see
it high and full all hours of the summer, not like it is here.
It's a brave sun up there. And you're an ornithologist going
to the Faroes."

Jonathan shook his head, but his mouth was too full
to contradict.

"You'll find plenty of birds up there. Why, it's a sports-
man's paradise. My mother was from there. Klaksvík. My
father shipped over there and he got caught in a storm. Lots
of bad storms off Klaksvík. He had to put up for weeks.
He was in her house waiting for the weather to shift off.
So he sent for her, when he got home. That was nearly a
year later. And she came. Never saw the Faroes again. But
she thought of it, I could see. She'd stand on the dock of
a time and look out. She never went back, even when her
mother died. I've been there." He stopped and looked intently at Jonathan. "It's a drear place, you know. But there's
something in it. Makes it hard to forget. Bad weather. All
the time!" He laughed and wiped his mouth.

"But it's a hard life, fishing," he went on. Jonathan,
mouth open, had been about to clear up the ornithology
confusion. "Hard life for a boy, harder for a man. You work
all the time. Where there's always sun, there's no sleep.
Fifteen years was enough for one man's life. I'm on the land
now, in my home." He surveyed his dining room. "But
Lars, he wants to see the world. I've told him, you'll see
only ocean. You'll see waves and more of them. But the
young don't listen to the old—or else, where would we be?
If they listened to us, time would have stopped long ago."

Jonathan's ears tingled. This had the ring of authentic
folk wisdom. He repeated it to himself. It justified his persisting in going to the Faroes against all his professors' pro-
tests that this was not a foreign culture; youth paves the
way to the future. But was he young enough to qualify as

"youth"? Since he'd passed twenty-five, the year before, Jonathan was prey to a sense of losing time, of moving too slowly. In bad moods he made depressing calculations about how old he'd be when he finished his thesis, which, depending on how bad the mood was, varied from twenty-eight to thirty-four.

"Johan," said the hotelkeeper, suddenly breaking off his narrative. "Johan, you are not an ornithologist, I think."

"No," admitted Jonathan. Now he felt revealed, as though he were a spy. "But how did you know?"

"Ornithologists look like birds. I've seen many of them. They come here to Iceland, and they all look like birds. You know, that'll happen with people and what they do, or their dogs, or their wives. I've seen husband and wife you can't tell apart. It's time as does it."

More folk wisdom. Jonathan decided to act like an anthropologist. "You know my name, but I don't know yours."

"Egil. Egil is a Faroese name, from my mother. It was her brother's name, who died in a storm once."

Was it possible to die twice in a storm? Jonathan feared it was. The whole world at this moment seemed a "drear place," with the rainy darkness now as oppressive as last night's low glare. Outside the dining room windows Reykjavík's main street was a solid, uninviting block of cement doubled by growing puddles on the tarmac.

"So. Are you a spy for the CIA?"

"Is that what I look like?" Jonathan had to laugh. This was too improbable, being taken for a spy in a dump of an Icelandic hotel. "I'm a student. I study"—here he paused, because he had formulated an exact description, and this was its inauguration—"I study the folkways, the things people do from the old days. If they still hunt whales and sing the old songs and dance."

"A spy," said Egil. "A spy into the past. Isn't it so?"

He laughed. Then he said, "These old ways, they are dead now. People don't want to think about these old ways now. You won't be getting much out of people on that score."

Jonathan had worried himself silly on this point for months already. "Maybe not here, in Iceland. But in the Faroes, they still dance and hunt whales. I know they do."

"Maybe so. Maybe they do." Egil nodded and poked at one of the dishes of herring. "And maybe they'll even talk to you of it. But maybe they'd rather be talking about progress, you know?" He popped a fat slice of herring into his mouth; Jonathan saw black stubs of molars marching back to his throat. "The Faroes are looking for their independence. They are thinking of their fish factories and their three-hundred-mile fishing limit and how to break from Denmark. They want"—here he couldn't cover a smile—"to have their own foreign policy."

"You have your own," Jonathan pointed out.

"The influence of Iceland on the world—it's like a mouse pissing into the ocean. And the Faroes! That's like a flea pissing. We are small countries." Egil's eyes narrowed. Was he looking at some large, influential country on a horizon Jonathan couldn't detect? "Small countries," he said again. "You know that small men make much of themselves."

"Like Napoleon?" The conversation seemed to be drifting away from Jonathan. He yawned. "I think I'm tired," he said. "I think I have to rest some more. I'm exhausted."

"Well, yes, you might be. And you've another long journey ahead of you. Rest up for it. You'll be leaving tomorrow, I think. These winds are shifting."

But winds in the north, though they rise up quickly, die down slowly, and two more days passed before Jonathan found himself again at the airport. His baggage had turned up in Copenhagen, the derisive ticket clerk told him, and would be arriving in the Faroes within the week. On his hotel bill, Jonathan had noticed, he'd been charged for half the lunch he'd eaten with Egil. Lars had accompanied him to the movies, where they'd seen *Serpico*. Lars and the rest of the audience said "Bang bang" at appropriate points in the action; this was clearly not the first time any of them had seen the film.

Overdoses of sleep, food, and Reykjavík had brought Jonathan to an expectant yet placid state of mind that seemed to him a good beginning to a journey. Long stretches of nothing-to-do had not activated a bad mood of the sort that had threatened during lunch with Egil. On the contrary, he had slipped into a tolerance of boredom that was nearly happiness.

This calm was useful in the airplane. Without doubt it was the most nerve-racking trip he had ever taken. The plane was a Fokker from World War Two converted to a passenger plane by the addition of ten unsteady rows of seats from a bus. The one stewardess hurtled up and down the aisle, a warning to all to stay in their places. Every fifteen minutes a pocket of air threw them down or flung them up, the sensation lasting many, many seconds more than any bump or drop Jonathan had experienced on the Eastern Shuttle. Many passengers prayed, some vomited.

After two hours of this the stewardess passed out tepid orange juice in paper cups and pieces of Wrigley's Spearmint Gum. The pilot's voice crackled from a loudspeaker— ridiculous, thought Jonathan; the cabin was so close the pilot could have talked to them over his shoulder.

In Faroese and Icelandic, he announced their imminent landing. For Jonathan's benefit, he repeated this in English. Then: "Would you be so good as to sit up straight with your seat belt around you, because I think it is going to be rough."

If the lurches of the rest of the trip had provoked no comment from the pilot, Jonathan did not like to imagine what "rough" meant. Crash landing on the ocean? Just let me see Mount Desert again, he said, too shy to address this request to anyone in particular.

He looked out the window: clouds, as there had been the whole time. Then came an especially deadly downward toppling, which overturned a number of juice glasses and provoked more vomiting behind him. Determined not to die, Jonathan stared fixedly out the window.

And below him, to prove he had been heard, the Faroes came into view. Long, soft, undulating, and green, great humps and valleys of land appeared. Above each height of land a crown of clouds poised white, its excess trailing down as mist to deep dips greener even than the tops. It was land ultimate, land eternal, huge and comforting, each piece defined by the ring of breakers at its edge, all stretched out on an ocean that, from this height, curved perceptibly with the globe's incline. The plane fell another thousand feet, and Jonathan saw a house, a bright red roof, a boat-dot on the vast green lawn that was the Faroes' salty front yard— then, in banging and darkness from another cloud, they landed, the engines screaming, the tires bumping and smoking. The pilot turned over his shoulder and said, *"Vælkomin til Føroyar."*

Admission

In the matter of his suitcase, Jonathan had passed through a number of the phases of grief: denial, in which he inquired after its arrival less and less hopefully from the desk clerk at the Seaman's Home; action, in which he besieged the Icelandair office in Tórshavn daily and oversaw the sending

of telexes to all cities in northern Europe; anger, in which
he wrote a stormy letter to the president of Icelandair and
stirred up small vortexes in the puddles on the street with
his tireless search for replacements for such banalities as
underpants and pads of paper—hoping to prove these unob-
tainable and thereby increase the amount of his reimburse-
ment from the airline. His success in this last effort was
small comfort. Like the rich man whose wealth cannot buy
him entrance to the kingdom of heaven, Jonathan loaded
down with kroner was still Jonathan with no access to what
he really wanted: his stuff.

After two weeks of this—fifteen days in which the
Faroes played only a cameo role, sod roofs and mysterious
cloud formations just the backdrop for his interior mono-
logue of frustration—he had come to a defeated acceptance.
The envelope full of fifty-kroner notes, passed across the
desk by Daniela of Icelandair, his telex co-author, had signaled the end of his resistance. Books, sweaters, little pieces
of home selected to buoy up a man during a long sojourn
in foreign parts, all had been distilled down to paper. The
patent inequivalency of the contents of the envelope and
the contents of his suitcase gave Jonathan a pang. It was
his first exposure to the reality of pricelessness.

Jonathan woke up one morning a rich man. His grant
for fieldwork had been enough to cover his airfare and a
few nights in a hotel—all spent in Iceland. He had two
thousand dollars from his parents, believers in higher education, and the bits of his teaching-assistant salary he'd
managed to squirrel away, though these didn't amount to
much. But he had calculated the Faroese economy to be
several centuries behind that of Cambridge and was sure
he could live his year in the minimalist style he'd grown
accustomed to as a graduate student. Now his loss, though
only several hundred dollars' worth, was in kroner enough
to keep him in the Hotel Hafnia of Tórshavn for half his
stay. Jonathan was practical, though, and, more than that,

in mourning. He remained at the Seaman's Home. He made a few preventive purchases—preventive in the sense of necessary and camouflaging. He had lost his American sweaters? Then he would have a Faroese sweater—and these were handmade and not cheap. He'd noticed that everyone wore black clogs with tire-tread soles against the streets' puddles and frequent lapses to mud; he bought some too. All the men wore old flannel shirts under their sweaters. He bought a flannel shirt, and he quickly made it old by wearing it every day for a week. With his blue eyes and his brown-tending-toward-blond hair he could pass for a native. He stared at himself in the rippled mirror on the wall of his small, mean room. An American abroad? A spy? An ornithologist, maybe? He ruffled his hair to give a more ornithological appearance.

There was so much money left he doubted he could ever spend it. Yet translated into the world beyond these islands, it was not enough to buy a round-trip ticket to England, where he could replace most of what he had lost. What he must do, therefore, was make friends and spend it on them.

It was time to make contact. Jonathan had one contact, from the professor who'd given him private instruction in Faroese. Professor Olsen was a Runic scholar, and an Old Norse scholar, and an Old Norseman himself. Norwegian, kindly, in a philological haze at his desk in Widener, he had for the year previous been Jonathan's only support. This was because he was not in the anthropology department. The anthropology department believed in snakes and wampum and tropical disease inoculations and the backwaters of Malaya. They did not believe in studying cultures that had newspapers, and the Faroes boasted seven newspapers, each the mouthpiece of a separate political party, one of which was edited by Professor Olsen's friend, Jonathan's contact, Eyvindur Poulsen.

But perhaps today he had other things to do? Jonathan

washed three of his four pairs of socks at his sink and hung them over the end of the bed. He didn't want to make contact. With all his money, he could disappear into the countryside, take a boat to the outermost island and hide, take a boat to the Hebrides and—how similar all these options were to each other and to the only choice he actually had. He was in the north, bounded by sea on all sides, pressed in by cloud cover, and here he would stay. He went downstairs to make contact by telephone.

Unlike telephones on the mainland of Europe, Faroese telephone was effective and prompt—rather American. Jonathan was talking to someone—*not* talking, that is—before he had time to prepare a speech. A woman was saying, "Hey, hey, hey?" Jonathan, befuddled, was thinking in French. "*Je cherche Eyvindur*," he snapped into the line. Then he blushed. Silence on the other end; he didn't blame her. His only concern was whether he had the courage to call back and attempt Faroese.

"Is it Jonathan?" a mighty voice boomed into his ear.

"*Oui, c'est moi.*" He realized that the only foreign language he had ever spoken over the phone was French. But that was no excuse. "Eyvindur—"

"You are coming for dinner?" This was in English.

"I couldn't—"

"You are coming for dinner. You like *spik*? You like it. Up the hill, number eight. You ask them. Congratulations on your departure."

"What time?"

"Number eight."

The phone was a sleek Danish model, streamlined to a lightweight black arc. Jonathan moved it from one ear to the other, but Eyvindur had gone. The desk clerk, who had listened to this multilingual exchange wide-eyed, said, in Faroese, "You are visiting Mr. Poulsen tonight? He lives on top of the hill above the sweater store. Number eight.

His house is the one with a sod roof. You are a reporter for the *New York Times?*"

"Something like that," said Jonathan wearily. He went back to his room to rehearse such phrases as "This is an excellent dinner" and "I would be grateful for your help in finding a house to live in."

Shortly before seven o'clock (the time Jonathan had decided he was expected), without flowers, a bottle of wine, or a letter of recommendation (first two unavailable in Tórshavn; third lost in his luggage), Jonathan set off into the evening to climb the hill to Eyvindur's house. The day's rain had given way to nearly warm sun that fell in long slats between the roofs and filled the bowl of the harbor with molten yellow foam. As he climbed upward, Jonathan's view of the town improved; from the crest of the hill Tórshavn achieved an almost Italian beauty, distance obscuring the messy winches of the fishing boats and revising to elegance the gnarled geometry of the streets. Could he come to love this view? He paused by a rock to consider. On closer investigation it relapsed to ugliness: an almost determined ugliness whose components were monotony of color (black, gray, dark green) and not enough monotony of form. Big new buildings loomed over small old buildings; shops with Danish Modern fronts of pale ash and plate glass stood next to black-painted stone houses. The twentieth century seemed to have squatted and left its spoor in an almost malevolently arbitrary path.

Jonathan knew he was a conservative in aesthetic matters, so he tried to reserve judgment on ugly, ill-planned Tórshavn. He was probably suffering some version of the anthropology department's reverence for "authenticity." Eighteenth-century Tórshavn would have found favor in his eyes: a string of low dark houses facing the harbor with windows shuttered against the cold. Bleak. Dreary. He thought of a sentence he'd read in a Danish guidebook to the Faroes: "The Faroese flora consist of approximately 300 varieties, many of which are moss." They were—he was— above the timberline. Not the timberline as Jonathan knew it, that point on a mountain marking the end of pine and the start of rock and scrub, but some larger, in fact, global, timberline. The Faroes did not support vegetable growth. Things grew down to some extent: potatoes, carrots, turnips. But things did not grow up. A sparse sort of privet struggled in front of a few houses, and outside of town he'd seen fields of angelica and Queen Anne's lace, but there wasn't a tree on the islands.

What a place! Jonathan sighed at the wonder and gloominess of it all. And it had begun to rain again. It was time for dinner.

Eyvindur had a brown goatee and was under forty. He was wearing an apron and holding a five- or six-year-old girl by the hand. "Jonathan," he crowed. "You are here. *Vælkomin*." He made a path through toys on the floor to the kitchen. "Here is Jonathan," he said to a woman who was feeding a smaller girl pieces of meat. "Anna," he said. "Anna and Jonathan."

Anna and Jonathan smiled wanly at each other. Jonathan could tell she didn't speak English; he was developing a sixth sense for that. Something about people's posture gave it away—a hunch, an apologetic slouch, a self-deprecatory, I-can't-communicate expression. In a fit of generosity Jonathan said, "Pleased to meet you," in Faroese. At this Eyvindur slapped the kitchen table.

"He speaks!"

"A little. Professor Olsen taught me what he knows."

"He knows nothing," said Eyvindur. "He is living in the tenth century. Anyhow, he is not Faroese." He waved his hand to brush Olsen away. "Marta"—pointing to the meat eater—"and little Anna." He lifted Little Anna's hand like a coach lifts a champion's. "You are married?"

"Uh . . ."

"Your wife, she didn't want to live up here in the middle of nowhere?"

"No, actually, I'm not."

"Good. You can marry a nice Faroese girl." Jonathan's face clouded. Eyvindur hit the table again. "You must forgive me. In reality, I am Italian. Anna is so disgusted with me because I do not behave. But tonight, for you, I will be very Faroese. We are eating *spik*. You know what's that?"

Anna reached into a cupboard and brought out a platter of gray slabs about three inches square. "Whale fat," she said in English, proud of her vocabulary. "With bread," she added.

"It's a joke," Eyvindur said. "We'll have a nice little smorgasbord. Traditional Danish evening meal. Traditionally, Faroese can't afford to eat in the evening. It's a joke."

Jonathan was befuddled. He had not expected wit, sophistication, jokes in near-perfect English. As he followed Eyvindur into the living room ("We'll leave Anna to her duties"), he wondered what exactly he had expected. According to Olsen, Eyvindur was a devoted Independence Party leader, ultranationalist, from whom Jonathan could learn everything about native culture and history. "Dedicated," Olsen had said, "to the preservation of the language and customs." And so Eyvindur had been cast in Jonathan's imagination as past fifty, pale, intent, consumed with his country's promise.

The living room walls were densely hung with large, dark, van Gogh-like paintings of houses and shorelines, all unframed. Jonathan did not like them, but he suspected that Eyvindur, or his wife, or his cousin had painted them and he felt under pressure to comment. "These pictures . . ." he offered.

"Yes. yes. You want to buy one?" Jonathan's money loomed in his conscience. "No. You cannot afford them. Now I am getting to be almost as famous as Ruth Smith."

"Who's that?"

"Ruth *Smith*. She was our"—Eyvindur was stymied here, but not for long—"our Great-Aunt Moses. Yes?"

"Grandma."

"Of course. She was that. She painted simple places, simple people, fishing, rain, just Faroese things. Very typical. Before, people tried to paint like Frenchmen—pink clouds all curled around. But we don't have those in the Faroes. You can imagine how stupid it was."

Jonathan hadn't an inkling. How exhausting he found these forays into alien culture. His mind would go flat and quiet. It didn't matter whether he was trying to buy socks or order lunch or find his way around town: a moment came when his concentration gave out. Human beings took the highest toll. Just the landscape and the smells of fish and motor oil and cold, rough sea were enough to force him back to his room at the Seaman's Home after a few hours. But here he was, and he'd been here only fifteen minutes, and Eyvindur was still talking. Jonathan pinched his thigh surreptitiously to restore sensation somewhere.

"I'm going to be on a stamp," Eyvindur was saying. "One like this." He moved toward a particularly dark and mysterious painting. "I sold it to the Parliament. It's there now. But it's like this, except it's bigger." He moved close to one of his windows and stared out into the pale amber evening of early summer. "This country," he said. "I have been to Italy. That's the way in which I found out that I was Italian. I am speaking in similes, of course. I went there to study painting. Do you know how surprising it was for me to go from here to there? Have you been there?"

Jonathan nodded. Hot, cramped, interminable trip from Paris to Rome in August, sharing his couchette with a self-confessed Fascist who missed the good old days; but the pots of oleander, the Alpine winds that cooled their passage, the gilded ceilings of churches and of noon—five days had been enough for him to know five years would not be enough. "How long were you there?" he asked.

"Two years. How I missed the Faroes! I suffered without the ocean. I went once, swimming somewhere on the Riviera. I had never swimmed before. You say swimmed?"

"Swum. Swim, swam, swum."

"I had never swam?"

"No. I swam, I have swum." Eyvindur scowled. "It's irregular," Jonathan said. "You just have to memorize it."

"Too many colors there, in Italy," Eyvindur went on. "But I stayed. I learned about all the colors. I learned to eat things I did not want to eat. Hah!" He pointed at Jonathan. "You will have to do the same."

"I guess so." Jonathan thought of the blocks of whale fat. Being forced to eat gnocchi didn't seem an equal hardship.

"There aren't enough rocks there," Eyvindur concluded, sitting down on his sofa beside a stuffed sheep.

Jonathan decided to take a different approach to the evening. He leaned forward. "Tell me about your political activities. Professor Olsen says you are an important figure in nationalist politics."

"Oh, I am bored with all of that. And you could never make sensibility of it. It's too complicated."

"But that's why I'm here."

"No. It's absurd. We are just pretending. I do it to make some trouble. In America you have baseball; we have politics. Who cares what we do here in this little country? You must study the old ways." He too leaned forward. "Study the dancing, study the stories, find the old people who are dying and ask them about the old ways. This politics, it's what we do to make ourselves feel real. You understand me?"

"No."

"Why are we getting all jazzed up—you say that, all jazzed up?"

"You can."

"All jazzied up about politics. We, the Faroese. It

doesn't matter what we decide. We teach Danish in the school, we don't teach Danish in the school; we get out of NATO, we stay in NATO—nobody knows. Nobody in the world knows anything about us."

"Jazzed," said Jonathan, "not jazzied."

"Okay. Jazzed. But you understand?"

"But self-determination?" Jonathan was the child of liberal parents.

Eyvindur lifted both his arms up and opened them, in the old gesture of offering, toward the window. "You see the sky? You see the ocean there? That is the Faroes. That is what we are. I paint that because that is what is very important and typical. And now"—his voice changed, became jaunty—"you will eat a very typical meal. I will describe everything. You must promise to try, even if you think it is nasty."

Jonathan felt uneasy making this promise. Professor Olsen's sole comment on current Faroese culture (in contrast to his lengthy and enthusiastic rhapsodies on Faroese philology) was a terse "What they eat! Oh, my God." But when in Rome: Jonathan squinted at Eyvindur, trying to imagine him in Rome. It was unimaginable. Jonathan had as yet no evidence of Eyvindur's Italianness. He was not what Jonathan had expected, but neither was he svelte, manifold of personality, perfected by centuries of social maneuvering and aesthetic supremacy. We are not in Rome, he told himself, but we are somewhere strange. I will eat whale fat.

Anna waited for them at the table; the girls had been put to bed. Several wooden boards were arranged diagonally in the center of the table. There were no forks and no glasses. Eyvindur pulled out a chair for Jonathan and began his inventory.

"*Spik*. Okay. This is whale blubber, and it's made with salt. That's how you preservate it. You scrape off the salt and you cut it thin and put it on bread. Also that's very good with *turrur fiskur*. Here's *turrur fiskur*." Eyvindur pointed at what Jonathan had figured to be a sort of napkin; it was white, shredded, and looked like clotted paper towel. "It's rotten fish, halibut is best. You hang it out and then it gets turned and then it gets fine like this."

"Turned?" asked Jonathan. He was determined to keep an anthropological stance.

"It gets softened by getting rotten but then it gets hard again. That's turned. It happens as well to meat. *Kjøt*. That's *kjøt*." What was indicated was a board containing small pieces of wood, possibly cherry, Jonathan had thought.

"What is it?" he asked.

"It's lamb. You hang it out and it gets soft. First it gets maggots. But they die. Then it's soft, then it's hard, after six months it gets really fine. Like this. Then you can keep it all year. It's very good with butter, but it's very good without too. Now here, this; it's *grind*. You know *grind*, of course."

Jonathan did know *grind*. *Grind* had been the determining factor in coming here. *Grind* was whale. *Grind* was whale meat, and schools of whale flashing in the sea, and the killing of whales by driving them onto beaches and attacking them with knives and then dancing medieval snaking lines of conquest until dawn. *Grind* was the savage heritage, the pagan bloodline, the native ritual par excellence; *grind* meant the difference between excommunication and begrudging tolerance from the anthropology department. Jonathan nodded at Eyvindur, who continued.

"This here's prune soup. It's just a stupid thing from Denmark. We eat it anyhow. It's pretty good. This is *drýlur*." Eyvindur lifted a flat, round, rocklike object. "It's bread. It's terrible. We Faroese ate this before we could afford to eat white bread. Nobody eats it now. Very typical. Here's some white bread, so you won't be hungry. You come another night, we'll have stuffed puffins. Even Olsen thought they were good."

"What do I eat first?" Jonathan asked.

"What do you want?"

"Isn't there some sort of order?"

"Eat," said Eyvindur. "Eat some *kjøt*." He picked up a slice, or chip, of the meat and passed it across the table. Jonathan shut his eyes and put it into his mouth.

Leathery, sweet with rot, salted by the salty air in which it had hung, this piece of meat seemed to Jonathan a consecrated tidbit, his admission slip to the Body of Elsewhere—the gray and cloudy archipelagic universe. Eating it, he knew himself for a carnivore in the simplest sense, and that simplicity of understanding brought with it a vision of the life to come. Faint still, as the outline of the harbor was faint under morning mist, the landscape of a new psychic country beckoned him. Its only discernible feature at that moment was happiness, and he had too little experience of happiness to conceive an image for it. Rather he sensed it as a miasma, a particularly benevolent species of fog that wrapped these islands, and Jonathan along with them, in its insubstantial but all-encompassing arms.

"It's good, isn't it?" said Eyvindur, interpreting Jonathan's beatific expression literally.

"I wouldn't go that far," said Jonathan, which made Eyvindur roar with laughter.

"Just wait until you eat some *spik*," he threatened. "Here. Eat some *spik*."

But Jonathan couldn't get it past his lips. Eyvindur suggested he add rotten fish to his bread and *spik*. "It's good. They are natural companions." Oddly, this proved to be true. The fish tasted exactly as it looked, like fish paper, but its dryness cut the oily slime of the blubber, in fact, demanded some sort of oiliness for ingestion to be possible. Having downed this less pleasant installment, Jonathan fell on the soup eagerly, hoping to wash his mouth out with something familiar. But the prunes refused to cut the taste of fish; if anything, they increased it.

"Is there fish in here?" he asked.

"Yes. That is fish soup with prunes. You make from cod heads a soup, then you can take the cod heads and stuff them with cod liver and you have something they like in the villages, *livurhøvd*, but I don't like it, so Anna doesn't make it. But that is fish soup in there. In Denmark, they make it without fish, so I suppose this is actually typical Faroese food."

"Can I try the *drýlur*?"

"No. No." Eyvindur grabbed it and held it to his breast. "Jonathan, I must make a confession." He grinned. "This is really a stone I have painted to resemble a *drýlur*. It's very good, no? I have done a beautiful job making it into a *drýlur*. I wanted to give you a full Faroese meal in all its typicality, Anna and I both wanted this. But Anna cannot make *drýlur*. Nobody can make them anymore. We've forgotten how, because they are so stinking bad to eat. They are just like rocks to eat. So, I decided, why not take a rock and make it into a *drýlur*? It's conceptive art, isn't it?"

"Conceptual," said Jonathan. "What are they made of, when they aren't rocks?"

"Barley. They are made of barley or rye. You have to cook them in ashes of pat."

"Ashes of pat? What do you mean?" Jonathan snagged a second piece of *kjøt*, which was, so far, the best thing on the table.

"Pat. It's everywhere." Eyvindur waved one arm, still holding the *drýlur* close with the other. "It's the land, it's—" He was stymied again. "You cut it up and it burns. The land. You understand? We here in the Faroes, we are so poor we have to burn our own country to keep warm and to cook."

"I'm sorry," Jonathan said, "but I don't understand you."

Eyvindur got up abruptly. "I will call Magnus. He

will know this word in English. I thought *pat* was right."

Jonathan and Anna were left alone with the food. They smiled at each other, then looked away. Fifteen seconds later they smiled again. Anna reached for the plate of *kjøt* and offered it to Jonathan. In slow, carefully articulated Faroese she said, "*Kjøt* is very good. It is good you like to eat it. It makes you strong."

Jonathan answered, just as slowly, "I like it very much." There was nothing more to say. Eyvindur was rumbling and crowing on the telephone in the hall, out of sight but surely waving his arms. Jonathan chewed meat and formulated the sentence, "What island were you born on?"

"Suðuroy," Anna answered. "That is in the south. We have a beach."

Jonathan tried to convey being impressed by raising his eyebrows and nodding.

"Peat," said Eyvindur. He pronounced it to rhyme with *Fiat*. Jonathan remained puzzled until Eyvindur spelled it.

"Oh, peat," he said finally. "I didn't know you still cut peat here."

"We don't, really. Now everybody has kerosene. Or heating. We have heating." He indicated a bulbous iron item in the corner. "But peat, yes, peat means pat. That's it." He yawned.

"I have to go." Jonathan scrambled to his feet. "I can't thank you enough."

"No, no. You haven't eaten *grind*. You haven't had tea. Sit. We have to find you a house to live in—but I have already found you this. Anna's father's brother's mother-in-law, she's dead, she has a house on Sandoy and you can have it. You have to pay, though. Can you pay? Here, eat *grind* while I tell you how much."

Grind tasted familiar to Jonathan. After a few bites he realized he'd eaten it for lunch one day at the Seaman's

Home, covered with lumpy brown gravy and served with
large, undercooked potatoes. These accompaniments had
identified it as beef in Jonathan's mind, though he'd thought
it a bad sort of beef. Naked and eaten with bread, it was a
worse sort of beef but a fleshy and appealing sort of fish.

"You like it?"

"Yes." Jonathan shifted the *grind* in his mouth. "It's
chewy, though."

"That happens when it gets old. So. It's five hundred
kroner."

"A month?" Even with his airline winnings this was
beyond his means.

"For the year. You are here for the year, aren't you?"

"Oh. Oh, that's fine." Quick conversion gave Jonathan
about a hundred and fifty dollars for a year's rent. "That's
too little, in fact."

"You want to pay more? You have fundings from the
CIA?"

"No. Five hundred kroner is fine."

"Hah. Maybe you have fundings from the United
States Government to explore the system."

"What system? Why does everybody think I'm from
the CIA? Why would the CIA be interested in the Faroes?"

"The bomb system up there in the mountain. *You*
know. Your country put it there."

"Missile silos?"

"I don't know what it does. I want to get rid of it. I
am making a big fuss in Parliament about it. I call everybody
on the telephone and talk about it. It's something from
NATO. It's a cancerousness on our country."

Jonathan perceived a smokescreen. Eyvindur even lit
a cigarette to add to the confusion. Neither said anything
for a minute. Jonathan took the opportunity to finish chewing his *grind*. Anna offered him a second piece, but he was
unwilling to embark on another seven-minute stretch of

chewing and declined. Eyvindur put his ashes on his plate and smoked with his head tilted back, sending smoke up to the ceiling in gray plumes.

"We won't talk about it," he said suddenly. "We are all friends. You are right, of course. The CIA would not be interested in the Faroes. So we will not talk about it." He put his cigarette out in a lump of butter on his plate; it hissed.

Jonathan decided it was time to leave. Offers of tea could not make him stay. "I must go," he said. "This has been an extraordinary evening. Absolutely—"

"Jonathan. Jonathan. You must not take offense because I have very black ideas. It's my Italian side. *You* are our friend. You are not from the CIA. I am just spitting up foolishness. Please. You will come back, we will have stuffed puffins and arrange your marriage. Everything in the Faroes is wonderful—you'll see. Maybe the food isn't what you like, but you'll get used to it. Ask other people. They will tell you I have black ideas and become unpleasant, but it doesn't mean I am unfriendly. You will come back and describe the university of Harvard to me and also Chicago."

"I've never been to Chicago, but I can describe Harvard to you for hours." Jonathan laughed. It was, he realized, the first time he'd laughed all evening. "Thank you, thank you both." He smiled at them, one on each side of the table, Anna nodding with sleepiness, Eyvindur debating another cigarette by tapping it on the fake *drýlur*.

"Okay," said Eyvindur. "Okay. *Vælkomin*." He and Anna stayed at the table as Jonathan walked down the hall to the door. "Thanks again," Jonathan called back to them. There was no response. He stepped out into the twilight of Tórshavn at one o'clock in the morning.

Twilight, two lights, thought Jonathan, looking at a sky too pale to permit a star but dark enough directly overhead to reveal the moon. All around the horizon—of which he could see three quarters from this hill—a pink glare with yellow highlights edged into what passed for night: a grayness dotted with grayer clouds. It was early June: fifteen or more days for the light to overtake the night. Jonathan wondered how much moon would be visible by midsummer. In a switch of the more usual metaphor, he felt himself being eroded by the approaching, increasing light, as though darkness were his territory. He sighed. A weight equal to the poundage of his suitcase seemed to have landed on him with its disappearance. He sat down on a rock by the side of the road and looked out over the harbor that had earlier failed to meet his standards of beauty.

How much easier to be a pioneer from the safety of his office in William James Hall. Resisting his professors was not so different from resisting some parental injunction: take a deep breath and do it. The world hadn't fallen apart. Jonathan had thought himself courageous. Indeed, he wouldn't have dared to come to the Faroes without that self-confidence. But his self-confidence was beginning to seem, if not exactly misplaced, then inapplicable. There was nothing here to resist or grab hold of—his two specialties.

Eyvindur, for instance: how was it possible to understand him? Both his chauvinism and his "black" mood seemed suspect to Jonathan. The native poses—the food, the rhapsodies over his view—were surely just that, poses assumed to spark the anthropological interest. His sophistication and his irony learned in Italy were transparent, barely covering someone quite different underneath: but who? The patriot incensed about nuclear devices in his territory? The tired father who sat with his equally tired wife looking at the dirty dishes? Jonathan was dismayed to find in himself the expectation that the Faroese people would be simple. But why shouldn't he expect that? A science that made much of such simplicities as who traded beans or feathers with what cousin or whether dinner was cooked in one pot or two was an inadequate lens through which to consider the mysteries of human motivation. Reductionist. Jonathan kicked mud off his clog.

The sun had now risen and hovered over the ocean. It was a quarter to two. Dinner churned inside Jonathan's stomach, which struggled noisily to process material it had never before encountered. If the people proved too complex, there was always the food. What myriad degrees of rot and raw were waiting for analysis and categorization. Jonathan tried to imagine a year of sniffing and tasting. Now how long did you say you hung this outside? It was ludicrous, but perhaps easier than trying to encompass the entire society in some sort of formal village study. Below him, lights were going out in Tórshavn; it appeared the natives waited until sunrise to go to sleep. Tórshavn was not a village, though. Life might be different, maybe more encompassable, outside the capital, in his house on the island of Sandoy.

Jonathan sighed again and wished for a beer. But there was no beer. This country had no nighttime, no trees, no napkins, no beer. Professor Olsen had lamented this to Jonathan several times. Instead of beer, they had national liquor allocation: those who paid their taxes got a certificate entitling them to buy a case of beer or four bottles of hard liquor (aquavit was most popular) each quarter, handed out to the law-abiding by government dispensaries. Outsiders such as Jonathan, however, were omitted from this system. And as the Faroese drank up each quarter's supply immediately in a two- or three-day binge, there was nothing left over to offer a visiting friend. A near-beer was available at the hotel, but it was thin and bitter and did not satisfy.

A dark, gloomy bar and a beer and a jukebox: all these things existed in the Hebrides, source of world-famous malts and brews. Why hadn't he gone there? Perhaps he could go there and the anthropology department would never know the difference. For didn't they also eat a sort of rotten meat? Didn't they fish and raise sheep and live gloomy lives under an overcast sky? Jonathan realized that this was the second time he had turned to the Hebrides as potential relief from the Faroes and was amused that within two weeks his standards had shifted to accommodate local ones. He knew he was right about the anthropology department; from the viewpoint of Cambridge, little distinguished Tórshavn from Stornaway. But he was no longer in Cambridge.

As if to prove this to himself once and for all, Jonathan stared out to sea, for the first time since he'd sat down, and gave himself over to the view. To the left was open ocean, frothing now from a wind that had risen with the sun, and tinted purple beneath the green. Below him was the capital, still ugly. To the right, a long dense spit jutted out, and beyond it a pale blue cloud of land appeared to be suspended above the water: his future home, Sandoy. As always in these islands, the very surfaces curved with the globe. Water and land described portions of circles as though molded from a malleable substance. But the arcs tilted in such a way that they seemed incomplete, tipping dangerously up into the air at one end so the land looked as though it might at any moment slide down into the ocean. It gave Jonathan a touch of vertigo.

More than beer, now, he wished for a companion. Someone familiar through whom he could filter all that was strange and by this make what was ugly beautiful and what was unknown and daunting mysterious and promising.

But Jonathan was alone in the world. And the reasons for this, like the reasons for his self-confidence, had been left in Cambridge. In Cambridge it was pleasant to walk through the familiar streets at his own pace, to sit by himself in the café where he ate lunch with the paper, to enter every party given by his classmates expectant and yet safe in his solitude. No broken heart motivated him; Jonathan's relations with women were few and cool and had not disturbed his life. Because he was tall and fair, intelligent, and possibly headed for success, he was sought after. His congenial, even responses deterred most women from persisting. Some few, evangelists of love, tried to take him on for reformation. He was not to be reformed. He could resist seductions of every sort, even the ringing of the telephone.

And the Faroes' seductions too were resistible. Jonathan's detached gaze turned momentarily to himself and were disheartened by the view. In plain terms, he thought himself a fool. Any of five women he knew at home would have been a warm, living creature to sit beside on this rock, to wonder at the sliding landscape with, to plan the next day's journey with. What arrogance to plan his life around his determination not to be trapped with another human being. Wasn't he trapped in himself? And wasn't something—either stolid or frightened—blocking his senses, so that he sat here on the rim of the world, on the edge of adventure, sulking and thinking of beer?

Insight, like pain, passes quickly and can't be accurately recalled. Jonathan at the bottom of the hill, where he shortly was, was Jonathan cursing the mud of the road and the volcano of dinner, with the siren voice of doubt fading on the wind.

Early Warning

Jonathan awoke with a case of nerves. Some schedule was not being met. He decided to go to the dock to find out when the mail boat went to Sandoy, but the activity there only confirmed his feeling that everyone else had something to do and he was a sluggard. Winches creaked, stacks of

crates grew as he stood on the concrete pier, open boxes of
silver fish alternately glinted and dimmed with the movement of the clouds. The harbormaster in his corrugated tin
shack told him the boat left daily at two, "except if the
weather prevents." He was eager to embark on a conversation in English, and Jonathan, to give himself the sem-
blance of involvement, was eager to oblige. They toured
the harbor together. The man showed no interest in Jonathan's reasons for being there; his attention was entirely
focused on the boats, their crews, and their cargos.

Másin, Ritan—the mail boats were named after birds:
the gull, the kittiwake. The fishing boats seemed to be
named after places: *Mykines, Eysturoy*, the islands of their
captains' births, maybe. Seven thousand pounds of cod lay
in each hold, some gasping still. And from here, where did
the fish go? asked Jonathan. To the fish factory, where some
was ground into meal and most salted to be sent to Spain.
"The Spanish like salt fish," the harbormaster said, "just
like the Faroese." Boats whose holds were filled with dis-
assembled radios, motorcycles, refrigerators, boats bringing
eggs and vegetables up from Denmark on a journey with a
high mortality rate, boats out of Scotland stopping on their
way to the best summer fishing in Greenland, these last
bobbing high in the water because their holds were empty.
Small boats whose crew of four sat on the edge of the dock
mending their nets, Danish Navy boats that disgorged
troops of nineteen-year-olds in white uniforms and blue
caps, boats beaten and chewed by the sea, boats that spar-
kled and gleamed, trawlers, tankers, rowboats, steamboats.
Smuggling boats. "What do they smuggle?" "Alcohol," said
the harbormaster. "I let them." "Why?" "It's not much. I
know when they are coming, and I give them two hours to
unload it. Then I come down here to the side of the boat,
so they know it's time to stop."

The harbor smelled of oiled machinery, a piercing

rusty odor, and fish dying, the odor of blood and brine. Mixed in with these was the smell of rope that had been soaked in salt and dried by wind over and over, a sharp tang. Here and there a blowtorch added its sulfur. And also here was the smell of movement, change, departure. Nothing was steady or fixed. In that rough water, even anchored, lashed vessels drifted forty feet out from shore and rode the waves the seawall couldn't hold back.

It all made Jonathan more agitated. He should be on a boat, heading for his new home. At the very least he should be on a boat investigating how "things worked"; who owned the boat, who had shares in the boat, who was related to whom, how the profits were divided.

"Tomorrow at two?" he asked the harbormaster, to indicate that he was leaving now, to return to the Seaman's Home and brood on his faults.

"And nine in the morning as well."

"Oh? You didn't say that."

"Yes. Nine and two. And you can come back at three-thirty, with the return of the two o'clock."

"Why did you only say two o'clock before?" Jonathan saw withholding of information and became curious and slightly insulted.

"Well, today, today you can only go at two. Because the nine o'clock has already left, don't you see?"

Jonathan saw that he was in a ridiculous mood in which everything was abrasive and disturbing. Here was a perfectly reasonable explanation, a down-to-earth, northern-sensibility sort of explanation. But he felt patronized. An American would have said nine and two, leaving it to Jonathan to figure he'd missed the nine; the harbormaster, wanting to spare Jonathan the pain of having missed the nine, was willing to pretend there was only a two. Following this line of reasoning—*un*reasoning—would only worsen his temper.

"Well. At nine, then," he said. "Do you sell the ticket?"

"On the boat. Everything on the boat. The *Másin*. If the weather doesn't prevent."

"Yes, the weather." It probably would, and then he'd have another drenched, hopeless day in Tórshavn.

Jonathan walked slowly back to the hotel for lunch, debating whether it would be boiled cod with boiled potatoes or what he now knew to be whale with gravy and boiled potatoes. Once there had been a fried fishcake. It was the only time he'd been able to make use of the HP Sauce that sat between the salt and pepper on each table; the Faroese put it on potatoes, but Jonathan didn't like that. It did, however, soften and improve the nearly impenetrable batter of the fishcake. He voted for cod.

Cod it was, cooked beyond necessity—beyond conscience—to a bleached stiff mass. Jonathan shut his eyes and wished for an artichoke, a little pot of hollandaise, a goose sausage, an endive salad: a roadside inn near Nîmes. The last green vegetable that had touched his lips had been an Icelandic one, many weeks before. A slow cementing process was occurring inside him; each day the amount he expelled decreased in comparison to the amount he ingested. Soon, at this rate, he would lose the ability to excrete. Modifying his intake didn't seem to help, and besides, boredom and anxiety made him hungrier than usual. Beyond that he was simply hungry—for anything that resembled a meal as he knew it. The more cod was heaped on his plate, the more he spent hours of his day conjuring dinners, actual and fictitious, that had given or could give him pleasure. Like a prisoner or an invalid, he lived in a world shrunk to the basics.

A shadow fell across Jonathan's plate, and a pale long hand took hold of the empty chair beside him. The substance of the shadow, as long and pale as the hand, was a man who looked familiar, though Jonathan had never seen him before. When he spoke, Jonathan realized why: he was American.

"Y'Amerrucan, right?" he asked. "They told me." He nodded his satisfaction and sat down. "Bart," he said, extending the other hand. This one had a ring. It was the sort of ring offered by senior committees to the graduating classes of large midwestern high schools—chunky, carved, set with a stone that looked like glass and was probably a low-grade sapphire. Jonathan put his fork on the table and joined hands with Bart.

"Whew." Bart sighed and said "whew" again. "Helluva place." Jonathan could only agree. "How's that lunch?"

"Not too good, but it's all there is."

"Don't care for fish myself. Seems like this is the wrong place to be." He laughed a whispery laugh, which slowly moved into a cough that kept him occupied for a full minute. Jonathan inched his chair away; he did not want to get sick.

"So," Bart said, when his cough had run its course. He looked at Jonathan. This was a question of some sort, but Jonathan couldn't formulate an answer. Stumped, he said "So" as well.

"Yup," said Bart.

This was an impasse. "What brings you here?" Jonathan asked. At the same moment, Bart said, "Where y'all from?" So they were at another impasse. Before they could get stuck again, Jonathan blurted, "Boston. How about you?"

"San Diego, by way of San Antonio. 'Course I flew over from Washington. But I'm based on the Coast." His shoulders shook; an as yet silent battle with the cough. "Whew." He had won, this time. "Boston? Never been there. Went to New York once. Craziest place I ever saw."

"It's not like that," Jonathan said, "it's smaller."

"Yup. So I hear."

Bart had close-cropped hair and a black suit and big,

shiny shoes, one of which nicked Jonathan's calf as Bart
settled in and crossed his legs. Adding up "Washington,"
the suit, "stationed on the Coast," and Bart's overall closed
demeanor, Jonathan decided he was from the CIA.

"You from the Company?" he asked, confident he'd
used the term that would guarantee an honest answer.

But Bart was either very dumb or very quick. "What
company?" He looked around the room. "Guess I'll get
some of that lunch there." He searched more determinedly.

"They'll bring it," Jonathan told him. "They know
you're here."

"Got here last night, you know, on the plane."

"Quite a trip."

"I've seen worse." Bart nodded. "Seen worse." He
nodded again.

"Yes?" Jonathan was sorry he'd interrupted, because
things had come to another halt. "You were saying?"

"Couldn't find a goddamned bar. Couldn't find one.
You know this place, don't ya? Point out the high spots to
me."

"I'd be glad to take you around. But there aren't any
bars."

"Whaddya mean? They got Prohibition here?"

"Sort of, yes. You can't buy liquor. You can only get
it from the government if you pay your taxes."

"I paid 'em."

"Me too," said Jonathan sadly. "But not to the Faroese.
So no booze."

"Well, I'll be. What do they do?"

"Pay, I guess."

Bart's lunch arrived and he fell to it. Like an old-timer,
he put HP Sauce on his potatoes and enjoyed it. "Not so
bad," he said halfway through, then, after a few more bites,
lost interest and sat silent, staring, his shoulders twitching
again. Jonathan was waiting for the arrival of the tea, which
was brought out approximately seven minutes after the fork

and knife had come to rest on the plate. He guessed Bart's presence had gotten the waiter off schedule. Bart began to cough in earnest.

"Got a flu?" Jonathan asked.

"Sure," said Bart, hopeless. "Had it for years." He grinned. He pulled a pack of Luckies from his shirt and lit one between spasms. "I'm down to three a day. One after breakfast, one after lunch, one after dinner. Can't quit, though. I even tried hypnotism, but I couldn't get under."

"Three's good," Jonathan said.

"So. They tell me you're an ornithologist."

"No. Well—" Jonathan debated leaving it alone. "Well, I'm actually studying the people. The culture, you know?"

"Like what? Prohibition?" Bart laughed a juicy laugh and heaved some more.

"Old stuff. Old songs they sing, native costume, that sort of thing."

"How long you figure on being here?"

"A year." It sounded like forever, and Jonathan sighed.

"You with the Army?"

"Army? No. Why would the Army be interested in that?"

"Beats me. I'm with the Air Force myself. I don't know what goes on in the Army. They've got the money."

"What are you doing here?" Jonathan asked idly.

"Checking the system."

"What system?"

"The one up there." Bart moved his head to the left. "Early warning."

"Warning of what?"

"Attack. Missiles. Catch the Russian missiles before they get to us."

"Jesus," Jonathan said. This put Eyvindur's paranoia in a new perspective. "You mean, it fires them back or something? Intercepts them? What does it do?"

"Classified," said Bart, stubbing his cigarette out on the plate. "It protects us. That's what it does." He looked at Jonathan. "They're all over the north. That's because that's the path the Russians set their missiles on, over the north. They got all their missiles up in Siberia aimed at us. Don't you know that? They got missiles aimed at every city with a population over half a million. 'Course, so do we."

A web of potential missile paths spread over Europe like a grid, some red (for the Russians), some blue (for the Americans), took shape in Jonathan's mind. It was a new geography; perhaps it was the only geography that counted. He shivered. "That's insane," he said.

Polite Bart pretended not to hear. He patted his belly, full of fresh, bad Faroese cod. "You gonna take me around this burg?" he asked.

"What do you want to see?"

"You're the expert. Show me what's important. All the native stuff." Bart chuckled.

This was just what Jonathan wanted—needed, in fact, to put his mood straight: expertness. No outright failure or foolishness can compare to the pervasive sense of incompetence engendered by being a foreigner—and a foreigner condemned to remain so into what seems the infinite future. In the strange algebra of human suffering, the condition of a sufferer is always improved by contact with one who suffers more. Bart, the ultimate foreigner, was, according to this formula, the worse off of the two.

But as they rambled through crooked and muddy Tórshavn, from the Parliament building to the street of sod-roofed houses to the bustling jetty, the happiness that had welled up in Jonathan at the prospect of relief from his chronic ineptitude ebbed away. Something was wrong. Bart didn't care. Jonathan was reluctant to fault him for not caring in the particular: Tórshavn had little to offer in the way of the marvelous and exotic. In a grand sense, however, Bart was unimpressed and uninterested.

He said, "Ummmmm," he said, "That so?," he said, "What do you know about that." He nodded or occasionally shook his head as Jonathan explained that there were no trees, that the economy had shifted from sheep farming to fishing a century before, that the islands were self-governing, that those wooden shacks were for hanging and curing meat. But he wasn't really there.

It started making Jonathan uneasy. Not because Bart didn't give two hoots about the economy, but because the totality of the place, its quasi-medieval, quasi-Appalachian atmosphere, didn't seem to register. After all, it was certainly strange, though it might not be wonderful. He was sure Bart had seen nothing like it before. In a scramble for recognition—of himself, of his efforts, of his passions—Jonathan said, "It's a far cry from San Diego, isn't it?"

They were back on the dock. It was the inevitable high point of any tour, the Scandinavian equivalent of a common. Everybody in town gravitated toward it, most because they had business there, but some, like the children, because of the commotion and vitality that were a contrast to the slow drip of rain on quiet streets. Jonathan looked out to sea and awaited Bart's reply, which he expected to be a low-key, down-home acknowledgment of the subtle fascinations of the north.

Instead, Bart yawned. "When you've been around as much as I have," he said, sourly, "it all looks the same. Fact is, it all *is* the same. Question is, Whose side are they on? That's all I want to know. Yes or no. For or against."

"Denmark is part of NATO," Jonathan said. It was a feeble response, he knew.

"I don't trust them. All those countries so close to Russia, they're all a little communist, you know? Free medicine. And pornography! You been to Copenhagen? Now that's something to see."

Jonathan had not been there. He looked at the winches

and the waves and the clouds colliding with the mountains and thought they were something to see.

Bart's cough came up along with a sharp gust of wind that made Jonathan shiver. He stood patiently while Bart shook and paled and flushed. A line of gulls on a roof was rearranging itself to make room for a new gull, who tucked itself in cosily, wing to wing with its neighbors. Some feathers dislodged in the process floated down to the cement pier. Then all the birds took off hooting in the wake of a small boat, bobbing in its diesel spume till it reached the end of the breakwater. At that point the flock lost interest and returned to the shed, settling again, dropping feathers again. All this time Bart coughed.

"Hey, Bart," Jonathan said, "I think you're sick."

Bart wasn't having any sympathy. "Let's get a drink," he said, turning back toward town.

So Jonathan had to remind him that they couldn't.

Bart pulled a cigarette from his pack and put it in his mouth. He chewed on it awhile before putting it back where it came from. "The base."

"Pardon?"

"Come up to the base with me. I'll bet there's a drink up there."

"No," said Jonathan. "I bet there isn't."

"Let's go see. Come on. You showed me round town, I'll show you round the base."

"Isn't it classified?" Jonathan didn't want to go but didn't know why.

"They'll never know. Bunch of Danish teenagers. I'll just tell them you're my assistant. Be more convincing if you got a haircut." He glanced at Jonathan's neck, where hair and collar connected.

"I'm not getting a haircut." A bad mood was threatening.

"Doesn't matter. Let's go. It'll be something to see.

And I'll bet you—I'll bet you five dollars we can get a drink up there."

Jonathan winced at "something to see." Clearly, all he had provided didn't qualify as that. He was tempted to refuse on principle, but imagining his room and his sulk and his afternoon slowly sliding down to dinnertime made him accept.

At the hotel Jonathan asked how they might find a taxi. Why, the desk clerk wanted to know, did they need a taxi? Irritated, Jonathan insisted that they did and that it was up to him, the desk clerk, to tell them how to get it. It depended on where they were going, he replied. Different taxis went to different places. Jonathan mumbled that they were going west; he had noticed early on that the Faroese did not use *here*, *there*, *right*, *left*, *up*, *down*, or any normal designations of direction: everything was according to a compass, as in, Pass me that salt on your east, please. He had spent an afternoon in his dim room twisting his map of the islands round and round and memorizing relative compass points between every important village.

"West," said the desk clerk. He smiled. "To the Place?"

Jonathan had to admit they were going to the Place. This was precisely what he had hoped to avoid. He didn't want to compromise his role as ornithologist/anthropologist. Damn Bart. Bart was chewing contentedly on another cigarette, musing perhaps on the drink he was shortly to get.

Símun would take them. Símun went west because his sister Maria lived in Vestmanna. Símun was in the Hotel Hafnia now having a *temun*. Jonathan shuddered at the thought of the *temun*—an inky cup of tea and a remarkably sweet doughy cookie available between two and five daily in the dining rooms of both hotels. He'd had it once on a rainier-than-usual afternoon.

"*Manga tak*." He toyed with the idea of explaining to

the desk clerk that he was going along as Bart's interpreter. But his Faroese wasn't up to it, and he knew that, even if it were, the desk clerk would nod politely and then spread the news that the American was a spy, just as they had thought. "Come on, Bart. We've got to go to the other hotel to get the taxi driver."

Jonathan and Bart had a silent ride in a creaking Rambler, at least twenty years old, through misty valleys and over naked hills where sheep licked lichen off rocks. Símun was silent too, respecting the secrecy of spies. After about ten miles they began climbing; Jonathan's ears popped and closed, and the mist on the ground mingled with thicker clouds from above, making a two-tone gray ether through which landscape, in smaller and smaller portions, was fitfully visible. No houses, no cars. Once a clutch of geese rose from a lake to darken the sky further. They were a premonition of the bout of hail awaiting them around the next hairpin curve. Three minutes inside a mad celestial pinball machine, then higher, into brief clarity that revealed high black cliffs beside the road, over which Jonathan could not bear to look. Even through the closed windows he heard the ocean roaring a hundred feet below.

Símun drove with reckless unconcern. His passengers knocked against each other as he blasted through the fog, honking his way around curves to warn the nonexistent oncoming traffic of his determination not to stop. Bart gripped the armrest; Jonathan ground his teeth. They avoided each other's eyes and apologized each time their legs or arms smashed together. Jonathan felt himself adequately punished for sloth and idle curiosity. If he had taken the nine o'clock boat. . . . Another prayer, to be returned in good health to Tórshavn, asked to be articulated, but he suppressed it; things, he told himself, were not that bad.

Indeed, they had arrived. A couple of flat-roofed low buildings nestled between a radio tower and a granite outcropping. Bart jumped out and fairly ran in the nearest door. Jonathan discussed the return journey; Símun would pick them up in two hours, after visiting his sister for another *temun*. The Rambler took off into the clouds.

Jonathan looked at the radio tower, whose top was misted over, and decided it was not the system. He had an urge to see the system. Behind one of the barracks—he assumed they were barracks—a single-lane road shot silver up the mountain; he buttoned his jacket and set out. Bart would doubtless find him, or find himself a drink and contentment.

It was perfect walking weather: fifty degrees, a light moist wind from the sea that parted the mist occasionally, enough dew or rainfall to lend the rocks some luster. In between rocks was what Jonathan knew to be tundra. It was not how he'd imagined it: springy, gray, patchy. Instead it was luscious and green, firm like a good lawn, and sprinkled with small white flowers, which, when Jonathan bent to examine them, seemed to be minute, perfect orchids. He put one in his jacket pocket for later positive identification and felt himself momentarily a genuine scholar.

Then an unpleasant thing happened. At first it was merely annoying. A very large brown bird (Jonathan took it to be a gull from the shape of its head) started to circle above him and scream and flap its huge wings. Jonathan ignored it and kept walking, but it circled closer and closer, shrieking and sometimes actually brushing his hair with a wingtip. Irritated and somewhat disturbed, he flapped his hands at it. At this the bird became incensed. It rose up high and then came bombing straight down at Jonathan, landing for a few horrifying seconds on his shoulders. Its cold webbed feet gripped his bones and its sharp, ammoniated bird smell filled his nostrils, making him gag. Then it took off, still screaming. Glancing back, Jonathan saw that it was heading his way again. He began to run. The bird had calculated its landing point on a slower target and missed him this time, just catching his cheek with the edge of its wing. Jonathan ran for about a minute. Then he ventured another look back. The bird was circling far behind him, hovering and crying over some sacred bird spot that looked, to Jonathan, the same as everything around it. His heart was racing. He sat down on the tundra—soft, cool, and comfortable—to calm himself.

But stopping was a bad idea. Fear, held at bay by motion, got loose and made him sweat and shiver. Alone on a mountaintop, with an angry bird on his tail and an armed nuclear device somewhere in front of him, Jonathan panicked. What kind of a fool was he to have set out alone in this country? Where was Bart? Why was that bird after him? He took some deep breaths. The air was salty and charged.

Then he heard the hum. Vibrating in consonance with one of the tones of the ocean's churning, it slid in and out of perceptibility in the way that the landscape appeared and disappeared in the mist. But by stilling his breath and, to some degree, his jumping pulse, Jonathan was able to pick it out, the low continuo in the cantata of sea and wind. Pressing his foot hard on the soft ground he was able to feel it thrumming. It was the machine pulse of the system, he was sure. Then he saw, not twenty yards ahead, its feet.

It stood on iron-gray cement blocks with the feet of a monster bird, long iron talons that dug into the base. As Jonathan looked upward the clouds moved upward also, revealing two towers topped with funnels that spun slowly, slowly, like eyes on stalks surveying all. The middle section—a sort of torso from which the towers emerged—was clad like a battleship in metal squares riveted along each edge. The hum seemed to grow louder as the clouds dispersed.

Jonathan wanted to approach it, but hesitated. Perhaps the surrounding terrain was mined? Perhaps his mere presence would "set it off"? He didn't know what this might entail: anything from a vast explosion to sirens and red lights flashing in a basement in Virginia, where bored recruits played checkers day and night on the off chance that something might happen. He walked gingerly across the space between them. Ten feet from it he saw a small white sign screwed into one of the base blocks. It said PROPERTY OF THE UNITED STATES GOVERNMENT. Well, he was a taxpayer, he could investigate what his government did with his money. Self-righteously he drew up next to it and, placing a trembling but determined hand on one of its girder legs, peered out over the cliff that was the machine's aerie.

For the third time in as many weeks Jonathan saw the Faroes in a long perspective. From the airplane, from the Tórshavn hills, and now from this windy perch beside his steel compatriot, he'd seen islands strung on the green silk of sea, and kept his distance in the distance: he had surveyed. But the greensward that softened and tinted the cliffs was made of individual blades of grass, the houses that were at best bright dots along the shore had people in them, the whitecaps buoyed and bounced trawlers whose wakes he could barely detect. Fifty feet above him, the funnels swiveled from left to right, a never-ending surveillance. The girder throbbed under his fingers. Jonathan let go his hold on the machine and took another deep breath. He cast one last glance at the big picture and then, turning around, descended through the clouds into the details of the landscape.

Home

Every morning when he awoke in his bed in his house and looked up three feet to his low ceiling papered in faded strips of trellised roses, Jonathan had to listen to a string of clichés: A house is not a home; Home is where the heart

is; A man's home is his castle; There's no place like home.
All lies.

Rising, washing his cold face in cold water in his bathroom with a view of three islands, he contradicted every
item. A house *is* a home. He put American toothpaste on
his toothbrush to demonstrate. Home is where the *coffee* is.
An elegant chrome coffeepot bought in Tórshavn jiggled
and hissed on the cast-iron stove. A man's home is his
castle—that was harder to refute: a parlor filled with an old
lady's collection of porcelain dolls, pink lampshades, stiff-
cushioned chairs, mangy rugs crocheted by relatives; two
bedrooms, three beds, none of which had a tolerable mattress; a refrigerator perched on a block of cement in the
hallway, a luxury much expounded on by Eyvindur, though
even Jonathan knew it was useless: the hallway itself was
an adequate refrigerator; a kitchen with a hot plate (two
burners), a kerosene stove, a good pine table, and a drawer
filled with antique hard-boiled eggs—all of this was his.

Jonathan waged a daily battle against the urge to retreat, to hole up in his castle and read the four Agatha
Christie mysteries he'd found in a stationery store near the
Seaman's Home or concoct field notes out of the movements
of his neighbor's dogs.

But. There's no place like home.

An ambiguous statement, in the same category as Feed
a cold and starve a fever. Was that: If you feed a cold you
will be starving a fever? Or was it two separate sentences:
Colds should be fed; fevers should be starved. On the home
front, the sentence refused to resolve into a Good Thing or
a Bad Thing. Like an optical joke, the "no-placeness" of
home oscillated between cause for relief and cause for dis-
may. And, complicating matters further, "home" was itself
ambiguous. Was home Cambridge? The Seaman's Home?
This purported castle on the island of Sandoy?

The real question was, was Jonathan any worse off

here than "at home"? Better here than at the Seaman's Home, that was easy. No whale meat masquerading as steak, no HP Sauce glowering at him from its greasy bottle, silently urging USE ME to the interloper in unWonderful-land. Astute use of his index finger at the village grocery had improved Jonathan's diet and, slowly, his vocabulary. He got fresh blocks of butter, bricks of smelly cheese, bread as crisp and crumbly as any he'd had in France, even, on courageous days, a few flat fish strung through the gills with twine from a three-toothed fellow on the dock. Pear juice, anchovy paste in a tube, and decent German salami were also available. And his daily foraging trip to the store three hundred yards of mud away was certainly an amuse-ment for the villagers. Jonathan was happy to please. They laughed at him but they said good morning to him, and each day the shopkeeper taught him a new word. Boot, string, screwdriver, toilet paper, apron, motor oil, pepper, aspirin: like every store, it was full of nouns.

Better here than in Cambridge? This was harder to say. On the negative side, it was very strange here, but he'd expected that. The village was small and mean, his house drafty and crooked, its cement walls having shifted over the years. The movie theater that had raised his spirits when he first saw it had proved a mirage, in that it was closed (perpetually, it seemed) for repairs. His Faroese, though impressive to the natives, still felt like gravel in his mouth and lead in his mind. Jonathan at home—in Cambridge—was a talker. He was witty, acerbic, full of opinions, most of them unasked for, many of them uncomplimentary. Abroad he was bereft of irony, allusion, metaphor: he was just another lunk, and one who didn't know the ropes, either.

And he seemed unable to learn them. In the first days he had taken on the groceries, the dock, and the post office, where each letter was weighed and the weight looked up in a book of prices, and then a new book, full of stamps, opened, and a stamp taken out; and the whole process was repeated for the next letter. Meanwhile, from one corner came the mouth-shuffling of an old man chewing tobacco— *rumpah, grumpah, wroompah, paaft!*—who then adjusted himself on his seat, a crate stamped FAROE FISH in blue on the side, and inserted a new morsel to accompany the next letter. His chin and lips were brown. When Jonathan got tired of looking at the postal officer leafing through his books he would look at those slack sienna lips and shudder. But these three challenges were the only ones Jonathan had to meet to survive. Everything else was above and beyond, extraordinary measures, work.

To avoid work, he took walks. And from these arose the question of in what way Cambridge compared. It did not. Cambridge did not offer anything resembling scenery. Nor did it offer serenity. And though he didn't understand why, Jonathan mute and foreign and tramping the tundra to escape his obligations to anthropology was serene.

The roads led roughly west or roughly east; just south of the village was a mountain, and the sea lay at its northern edge. The eastern road passed through a village named Húsavík on its way to the third village, Sandur, and was heavily trafficked by trucks of chickens, bread, boat fuel, and cousins on visiting jaunts. Skopun, Jonathan's home, was where the mail boat landed, so anything requiring transportation off the island had to get there—*mail* in this case being interpreted so loosely as to include cars, a bride-to-be on her way to her wedding in Tórshavn, and all the wool that had been cleaned and carded in the village of Sandur over the winter and was now bound in hemp sacking for delivery to the sweater factory in Klaksvík, two islands farther north. An afternoon dodging mud and stares on this road had given Jonathan a preference for the other one.

He probably would have preferred the western road in any case. Even on a slow day, the eastern road had a destination; the western road did not. It died out slowly, dwindling to one lane, becoming dirt (both roads were paved with a narrow macadam strip that perched tentatively on the mud), and resolving to a trodden grass swath. On the high fields that crowned the island's outermost cliffs, all Jonathan could see before him was the road. At least, this was how he phrased it to himself, amazed to know, finally, that anything could lead somewhere, once you got off the track.

Jonathan was definitely off the track. For the first time in his life he had nothing to do. That is, having made an uneasy peace with his inability to do anything that resembled his idea of anthropology, he was left aimless but alive on the Faroe Islands. He had to fill his days, and his days were remarkably long. The sun rose from its half slumber at one-thirty in the morning and glared down with an insomniac sheen until well after eleven at night, when it wilted below the edge of the mountain, leaving the sky streaked with pink and yellow announcements of its imminent return. The solstice had come and gone, but the sun seemed intent on being a permanent fixture. Like Jonathan on the hills.

Jonathan walked, initially, in the afternoons, fortified by lunch and by having "interacted" to the degree he was capable: purchase of cheese, inquiry after mail, stroll along the dock to watch the gutting, filleting, cleaning, repairing, weighing, embarking, and unloading that constituted the Faroese economy. He made sure to be home by seven in the evening to listen to the BBC news on his shortwave radio (purchase funded by Icelandair). Through the fuzz and burble he heard mostly about sessions in Parliament, but it was in English and comforting. He hoped each day to tire himself enough to be able to sleep. He failed. He read all the murder mysteries. He twiddled his dials and listened to Radio Glasgow, Radio Bergen, Radio Free Europe, which played the blues late at night, making servicemen in Frankfurt, teenagers in Budapest, and Jonathan in isolation sad and frustrated with the interference. Was it natural or communist generated? Whole verses would drop out, leaving a mournful hum that was the technical equivalent of the lonesome guitar riffs it had replaced.

And so he began taking longer walks. He packed his lunch and ate it on bluffs above the Atlantic, lying afterward on the orchid-studded blanket of grass and looking at the shapes of the clouds. Childhood games with clouds came back to him: a fish, a fleet of ships, a country composed of islands—the celestial mirror world held, in the end, nothing so different from the terrestrial one. He pushed farther down the road each day.

One day he came to the region of sheep. He'd wondered where they were. A small but thriving wool industry supplemented fish in the Faroese balance of trade. Faroese wool was prized enough to be advertised as such in sweater stores in Iceland: HANDMADE IN FAROE WOOL read labels in pullovers he hadn't bought during his waiting period in Reykjavík. But Faroe wool on the hoof was somewhat intimidating. Jonathan's only previous experience with sheep had been to look at them through train windows in France and to dismiss them as dumb for getting in his way when he was riding a bicycle through a flock from a neighbor's farm on Mount Desert. Jonathan was the interloper here, and the sheep knew it.

They were tall, for sheep, and uncouth, with excrement and mud matted into their luxuriant, pricey hair. The rams' horns curled round and round, sometimes growing so tightly to the head that they seemed about to pierce the eye. The ewes' teats hung low, tugged down by lambs who, despite their smallness, were not cute the way lambs were supposed to be. These were clearly wild animals. They looked Jonathan in the eye and snorted with disdain and menace. A few of the bigger rams pawed the turf and butted the air in his direction the first time Jonathan appeared. He stood his ground. He had survived the avenging bird and he would survive sheep. To keep him in his place, though, two rams staged a battle for his edification. Stamping and snorting, they rushed at each other and bashed their heads together with such force that Jonathan was sure sheep brains would fly. But the sheep were apparently as hardheaded as he. After five minutes' smashing and crashing, they went back to lunch.

Jonathan was impressed with the display, but he didn't want the sheep to think he was scared. He sat down on a rock to eat his lunch too. After all, the sheep were company, of a sort.

Jonathan and the sheep ate lunch together for several days, during which they observed each other closely. Jonathan counted forty-five sheep: seven rams, twenty ewes, and eighteen lambs. About half the population was black, a quarter white, and the other quarter various shades of brown. He wondered if wool prices reflected this division (NEVER DYED had been the second line of the label in the sweaters in Iceland). The lead ram was getting old and fat; his authority was challenged now and then by a spry gray ram (the only gray in the herd), who would sidle up to the old sire and horn in on his patch of grass. Stamping and snorting; then they'd munch side by side for a while. After lunch everyone took a nap in his own fashion, Jonathan on his back, rams nodding and drooping on their feet, ewes on their sides mauled by sucking lambs, who'd fall off the nipple midstream into open-mouthed dreams of milk. The end of naptime was announced by the leader, who roused the herd to a trot toward unclipped fields farther west. They chewed their cuds as they walked, sticking their necks out more like chickens than like sheep, and left Jonathan at the rear, seeing a white herd of a friendlier species in his clouds.

Jonathan concluded they were harmless. They must have concluded the same, for by the third day a few raised their heads in what seemed a greeting at his footstep. And one came close to sniff at his bread and cheese, bringing to Jonathan's nose the musky smell of wild meat, then belching a breath that reminded him of mown lawns on summer evenings. Curious, he reached out to pat it, thinking to scratch it on the forehead the way a dog likes to be scratched. The sheep—she was a young ewe—bucked backward away from his hand, looked up at him darkly from under her bony brow, and stood four feet off, still sniffing, with her neck extended. Jonathan tossed a hunk of cheese at her. She ate it and glared at him.

"Do you want more?" Jonathan asked. He repeated the question in Faroese. The ewe burped again and went back to her companions.

Having broken the silence, Jonathan was seized with a desire to speak. It was an activity he didn't indulge in much these days. He had to ease himself into it, saying in an undertone, "Well, what do you know," several times to accustom himself and the sheep to the sound of his voice.

"What *do* you know," he said, shifting his emphasis slightly to recapture for his lonely ears the sound of irony, subtlety, so entirely absent from his daily requests for bread or letters. "Who would have thought," he continued, "that I would be eating lunch with sheep. Not"—he bowed slightly toward them—"that I object to your company. Far from it. I mean, beggars can't be choosers. No, I don't mean that. In fact, I think on the whole I would rather eat lunch with you than with anybody else on this island. But whose fault is that?" Jonathan lifted his eyes to the clouds, then readdressed himself to the sheep. He was gratified to see that they were all quite attentive, standing still on their pronged feet and chewing their balls of grass. "It's not what I expected, though. Well, what did I expect? Did I think I'd have fun?" He sighed. "But you know, I am having fun, sort of. In fact, I'm definitely having fun. This is fun. Who wouldn't enjoy sitting on top of a cliff covered with tundra eating bread and cheese with fifty animals that smell bad? No." He kept getting it wrong. "Okay, so they smell bad. Or they smell like sheep."

He stood up for a different approach.

"I have left the world," he announced. Stunned by the truth of this, he sat down. Was there anything else worth saying? The clouds scudded above him, soundless and active, casting shapely shadows on the earth. Jonathan got to his feet again. "And in conclusion," he said, "I would like to express my gratitude for your faith in me, and all your hard work, and assure you that I will keep your interests in the forefront of my concerns and will do my level best to represent you fairly in our nation's capital." So help me God, he added mentally.

The next day Jonathan changed his schedule. He braved the dock, bought some fish called *scrubba* from a man who had a crate full of them, flipping and flopping over one another, cleaned them at his sink (fins and scales flying, sticking to his hands, guts tearing while being extracted, fish bile steaming his eyes to a squint), and ate the lot— eight fillets—for lunch. He used half a pound of Danish butter to fry them. The kitchen stank. He wrote a letter to his parents while digesting; it described the nature of political parties in the Faroes and was monotone, as if written by a robot. Jonathan had learned all the information in the letter six months before leaving Cambridge. He reread the first two chapters of one of the murder mysteries and tried to reconstruct the outcome. He washed some of his socks in the plastic dishwashing tub and cursed soap flakes. "What you need is detergent," he said as he arranged the socks on a line he had strung above the kerosene stove. It was two-thirty. At four, he had decided, he would go.

He sat at the table waiting for four o'clock, which seemed slow in coming. It occurred to him that it might be nice to take a candy bar along; he'd noticed some Lindt bars in the store. Leaving now (it was three) in order to have

time to buy candy was permissible, wasn't it? By the time
he'd waited in line and learned the word for chocolate it
would be three-fifteen. Or was buying candy part of the
trip itself? On such fine points our lives pivot—but how
else was he to keep up discipline? He would mail the letter,
which would take at least ten minutes, then head for the
store, slowly, saying good day to everyone—well, at least
two people.

Resolved. He checked the pilot in the stove to be sure
it was burning blue; a yellow flame meant the kerosene was
running low. Blue. Tonight he would listen to Radio Free
Europe. Last night he'd heard "I'm a Diving Duck": Dive
to the bottom, honey, and I'll never come up.

In the store he found Cadbury's Fruit and Nut, better
than Lindt. Jonathan in Cambridge was a chocolate con-
noisseur. Lindt tended to a dusty aftertaste. *Chocolate*, like
Mama, was the same word the world over. The tobacco
man from the post office was up and about today and greeted
him before Jonathan had a chance to say *Góðan dag*. "Good
day the American!" he said in English. All in all, an auspicious sendoff.

Jonathan had decided to walk to the end of the island—
the outcropping due west of the village known as the Troll's
Head, which on a map looked about ten miles away and
jutted out from the mass of land like a finger pointing toward
America. Foremost among his reasons was the desire to
walk at night, to be out of the house in the sun-spattered,
long-shadowed false twilight of ten-thirty on a Faroese summer's eve. But he had also begun to justify his wanderings
by considering them exploration rather than retreat, and
this was a place he had not yet been. Finally, in an acknowledgment of his possible alternate career, he was looking for the birds.

The Danish guidebook he had plodded through with
a dictionary the month before he left home, scanning it for
hints about the climate and the local habits that would help

him figure out what to take (all those hand-selected items in the perished suitcase), had, like every other foreign commentator on the Faroes, emphasized birds. He would find them, it said, "on the rocky headlands of the islands, nesting in the cliffs and grass. Fulmars, kittiwakes, gannets, guillemots, and puffins nest in abundance," the guide had continued, "in addition to countless species of gull." So far, Jonathan had seen: the avenging bird, whose species he did not know; five herring gulls who'd trailed the mail boat from Tórshavn to Skopun and their brother herring gulls on the roof at the Tórshavn pier; some sparrows taking a bath in his neighbor's backyard dust.

Their names were romantic, tasting of salt winds on the tongue. Kittiwake, fulmar, guillemot, he repeated to himself as he walked out of town, past the cement breakwater, past the last houses, the fields fenced in wire draped loosely between sticks, over the first hill, off the macadam, onto the dirt, past the sheep, who watched him go by without comment. Gannet and puffin. The great black-backed gull. And the mysterious booby, the shy, big bird who spent half its life in circumnavigation, who bred near the Arctic and wintered off Tierra del Fuego.

Jonathan pushed onward into the unfamiliar. Here, beyond the range of sheep, the tundra was thicker, studded with more, and more varied, flowers: daisies, black-eyed susans, orchids tipped purple and red, mosses with white-star blossoms, buttercups, and heathers. The day, like all the days since he'd arrived on Sandoy, was bright and breezy, high gusts of the sea lifting toward him, sweet smell of warmed earth rising at each step he took. No trees swayed to tell which way the wind blew. He tracked its passage in the grass instead, where each puff bent a momentary pathway, as though a phantom traveler accompanied him.

It was a silent region. Far below, three hundred feet down the cliff, the sea and the rock met and parted angrily, but this ocean was so violent that the sound was continuous and therefore unnoticed. And Jonathan's feet on the loamy carpet made no noise. A passing fly could have been a helicopter for the start it gave him. He was beyond the reach of airplanes (for it was Wednesday, and airplanes came only Tuesdays and Thursdays); beyond the laws of light and dark (for it was getting on toward eight, and the sun still stood above); beyond, it seemed, the realm of words. For Jonathan sensed a profounder silence: an internal one.

In Jonathan the need to observe and take note of the world was so pressing that even a trip around the corner in Cambridge generated the equivalent of five pages of commentary—not mere notation, but speculation and attempt at synthetic description: that is, a description that reveals— as though his internal life were a perpetual effort at writing a case study of Jonathan and his perceptions. He did not know to locate his unhappiness in this effort, but the traces of this very exertion on his face and character were what revealed him to those others wise enough to read the signs as miserable.

Jonathan's life was entirely filtered through words. Words were his sixth sense, a brushing of his consciousness against the world that was necessary for experience to be felt. Nothing could be known that was not named.

The magic of naming: a name can conjure, halt, speed onward, locate; make the vague distinct, make the ominous merely eerie; mostly, tame the new, the wild, the never-seen and cage them with the understood. "The words to wrap around the thing," Jonathan had said once in conversation with Professor Olsen, who'd cocked his head, alerted to something. But Olsen had let it pass. That wrapping Jonathan struggled with—it's rotund, he'd say of a smell; it's ambivalent, of a symphony: he was working on a very high level—had the effect of dulling the impact of life. Yet for him it *was* life.

Jonathan's home was the English language, a large mansion. He roamed its deep German basement, leaned against its Latin pillars, admired its Greek buttresses and joists, disliked but was familiar with its French interior furnishings. And throughout his roamings he kept his ears wide for the old, the very old, what he considered to be the root—Anglo-Saxon—not willing or able to see the whole as something other than the sum of its parts, reducing always, wanting this complexity to have its source in one pure well. Everything else he considered adulteration. *Sang-froid* was spit in the beer. Why say *cogitate* when you could say *think?*

This language love had led him to the Faroes. Jonathan had spent many late nights and weekend afternoons reading the dictionary, moving from AUTHOR to AUTHORITY, mulling over AUTOECIOUS (having all stages of a life cycle occur on the same host; did this apply to humans living on earth?). One Sunday he'd found a chart of Indo-European languages at the end of the introduction. Slovene, Serbo-Croatian, Macedonian, Old Church Slavonic; Dard; Tocharian A and B—what a host of unthought-of, unlearnable-because-no-longer-extant languages. Oscan and Umbrian, indeed! But there, tucked between Icelandic and Norwegian, and tracing its ancestry in one straight line back to Old Norse, was Faroese. Pure. Closer, in terms of forkings and dilutions, to the source (Germanic, some proto-tongue probably never congealed enough at any period to be called a language) than poor beloved English, which had been squeezed out through West Germanic, Old English, and Middle English, with countless blendings and borrowings from other branches along the way.

He looked up FAROESE and found one of those circular definitions that compose the bulk of dictionaries: Language spoken by inhabitants of Faroe Islands (see). He saw: A group of islands in the North Atlantic Ocean between the Shetlands and Iceland. They didn't account for much on the map of northern Europe, his next stop. A map of Scandinavia offered the Faroes in insert, floating above Norway in a green box and looking larger than all of Sweden. The Widener card catalogue listed the Danish guidebook, a number of eighteenth- and nineteenth-century travelogues also published in Denmark, an epidemiological monograph on measles (this was translated), and a volume of "studies in island life" by Nelson Annandale called *The Faroes and Iceland*. Oxford had published this, giving Jonathan momentary hope he'd stumbled onto something worthwhile. He charged into the stacks and came out half an hour later with measles and Annandale. The next day he bought a Danish dictionary, withdrew two of the travelogues, and stayed up late trying, with the aid of his high-school German and his years of reading etymological notes pertaining to Old English in dictionaries, to make sense out of the language. By the end of the week he'd written a proposal for a village study. Its main point—the one he reiterated to every tight-lipped professor in the department over the next year—was that no modern anthropologist had ever been there, that the literature (such as it was) stopped in 1905 with Annandale, who hardly qualified as an anthropologist.

But then, neither did Jonathan. He knew it, and his professors knew it, though their explanations of it differed. He did not have a scientific mind; he was really a historian; no, he was really a psychologist and should move down a floor to join the rest of them; he was unable to focus on facts—well, rejoined the professor who had proclaimed him not a scientist, that was my very point. Thus the professors, among whom the only consensus was that he did not "fit." Jonathan's explanation was that only a fool would believe in anthropology, and not being one, he did not believe. He didn't have to articulate this opinion to make enemies; sighs and coughs, wrinklings of his brow, and inappropriate smiles did the trick. But his failure to believe extended to history, psychology, philology (Olsen's companionable muddle notwithstanding). Why not then be an unbeliever in the discipline that embraced everything? Out of its vast, codified mishmash he was sure to find some trail to follow.

So he'd found it. It had begun in language and it petered out on a cliff in silence. All around him was quiet, green nothing. And within him, the same. Jonathan felt light-headed. He reached for his chocolate bar and took a bite, standing still and looking out to sea. The sharpness of the taste was so intense that he made a noise of surprise. It was like, it was like—he didn't know what it was like. It was amazing. Too amazing to take a second bite, though at other times he'd eaten two bars in one sitting, he liked them so much. He wrapped it up and put it back in his jacket. It was eight o'clock. In half an hour, he figured, he would reach the headland.

Ornithology

The greater part of this world is water. Salt, cold, fresh, temperate, blue, brown, stagnant, or choppy, it holds another world, on which we prey. And we are neither its sole nor its most accomplished predators. Plovers and phalaropes skimming the sand, puffins and pelicans skimming the sea, kingfishers waiting by a stream, petrels, shearwaters, frigate birds, skuas riding the gusts above the swells, climbing higher as if height gave them an equal depth of vision down below the waves: all of them are fishers. Some fish algae and some fish herring, some snatch fish others have caught, some snag crabs and drop them on rocks, some eat eggs of other birds occupied, at that moment, by fishing. Some dive, some hover, some only wade in to their knees. Some spend most of their time ashore. Some never come home to land.

From Gander to Kap Farvel to Tromsø, and on all the islands, rocks, fjords, and straits of the subarctic seas, birds nest in the cliffs. A few homebodies like the puffin and the guillemot spend their whole lives on the cliff where they were born, perfecting a grassy cleft in the rock and feeding their young from what swims at their feet. But most are wanderers. Some do not wander far; gulls who breed in Greenland may winter at sea off the Faroes. Many, however, travel long distances to get precisely nowhere: pelagic birds, they spend half the year bobbing on the ocean out of sight of land, a thousand miles off Florida, Brazil, India. The arctic tern breeds in Alaska and heads in fall for the Antarctic; it never sees night.

The long days of northern summer teem with birds, and the Faroes' rocky shores are one of the busiest breeding grounds in the world. One steep cliff may be home to many thousand adults and fledglings, different species and their different habits side by side. The puffin, whose Latin name means *arctic brother*, who looks like a cross between a parrot and a small goose, is a bad flyer but a good swimmer and feeds its single baby whole herring, which it brings up by the dozen laid crosswise in its orange beak. The Faroese hold it bad luck to catch the "herring bearer"—the puffin feeding its young. Only empty-beaked puffins are fair game for the butterfly nets of the bird catchers. A puffin baked and stuffed with cake is a summer specialty. The fledgling

fulmar is even more prized and a good deal easier to catch
than a puffin, no matter how awkward, on the wing. Young
fulmars, fed to absurd stoutness by their parents, are pushed
out of the nest into the sea, where they float, too fat to fly,
until they lose enough weight to move—which takes at least
a week. During this week Faroese men in boats thread their
way through the water picking up the immobile young,
which they boil and eat with bread to soak up the fat. The
kittiwake fledglings, though they scream at intruders, can't
fly out of the nest; these too are taken home and baked.
The adults, with their streak of black eyeshadow and their
catlike cry, are the swallows of the north, darting and
swooping in every boat's wake, filling the sky as soon as
land is out of sight.

   And the skua, with whom Jonathan tangled briefly,
who nests in the tundra and harasses smaller birds, dive-
bombing them until they drop what's in their beaks; the
big slow gannet with its amazing jet takeoff; the Iceland
gull, the ring-billed gull, the glaucous gull, Thayer's gull,
the familiar herring gull; the murre, the guillemot's cousin,
with its fine-featured head and its stumpy body: Faroese
people number in the thousands, Faroese birds in the mil-
lions.

Sooner than he had expected—it's hard to calculate how
far away another world lies—Jonathan was among them.
The natives: screaming and cawing, circling above him,
smelling, in their scores, so sharply alien that his stomach
turned. The air was white with them. The ground along
the top of the cliff was perforated with their burrows and
littered with their feathers. And in the lower air, the warm
currents that grazed the top of the tundra, curling tufts of
down hovered in a dance that duplicated the crisscross, dart,
and soar of the birds above, whose breasts they had recently
warmed.

   Jonathan slid a few feet down the cliff to a rock that

could serve as a seat. The sea wind and occasional spray diluted the smell. He was facing northwest, a lookout searching for sunset or for a gust of wind from home. But home lay south, far south, and the sun was nowhere near setting. At his feet a puffin popped itself into its hole; he heard the young one screaming its thin screams in the earth. Mom—or Dad; they were not dimorphic, so it was difficult to know—came out orange feet first and tumbled into the ocean, flailing stubby wings. A minute later it was back with a beakful of food. More screams, then the peace of dinner, then out again, down again—Jonathan realized that this was the totality of puffin life.

Like a puffin, Jonathan was an only child. In the animal world this meant that a species had few natural predators. But humans had so many: fear, doubt, boredom. From his parents he had learned to fear this last the most. He's so boring; that's a rather dull theory; I found that party tedious: dullness was the harbinger of mediocrity, the Medusa of academe whose touch could turn a career to stone. By the age of five Jonathan had learned to entertain and impress his parents. This had never before struck him as odd, but something about the repetitive caretaking of the puffins all around him made it seem so now. Listing the differences between his parents and these puffins did not stanch the sudden flow of memory. The facts were that there were two of them and he was their only child, that they had fed and sheltered him—but oh, how differently!

Jonathan had the distinction of having not one but two professors for parents. Gerda Brand, a sociologist, had been tenured at Wellesley when she was five months pregnant with what was to be Jonathan, who didn't yet "show." Had he been conceived two months earlier, perhaps Gerda would have been a high-school teacher of American history; or so Gerda speculated occasionally, with a fond look at her husband, Bear, and her child, as though she believed she owed her good fortune to a conscious sensitivity on their part—a sensitivity she counted on them to maintain.

In fact, it was all happenstance, as Bear the Realist explained to a first-grade Jonathan. "We'd been trying for two years, and we'd just about given up." They were walking together to school, son to Buckingham, father to Harvard. Gerda had explained sex already. In Jonathan's mind it was a version of cooking, with genes as the ingredients; he had images of his parents kneading each other's bodies like dough. His mother had talked about people pressing together. "What makes it work, Bear?" Jonathan asked of his father's thigh. This thigh was bigger than Jonathan's torso and wrapped in itchy tweed. "Well, it depends on whether the egg has descended fully down the Fallopian tube," Bear said. "Oh, I see," said Jonathan. His mother had not mentioned the egg, but it fit in with his culinary understanding.

Not only both professors, both professors of sociology. Bear (originally Albert), despite his Marine-like bulk and Midwestern plain speaking, was highly regarded by his shorter, thinner Eastern colleagues for his work on closed institutions—prisons and the like. Gerda had made some suggestive correlations between voting behavior and buying behavior, long before anyone else had thought to link them.

Like the anthropologists Jonathan had now to deal with, the Brands put great stock in being scientists. Gerda especially brooked no foolishness about instinct, emotionalism, mysterious goings-on. Typical was a scene from his second-grade year in which Jonathan kicked the refrigerator in a rage over a birthday party he didn't want to attend, while his mother relentlessly repeated, "But you must have some reason, what is the reason?" The reason was nothing but Jonathan's revulsion for the party giver, Paul, who smelled funny and liked to pick his nose and show Jonathan the boogers because he knew it made Jonathan feel sick.

But seven years of life with Gerda and Bear had been enough to convince him this wasn't a reason. "I hate it, I hate everything!" Jonathan yelled. To which Gerda, in an even voice, said, "I don't think you really mean that, Jonathan." Bear could be counted on to back her up. Ambling into the kitchen, he said, "If you could explain just what the problem is, perhaps we could understand." But it was all, in retrospect, like trying to explain a joke; his parents seemed exempt from unwieldy emotions the way some people are exempt from humor.

They shared a study in what was meant to have been Jonathan's brother's or sister's room, to which they retired after dinner and all day Saturday. Sunday was reserved for family activities: the Museum of Science, the flower-hung courtyard of the Gardner, ice skating on the flooded Common in the dark January afternoons, Gilbert and Sullivan at one of the Harvard Houses. Jonathan did his own studying in the evenings. *Gods and Heroes*, *A Book of Discovery*, children's editions of the *Iliad* and the *Odyssey* were his companions as he listened to the rustle of articles being leafed through and the scratch of notes being taken on three-by-five cards. Soon enough he left Buckingham for Browne and Nichols and had real homework. He found it dull, but when he complained, he was told that this signified only his own dullness. "If you are bored by it, it's because you haven't made the effort to interest yourself in it. There's nothing boring about history." Or biology, or algebra.

What was amazing—and it had amazed him even then, he thought, sitting on his rock—was that they never descended to his level. He was always expected to reach theirs. Difficult enough; but more frustrating was that he could not irritate them, drive them crazy, make them whack him or at least yell something ridiculous the way other parents did. Nobody ever said those magic words, *Because I say so!* to Jonathan. Consequently, he never had license to say the child's equivalent magic, *Because I don't want to.* Jonathan twenty-six made a fist, thinking of Jonathan eight, nine, fifteen and always struggling to move beyond feeling into analysis or documentation.

His efforts paid off eventually. By the time he started college, he had perfected a veil of equanimity and maturity. Under these auspices, he graduated with a magna and sank immediately into a funk.

Was he still in it? Of course he was; he barely needed to ask himself the question, though he often did. But asking it in these circumstances—with homeward-bound birds trailing clouds in their wake, and clouds trailing intimations, finally, of evening—was odd enough to skew the answer off the expected. He was in a funk, but this fact didn't seem as interesting as it had been for the previous five years. The real question was, How to get out of it?

The intermediate question, of why he was gloomy, didn't interest Jonathan. That is, he had considered it and he knew why. He had read Freud; he had read Jung and Harry Stack Sullivan as well. He consigned all this to the mumbo-jumbo heap along with anthropology: pretensions to science. Perhaps from a sense of his similar troubles with the need to describe, Jonathan had detected the problem with psychology and its terms: no matter what you called it, misery still plagued people. Telling himself he had too effectively internalized his overbearing parents didn't change a thing; it was just a title for some aspect of despair: codification of the ineffable. Ornithology—that was real science.

From a bird's-eye view of his present situation, Jonathan told himself with amusement, he certainly looked like an ornithologist. But despite local attempts to cast him as such, he wasn't. Nor could he be, he knew; looking at the activity on the cliff provoked him only to wonder if these birds were happy living on the Faroe Islands. It would be even harder to pinpoint the marks of unhappiness in a bird than in a human. And ignoring that question entirely was what gave ornithology its purity.

He made his way back up to the rim of the cliff, legs stiff from sitting for so long. It was bird bedtime; heads and tails were disappearing into burrows, bigger, whiter birds were squatting on the grass up top, ruffling and re-shuffling their feathers in preparation for sleep. It was probably his bedtime too. The sun was now level with the edge of the sea, which meant that it had nowhere to go but up.

Jonathan felt he also had nowhere to go but up. He trudged back to the village fingering his funk, poking his sore spots and telling himself to get going on anthropology. Armed with his note pad, he could pursue the question of whether the Faroese were happy living on the Faroe Islands and, if so, how they managed this in such a "drear" place. And ask as well the inevitable next question: Could he learn to do the same?

Labors, Herculean and Other

Sigurd, proprietor of the store with the salami and occasional language instructor, would be a good informant, Jonathan decided. He chose a balmy afternoon when he hoped there would be few customers for the initial interview. His audience was indeed small, but it was rapt: a toddler whose hand was held by a girl too young to be her mother; two eight-year-old boys in hip boots who leaned together and giggled at everything Jonathan said; and Tobacco Man from the post office, whose secondary headquarters seemed to be a box in the corner of Sigurd's store.

It began badly.

"My name is Johan," Jonathan said.

Sigurd contradicted him immediately. "Your name is Jo-Na-Than." He gave each syllable equal weight. "Jo-Na-Than Swift," he added. Then, to clarify further, *"Gulliver's Travels."*

Not far from true, thought Jonathan, though he wondered if he was being mocked. He looked into Sigurd's eyes for disdain or distance; he saw only curiosity. Everybody in the store was waiting for him to say something else. He had a little speech prepared, so he gave it. "I am here to study the way people live, and the history. I hope you will talk to me about these things."

"I don't know any history. You should talk to Jón Hendrik." Sigurd leaned his head toward the box in the corner. "Jón Hendrik," he yelled, "tell this man some history."

"The way you live now is more important," Jonathan said quickly. He didn't want to deal with Jón Hendrik and his dribbly brown mouth. Luckily, it appeared Jón Hendrik didn't want to deal with him either. He spat and growled and chewed and mumbled, "Another time, another time."

"Too bad," said Sigurd. "He knows everything." He leaned over the chipped wooden counter and said softly, "If you bring him some brandy, he'll talk to you."

"I can't get any," Jonathan said. "I don't know how to get it," he amended.

"Yes," said Sigurd.

Yes, what? Jonathan scowled. But scowling wouldn't help, was, in fact, just the sort of thing he'd resolved not to do. "Can you—" he began.

But Sigurd, who'd been staring out the small window beside Jón Hendrik, started talking rapidly to the young woman about, as far as Jonathan could tell, a boat of her father's that was currently under repair in Sandur, the town on the other side of the island. The word *brenevin*—Faroese for liquor—cropped up occasionally. Jonathan stood on one foot, on the other foot, put his hands in his pockets, leaned on the counter. Was his conversation with Sigurd over? Was he supposed to leave? Nobody else was leaving; Jón Hendrik was chewing comfortably, the little boys had their heads together and were discussing Jonathan—he supposed—in frantic whispers. The toddler had not taken her eyes off Jonathan's face from the moment he'd walked in, and she still stood gaping at him, her head lolling back on her short, soft baby neck. Sigurd and the girl talked faster and faster, the boys' whispers got louder and louder, and Jonathan felt himself being obscured by a cloud of words— two of which popped out distinctly: "potato head."

Sigurd heard them too. He turned around and put his face right between the little boys' cheeks. "Don't you talk that way about a stranger." The boys' eyes widened and blinked. "Ever," he added. He straightened up and brought both hands down on the counter with a thump. "So," he said, and smiled abstractedly at a point above Jonathan's head.

Cast in the archetypal role of Stranger, Jonathan saw the interview in a new light. He was being humored, perhaps played with a little, mostly being checked out—but all under the protection of an ancient code of hospitality. Like all fierce, combative peoples, Vikings had had strict rules about how to treat foreigners, interlopers, ambassadors. You couldn't kill your enemies while they were in your house. A sort of Bronze Age Geneva Convention. He sighed. He wasn't going to get very far as long as he remained a stranger. But what else was he? He looked at the six faces around him, which ranged over the whole life span, and despaired of knowing what animated them. Their blue eyes, which daily saw sea and clouds and one another, had never seen what Jonathan considered the world. To know them, he would have to know a world in which *this* was the world—and that was impossible. He might as well have been a visitor from another planet.

This same thought must have been in the girl's mind, for she let go of the toddler's hand and poked Jonathan gently in the arm, as if checking his substantiality, then asked, "You are from America?"

"Yes," said Jonathan, noting that she'd used the polite form of *you*, which he hadn't mastered.

"What is the name of your village?"

"Boston." Jonathan had an inspiration. "It's a fishing village like Skopun, but it's bigger."

"And your father and mother live there?"

"Yes."

She shook her head. "They must be sad that you have gone so far away from home."

Jonathan conjured parents who might be sad about such a thing and nodded. Then he decided to meet his language problem head on. "I did not learn how to say *you* in the polite way—" he began. Everyone in the store laughed.

"That's very good," Sigurd said. "Then you will be a real Faroese. We don't ever use that *you*."

"But you used it," Jonathan said to the girl.

"We use it with Danes," she said.

"Danes like it," Sigurd said.

"I'm not a Dane," said Jonathan. Being a Dane was bad. Danes were colonial overlords. Better to be a Martian.

"Jo-Na-Than Swift," said Sigurd. "But he was Irish, wasn't he? He wasn't from your country."

Jonathan was struck by Sigurd's making a fine distinction not usually important to outsiders, between Irish and English; did the Faroese consider themselves the Irish of the Arctic, oppressed and misunderstood? This was a trail worth following.

"Well, what about the Danes?" he asked, liking the open-endedness of the question. "Nondirective" and "open-ended" were terms heard often in the anthropology department. Woe to the anthropologist who determined the outcome of his research by witlessly asking questions that led straight to answers.

Nobody wanted to talk about the Danes. "Danes," said Sigurd, making it sound like a curse. And Jón Hendrik gargled in agreement.

"In America, are there trees?" One of the little boys had ventured out from his pal's arm and come a few steps toward Jonathan. Everybody turned expectantly, waiting for his answer. They didn't want to talk about Danes, he realized, because they wanted to hear about America, his native planet.

"Yes," he said, "there are trees everywhere."

"In America," said Sigurd, "there is everything. Am I right?" He cocked his head at Jonathan.

"There aren't any Faroese people in America," said Jonathan, pleased with his own diplomacy.

But Jón Hendrik had something to say to this. "There are hundreds of Faroese in America. *You* just don't know them, because you don't know anything about the Faroes." He shot a nearly black stream expertly into the corner behind him.

"Where are they?" Jonathan was skeptical.

"In Dorchester," said Jón Hendrik, "and in New York City."

"What do they do there?" Jonathan couldn't imagine a Faroese in New York City, or Dorchester, for that matter.

"They *fish*," said Jón Hendrik. Then he shut his eyes to indicate he wasn't giving out any more information.

"Can you eat trees?" asked the little boy.

"No. They're pretty to look at, that's all." Jonathan

reconsidered. "You can climb up them. Sometimes you can make a little house in the branches and sit up there."

The boy's mouth opened at this idea, urging Jonathan to greater heights. "You can make things out of them. Like this counter." He touched it. "This is made from a tree." He looked around the store for more examples, but the floor was concrete and the walls were cement block. A broom hanging on the wall behind him offered itself. "This handle is made from a tree." He thought for a second. "Trees are good to stand under when the sun is too hot."

"Too hot?" This was the girl.

"Sometimes in America in the summer, the sun is very hot."

"Are you closer to the sun than we are?" asked Sigurd. "You can't be. We have more sun than you do. We have daytime all night here."

Jonathan couldn't explain why this was so, though he had a vague notion that it had to do with the shape of the earth. Instead, he produced information he was sure of: "There used to be trees all over the Faroes too."

"When?" This was from the other little boy.

"A very long time ago."

"Did you see them, Jón Hendrik?" asked the boy, peering over the counter.

"He thinks he knows Faroese history," was all Jón Hendrik said.

"If you wouldn't be so unfriendly, he could learn Faroese history from you," said Sigurd. He leaned over the counter again. "He'll come around when he knows you better. It's just his way."

Jonathan nodded. He didn't care if Jón Hendrik never "came around," though he knew he would be the perfect informant. Sigurd, with his blue overalls and his literary references and his hardware-grocery-stationery-ship's-chandler emporium, appealed to Jonathan much more. But he wasn't here to make friends.

With that sobering thought, a desire to get out of the store arose in Jonathan. Surely he had overstayed his welcome, if he'd ever had one. On the dock and in the post office, Jonathan had watched people taking leave of each other, so he had an idea of how to do it. First, take hands out of pockets; second, say "So, so, so"; third, look at the floor—or ground; then, another "So, so, so," accompanied by reinsertion of hands in pockets. The point of no return was signaled by the phrase "I reckon so," addressed to the clouds and, if the other person were older or in some way venerable, repeated with nods and, rarely, a smile. But this was only one side of a streamlined version; when you got two people going, it could take up to twenty minutes, what with comments on the weather and the trading of "So, so, so," until both parties were satisfied. Still, there was nothing for it but to launch in.

"So, so, so," he ventured.

To which Sigurd in instinctive response said, "So, so, so."

Jonathan took his hands out of his pockets (which he had omitted to do at the start) and put forth another "So, so, so."

Going for the long version, Sigurd said, "Good weather."

"Today," said Jonathan. An inspired response, he was sure. He was still waiting for Faroese weather to turn on him; so far, soggy weeks in Tórshavn notwithstanding, he'd seen none of the fabled storm or drear.

"Today," repeated Sigurd. He laughed. He turned to Jón Hendrik and shouted, "He says the weather's good *today*."

"He'll see," growled Jón Hendrik.

"He sees plenty," Sigurd stated.

A balm of triumph suffused Jonathan; one person, at least, did not think him a boob.

"So," said Sigurd.

A single *so* wasn't in the script. And to confuse things further, the girl, pulling the child in her charge closer, chimed in with "I reckon so."

Jonathan really did want to go. "I reckon so," he said, hoping he could ride out on the girl's coattails.

But, as he had suspected from his research, women's scripts were different, and with a quick "So, so, so," she was out the door, leaving him to thread his own way through the maze of farewell. And between his incompetence and Sigurd's boredom (Jonathan could see no other explanation for Sigurd's embarking on the epic version of goodbye), this might have taken the rest of the afternoon. They were rescued by the arrival of two fishermen in yellow outfits who needed tobacco and lubricating oil. Jonathan scuttled out into the street with a "Good day" and an all-American wave. This gesture evidently struck Sigurd as mysterious, for in Jonathan's last glimpse of him, through the window beside Jón Hendrik's head, he was open-mouthed and inattentive to his customers.

Pleased with his productive afternoon, Jonathan went down to the dock to watch the mail boat load for Tórshavn, which took ten minutes, then went to the post office. Improbably, Jón Hendrik had in those ten minutes transported himself to his major headquarters and was chewing in the corner when Jonathan arrived. "Good day the American!" he said. He tendered this greeting as if they had not been at loggerheads only fifteen minutes before.

Devilish, Jonathan said, "Fine weather." But Jón Hendrik did not reply. There was mail: a letter from Professor Olsen and a bank statement from the Cambridge Trust Company, with Gerda's tidy script forwarding it to the Faroes.

Feeling a little tired, Jonathan decided to go home and read his letters (a bank statement qualified, in these circumstances, as a letter) and then make himself corn muffins for dinner. And take notes on the day.

Jonathan's preferred spot for letter reading was the toilet, so there he repaired. A pleasant twenty minutes passed during which he learned that his balance was $2,500 and that Olsen was thinking of coming to the Faroes at the beginning of September. (Jonathan doubted he would. Olsen had, in his two previous letters, announced that he was thinking of coming to the Faroes at the beginning of July and the beginning of August; Jonathan figured it was his way of assuring emotional support.) Gerda had enclosed a hurried note on the order of *We miss you, weather's been lovely, off to Maine in twenty minutes, do write*. What was puzzling was that she had gone to the trouble of carefully opening the bank statement, tucking in her note, and sealing up the whole in such a way as to be nearly unnoticeable: was it meant to be a surprise? Or was she somehow apologizing for opening his mail?

Jonathan hitched his pants up and looked out the window at his view. It was magnificent. Never, in all the world, had there been such a well-situated toilet. The house was on the higher of the two village roads and in addition stood on a little rise of its own, so from this second-floor window Jonathan saw miles across the broad fjord to Streymoy, the main island, and up to the Troll's Head where the birds' kingdom lay. His daily twenty minutes in the bathroom were dependably enjoyable—he had even considered making the bathroom into his office. It was big enough; clearly, before indoor plumbing, it had been a bedroom. Even now, since it lacked a bathtub, there was room for a desk. But: Don't shit where you work. Or something along those lines. He leaned over to flush.

The toilet, a new Danish model, had a roaring cataract of a flush that could sweep his shit to Tórshavn. But now it did not flush. The handle that usually sprang at his touch, unleashing a tremendous *whoosh*, refused to move. Jonathan scowled and tried again. Nothing. He jiggled the handle this way and that, ran some water in the sink to make sure there was water (there was), opened the back of the toilet looking for obvious problems, tried again. This time a thin trickle made him hopeful. Several tries later, though, he had succeeded only in filling the bowl to the danger point, contents still afloat.

He shut the door on the situation and went downstairs to make muffins. Like many unmechanically minded people, Jonathan believed that if you gave the machine time to recover it would perform properly. He would let the toilet rest. He could piss in the sink, and probably by morning the toilet would somehow have healed itself.

In the morning, his production of yesterday greeted him when he stumbled into the bathroom. Tentatively, he tried the toilet handle; it was as rigid as it had been the day before. Pissing into the sink, Jonathan considered his options: wait for the miraculous self-healing process to begin; ask for advice; ask for somebody to fix it. The first seemed foolish; the second pointless (Jonathan knew his limits, and he doubted his ability to fix a toilet in English, never mind Faroese); and the third involved getting rid of the current contents of the toilet. Breakfast first, he decided.

Breakfast, with its accompanying internal rumbles, only brought home to Jonathan the fact that much of what humans eat is returned to the world as shit and confirmed his initial sense that option three was the way to go. But where was he to put this all-too-obvious evidence of his humanity? In a plastic bag, and then in the trash barrel outside the house. But the bread came naked from the bakery on the other side of the island; the cheese, cut from a big slab, was wrapped in brown paper; the fish was fresh out of the sea. All the traditional American locations for plastic were here so reduced to their origins that there was no need for Baggies. Then he remembered that salt cod, of which the Faroes produced most of the world supply, came in a thick plastic bag stapled shut at the top. He would go to the "other" grocery store and purchase some, throw out the contents, and use the bag. Then he would find himself a toilet fixer.

Within an hour Jonathan was ready to find help. He had made a new friend in the proprietor of the second grocery store, a red-faced woman who was delighted that Americans ate salt cod—as Jonathan assured her they did, in order to cover his tracks. And he had for the first time sensed the life of the village: she and everyone in her store (the usual assortment of lounging kids, bored young mothers, and hurried fishermen) knew he was the American who had come to live with them. Everybody in town knew him. Of course: in a village of four hundred people, a visitor from outer space would not go unnoticed. He found a certain comfort in this, for it relieved him of the burden of self-explanation. A deeper comfort lay in this evidence that the tree falling in the forest made a noise. Life was not restricted to what went on in his head; life surged along on a tide of gossip and common interests, one of which was his unaccountable but real presence.

So, he had a verifiable existence. Cheered, Jonathan went over to Sigurd's store to get help.

Sigurd diagnosed the problem immediately. "Full septic tank," he said. But *septic tank* in Faroese wasn't within Jonathan's ken, so there was an interlude of diagram drawing on a scrap of brown paper. Particularly explicit was the overflowing heap of turds Sigurd inked into his cross-section of Jonathan's front yard, stopping occasionally to hold his nose so there would be no doubt what he was representing. Pleased with his drawing, Sigurd beamed at Jonathan and said, "Full, completely full of shit." *Shit*, an Anglo-Saxon word, was easy to recognize.

"What shall I do?"

"Empty it." Sigurd nodded. "With a wheelbarrow." *Wheelbarrow* necessitated another sketch.

This must be a joke, thought Jonathan. "That would take forever," he objected. "Also, I don't have a wheelbarrow."

"I'll send my brother Jens Símun."

"He'll help?"

"He has a wheelbarrow."

"Where am I going to put it?"

"In the sea," said Sigurd.

Jonathan went home in a downcast mood.

Jens Símun had one blue eye and one brown eye, and he was in Jonathan's kitchen before the water for tea—which Jonathan had put on as soon as he got home—had come to a boil. He was bigger and rougher-looking than Sigurd, but these seemed to Jonathan good qualities in a person who was going to demonstrate shoveling shit.

"So, so, so," said Jens Símun, shutting his blue eye. He sat down at the kitchen table. "A *temun*," he said.

Jonathan produced a bachelor's *temun:* bread, butter, plum jam, tea with plenty of milk. Jens Símun ate three pieces of bread with condiments, then asked for cake. Cake was the real point of a *temun*, Jonathan knew. What was it about island living that nourished a sweet tooth? He thought of the English and their treacle, the ranks of bad eclairs in the bakery on Mount Desert.

"I'm sorry, but I don't have any cake."

"So, so, so." Jens Símun took another slab of bread.

"What am I going to do with that?" Jonathan asked, leaning in the direction of his front yard.

"I have to look at it, to see how bad it is." He chewed his bread slowly. "Sometimes you have to stir."

"Stir?"

"Sometimes it's too hard to get it out."

Jonathan shut his eyes and hoped he wouldn't have to stir.

But, of course, he did have to stir, Jens Símun proclaimed after lifting what looked like a big manhole cover at the edge of the lawn. He shook his head: this was a very bad case indeed. As they stood looking into the dark depths, Jonathan's next-door neighbor, with whom he had never exchanged a word, came out and joined them. He and Jens Símun flanked Jonathan, both shaking their heads. Then the neighbor disappeared behind his house and returned a minute later with a hose, dripping water, and a long pole. He handed these to Jonathan.

The idea was to run the water into the tank while stirring with the pole. This would "soften things up," Jens Símun explained, and make it easier to remove the contents with the shovel that the neighbor, Petur, had brought after a second trip behind his house. Then, fill the wheelbarrow and take it down to the sea.

"Where?" Jonathan didn't think he was supposed to dump it right into the harbor alongside the boats.

"Oh, to the west," said Jens Símun airily, waving his hand toward the Troll's Head.

Petur was more specific. "You see where the break-water ends?" He pointed to a concrete wall jutting out from one of the arms of the natural harbor. "You go down there and dump over the wall, into the sea." He turned back to his house. "Dump to the west," he added, "because the current runs to the west."

So Jonathan began his labors. Hercules, he remembered from *Gods and Heroes*, had diverted two rivers to wash away his piles of manure; Jonathan had only his hose and his hands. After the first trip to the breakwater with a full wheelbarrow, he decided that Sisyphus was a more appropriate role model; after the second trip, he stopped thinking.

For the early part of the afternoon, Jonathan worked steadily, achieving a rhythm: stirring was hard, but not as hard as excavation and loading the barrow; his recovery period was his walk to the sea. Though in the beginning

he'd feared the wheelbarrow would tip over, he soon realized that it had an implacable stability, and he was able
to look at the scenery as he walked instead of peering anx-
iously at the front wheel. It was the dead time of day before
the second mail boat arrived, when all the men were working and all the women were washing the lunch dishes. Jonathan and his noxious cargo were unobserved on their
rounds.

He returned from his eighth or ninth trip to find his
septic tank surrounded by visitors: Jens Símun, Petur the
neighbor, a man he didn't know, and the two little boys
who had likened his head to a potato. The opportunity for
a pause was welcome. Jonathan smiled, but nobody smiled
back. He let the wheelbarrow drop to the ground with a
thump and sighed. Jens Símun and Petur moved aside to
allow him access to his hole.

Jonathan's will failed him. This was not a task he could
perform under observation, and clearly these people were
here to watch. Didn't they have anything better to do? No,
they didn't, Jonathan realized; there was not much to do in
Skopun on a long summer's evening. Whatever Jens Símun,
Petur, and the third man worked at, they were probably
finished by now, four-thirty. And boys of eight are famous
the world over for having nothing to do. His septic tank
was the newest movie in town.

But did that mean they had to stand so close? Jonathan
the Anglo-Saxon liked to keep a few feet between himself
and other people. As he set to stirring and shoveling again—
for that seemed the only thing to do, and his pride, which
would not let him walk away, was an adequate substitute
for will—he had to be careful not to dump shit on their
shoes or jab them with the handle of the shovel.

Now and again one offered a comment: "Tough work";
"Badly clogged"; "This happened to Johan Heinesen over
on Nolsoy." The little boys declined the chance to call
Jonathan a shithead, for which he thanked God, or whatever

force had inflicted this situation on him. He felt that he was being tested. His patience was certainly being tried. And more and more he felt himself fulfilling—or attempting to fulfill—one of those tasks that in fairy tales win the maiden for the young knight and in myth win the favor of the gods.

Under their blue eyes, he'd loaded another barrowful. As he wheeled off down the road, he wondered if perhaps he'd return to find Jens Símun stirring for him. An idle hope, he supposed. Indeed, when he got back, nobody had moved. Not completely true, he saw; they had moved the number of inches necessary to accommodate the addition of Jón Hendrik's thin, cranky body to the circle.

"In America, you hire people to do this, hah," said Jón Hendrik in perfect English.

"In America, we have a sewage system," Jonathan spat out, in perfect Faroese. He'd been looking up words in his dictionaries (English-Danish, Danish-Faroese) the night before.

"Now you are here," Jón Hendrik said.

"*Vælkomin til Føroyar*," Jonathan said, resuming his shoveling.

This remark, made in bad temper, was a big hit. Jón Hendrik laughed and stamped his foot on the ground in delight. Jens Símun's multicolored eyes watered with tears, Petur slapped his thigh, and the unknown man had to lean on Petur for stability while he chortled. Jonathan was so surprised that he stopped working and stared at them.

"What's so funny?" he asked.

"You are beginning to understand our country," said Jón Hendrik. And as if this was what they had all been waiting for, the group dispersed. Even the boys wandered off to stare at somebody else.

Two wheelbarrows later one of the little boys came back into the yard and said, shyly and very softly, "Papa says you are to come for dinner."

"Oh," said Jonathan. "Where do you live?"

"There." The boy pointed next door, to Petur's house.

"Your father is Petur?"

Nods.

"Is that your brother, the boy you walk around with?" Jonathan figured he might as well get going on a kinship chart.

But this made the boy giggle. "That's my *cousin*," he said, as if only an idiot wouldn't know.

"When should I come?"

This the little boy didn't know. "Mom!" he yelled. A woman's head popped out a window. "The American wants to know what time is dinner."

"When he comes."

"When you come, we'll eat," the boy repeated.

Jonathan leaned on his shovel. "I think I'll come soon," he said. "What's your name?" The boy didn't answer. "My name is Jonathan."

"I know that," said the boy. Then he skipped off into his house.

Twenty minutes later, sponged off in tepid water and dressed in clean clothes, Jonathan was knocking at his neighbors' door. He could hear voices and kitchen noises, but nobody answered. After a few more knocks he opened the door and walked in.

He was in a kitchen similar to his own, but with life in it: framed embroidered mottoes on the wall, a row of cacti on the windowsill, a tablecloth, steam from cooking, noise from the conversation of Petur and a number of other people at the table and from the radio blaring in Faroese about tomorrow's tides.

"Good evening," said Jonathan.

"Jo-Na-Than," said Petur, intoning it in Sigurd's fashion. He stood up and began the introductions.

Maria at the stove was the wife, the nameless boy was Jens Símun, the cousin Jens Símun went around with was

Petur, a young man of about twenty was Heðin, another young man who looked a year or two older was Olí, and the girl from Sigurd's store, minus the toddler, was Sigrid. Jonathan's head was in a whirl. Petur concluded the introductions by clapping Jonathan on the shoulder and announcing, "And this is the American!"

Jonathan sat down and smiled feebly. He was hungry, tired, and puzzled by what all these people were doing in Petur's kitchen. Everyone had a plate, so they were all staying for dinner; the question that interested him was whether they ate together every night. Plunging headlong into anthropology, he asked, "Are you all related to each other?"

Heðin or Olí—Jonathan had mixed them up immediately—said, "In America, you don't have such big families?" Then everyone laughed.

But Petur, in the same sober way he had explained to Jonathan where to dump his wheelbarrow, outlined the connections meticulously.

"Heðin and Jens Símun are our sons, and Petur is Jens Símun's son, my brother—"

Jonathan interrupted here. "You and Sigurd and Jens Símun are all brothers, then?"

"Yes. And Sigrid is Jens Símun's daughter."

"Your niece," said Jonathan.

"Yes."

"Petur's sister." Jonathan wanted to be sure he had everything straight.

"Yes. And Olí is working on the boat with us. He's from Streymoy, from Vestmanna; he's Maria's little brother."

One thing bothered Jonathan. "How do you tell little Jens Símun from big Jens Símun, and little Petur from you, big Petur?"

"We just look at them," said Petur. Everybody laughed again. Jonathan gritted his teeth and persisted.

"When you are talking about them, I mean."

"Oh. Yes. My Jens Símun is Jens Símun *hjá* Petur, and Jens Símun's Petur is Petur *hjá* Jens Símun. You see?"

Jonathan nodded. He saw. *Hjá* was the Faroese equivalent of *chez*. He saw also that this could be a long evening. Information was lurking everywhere, teasing him, urging him to work when what he wanted was dinner and company.

Maria was concerned that he wouldn't like the dinner. "It's *livurhøvd*," she said. "You know what that is?"

Jonathan remembered that Eyvindur had given this dish bad press. "I've heard of it," he said. He hoped it would be edible.

It was extremely unpleasant: boiled cod heads stuffed with cod liver, unseasoned, gelatinous, contents and container reduced to soft masses distinguishable by color only. He poked at it. Luckily, there were lots of potatoes, also boiled, and some shredded red cabbage that tasted of a can. Heðin, who was sitting beside him, noticed he wasn't eating the *pièce de résistance*.

"It's not a good thing to give a stranger for dinner, Mama," he said. "You would have to be Faroese to like this." He smiled at Jonathan. He had terrible teeth, stained and crooked, and a wonderful, wholehearted smile. He removed the *livurhøvd* from Jonathan's plate with his fork. "I'll eat it. You don't have to eat it."

Maria stood up. "I'll make you an egg," she said, opening a cupboard and taking out six eggs.

"No, no," said Jonathan. "Really, I'm happy with potatoes."

"Nonsense," said Petur. "You worked hard today. You must eat."

"How many eggs?" Maria asked.

"Two. Two is fine," said Jonathan. "But please, wait until you have finished your dinner. You know, I can cook them myself." He stood up.

"No." She moved in front of her stove to guard it. "You are my guest. I will make you some eggs."

All of this was making Jonathan uneasy. He was an impolite foreigner who disdained local cuisine, he was causing extra trouble and mixing up what should have been a simple family meal. It was taking away his appetite, already compromised by the *livurhøvd*.

"You should eat more than two eggs," Petur said.

"Mama, I don't like *livurhøvd* either," said little Jens Símun. "I want eggs."

Jonathan waited for a storm to break over Jens Símun's head: You eat your dinner, you just want to be special like the American. Instead, Maria asked how many eggs he wanted.

"I want three eggs," said Jens Símun.

"Give me your *livurhøvd*," said Heðin.

"You have the American's," Olí protested. "I want it."

"Okay," said Heðin. *Okay*, Jonathan noticed, had passed unchanged into Faroese.

"Sigrid, do you want some eggs?" Maria asked.

"I like *livurhøvd*," Sigrid said.

"I think usually men like it better than women," Petur said, to nobody in particular.

The eggs were ready. "I made you three," said Maria, as she served Jonathan, "because you worked very hard today."

With Jens Símun and Jonathan reprovisioned, dinner continued. Jonathan was glad he had three eggs; now that the *livurhøvd* was off his plate and the atmosphere calm, he realized he was remarkably hungry. They were right: he had worked hard. Probably tomorrow would be the same. He'd tried the toilet handle before coming to dinner, and it still resisted his touch. Another eight hours of shoveling awaited him. Jonathan found something comforting in this: one day, at least, was scheduled for him.

Sigrid cleared the plates and brought everyone tea in

mugs. Maria took a bowl of cookies from the cupboard and put them in front of Jonathan. And Petur went into another room to fetch an item Jonathan hadn't seen for a good many weeks: a bottle of liquor.

"Aquavit," he said with reverence. This also came to rest in front of Jonathan.

Jonathan took a cookie, which he didn't want, and passed them to Heðin, who took two. Petur was waving at him to drink, but he couldn't figure out whether he was to put the aquavit in his tea or drink it from the bottle. "Drink," urged Petur. Jonathan opted for the direct approach and took a swig. Fiery stuff. He wiped the neck with his hand, having seen this in cowboy movies, and passed to Heðin.

Heðin was impressed with Jonathan's drinking method. "We put it in the tea," he said. "That's how you drink in America?"

"Sometimes," said Jonathan. His throat hurt from the liquor. "Or in glasses."

Heðin drank in the American way: "Too strong." He shook his head. "Try it, Papa."

Petur declined. "I'll just put it in my tea," he said.

The aquavit went around the table and into everyone's tea, even little Jens Símun's. Jonathan too infused his cup, though he wondered first if they'd think him greedy, second, if he could survive such an amount of aquavit. His limbs, tired and puffy-feeling from the day's exertions, began to sing and twinkle from the alcohol. He would get drunk—he was gettting drunk. He realized he wanted to be drunk. He took a great gulp of tea to speed the process.

"So, so, so," said Petur, breaking the general silence that had accompanied the drinking of aquavit. "You are a hard worker."

"Thank you," said Jonathan.

Petur said "So, so, so" again and put his hands around his teacup. They were huge hands, the hands of a man who was a hard worker, who'd had a life full of hard work. "Will you come out to drive sheep with us?"

"Yes." Jonathan was pleased. "When is that?"

"When you finish your job"—here Petur grinned—"we'll go."

"And what do you do when you drive sheep?"

"We must shear them now, before their wool gets too thick, and decide which ones we will kill in the fall. We have to bring them in from the outfields. It's not easy." He looked at Jonathan. "Can you run?"

"Yes." Jonathan considered himself a good runner; his only genuine participation in the anthropology department had been on the softball team, where his running was appreciated.

"Sometimes you have to chase them. But we have dogs, too. You know"—Petur paused and sighed—"sheep are not so intelligent as cows. Cows know the way home. Sheep never learn this."

"How many sheep have you got?" Jonathan asked.

"Five. This year I have five."

"Oh. Then it won't take very long to chase them in."

"No." Petur shook his head. "We are driving in all the sheep—everybody's sheep—because it's time to shear them."

Now Jonathan was confused. "Are you the head of sheep driving?"

"Everybody's driving in sheep—at least, everybody who's here, who's not out fishing."

"And I'm going out fishing," interjected Heðin. "I hate to drive sheep."

"You can go," Petur said. "We have Jonathan."

Jonathan was startled to feel tipsy tears in his eyes. He was an asset—here, in this peculiar country that he didn't understand. Doubtless, anyone who could be enlisted to run after sheep would be considered an asset; still, something in Petur's voice—a proprietary sort of approval—had given Jonathan the feeling that he was, finally, welcome.

He looked at the faces around the table. None were beautiful, though the children—Jens Símun and Petur—had pale, translucent skin that was appealing. Sigrid, on the cusp of adulthood (Jonathan figured her to be about fifteen), had lost that baby clarity but had not attained the comforting solidity of the grown-ups. Petur and the two young men had rosy cheeks, perhaps enhanced by aquavit at this moment, and the dreamy gaze that Jonathan was learning to associate with fishermen. Petur's brother Sigurd didn't have it, being a land-bound shopkeeper. This gaze looked through and far beyond whatever was at hand; it was panoramic and comprehensive and nonjudgmental. And it was a strange vein of abstraction in otherwise concrete characters. Petur in particular emanated rootedness and dependability; his speech was to the point, his movements economical, slow, and confident, and yet he was at moments awash in the away, in the elsewhere, in the featureless, ever-changing country of ocean where everything was reduced to nothing, or at least to nothing much, and where an innumerable series of nothings—wind, current, temperature—combined to create the vast frothy something that was the Atlantic: Petur's office. Heðin and Olí, though twenty years younger, had already been affected. Jonathan coveted that gaze, because it seemed to him the look of peace.

Also desirable—though not as fascinating—was their firmness, what Jonathan thought of as their *thereness*. Maria and Petur seemed more adult than adults in America—as if they had become what children always imagine adults to be and are always disappointed to find they are not, when they become adults themselves. Petur and Maria gave Jonathan the impression that they understood life and how to live it. How had they done this? Had they, in fact? Jonathan tried to look beyond his wishes and his cultural blinders and his happy aquavit haze and determine what these people were *like*. He saw in a flash: they were like trees. They were, actually, the trees of the Faroes. They grew from this soil, they gave shelter and comfort, they were useful, and he—Jonathan—could make a little house in their branches and call it home.

With this he realized that he was well and truly drunk. He had a long day ahead of him. It was time to go. He stood up, a bit unsteady. "I think it's time for me to go to bed," he said.

"Let's look at your hole," said Petur. "Maybe you'll finish tomorrow." The entire family followed Jonathan out the door.

In the greenish half-light of midsummer night, his hole was mysterious and bottomless, and the wheelbarrow resting atilt on a hump of earth with the shovel laid across it looked phantasmal—as did the seven people grouped in the yard. Not a star was in the sky, not the faintest trace of moon. Jonathan felt himself waking up, partly revived by fresh air, partly by the endless light. He had the urge to get back to work. He could probably finish by tomorrow morning—by the time the sun shone yellow again.

Jens Símun said, "Puuh. It smells."

"What do you expect?" said his father. He peered in. "You'll finish by tomorrow evening," he told Jonathan.

"What a beautiful night," said Maria. "Well"—she sighed and turned to go back to her house—"soon we'll see the stars again."

"Soon?" Jonathan missed them.

"By August. We start to see them again then." She took Jens Símun by the hand. "Then you won't stay up so late, will you?" She wiggled his arm, and they both laughed.

"Oof, I could sleep all winter," said Olí. "Because you make me work so hard all summer," he went on, turning to Petur. Petur grunted and kept looking in the hole.

"You might need a longer shovel," he said. He took the hose, which was lying on the ground, and put it in the hole. "If you leave this in overnight, it'll soften more. But just a trickle, because you don't want shit soup in the morning. Then you'll need a bucket."

"So, so, so," said Heðin. The signal to go.

Without saying goodbye, they all trooped back into the house. Jonathan stayed in his smelly yard admiring the world. Five minutes later, young Petur—Petur *hjá* Jens Símun—came out of the house and set off down the road, an elfin eight-year-old on his way back home at midnight. He walked slowly, kicking stones and singing to himself as he went. Jonathan could just make out the words, thin and sweet in the thin, clear air:

> When I get big, it'll be good,
> Oh, how I'll be happy.
> I'll go to sea day and night,
> As a fisherman.
> Here is the land that suits me.

"Petur, wait for me," called Sigrid, running out of the house. But Petur scuffed along, still singing, speeding up a little to tease his sister. As Jonathan turned to go into his house, he heard the song still, and Sigrid still, saying "Petur," in the voice girls reserve for their younger brothers. He shut the door. The song persisted: *Here is the land that suits me.*

By the next evening Jonathan had reached the bottom of the septic tank as Petur had said he would, had made a nearly ceremonial use of his toilet (flushing first to be sure it worked), had given himself a more thorough washing (this involved bringing an enormous pot of water to the boil, hauling it upstairs, and then mixing it, in pitcherfuls, with cold tap water as he stood in a baby-sized plastic tub and shivered), and had left his shit-stiffened jeans to soak in that same tub. Dressed in ill-fitting beige corduroys bought in

Reykjavík and his handmade Faroese sweater, he sat stupefied next to his stove and wondered what to eat. The un-
accustomed labor, which yesterday had given him a sense
of well-being and pleasant tiredness, today had made his
muscles ache, his back hurt, and his hands raw. A serious
blister had formed on his right thumb from the shovel, and
he had several times gouged himself on some part of the
wheelbarrow—small but deep wounds into which he feared
he had gotten shit.

For dinner he could have eggs again, dehydrated soup
(beef with barley), or bread and jam. Or perhaps all of the
above. Alternatively, he could go to bed dinnerless and sulk.
Or just prop himself up by the stove and sulk there—why
bother going to bed? He shook his head at his own idiocy;
this was a major bad mood, he could tell. Sometimes the
best remedy was to indulge all his ornery impulses. His
self-hatred did have its limits, and if he pushed hard enough,
he might reach them and find the elusive but sober inner
Jonathan who wished him no harm. But that was the longest
distance between two points.

He turned on the radio. It was too early for the blues,
but maybe he could hear some English. The BBC was
broadcasting the usual parliamentary twaddle; Radio Glasgow had vanished into the fog bank that had added drizzle
to Jonathan's final hours of excavation. All he could bring
in was a mesmerizingly stupid program of Italian popular
love songs from Milan, crooners interrupted by agitated
hucksters of Fiats and a yogurt named Yomo.

"Oh, shut up," said Jonathan, and turned off the radio.
This made him feel slightly better, so he walked around his
kitchen saying "Shut up" to his stove, his drawers, his sink,
and giving them a kick for good measure.

He was bored. He was lonely, was the truth of it. His
evening at Petur's had put his isolation in a spotlight. Was
he really going to spend the next eleven months swearing
at his furniture? He sat down by the stove again and in-

dulged himself in a fantasy: he would meet Sigrid's older sister (he didn't know if one existed, but never mind), she would be drawn to the Outsider, they would fall in love, he would explain to big Jens Símun that he wasn't going to take her away, they would live half the year in the Faroes, they would embrace when everything was settled with her father; the embrace grew warmer, more entangled—Jonathan's imagination went on a rampage of kissing, licking, nibbling, and undressing that startled him with its intensity and vividness. And now, having been fired by these images, his mind went wild: first Petur's wife, Maria, then Sigrid herself, then a girl with a big mouth who'd been in the post office one day successively succumbed to the voracious and compellingly attractive Jonathan. His head spinning, Jonathan retired dinnerless to bed; other appetites seemed more pressing.

An hour later Jonathan was awakened from a deep sleep by someone calling his name. He opened the bedroom window and looked down, thinking to find the caller at his door, but nobody was there. He pulled on his clothes and went downstairs, where Sigurd was sitting at the kitchen table.

"You had a long day," said Sigurd, and laughed.

"Uumph," Jonathan said. He was hungry.

"So. You've got a telephone call."

"What?" Jonathan couldn't make sense of this. "Where? What do you mean? Who's calling me?" One of his parents must have died. "Where?" he repeated.

"At my house. Come on."

"What time is it?" He was trying to remember how many hours earlier it was in America.

Sigurd had already walked out and was waiting for him on the road.

"Where is the telephone?" Jonathan persisted. "Is it in your store?"

"In my house, I told you," said Sigurd. "It's not very late, you know. It's only eight-thirty. You're not used to working so hard, I reckon."

"Mmm," said Jonathan; he was reluctant to admit this.

The telephone was off its hook, waiting for Jonathan to pick it up, on a table in Sigurd's parlor, a place jammed with uncomfortable-looking furniture and lined with a shelf of peculiarly ominous dolls dressed in native costumes from around the world. Sigurd courteously went into the kitchen and shut the door almost, but not quite, all the way.

"Hello," said Jonathan. His heart was pounding.

"Hah! There you are," a familiar voice boomed. "You are famous now in Skopun. Everybody knows you, the American with the Broken Toilet. And you are such a prodigiously hard worker! But now we have some puffins, so it's time to come for dinner."

Jonathan was delighted. "Eyvindur, how did you find me?"

"Anna's father's brother's father-in-law—who used to live in your house—he is the grandfather of Sigurd's brother's wife, so I called Sigurd."

Jonathan failed utterly to follow this, which also contradicted the information he remembered getting from Eyvindur when they'd first talked about the house. "I thought you'd said it was a mother-in-law and that she was dead."

"Well, it was. He was married to her, then she died and he moved out, in with one of his grandchildren, Sigurd."

"But you said he was the grandfather of Sigurd's brother's wife."

"Both! Both! Isn't it complicated?"

"Wouldn't that be incest?" Jonathan had been scribbling a kinship chart on a pad lying on the table.

"No, he had two wives, and it was the second who

was Anna's father's brother's mother-in-law and the grand-mother of Sigurd and his brothers. The other one was the grandmother of the brother's wife."

"Eyvindur, you're joking with me, aren't you?"

"Jonathan." Eyvindur drew a deep breath. "I *never* joke about Faroese matters. Now. You are coming for dinner, you are coming on Sunday night because you must first drive sheep and then rest. Wear nice clothing, because I have invited your future wife. Have you got nice clothing? A nice American shirt?"

"No. It's all gone in the lost baggage."

"It doesn't matter, nobody cares, everybody under-stands that you lost your clothes. But don't wear a Faroese sweater—you understand me?"

"Why? It's what I've got."

"Don't wear it. She is very interested in rocky roll and American things, and at least you can pay homage to her by not wearing a Faroese sweater."

"Rocky roll?" Jonathan giggled.

"Your music."

"Eyvindur, how old is she?" Jonathan felt his heart, which had momentarily lifted at the prospect of meeting a woman, sink.

"She is fine, she is *perfect*. She is descended from very important people. And Anna has already agreed that we will make you the wedding dinner. So. But dress Ameri-can." With that, the line went dead.

Sunday night. Four days from now—and between now and then, he would have chased dozens of sheep and failed to find a substitute for his sweater. Perhaps he could go to Tórshavn on Saturday and buy some more clothes. He was looking forward to this dinner. Whatever the "fu-ture wife" was like, she would be someone new, someone female; and Eyvindur was good company. Jonathan smiled. He could show off his improved Faroese. He rapped on the kitchen door. "Thank you," he called.

"Come in, come in," said Sigurd. "Have a *temun*."

Sigurd and Jón Hendrik were sitting at the kitchen table playing cards. A bottle of brandy stood between them.

"Sit, sit," Sigurd said. He slid the bottle toward Jonathan. "Have a *temun*."

Jonathan had hoped for a genuine *temun*, with cake and milky tea to take care of his growling stomach. But this was bachelor life: dishes stacked haphazardly in the sink, a fishy platter left next to the radio, the gray, sticky deck of cards that made their nightly appearance with their co-star, the bottle. The scene struck Jonathan as sad. Yet they were not sad. Jón Hendrik in fact seemed more cheerful than usual, certainly more friendly.

"So. Welcome to the American," he said, in English.

"Where did you learn your English?" Jonathan asked.

"Well, now, that's a long story," Jón Hendrik answered. He leaned back in his chair. Jonathan doubted he could sit through a long story without something to eat. Jón Hendrik looked at the ceiling, and Jonathan felt something nudging his foot. It was Sigurd's foot.

"I told you," he whispered. "He talks when he's got brandy. Now you will learn everything. Grandpapa"—he turned to Jón Hendrik—"you tell him history. He's here to learn about history."

Jón Hendrik, though, was reconstructing the story of how he had learned English. "When I was fifteen," he began. Then he stopped. "No, I was fourteen." He nodded. "When I was fourteen I went out fishing with my father to Iceland." He stopped again. "I am going to tell the story in the Faroe language. I don't remember enough of your language now. It was many years ago."

"He's eighty-four," said Sigurd. "Aren't you eighty-four now?"

"I'm eighty-five," said Jón Hendrik.

Sigurd's foot was nudging again. "He's lying. He likes to say that he's eighty-five but he's only eighty-four."

Jonathan decided he needed a shot of brandy.

"When I was fourteen I went out fishing with my father to Iceland. But we got in a big storm and he went overboard trying to haul in the lines. So I had to go on alone. Iceland was close, so I went there. There were many people from the Faroes there putting up from fishing, and with them I sent home the message of my father's death. And I gave one man our boat to take home, because I had got a job on a big boat that was going to America. It was a boat from Newfoundland, and it was going back there. We fished all summer under Greenland. And I had to learn to speak your language, because these were all Newfoundland men, and they could say only *thank you* in Icelandic. I could understand because Icelandic is almost the same as the Faroe language. Did you know that?'" He looked with a sudden fierceness at Jonathan, who nodded. "So we came finally to Newfoundland. And I went ashore and lived there awhile, working on the dock. I lived there maybe six years." He stopped again. "I lived there six years," he repeated, sure of his information now. "And I had a friend, a crazy Faroe man, his name was Egil. He got into his head the notion that we should go down into America and look at the cities. He had come to Newfoundland from—" he paused. "I can't remember how he had come to Newfoundland. So. Anyhow, we went down there, the two of us, fishermen, and we went to Boston. Now that's a very big city. Have you been there?" Jonathan nodded; he didn't want to stop this flow. "And we were so bothered by the noise of it, we gave up the idea of seeing the other cities. We went down to the dock looking for Faroe people. And we found them. Wherever there are fish there are Faroe men. So we stayed with them awhile."

"How long?" Jonathan interrupted, expecting Jón Hendrik to say, "A year or two."

"Oh, I think it was a week. We found a boat going

home. So we worked on that boat and we came home, to the Faroes. Egil was from Klaksvík. He's dead now. And that's how I learned your language."

He looked back up at the ceiling. Then he began to sing, in a most gravelly voice, "God Save the Queen." "I learned that from the Newfoundland men," he said. "That's their important *kvæði*."

Jonathan's ears pricked up at the word, though he was surprised to hear it in this context. A *kvæði* was a ballad recounting the doings of such legendary figures as Sigmund, Siegfried, or Charlemagne. Once the living historical record of Europe—Homer had sung a Greek equivalent—they survived exclusively here, in the Faroes. But the Faroe-centricity of Jón Hendrik's worldview was evident in his classification of the British national anthem as a species of *kvæði* and his intimation that Icelandic was merely an odd variant of Faroese. Here indeed was a rich lode for Jonathan's mining. But not now, he pleaded with Fate. Now he just wanted to go home and get back into bed. And take some notes, if he could stay awake.

"So," said Jonathan, preparing to propel himself out the door.

Sigurd wasn't ready for him to leave. "Ho. You want some cake?"

"Yes, cake," Jón Hendrik chimed in.

Jonathan didn't want cake anymore. "I'm really tired. And tomorrow I am going to drive sheep—"

"No," said Sigurd. "We're driving sheep on Friday."

"Oh?"

"Tomorrow it will rain. So have some cake."

The logic was irrefutable; the cake, when it was extracted from a dank shelf beneath the sink, was awful: hard, dry, speckled with pebbles that once were nuts, tasting mostly of dust with a soupçon of soap flakes.

Two days of terrible food and hard work: it was

enough. Jonathan was determined to go home, even if he had to be rude. He ate a few hunks of cake and stood up, saying "So, so, so," as he did.

Sigurd nodded. Jonathan was encouraged to move to "I reckon so." Sigurd nodded again. Was he too fuzzy from brandy to do his part? "Thank you," said Jonathan, "thank you for the cake and the phone call."

"Now how do you know Eyvindur?" asked Sigurd, disregarding Jonathan's leaving procedure.

Dog-tired, Jonathan said, "I met him in Tórshavn." This ridiculous answer satisfied Sigurd long enough for Jonathan to get to the kitchen door, where he stood and announced "Good night," sternly. He could almost see another question forming in Sigurd's mind. Before it could take shape, he opened the door and left.

The following day brought the predicted rain and, with it, a gray, leaden mood that drizzled self-doubt on Jonathan's head. Kicking the stove and snarling at the furniture wouldn't help; this was no access of petulance. His conscience—a composite figure with the body of his father and the voice of doom—had decided to hold an inquisition.

A skilled torturer, his conscience moved deftly between the general and the particular, between statement and question, obscuring the boundaries of reality and asserting—often successfully—that black was white.

Who do you think you are? was the first question, rapidly followed by an assertion designed to invalidate any answer Jonathan could come up with: You don't know *anything*. Just what do you think you're doing? Do you have a plan? Jonathan didn't have a plan. Why didn't you take notes last night? You didn't even take your notebook to Sigurd's. All that stuff Jón Hendrik was saying is *gone*. That was true, but he'd been half asleep when he'd gone over there, for God's sake. But you weren't asleep when you got home; you could have taken notes then. True. Well, now. Notes could be made now. He pulled the notebook out of

the drawer in the kitchen table to underscore his good intentions. You didn't take any notes on dinner at Petur's
either. And how about that kinship information from
Eyvindur? And what do you think you're doing, anyhow?
You haven't got a clue.

Are you on some sort of cultural joyride here? He
couldn't be accused of having fun, really now. You couldn't
be accused of doing any work, either. I know you think
you just got here—but you know, the truth is you've been
here a month. And you haven't done diddly-shit. Pretty
soon it'll be September, and then November—All right,
Jonathan interrupted. But the conscience did not tolerate
interruption. Then December, and you'll be sitting in your
kitchen feeling sorry for yourself or jerking off in the middle
of the afternoon—All right! Jonathan said.

So, the conscience said. So. What have you done that
you're so proud of? Split second of silence for Jonathan's
answer; no answer; conscience rolled on. You are so smug
and self-satisfied and self-deluding. You can't think straight,
that's your problem.

You know what the real problem is? Jonathan was tired
but fascinated; his conscience was always announcing the
"real problem," and Jonathan could not relinquish his hope
that someday he would be enlightened by something the
conscience said. The real problem is, you don't like these
people. You don't like this place. Now that's just completely
wrong, Jonathan protested. This is a great place. If it's such
a great place, why aren't you doing any work? Jonathan
knew this was drivel. That's drivel, he said; that doesn't
follow at all.

This stopped the whole procedure, and Jonathan had
a few minutes of peace, succeeded by a queasiness more
penetrating and intolerable than the pain of inquisition. If
the conscience was "wrong" and even negligible, then what
was left of *consciousness*? A strand of primitive consciousness—I'm hungry, I want to take a walk—remained intact,

but all that Jonathan took to be the hallmark of civilization, reflecting upon one's actions and musing on the actions of others, seemed bound up in this Nagger. Much of the time it slumbered, but its sleep was never deep, and any venture into the realm of thought might waken it and provoke its rantings. Yet without it Jonathan felt one-dimensional.

He spent the day alternating between a flat, unsettling silence and bouts of interrogation. Only one thing was solid: his need to eat. He went to the dock to get some fish; from the steady rain and the slow bobbing of the boats on oily, choppy water, he had his first insight into the components of "drear," which he saw could be a formidable enemy.

Toward evening Heðin put his head into the kitchen to say they would be leaving at eight the next morning. "I'm coming," he said, "to show you what to do."

Jonathan broke through his stupor enough to say, "I thought you hated to drive sheep."

"Yes, but the currents are bad for fishing, and I'll show you what to do. We'll have fun."

This might be irony; Jonathan peered at Heðin's face, but he couldn't tell. "Fun?" he asked.

"It's just work," said Heðin. "Eight o'clock."

They rode out in a flatbed truck under skies splashed with clouds that moved swiftly, peeling off white to show pale blue bright swatches between puffs. The wind was high but moist; the sea was lavender and gray between swells. A charged, metallic smell blew over the hills, greener now than they had been when Jonathan took his walks. Petur and his two sons in the front were silent; Jonathan, in the back with Jens Símun the elder, voiced an occasional grunt of admiration or surprise as the view or the bumps in the road hit home.

A pen improvised from a circle of trucks and some tired-looking lumber was teeming with sheep when they

arrived. Small, collielike dogs and boys ran around the outside, barking and yelling. Inside, two men were wading
among the sheep, one brandishing shears, the other a paintbrush. In their distress at being penned up, the sheep were
shitting and bleating and kicking each other. Jonathan felt
a surge of sympathy. They were a far cry from the noble,
disdainful creatures he'd eaten lunch with, and he pitied
them for their captivity.

Petur added his truck to the circle and everybody piled
out. Little Jens Símun immediately joined the ring of bark-
ers and yellers, where his cousin, Petur, yelled loudest and
ran fastest. Their fathers stood next to the truck, dividing
up the territory: they would go north, Heðin would take
Jonathan south and show him what to do, then continue
west.

"And east?" asked Jonathan.

"East is home. The village," said Petur. "No sheep
there."

Heðin and Jonathan set off, walking shoulder to shoulder on the turfy road. After ten minutes' walk Heðin halted,
sat down on a boulder, and rolled a cigarette. "Want one?"
He offered his tobacco pouch. Jonathan took it and rolled
a misshapen, nearly triangular object. Heðin shook his
head. "That's terrible." He unrolled it and dumped the
tobacco into a fresh paper, which he rolled slowly, explaining what he was doing. "You must roll evenly, roll all your
fingers at once, and push from the middle, otherwise you
make that messy thing you made. Here."

Jonathan was an infrequent smoker, and he felt a bit
dizzy from tobacco so early in the day. But sitting in the
speckled silence with Heðin was pleasant; they seemed like
friends.

"Oh, I hate to drive sheep," Heðin said. "You know,
it's very hard work. They can run fast and they never want
to go where you want them to go."

Jonathan said nothing; he was content. The sun was warming him, and the air was clearing his head of all the vapors of the day before.

"Well, time to go." Heðin sighed. "Off into the *hagi*. Do you know what that is?"

"It's the outfield, isn't it?"

"Yes. The *bøur* is the infield, where we are now, just on the edge of it." He paused. "In the winter, the sheep come into the infield. But in the summer, they live in the outfield."

"I know," said Jonathan. If Heðin had decided to set himself up as an instructor, he was certainly starting at a first-grade level; these were facts Jonathan had learned from his Danish guidebook.

"Do you know who else is in the *hagi*?"

"No."

"The *huldufólk*. Do you know who they are?"

"No."

"They are the gray people who live in the *hagi*."

Jonathan cocked his head. "Elves?"

"No. They are people, except they are all gray. They have gray clothes and gray boats."

"Have they got a village out here?" Jonathan couldn't tell if these people existed or what.

"No. They live in rocks." Heðin nodded several times.

"Oh. Then they are a sort of elf."

"No. Elves are smaller. Also, elves live in town, mostly. But the *huldufólk* live here—there." He gestured into the green beyond. "You have to be careful."

"Why?"

"This is their land. Sometimes they don't like us coming out here. Sometimes they get angry when we come out to get the sheep."

"Then what happens?" Jonathan felt a faint stir of unease.

"They can do surprising things. You'll be walking

along and all of a sudden there's a *huldumaður*—a gray man—
walking beside you. Or sometimes you're catching hold of a
sheep, and somebody else is pulling it away from you—because it's a sheep that belongs to the *huldufólk*."

"What do you do then?"

Heðin laughed. "You let go."

Jonathan hesitated for a moment, then couldn't forbear
asking, "Do you really believe all this?"

"Jonathan, I am telling you this so you know what to
do if it happens. And so you won't be scared if a *huldumaður*
appears. They don't hurt us. They live here and we live in
the village. It's just sometimes they don't like visitors. So you
must be polite and remember that you are on somebody else's
land." He stood up. "Come on," he said.

This region was one Jonathan had not explored on his
walks, but it looked familiar: green, lumpy, flowery. Soon,
however, the terrain became more hilly; stony outcroppings
shaped like miniature mountains made a hike of their progress,
leaving Jonathan out of breath and trailing behind Heðin. His
wind was not good; sitting around in hotels and kitchens
sulking and brooding had not kept him in condition. He
hoped his running was up to scratch.

On the crest of the next ridge Heðin was waiting for
him. "There," he said, as Jonathan wheezed up beside him.
A herd of sheep grazed in the valley below. "We'll get
behind them," Heðin said, "and I'll scare them. Then we'll
chase."

Scaring meant throwing stones into the middle of the
herd and yelling "Oopla!" Jonathan joined in. The sheep
paid no attention. "We'll have to push them," Heðin said.
He walked right up to a fat ewe and pressed his knees into
her rump. She baaed and moved away, sending Heðin into
a lurch. "Stupid sheep," he muttered. He leaned down and
put both hands on her back, propelling her forward in the
direction of the ridge. This worked. The ewe took off,
spraying chunks of turf as her hooves dug in for the sprint.

"Push another!" yelled Heðin.

Jonathan put his hands tentatively atop a white ewe, who promptly shot a burst of pellets on his feet. "Dammit," he said; he kicked her gently in the backside, mostly to repay the favor. But it had the right effect, and this ewe too ran toward the ridge.

"Two more," called Heðin, "then they'll all go."

In unison, Jonathan and Heðin each pushed a sheep. And the entire herd, stirred by some critical amount of movement, followed in the wake of the last two. "Run!" Heðin yelled. He circled around to the back of the herd and pointed Jonathan down toward the opposite side. "Get over there and run!"

And so they retraced their leisurely journey, both of them panting now, Heðin directing Jonathan's movements and position like a football coach: "East! Down! Harder! Watch that black lamb!" When they reached the rock where they'd had the cigarettes, Heðin stopped and flopped onto the ground.

"Leave them here," he said between gasps.

Jonathan thought he might faint. He stood still while the world spun around him in black and green flashes. When his blood had slowed to a steady thumping, he too dropped onto the grass.

"Why don't you use dogs?" he asked.

"Sometimes we do."

"Why not today?"

Heðin laughed. "I told you it was hard work."

The sheep were a ways in front of them, grazing again. "Should we take them to the pen?" Jonathan asked.

"No, they'll stay here. They're in the *bøur* now. Somebody will get them, or we'll get them later. So. Do you think you can do it?"

"Sure," said Jonathan. This was pure bravado. He doubted he could ever run again. And he doubted he could agitate enough sheep to set a whole herd running. "I just have to rest another minute."

But Heðin stood up. "We'll walk back out," he said. "It's farther."

It was much farther. They walked for half an hour before reaching the next group of sheep. Jonathan was worried. "I don't think I can run all this distance," he said softly.

"When you stop, they stop," said Heðin, "so you can rest. Then you have to get them going again, but sometimes it's better that way. This is too far to run, so you'll have to stop. But watch out that one doesn't get away. Sometimes one keeps running." He nodded. "That can happen."

Jonathan could only hope it wouldn't. Heðin had lighted another cigarette and was picking up rocks. "Here." He offered Jonathan a fistful. "If you run at them while you throw the rocks it works better." He walked away.

"Are you leaving?" Jonathan heard a note of distress in his own voice.

"I've got to get the ones to the west," said Heðin, waving his arm toward America. He threw a rock into the herd, stirring up a little movement. "I got them started for you," he called over his shoulder.

Alone with his charges, Jonathan had a rush of worries: the sheep would trample him, the sheep would refuse to move and he'd be out all day and night trying to budge them, he'd pass out from overexertion on some hill, where he wouldn't be found till morning. Lurking behind all this was the specter of the *huldumaður*, that otherwordly shepherd in gray who might at any moment appear to reclaim his stock. A thrill of fear shot up his spine; wasn't that a movement over there, just beyond the herd? Jonathan stood very still and stared at the spot where he thought he'd seen something: nothing. Of course, he told himself. He was being ridiculous. With the energy anxiety brings, he threw several rocks at the sheep and ran at them, yelling "Git!" as he went. They got; in seconds most of them were charging over the hill.

The rest period and the reanimation of the herd went off without incident, and within an hour Jonathan was walking back out to the *hagi*, with a doubled number of sheep munching in the *bøur*, his dutiful children waiting for his return.

Finding sheep on his own, though, was hard. Heðin must have known where they were; Jonathan walked for what seemed miles without running into anything alive. The reliable guidebook had mentioned the lack of animals: no snakes, no squirrels, no badgers, no owls, no deer, no mountain lion to live among the trees that weren't there; no hedgehog, no elk, no arctic fox to burst into his path with its shining tail. Like the absence of trees, this vacuum was one thing when described and quite another when experienced. A pre-Edenic silence and stillness reigned here, in this vegetable and mineral universe. Time was fixed at the fourth day of creation: water, earth, grass, and herb yielding seed, and lights in the firmament, but the fowls and great whales of the fifth day were not in evidence, though in other parts of the island time had progressed that much.

Jonathan was not sure he liked this version of the world. God had been right to put man into a place already populated by moving creatures. Even two days as the only form of animal life would be enough to cause permanent loneliness—and, Jonathan guessed, a permanent delusion of grandeur.

So it was with relief that he heard, faint and far away, the bleat of a ewe calling her lamb to her side.

He followed the trail of the sound, which led him suddenly to the brink of a cliff. The sight of the sea crashing and seething below was as heartening as the noise of the sheep: Jonathan knew there were fish in the water. And a clutch of guillemot took flight at his step, spinning black and white in the pale air. He realized he'd been holding his breath as he walked, taking in small gasps when necessary. He let his chest relax. The ewe was perched on the edge of the cliff, tearing at a tasty clump; her lamb was right beside her. They were both gray.

"Git!" he yelled. The animals lifted their heads and stared at him. "Uh, go home," he tried, as if to a dog, waving his arms in the direction he hoped they would go. The ewe backed away, looking at him as she placed her feet gingerly on the fine grass at the cliff's rim. She stepped on the lamb's leg; it bleated and started to totter. Still staring at Jonathan, she pushed the lamb to higher ground with her hindquarters, flicking her stubby tail on its back to get it moving. With the lamb positioned away from the cliff, Jonathan felt safe making his move. He ran a few steps and then lunged after it, hoping to catch hold of its fleece with his outstretched hands. But the lamb bounced away, bounding off in its rocking-horse motion across the tundra. It was quite young and small, and like all young and small beings it looked like something good to hug. Jonathan was determined to get his arms around it—as much for the pleasure as for the fulfillment of his duty.

The lamb ran him in circles out into the landscape, bobbing up and down, pausing long enough for Jonathan to approach and try, and fail, to catch it. Winded and irritated after three tries, he lay down for a rest. The ewe ambled up to him and sniffed his shoes. He wasn't worried about her; he was sure that if he captured the lamb, the ewe would follow. If he had to, he would carry the damned animal back in his arms, five miles through the country, till he reached the safety of the *bøur*. The lamb had begun to graze again, with its mother nearby.

Jonathan turned onto his belly and started moving across the grass like a snake, slowly, wiggling, breathing steadily. He would come at the lamb from behind and grab it. He inched along, willing the sheep to keep their heads down in the grass. They obeyed. When he was two feet behind his prey he rose, gently, to his knees and then thrust himself forward onto the lamb's back.

It was warm, much warmer than he'd expected—but how long since he'd held a living creature in his arms! And it wriggled and kicked and cried so piteously that Jonathan was almost moved to let it go. Almost, but he pulled it closer to prevent himself; he had succeeded, and he intended to bring his booty home.

He rose to his knees with the lamb clasped to his chest. Once stable in this position he tried to stand up; but that was hard to do holding a squirming twenty-pound bundle of wool and meat, and his first attempt ended with both parties on the ground again, though still attached. Adjusting the lamb in his arms, Jonathan achieved a semi-upright position once more and rested on his haunches, considering how best to get vertical. Suddenly the lamb jerked in his grasp, rising up a few inches.

"Hey," said Jonathan. He tucked it down with a pressure on its head from his chin. "Stay put, buddy."

But the lamb wouldn't stay put. Another jerk, this time releasing both forelegs from Jonathan's hands. Then a slow but insistent movement out of Jonathan's arms, as if somebody were pulling . . . Jonathan's blood froze.

The *huldumaður*.

Gray ewe, gray lamb, just the two creatures alone by the cliff, this nowhere, nobody, nothing part of the island: all of it made sense.

Jonathan let go of the lamb and tore off for home.

By the time he reached the herd he'd gathered with Heðin, Jonathan wasn't sure what had happened. Maybe he'd just spooked himself. He felt a mixture of pride and embarrassment: proud to have had, so early in his stay, an encounter with the supernatural; embarrassed to have been so easily convinced of its existence. He couldn't decide whether to tell anybody about it or not. But the opportunity, which came immediately, was too tempting to resist. Heðin was standing on the far side of the herd, rolling himself a cigarette; Jonathan jogged over to him.

"I met a *huldumaður*," he announced.

"Oh," said Heðin.

"He took a lamb away from me."

"Mmm," said Heðin, putting his cigarette in his mouth. "Didn't you get any more sheep?"

"I only found these *huldufólk* sheep. They were gray, they were all by themselves, and when I tried to catch the lamb, the *huldumaður* took it away."

"Oh, well," said Heðin. "Let's get some lunch." He kicked a stone into the herd and got them moving in the direction of the pen. He walked off at their rear, urging them on with an occasional toss.

Jonathan stood dumbfounded for a minute, then ran after Heðin. "I met a *huldumaður*," he said.

"So you said." Heðin offered the tobacco pouch.

"Don't you believe me?" By repeating the incident, Jonathan had completely converted himself, he realized, and now took anything less than enthusiasm as scorn.

"You like *skerpikjøt*?"

This word rang a bell: it was that dried meat he'd had at Eyvindur's. "*Kjøt*—yes, I love that."

"We eat that when we work hard, because it's very good food." He grinned at Jonathan. "Makes you fart."

When they got to the pen, men and sheep were converging on it from several directions, Petur and Jens Símun driving the foremost herd. There was a noisy and terrified traffic jam at the entrance, some sheep swarming over the backs of others in the effort to get away. A second pen had been set up, where sheared sheep, looking like huge rats,

were being daubed red by the man with the paintbrush and
squirted with white liquid by a man with a bucket and a
hose. The smell of fresh dung was overpowering.

"What are they doing to the sheep?" Jonathan asked.

"Delousing them. And we mark them too, to show
they belong to Skopun. Sometimes sheep will wander into
the *hagi* that belongs to Sandur or Húsavík. Every village
has a mark."

The backs of the trucks had been piled with wool;
detached from the sheep, it looked unappealing—dirty,
matted, lifeless. "And you slaughter some of them?"

"In October," said Heðin. "We slaughter the lambs.
Where do you think we get the *kjøt*?"

Jonathan sensed Heðin's patience was thinning. The
role of instructor could be a tiresome one. Jonathan recalled
his own impatience with the freshmen in his Introduction
to Anthropology sections the year before. But was he such
an unrewarding student? His students had known nothing—in Jonathan's terms. One had insisted that Homer had
written the *Aeneid,* causing Jonathan to omit the classical
references that he'd thought would humanize anthropology.
They had never read *Anna Karenina* or *Huckleberry Finn.*
They lived in a cultural void. He supposed, though, that
not knowing why sheep were sprayed various colors or
when they were slaughtered put him into a similar cultural
void, from Heðin's point of view.

But he wanted to learn. Didn't that count for something? And didn't the fact that he was willing to rush around
after sheep indicate his good intentions? And what about
the *huldumaður?* Didn't his appearance mean that the supernatural residents at least had found Jonathan acceptable?

Petur put a stop to this huffy line of reasoning by
coming over and clapping Jonathan on the shoulder. "Did
you enjoy yourself?"

"He runs fast," said Heðin, but begrudgingly, Jonathan thought.

"So. Hard work, eh? Now we'll eat." Petur steered Jonathan over to their truck with his big hand.

"I met a *huldumaður*," Jonathan said. Clearly, Heðin wasn't going to mention it.

Petur stopped short. "Where?"

"By a cliff. He took a lamb away from me." Jonathan didn't feel as sure of this as he had when he described it to Heðin. "I think," he added, lamely.

"Did you see him?" Petur was stern.

"No. I just felt him pulling."

"Hah," said Petur. Jonathan couldn't tell if this was surprise or doubt. "But you didn't see him?" Petur repeated.

"No." Jonathan waited for Petur to tell him that there weren't any *huldufólk*, or that he must never go back to the *huldumaður*'s cliff, but he just said "hah" again.

Lunch was hunks of lamb, hunks of bread, and hunks of raisin cake. A thermos of tepid tea was passed around after the cake. Then everyone rolled a cigarette, including Jonathan, who did better this time. Petur and Jens Símun chatted in low voices, leaning against the side of the truck; Heðin leaned on the hood, keeping his distance from Jonathan, who perched on the open tailgate watching little Jens Símun and little Petur making scary faces at the sheep in their pen.

Jonathan was tired, sleepy from lunch, and depressed in some way that he couldn't pinpoint. The whole lamb episode had affected him oddly. He'd scoffed—gently—at their beliefs, and then been scoffed at—possibly—for becoming a believer. And the question of whether there were or weren't gray people living on the outer reaches of the island had now taken on a jumpy, bifocal quality: there couldn't be such people; he'd encountered one of these people; he must have made it up, it was autohypnosis; but the lamb had been lifted right out of his arms; he had probably just let go of it from fear and it had jumped out; and so forth.

All afternoon he pondered, strolling out to find sheep,

racing them back to the pen. From the details he moved to
the wider concerns, which were with faith. Did he believe
in *huldufólk*? More pertinent, did the Faroese? If they did,
why? If he did, then what? Belief opened a door Jonathan
had been trained to keep shut: the door to mystery. His
parents' rationality had easily revealed to him its opposite,
irrationality, and this, in his sulks and self-absorptions, he
knew well. But mystery was something other. Its opposite,
Jonathan now saw, was despair—just the sort of despair
that plagued him and wreathed his parents in an ineffable,
omnipresent sadness that the world could not cure because
the world had generated it. Marriages would fall apart,
nuclear weapons would be built, tyrants would seize power
in hot countries, warranties would expire a week before the
toaster broke: life was like that. But there were explanations;
everything had an explanation. Male psychology, scientific
curiosity, greed, capitalism—all this could explain why life
was like that. Knowledge was his parents' god and his own.
But knowledge brought sadness.

Riding back to town on a heap of wool, Jonathan
looked hard at Jens Símun: Was he sad? Tired; his two-
tone eyes were half shut, his workman hands hung loose
between his knees. Jonathan couldn't determine anything
about Jens Símun's mood. His own mood, though, was
improving. He'd run fast, he'd found more sheep, he was
going back to Petur's for dinner, he was looking forward to
Eyvindur and Tórshavn. And the *huldumaður*, along with
the thoughts he had provoked, had lifted the edge of Jonathan's veil in some way. The Unknowable beckoned, glim-
mering with the promise of a respite from explanation. His
mind fixed on that small beam of light, Jonathan fell asleep
as the truck bumped home.

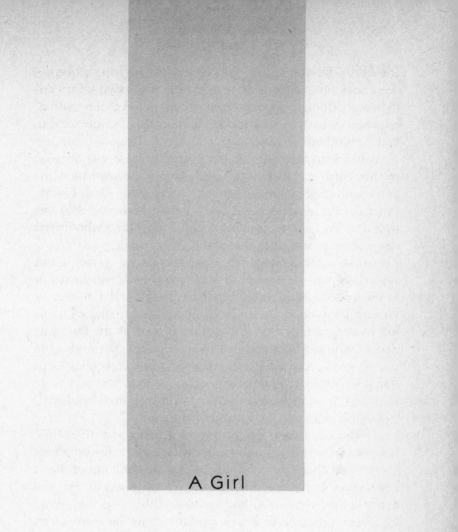

A Girl

The shifting clouds of the latter part of the week had turned to a gusting, driving rain by Saturday, when Jonathan stood on the dock waiting for the afternoon boat to Tórshavn. People in city clothes moved from foot to foot, trying to preserve their shoes from the wet. Jonathan's American

sneakers—his sole concession to Eyvindur's instructions—
were soaking up rain like sponges. He was looking forward
to luxury, though. He'd booked a room in the Hotel Hafnia,
Tórshavn's best, with a private bath. There he intended to
take a two-hour shower.

   The boat was late. People were saying it was because
of the weather. "Bad tides," he heard. One woman whispered to another, "I'm going to be sick, oh, my God, I know
I'm going to be sick." "Maybe it won't get here," said her
friend. This worried Jonathan. But the woman who feared
she'd get sick was sure the boat would come.

   It did, though not before everyone was sodden and
chilled. It was chock-full of sacks of flour, mail, boxes of
canned goods, used tires, relatives from Tórshavn over to
visit for the weekend. In a burst of confusion, all the board-
ing passengers attempted to get on as soon as the boat was
docked; those who were on the boat looked pale and more
than eager to get off it, which they were prevented from
doing by the onslaught of embarkers. Many wet feet were
stepped on, and a few were rolled over by a dockhand with
a dolly who attacked the cargo with vigor.

   When Jonathan got on board he saw why there had
been such a rush. The small cabin had seats for about
twenty; another ten were perched on laps and knees. He'd
last taken this boat on a balmy day. He'd stood in the bow
and watched the birds, and when he'd tired of that view,
he'd sat on a piece of heavy machinery in the front cargo
area. It had been a beautiful trip, and in his enthusiasm
he'd imagined himself standing at this prow in later months,
the Anthropologist Who Is Accepted, riding the waves back
to "his" village. He had disregarded the fact that the weather
would change.

   Seatless, Jonathan stood near the door of the cabin in
his squelchy shoes. The engine roared beneath his feet, and
the smell of fuel seeped up through the floor, hinting at a

terrible, close atmosphere to come once the door had been shut. As they got under way, the ticket taker latched the door and turned on a heater that blew foul air onto Jonathan's head. Within ten minutes the cabin was dense with breath, wet clothing, and diesel fumes. Jonathan leaned against the door, where sea air occasionally burst through the crack. But it wasn't enough. His head was clouding up. He went out and stood on deck, gulping in the freshness.

They were riding into the wind, so Jonathan made his way to the back of the boat, where, he reasoned, he would be somewhat protected from the elements. He was glad he hadn't listened to Eyvindur about the Faroese sweater; he would have been freezing without it. He took a position under a small overhang and stared back at Skopun in the mist; the boat's wake was wide, and its course was a straight one, giving Jonathan the illusion that they were towing the village along with them.

He was beginning to enjoy himself when the boat changed direction and started riding over the sea at a new angle. The waves that had bobbed them up and down gently, predictably, now hit them broadside and made a dizzying zigzag of their course. There was no rhythm to the boat's rise and fall; it would skid sideways as if planing on the surface, then sink deep into a swell that, as the boat rose again, washed half over one side or another. An especially large wave dumped water at Jonathan's still-wet feet. He pressed against the cabin housing and wondered if he was safe.

"Hey," somebody said. Jonathan jumped. It was the ticket taker, all dressed up in yellow rain gear. "Get inside."

"Me?" asked Jonathan.

The ticket taker came closer to see who was such a fool. He peered at Jonathan from under his rubber hat. "Oh. You. You go inside. It is dangerous out here. You understand?" Then he took Jonathan's arm and pointed at the cabin, against whose outer wall they both sheltered. "In. In. No good here," he said, his faith in Jonathan's Faroese waning by the moment.

"I understand," Jonathan said stiffly. "I'm going."

"You could fall right in and die. You could get taken away by a wave." Assured of comprehension, the ticket taker went on a tear. "Nobody would ever know. Do you know this happened only last year? A little boy, it was Páll *hjá* Jørgen's youngest, he was washed overboard—we think. It was a July storm just like this. Nobody saw because nobody with more than a herring's brain would be out here." He shook his head. "Go."

Jonathan scrambled back to the cabin with the ticket taker on his heels. Drawing in his last real breath, he opened the door.

It was worse than he remembered it, or perhaps it had worsened in his absence. Something sweet yet horrible had been added to the brew. Within moments, a sound identified it for him: vomit.

The woman who had insisted she would be sick was being sick, profusely, into a paper cone. And she was not the only one. Mothers were holding cones for children, husbands for wives, sons for fathers who looked like fishermen impervious to seasickness. Full cones were held at arm's length, carried to a window, and thrown into the sea. But the pitching of the boat and the juiciness of the cones' contents made this a hazardous operation. Mishaps dotted the floor.

Vomiting, like yawning, is contagious—nearly irresistible. Jonathan felt that strange dissociation of head from stomach that is the harbinger of nausea. A gulf several miles wide seemed to have opened between his throat and his belly. And yet they were connected—too connected, in fact—by what felt like a thick rubber band that stretched and contracted with the movement of the boat. He clamped his teeth together and defied fate. Gushes of bile flooded his mouth, black dots danced before his eyes, he swayed against the door and then, unable to stop himself, puked all over his sneakers.

Tears of embarrassment and pain (his vomit had been acrid and harsh, probably because he'd eaten leftover fried fish for lunch) sprang to his eyes. What was he to do now? He looked disconsolately at his shoes. What a foreigner! He couldn't even vomit into a cone. What must they be thinking, these green-faced, sober people who sat quietly chucking up their lunches without any fuss.

One of them, less green than most, a fisherman, Jonathan figured by his slicker and his vacant expression, lurched off the bench and approached him with a handful of paper towels. He thrust these into Jonathan's hand and was replaced on the bench by a sudden heave of the sea. "Bad storm," he said to Jonathan; he imitated the motion of the boat in the waves with his arm and then mimed throwing up. He pointed to Jonathan's spattered shoes. "Clean, clean," he said, wiping the air in front of him with another pile of paper towels, which were stacked on the ledge behind him.

Jonathan was touched by this interest. "Thank you," he said, smiling as best he could. The fisherman repeated "Clean, clean," in a commanding tone, so Jonathan bent over and got to work. The paper towel reminded him of toilet paper in France: shiny, brown, slippery, unsuited to its task. The whole handful wasn't enough to clean half of one sneaker. "Can I have more of those?" he asked.

The fisherman was impressed. "You speak very well," he said. He turned to a retching fellow beside him and said, "You know, that's an American man. He lives in Skopun. But listen to him speak!" The retcher filled his cone, made his way to the window, disposed of it, sat down, and looked at Jonathan, who was still waiting for more paper towels.

"Fucking asshole," he said, in English. He smiled broadly. Jonathan bristled. "Fuck, shit, stick it in your ear," he continued. He was showing off, Jonathan realized.

"You worked in America?" he asked, in Faroese.

The curser nodded. "Shit, damn," he said, grinning. "New Bedford. Goddamn son of a bitch," he concluded.

The first fisherman handed Jonathan another pile of towels. "He speaks your language well, no?" Jonathan, busy with his shoes, only nodded. What his sneakers required was a bath; perhaps he would wear them into the shower. If they ever reached Tórshavn.

They spent another half hour on the choppy sea before the boat again changed direction and rode with rather than against the waves. The ticket taker signaled their imminent arrival by opening the door to let in some fresh air. The passengers started straightening themselves—combing hair, wiping pale, sweaty faces with handkerchiefs, adjusting clothing rucked up during vomiting. Jonathan made a few more passes at his sneakers. He looked at his watch: only four o'clock. If he hurried, he might be able to buy a non-Faroese sweater.

In his palatial room at the Hafnia—two beds, view of Tórshavn's main street, wall-to-wall carpeting, a heartening list of breakfast choices laid on his down pillow—Jonathan unwrapped his packages: a Shetland sweater, navy blue; four new murder mysteries; a pair of Nikes, black and white; a package of airmail envelopes; a small watercolor set; the *Herald-Tribune*, six days old; two long-sleeved T-shirts; an overpriced and weighty picture book about the Faroes; a second Faroese sweater, light brown with dark brown designs; a pot of geraniums, pink.

He had spent a fortune. He didn't care. He piled his purchases on one of the beds and looked at them from the other bed. The watercolor set made him especially happy. Jonathan couldn't remember painting since he was in grade

school, but the moment he'd seen the little red box in the
stationery store, he'd coveted it. He would go off walking
with his paintbox in his knapsack, out to the bird cliffs,
and sit there, in the mild sun, painting the sea and the sky.
He got up and moved next to his piles of stuff, fingering
his sweaters, his T-shirts, his crisp, thin, blue envelopes.
The second Faroese sweater had been a wild extravagance,
but it was much more beautifully made than his first one,
and he knew he'd be happy to have it in the future, when
Faroese sweaters would be unavailable. Other anthropologists came back with spears and shields, drums made of
human skin, wooden statues that required elaborate crating;
he would return with sweaters.

And now, the shower. Jonathan regretted he hadn't
bought new pants as well. All his clothes had an aura of
vomit. He opened the window and hung his old Faroese
sweater and his blue jeans over a chair to air. Then, sneakers
in hand, he went into the bathroom.

Twenty minutes later, faint from too much steam and
heat, he reeled out and flopped onto the bed. Naked and
with hot moist vapors rising from his body, he read the
Herald-Tribune. The crackle of the pages recalled Paris and
made him wish for the croissant and café au lait that had
been his daily accompaniment to the news. Perhaps he
would go to Paris. It wasn't that far: a boat to Copenhagen,
then a plane. He could be there in three days. He could be
there in one day if he took a plane to Bergen, in Norway,
but he feared it would be the same sort of plane—and the
same sort of trip—as the one that had brought him to the
Faroes. The boat would be nice; he would take the boat.
Perhaps spend a few days in Copenhagen, where the food
was rumored to be good. No, better go straight to Paris,
where he knew the food was good. He could buy an old
map on the bank of the Seine. He could have a Pernod, he
could have steak au poivre, he could go to an American
movie on the Champs-Élysées.

A cool wind blowing the smell of fish in the open window brought him back to reality: he was in the Faroe Islands doing fieldwork; he was chilly; he was not going anywhere.

Maybe he'd be better off never going out of Skopun. Jonathan remembered dreaming of leaving the country the last time he'd been in Tórshavn. Something about the place provoked the urge to get out. In Skopun, the rest of the world seemed to fall away; he was stranded there, but the exigencies of living so occupied him that he didn't have time to think about being stuck. Or perhaps it was merely that nothing in Skopun reminded him that he was, technically, in Europe, whereas here everything was a sad, bedraggled version of life in a European city. Like Rome or Paris, Tórshavn had too much traffic, but a hundred cars were enough to qualify as too much; as in Marseilles, sailors on shore leave roved the streets looking for excitement, but here they found none and were sober while looking; the weather patterns that made London a mystery of mists and fogs made Tórshavn a muddy, soggy hole: all Ireland might be washed in the Gulf Stream, but Tórshavn was drowning in it.

Jonathan folded the pernicious *Tribune* with its memories and its advertisements for villas on the Riviera and Swiss watches. He told himself he was lucky not to be in Sarawak with malaria and a shortwave radio and nothing else, but this had never been a convincing argument for happiness in the past and it failed to raise his spirits now. Every anthropologist gets the culture he deserves, had been the wisdom in Cambridge. To the pacifist, the warlike tribe; to the squeamish, the aboriginal bug- and snake-eaters; and to the sophisticate, evidently, the fourth-rate, hopelessly provincial, downright grubby Faroes.

Only half an hour earlier he'd found his room charming. Looking around it now, Jonathan failed to see what had appealed to him. The prospect of a shower, doubtless, but now that he'd had one, there seemed nothing in the world to look forward to or enjoy. He picked up the breakfast menu. It was a list of cereals and methods of egg preparation; no grapefruit, pancakes, blueberry muffins, or anything else Jonathan craved. And he noted that it did not proclaim the availability of room service. He would have to go to the dining room to get his morning coffee. Jonathan loathed drinking his coffee in company and was always willing to pay the surcharge for room service in the morning. Not only in the morning; he would happily pay it at this moment to avoid seeing and sitting with the people who were destined to be his dinner companions.

If this were Italy, he could bribe a maid or bellboy to bring him a plate of food. If this were France, room service would be available. But in the obedient, unhedonistic north, his only choice was to go downstairs or to go hungry.

He put on some of his new clothes and went downstairs.

Dinner was a smorgasbord, a fairly extensive and appetizing one, laid out on a long table near the windows. Jonathan helped himself and indulged in the luxury of an orange soda, which for once he would drink during dinner. He couldn't accustom himself to the Faroese practice of not drinking until after the meal. As he ate his herring and his Havarti, he sized up his fellow diners. There were a couple of families with young children, out to dinner on a Saturday night; the inevitable sprinkling of middle-aged men who every night eat dinner alone in hotel dining rooms throughout the world; three Danish Navy recruits (from the early warning station, perhaps); and a slight, pale man with a large head, who looked about Jonathan's age and was reading a book while he ate. Jonathan always wanted to know what other people were reading, so he made a detour past the pale man's table on the way back from refilling his plate. The book was T. E. Lawrence's *The Seven Pillars of Wisdom*.

Chewing his second helping, Jonathan chewed also on

the puzzle of this person and his book. It was in English, so he was at the least an English speaker; probably he was a native speaker, because Lawrence's swashbuckling yet self-denigrating account of his adventures would be incomprehensible—and uninteresting—to a foreigner. As an American, Jonathan had found it dull, suggesting that the pale man was English and aspired to be a suntanned, intrepid version of himself.

Jonathan debated going over to his table to say hello. He wished he'd brought a book also. Then they could peek at each other's books and determine that they had a language in common. He could have brought the *Herald-Tribune*. But did he really want to meet this person? He looked over to find the pale man looking his way. Jonathan smiled. The pale man put his book on the table, with a spoon to mark his place, and walked over to Jonathan.

"Swithin," he said, extending his hand. "Frank."

"Jonathan Brand," said Jonathan. They joined hands for a moment.

"You're an American, aren't you?"

Jonathan nodded; Frank Swithin had a full-blown upper-class accent, something Jonathan enjoyed.

"I thought so when you walked in, and then, of course, the way you were eyeing my book—have you read it?"

"I did, yes." Jonathan paused. The English didn't mind contentiousness. "I thought it kind of went on."

"Um." Swithin was noncommittal. "You must be the anthropologist living on Fugloy. I'm glad to meet you, because I'm heading up there soon and I was hoping to stay with you."

"I'm living on Sandoy," Jonathan said. "I've got lots of room, though."

"Sandoy? I was sure—" He rummaged in a pocket. "Here. Fugloy." He had a piece of paper. "Oh, hold on, this fellow's name is Jim. You did say your name was Jonathan? Perhaps they've got it mixed up."

"Let me see." Jonathan held out his hand. The piece of paper read *Jim Wooley, Fugloy*. "That's not me."

"Well, you've got a double, then." Swithin emitted a short laugh.

"Where did you find out about him?"

"At the Folklore Institute."

The Folklore Institute was news to Jonathan. "Are you an anthropologist too?" he asked.

"Oh, no, ornithologist. But I am somewhat curious about the bird legends, so I stopped over there. I also hoped they would be able to tell me the best observation spots, and as it turned out, there was a most helpful fellow who does a bit of amateur watching. At any rate, he recommended Fugloy—you know the name means 'bird island'—and mentioned this Jim Wooley, who's been living here since last winter."

"Last winter?" Jonathan was not feeling well.

"You don't know him? Surprised. I wouldn't think that two American anthropologists in this place could miss each other." He shot out another little laugh.

"How long have you been here?"

"A week." Swithin glanced over at the food table. "Why don't we have some tea," he said. He was looking at a tray of cakes that had appeared at one end.

Settled down at the table again with cakes and tea, Jonathan said, "Tell me about this Folklore Institute."

"Hardly lives up to its name," said Swithin. "Two old chaps and the spry assistant who helped me out. They're working on a collection of Faroese legends and ballads. They've done one volume; took them ten years. Magnus Mohr and—I can't remember the other one's name. Jens Pauli something. The assistant's name is Smith. Isn't that funny? Marius Smith. Told me he's just a secretary, really. Spends most of his time transcribing the old fellows' scrawls and jottings."

"Where did you find out about them?"

"Bothers you, eh?" Swithin looked into Jonathan's eyes for a second. "Up here for the doctorate?" He smiled.

Jonathan did not enjoy feeling exposed. And he didn't know if Swithin was prodding him or merely commenting on the obvious.

"I know how it is," he continued, when Jonathan said nothing. "I got out of it myself. You would never have heard of that institute in America. It's sheer luck I found out about it. I've a Norwegian friend in London who was at Oxford with me, a folklorist, who had been up here years ago, when they were just starting to collect ballads. He told me to look up Mohr and send his regards and all that."

"I'm at Harvard," Jonathan blurted. Then he blushed. But it was too much: the institute, the other anthropologist, Oxford. To regain his composure, Jonathan turned the conversation back toward Swithin. "You were in graduate school?"

"I was working toward the doctorate, yes, in history. Terrible life. I canned it, moved down to London, got a job with a bird society. Banding, population estimates, that sort of thing. Peaceful. And I like the travel."

"How did you learn it, though? I mean, if you were studying history."

"In the blood." Swithin smiled again. "My father's a devoted birder. I grew up counting wrens and rooks. Really, though, it's easy. I took classes in the evening."

Jonathan had calmed down somewhat, and he wouldn't have minded a few questions about himself. But Swithin was occupied by eating cakes. "People took me for an ornithologist when I first arrived," Jonathan said, offering an opening.

"Did they now." Swithin chugged down a cup of tea. "How long have you been here?"

"Oh, a month or two," Jonathan said. It had been five weeks almost to the day. He waited for more questions.

Swithin stood up. "Good to meet you," he said. He

had powdered sugar on his cheek. Jonathan had an impulse
to invite him to come along to Eyvindur's. They might
appeal to each other, and his presence would provide a
distraction should the future wife prove dull or unaccept-
able.

"Will you be here tomorrow night?" Jonathan asked.

"No. I'm going to Mykines tomorrow. Main booby
nesting grounds. I'll see you at breakfast, though." He
bobbed his big head up and down. "Au revoir," he said.
Scooping up his book, spoon still in place, he left the dining
room.

Before dinner Jonathan had been merely sad; now he
was in trouble. Room service would have protected him
from the terrible news that he was not the only anthropologist on the Faroe Islands. What was he to do? Back in his
bed, he located Fugloy on the frontispiece map in the picture
book: far away, far up north, with only two tiny dots of
villages. Bush—or as close to bush as you could come in
the tundra. Skopun, with its choice of grocery stores and
its bustling harbor, was New York City compared to Hattarvík or Kirkja. Things were grim. This Jim Wooley had
probably already written his thesis, if he'd spent a whole
winter here. He was bound to be a live wire from the
University of Chicago, tough, self-sufficient, inured to the
rigors of fieldwork from undergraduate stints in jungles with
his mentors.

Jonathan shut his eyes. He would have to enlist Frank
Swithin's aid. He was going up there anyhow. He could
give Jonathan a report on Wooley's activities and research.
Whatever it was Wooley was doing, Jonathan would do
something else—no hardship, as he hadn't started yet. If
Wooley was doing kinship on boat crews, Jonathan would
do *huldufólk* beliefs; if Wooley was doing folklore, Jonathan
would do political party alignment within families.

But whatever he did, it would be diluted by Wooley—
negated by Wooley, in fact—as Wooley had the jump on

Jonathan and surely would finish first. Jonathan's secret dreams of being asked to publish his thesis, of the scholarly world brought to attention by his seminal analysis of this little-known, well-nigh forgotten corner of Western Europe, now looked like hopeless fantasies rather than slightly exaggerated visions of his future. He groaned.

Swithin would help. Swithin had seemed sympathetic to academic troubles of this sort. But perhaps he would prefer Wooley and would side with him? After all, Wooley's island was a better bird-watching spot. And Wooley would be his host. Jonathan determined to invite Swithin to Skopun first; there was nothing wrong with the birds out at the Troll's Head. Calmed by this resolve, he turned his attention to the next night's dinner.

Jonathan quickly realized that he had better stop thinking. The girl would be ugly and stupid; the girl would be delicious and find him lunky and dull; the girl would not come (this seemed the best alternative he could imagine).

He went into the bathroom to check the condition of his sneakers, which he'd left to dry on the edge of the sink. They were soft, moist, and expansive, as if they had been transformed into a pair of large mushrooms. He sniffed one; it smelled of warm rubber and shit. His Keds, from the five-and-dime on Mount Desert: their death increased his sadness. He had his new Nikes, but the Keds were one of his few representatives of home. It seemed wrong to leave them in a wastebasket in Tórshavn. He put them on the radiator next to the bed. Maybe a good baking would revive them.

In the morning Jonathan drank three cups of thin mean coffee and made revisions to his invitation to Swithin: Please come and stay with me this week, I think you'll like my birds (too eager); did you say you were looking for puffin colonies, because we've got a big one (Swithin had said nothing of this); you must stop off in Skopun on your way back from Mykines (this suggestion defied geography); I

need your help—why not? Why not just tell the truth? He
ate bread and cheese and kept his eyes fixed on the door to
the dining room. By ten-fifteen his nerves and the coffee
had put him into a sweaty, shivery, buzzy state. He went
to the front desk to find out Swithin's room number.

"The English?" asked the clerk. "He has left."

"When?"

"Very early. He had coffee in his room."

Jonathan didn't move.

"He went to Mykines," said the clerk.

"I know," said Jonathan. Coffee in his room. He decided to go for a walk.

The storm had blown off during the night, leaving
high, thin clouds that either presaged the arrival of the next
storm or signified enduring calm weather; natives could read
the clouds' language, Jonathan could not. But even an il-
literate such as he could enjoy the sun, the brisk winds that
twirled through the streets, the air freshened and distilled
by rain. Many others were out walking too: elderly people
dressed in black leaving church arm in arm; young men
recuperating from exasperatingly sober nights-before; packs
of little boys darting up and down hills, chasing cats from
their spots in the sun. And couples in love—a Nordic version of love.

This love did not hold hands, did not kiss on the street,
did not coo into an ear or let a hand stray to a buttock.
This love was evident only in a fine thread of tension between two people, a quivering, taut connection that en-
forced a distance at the same time that it ensured a link.
Couples in love always emitted some sort of glow; Jonathan
had often enough been set to grumbling internally from
seeing it. But Faroese couples seemed to inhabit their own
pulsing electrical field, sparking out warnings to everyone—
including the beloved—to stay away.

Watching two teenagers at the pier who were so besotted that they couldn't look at each other and stood poised

side by side, listening—or so it appeared to him—to the crackle and hiss of their high-voltage emotions, Jonathan wondered if such a dangerous and powerful connection would be waiting for him at Eyvindur's. He admired the usually phlegmatic Faroese for their all-out engagement in the business of love. Let the French neck on the boulevards, let the Italians pinch every passing bun, let the English talk their heads off over drinks while fantasies rolled past their eyes: the Faroese had passion with dignity. What captivated him most was the sense of their privacy, their unwillingness to display anything. Some might call their unwillingness an inability and think them repressed; Jonathan thought them only serious. And weren't they right? Wasn't love too serious to toy with or show off?

He hoped so but he didn't know. Love in Cambridge was offhanded. It lacked both Continental form and Faroese substance. From his parents' marriage he had learned that it was possible to connect and stay connected, but examples of *how* to do this were unavailable. His fifteen classmates made the rounds through one another's beds sequentially, unceremoniously. Jonathan himself had gone a quarter of the circuit. He couldn't claim any credit for finding this distasteful; he had found it too much trouble. Even the minimal wooing needed to bed a level-headed girl graduate student was more effort than Jonathan was willing to put out. Eight of his classmates were women; after he'd made love to three of them, he quit. They were all the same. Like him, they were entirely fixed upon their futures, their qualifying papers, "their" tribes. Their minds were not on him—any more than his mind was on them. And mindless conjunction was hollow, Jonathan had realized. He had also realized he wanted no other sort of connection.

So Jonathan had put love off until the future. Sex became dimmer as it slipped further into the past. He had an adept if predictable partner at home, and the life of a graduate student, with its competitiveness, jockeying for

position, and deadlines for achievement, was an anti-
erotic one.

But the world, even the gray, undemonstrative Faroese
world, was full of sex and love and confusion. Some of these
might be heading his way, might be at this moment walking
around Tórshavn wondering how dinner would go and how
she would like the American. Jonathan smelled a whiff of
hope and chided himself: expect nothing, never be disappointed. Anticipation was alluring, though. She might be
beautiful. She might be, in fact, his future wife. Jonathan
projected himself five years into the future, telling his colleagues the story of meeting his wife one evening at dinner
in the field. But this assumed a transplantable girl. She liked
rock and roll; didn't that suggest a fondness for America
and possibly a yearning to go there? On the other hand,
maybe he was transplantable. A sod-roofed cottage in the
old section of Tórshavn, work at the Folklore Institute, the
annual visit to the States, which each year would seem more
foreign. Walking the cold cement pier into the wind, Jonathan doubted he could become Faroese. More than the
food, the language, or the customs, the very land was alien.
Could he ever stand at the end of this jetty looking out to
the dark swatch of island across the fjord, watching the
clouds drift down onto the crests of the cliffs and the light
banding the ocean purple, blue, black, purple, and say, in
the words of little Petur's song, Here is the land that suits
me? No sun speckled through the trellis of deciduous
growth, no thick, tar-heavy summer air, no January drive
on roads cushioned and battened by snow, no pulse of city,
dangerous, melodic, that symphony of cars and radios and
population that is the real American music. Here silence,
shot through with bird cries, and the visual equivalent of
silence, these naked scarps of earth, monotonous, magnificent, and empty.

Thoughts of home stirred in Jonathan an urge to make
trouble—an urge he had rarely indulged in America, where

there was a wider scope for it: a few teenage trips to the beach in the small hours with beer and a companion willing to neck with him until the sun came up and the mosquitoes woke; a marijuana-fuzzy month in his sophomore year. He now wanted intrigue, deception even, secret trips, late nights, coffee at one in the afternoon in a bathrobe: dissolution of some sort. Or its opposite: dangerous action. Perhaps he could join whatever group was protesting the early warning station. Or go home and pour blood on government documents.

He would not, he knew. These longings were only today's installment of Tórshavn malaise. Discontent was endemic here, as dysentery to Bombay. And he had additional sources of misery in the discovery of Wooley, King of the Faroes, and the imminent encounter with the unknown, the girl. Momentary encounter—for, looking at his watch, Jonathan saw he would be late if he didn't hurry. Lacking all-American clothes, he had resolved to shower at least before putting on Faroese ones.

He went back to the hotel in the liquid yellow afternoon light of 6 P.M., washed, dressed himself in navy blue, chucked his Keds into the trash with a brief farewell, grabbed the geranium, and trotted uphill in his Nikes to Eyvindur's house.

Daniela of Icelandair, with whom Jonathan had written the fruitless telexes searching for his suitcase, was not an improbable choice for his future wife. She spoke excellent English, he remembered, and had struck him as intelligent. She had not, however, struck him as particularly attractive, but he prepared himself to change his mind on this point. She was more appealing out of her uniform, a stiff, dark-blue woolen suit with a military aura. She was dressed now in genuine Levi's (in honor of his presence?), a "professional" silk shirt with a bow at the neck, and black pumps whose soles had curved upward from hundreds of soakings by Tórshavn's rain. This garb didn't catch Jonathan's fancy, but it did reveal her figure—curvy, though on a small scale. Jonathan noticed she didn't reach even to his shoulder. In previous encounters, they'd been sitting at her desk in the office.

Anna emerged from the kitchen to watch the momentous meeting. Always awkward with gifts, Jonathan thrust the geranium at her and mumbled, "This is for you." She barely looked at it; she and Eyvindur were hopping with excitement. As Jonathan and Daniela shook hands—her hand was dry and warm, almost fevered—Anna clasped the geranium with one hand and her husband's arm with the other, the two of them nodding and exemplifying, Jonathan thought with irritation, the ideal of the happily married couple that was supposed to spur him to action.

To her credit, Daniela seemed uneasy with the fuss the Poulsens were making. She sat down on the sofa as soon as she'd let go of Jonathan's hand. Then she kicked off her curly shoes and tucked her feet up under a pillow, as if to announce that she was now off duty. The ball seemed to be in Jonathan's court.

"You know that we know each other," he said to Eyvindur.

"But of course! Do you think I would have you marry somebody you didn't know?" Eyvindur beamed. "But you know her *professionally*. Now you will know her *privately*." He winked. Jonathan winced and looked over at Daniela.

She was shaking her head and smiling to herself, looking not at the three people to her left but at the floor, where the toys that had tripped Eyvindur the last time Jonathan was here still lay. She leaned over and picked up a stuffed giraffe. "Are the children asleep?" she asked.

"No, no. Go and say hello to them," Eyvindur said. "Go." He pulled away from his wife's arm and shooed the women out. Anna raised her eyebrows but obeyed; Daniela, leaving her shoes behind, got up and followed Anna down the hallway.

Eyvindur grabbed Jonathan's shoulder and pushed him onto the sofa. "Now listen," he said in English, "she is the most perfect person for you. Why? Because she is very cultured, she speaks English, she is very Faroese but with a Continental flavor, just as I am, and she is so fucking beautiful. No?"

"Well," Jonathan began.

"And listen to this. She went to school in Denmark and lived in Paris and she is descended from the very famous painter I told you about, Ruth Smith, the most famous family in the whole Faroes, everybody in the family is famous and special. Her brother runs the Folklore Institute, her father is a member of Parliament, her mother—" Here Eyvindur ran out of steam, or perhaps the mother was not as notable as the rest of the family.

"I'll have to get to know her, Eyvindur," Jonathan ventured. "I'm sure she's as wonderful as you say. I am looking forward to—" He paused. What was he looking forward to? Eyvindur's broad, affable face, intent on him, was poised five inches away. Eyvindur's efforts to find him a mate were oppressive yet touching, and Jonathan felt the burden of gratitude for something he wasn't sure he wanted. That is, he wanted it abstractly, but as embodied in Daniela Smith it was not quite right. Wasn't it best to forestall disappointment on all sides and admit this early, before the situation got too complicated? "I think it's best to say—" Jonathan started.

Eyvindur cut him off. "Jonathan, are you a homosexualien? Is that why you don't have a wife?"

"Homosexual," said Jonathan automatically.

"What is it like?" Eyvindur leaned even closer, eager.

"No, I meant the word is homosexual, not homosexualien. I'm not."

"You can tell me. I don't care. I am very broad-headed."

"I'm not. Eyvindur, I'm just not sure about Daniela. Well, I guess I'll have to get to know her."

"Okay." Eyvindur sounded dubious. "It's really fine if you are. I won't tell her." He frowned. "But it would be better, because then she would not think that perhaps you do not like her."

"I like her! I like women. I'm not interested in men. I like her." Jonathan put his hand on Eyvindur's knee to emphasize his sincerity. Eyvindur pulled his head back a little and Jonathan burst out laughing. "Honestly, I'm crazy about women. It's just that after you and Anna have gone to all this trouble, I don't want you to be disappointed if Daniela and I don't get married."

"Well, no, of course, you have to get to know her," Eyvindur said soberly.

"I'm sure we'll be friends. Maybe we will fall in love. Who knows? She's lovely, Eyvindur." Jonathan felt that he was complimenting Eyvindur on a painting.

"Yeah, she's so fucking beautiful," he said with a leer. "I like her boobles."

Daniela's "boobles" had not seemed especially wonderful to Jonathan, but they were more evident than Anna's, and he had the uncomfortable insight that he might be Eyvindur's stand-in. This, however, was mitigated by Eyvindur's apparent acceptance of his heterosexuality: only two regular guys would talk about breasts. Chucking sincerity in favor of expedience, Jonathan said "Yeah" in as heartfelt a tone as he could manage.

"What can be keeping those women?" Eyvindur said. He was done with the man-to-man talk, Jonathan guessed. "I'm hungry."

"Me too," said Jonathan. "Puffins?"

"Puffins from Mykines—the best. For you."

Mykines made him think of Swithin and Wooley. "Did

you know there is another American anthropologist here, living on Fugloy?"

"No, there isn't. I would know. Who told you that?"

"An Englishman I met at the hotel."

"He is joking with you. If there was another American here, I would know about it. This"—he leaned close to Jonathan again—"is a very small country."

"The one on Fugloy?" asked Daniela, who'd come into the room while Eyvindur was talking.

Jonathan's brief respite from competition—maybe Swithin had invented Wooley, maybe he himself had invented Swithin—ended. "Do you know him?" Probably, he thought, Wooley was Daniela's lover; though two minutes before he'd been scrambling out of her metaphorical bed, he now felt possessive and trespassed upon.

"I met him when he arrived, last October. Isn't his name Jim?"

"How did you meet him? Did he lose his luggage too?" Jonathan was hopeful.

She laughed. "No. I met him through my brother, Marius."

"Her brother runs the Folklore Institute," Eyvindur said.

"My brother works at the Folklore Institute," she corrected.

"Everybody else there is half dead," said Eyvindur.

"Should I go talk to them?" Jonathan asked. "I don't understand what they are doing, exactly."

"Well, Jonathan"—Eyvindur puffed himself up in the chest and expanded on the sofa—"they aren't doing very much. They did good things when they started ten years ago. Jens Pauli and Magnus collected the *kvæðir* and wrote them down. That was good. Because now nobody can remember them and they have to look up the words in the book before they go out dancing."

"Really?"

"Almost," said Eyvindur.

Jonathan decided not to pursue it. Eyvindur was probably the least reliable informant in the history of the world.

"But what they are obsessed with now—and Jonathan, it is an obsession—is the purity of the language."

"Oh, Marius thinks that's silly," said Daniela.

"But for Jens Pauli and Magnus, it is a *mission*. They are language police. They study old documents and old newspapers and they are always hunting around in little villages for original Faroese words. They are trying to eliminate Danish words from the language. And when there is a word that there never was an old word for because it didn't exist—like for a truck that makes cement—then they invent a Faroese word and tell everybody they have to use this instead of the normal Danish word. They are on the radio once a week to tell people how to talk. Each week they invent new words and tell people to use them."

"But I thought you were such a champion of Faroese things," said Jonathan. "This sounds like something you would approve of."

"Jonathan! I am not an idiot. We live in the modern world. We are not a godforsaken, isolated colony in the middle of the ocean anymore. We have a balance of trade. We catch many tons of fish. We are in NATO."

"I thought you disapproved of NATO."

"I do, but we are in it. These two language policemen are living in a dream—like your professor, Olsen. He kept asking me where the runes were. There are no runes here." Eyvindur shook his head.

Jonathan looked at Daniela to see what she made of all this. She was smiling her secret smile for the floor. "Your brother isn't interested in this language business?"

"No. He's working on a collection of folk tales, which Magnus gathered years ago and never organized."

"Marius is a music jockey," said Eyvindur. "He has many talents."

Before Jonathan could ask what a music jockey was, Anna summoned them to dinner.

A robin-sized roasted bird lay on each plate, with its wings and feet tied together so that it resembled a trussed calf. Daniela showed Jonathan how to undo the string and open the breast cavity, which was stuffed with a crumbling, raisin-dotted mass. Eyvindur was busy heaping boiled potatoes on his plate. Jonathan leaned close to Daniela and whispered, "What's a music jockey?"

Her breath brushed his cheek as she answered. "He means disc jockey."

She smelled good, of clean skin and soap. Because he wanted another whiff of her, he whispered a second question: "What's in here?"

"It's cake," she said.

In between bites of cake and puffin, Jonathan glanced at Daniela. Her self-sufficiency interested him. He liked her private smiles, her lightly mocking attitude toward Eyvindur, her direct answers to questions. Most of all he liked the fact that her expectations of the evening appeared to be even lower than his. She seemed to take the matchmaking as a joke, another one of Eyvindur's eccentric ideas.

"Is this not the best food you have eaten in the Faroes?" Eyvindur boomed out.

Jonathan was able to answer yes. Although slightly tinged with fish (not surprising, as puffins subsisted on herring), puffin meat was delicious, somewhat like Cornish game hen. Jonathan was not as delighted by the cake, but the dinner was nonetheless an easy winner in the Good Food in the Faroes contest. A little salad would have been nice—but, he chided himself, there was going to be no salad, and he should be happy he wasn't eating *livurhøvd*, served to further his culinary education. "Absolutely the best," he said.

"You will never eat it again," Eyvindur intoned.

"Why?"

Daniela giggled.

"Don't laugh!" Eyvindur waved his fork, distributing cake crumbs. "You will be gone, you will be home in America, next year when the puffins come again. You will always remember this evening when you ate stuffed puffins."

"But I might eat them in Skopun," Jonathan protested.

"Who is going to give you puffins in Skopun? Are you going to catch them yourself? No."

"Can't I buy them?"

"Faroese food is not for sale."

"I don't know what you mean," said Jonathan. He thought of the bags and bags of salt cod stacked in Sigurd's store, the canned red cabbage that flanked the block of cheese where two flies ate lunch.

"Real Faroese food," said Anna. "Lamb and puffins. You must catch those yourself. I don't get them in the store."

Jonathan doubted Eyvindur spent much of his time out on the cliffs trying to snag puffins in a butterfly net. Eyvindur interpreted the furrow in Jonathan's brow correctly.

"Anna's cousin in Vestmanna, he sends things to us. Puffins in the summer, and fulmars, and part of a lamb."

"And *grind*?"

A general sigh went round the table. "No. He doesn't send that. And we don't get much *grind* in Tórshavn. The whales don't come here often now, because the harbor is too busy." Eyvindur shook his head. "And you know, you can buy *grind* now. In a store. I think this is terrible. People on other islands are selling off part of their *grind*."

"But if they didn't, you wouldn't get any," said Jonathan.

"Yes, but it is not right. It is not proper Faroese behavior."

"I buy it," said Anna. "I want to eat it, so I buy it."

Eyvindur pointed his fork at his wife but said nothing.

"How long are you staying?" Daniela asked.

"A year."

"You must stay three years," said Eyvindur. "Four years. Forever!" He grinned at Daniela. "Make him stay."

"And how do you like our way of life?" she continued.

Jonathan was taken aback. No one had yet asked him this question. His admiration for Daniela increased immediately. Eyvindur, for all his Italian sojourn and his chat about the modern world, was as Faroe-bound as old Jón Hendrik in Skopun. Neither one of them believed that the Faroese way of life was just that—a way of life. It was *the* way of life, and all others were divergences or variations. The Faroese generally seemed to feel about their culture the way evangelists feel about their religion: they didn't see how a newcomer, once exposed, could fail to be converted. So Daniela was unusual. Jonathan wondered if she knew it, and, further, if she found it uncomfortable to be an atheist—at least, an agnostic—among so many true believers.

This curiosity led him to respond, "I don't know much about your way of life yet. How do you like it?" She didn't answer, so he went on. "Eyvindur tells me you lived abroad."

"Yes." That seemed to be all she was going to say without more prodding.

"In Paris?" This didn't even warrant a word; she nodded. "Did you have a hard time adjusting to life there?"

"Don't you find it difficult, adjusting?" she asked.

"You would make a good anthropologist," said Jonathan, with a smile. "You know how to answer a question with another question." She smiled back. Jonathan decided they were flirting. "So," he said softly, "did you?"

"I knew some people. My great-aunt had friends there, and they were kind to me."

"Ruth Smith, the famous painter," Eyvindur said.

"She studied in Paris when she was young. But then she came home to paint her own country."

Jonathan wished Eyvindur would let up a little. Daniela had taken cover again and was gnawing on puffin bones with an abstracted expression on her face. Anna seemed to share Jonathan's feelings; she scowled at Eyvindur and shook her head. But Eyvindur was on a roll.

"You know Ruth Smith?" Jonathan didn't bother answering; they'd had this conversation the last time he'd been there. "She is world-famous in Denmark! You don't know her?"

"No."

"She is very influential. Without her, I would never have become a painter."

"Why did you go there?" Jonathan asked Daniela.

"Oh, Paris," she said, as if this were explanation enough.

"She is a painter too. She is a very excellent painter."

"Oh, Eyvindur, I am not good. And I don't paint anymore. That's finished."

Was this modesty, depression, or the truth? Jonathan tried to get a look at Daniela's face for a clue. Obligingly, she turned toward him. What he saw told him nothing. Her wide-set blue eyes were friendly but blank; her mouth, with its full lower lip, a little chapped or bitten (he'd noticed her fingernails were bitten down when she helped him with the puffin), was almost smiling but not quite. If her face had any message, it was *You will never know me.* And while on an American face this would have been a challenge, on Daniela's face it was merely a fact.

The familiar cultural exhaustion was sneaking over Jonathan. In deference to Anna, the dinner conversation was in Faroese. And discussing Paris and painting in Faroese was more tiring than discussing sheep driving—perhaps because he'd never had occasion to talk about sheep in En-

glish. Flirtation in Faroese was apparently beyond him,
though he had to admit that it was hard to know where to
locate the blame for flirtation's failure tonight. Jonathan
knew he wasn't going to marry Daniela, but he would have
been willing to go on flirting with her—to flatter her, himself, their hosts. She wasn't having any.

Jonathan rearranged himself mentally. If no flirtation,
then information. And alertness! A cup of coffee—but that
was in the same universe as salad, some unreachable universe where food made sense and girls enjoyed a little attention at dinner. In this universe, puffins, the never-ending
daytime of evening, the burden of anthropology to be done.

"What's Wooley like? The other anthropologist," he
asked Daniela.

"I spent only one evening with him," she said.

But she seemed to have no trouble figuring Jonathan
out in half an evening; he was beginning to feel frankly
spurned. "Did you enjoy him?" he asked, somewhat nastily.

"His Faroese is not very good," she said, "not like
yours."

Jonathan was not to be wooed. "What university is he
from?"

"I don't remember him saying anything about that.
Marius might know."

"You should go visit him, Jonathan," said Eyvindur.
"Aren't you lonely for a countryman?"

"Not yet," he answered. He couldn't imagine ever
being lonely enough to visit his rival.

"Now, Marius could fix your homesickness," Eyvindur said.

"I'm not homesick."

"He has a radio program of your music," Eyvindur
continued, paying no attention. "He has hundreds of American records. He plays them on Thursday afternoons."

"Wednesday afternoons," said Daniela. She ran her
fingers through her hair and looked at Jonathan.

She *was* flirting. He smiled. She looked away. On impulse, he let his leg fall against hers under the table. She didn't flinch, but he, startled by the sensation, drew his leg away immediately. What was ailing him? He couldn't tell if his skittishness was a sympathetic imitation of hers or something of his own. Either way, it was making the evening confusing.

Eyvindur was smoking and watching the two of them. Anna had begun to clear the table. Jonathan stood up to help her; movement would dispel his discomfort, he hoped. But Anna protested.

"Sit, you are a guest."

"I like to help," said Jonathan.

"In America, do the guests wash the dishes?" Eyvindur asked.

"Sometimes. If you are friends with the host."

"A democracy. We are not a democracy." He was in his smoking pose, leaning back in his chair, head tilted up, nostrils pluming smoke as if he were a dragon in a saga.

"Oh?" said Jonathan. He knew that they were, a sort of parliamentary democracy. But Eyvindur was probably about to make a sweeping generalization, and this was his buildup to it.

"We are not free," said Eyvindur.

"That's ridiculous," said Anna, clearing Eyvindur's plate. She turned to Jonathan. "We are free. In the Faroes, everybody can do as he pleases."

"We are not free," Eyvindur repeated.

"What do you mean, exactly?"

"What I mean is real freedom, Jonathan. We have a free press, yes, we have votes, yes, we can live where we like and say what we like. But what kind of a life can you have here in this country? Tell me that." He leaned forward, his cigarette dangling at the corner of his mouth. "Hah! You can be a fisherman, or you can be a farmer, or you can be an institutionalized outlaw like me—that's what I am. You have a wife who washes the dishes: very nice. You have your little home all paid for: very nice. You have your disability pension if you get hurt while you are out fishing. And let's say you don't want to work, you are a crazy person who wants to roam around talking to yourself—fine! Just go to the pension office and say, I am a crazy person who doesn't want to work, and they give you money. I get money because when I was young I had tuberculosis and I couldn't work. That's how I could become a painter. Everybody knows I'm not sick now, but I still get money. This is because everybody must be inside the system. No exceptions." He leaned farther over the table and put his cigarette out on Daniela's plate, which Anna hadn't yet removed. "We're always taken care of."

"And this means you aren't free?" Jonathan asked.

"Sometimes he gets into this mood," said Anna. She picked up Daniela's plate.

"It's not a mood. It's the truth. We are in prison."

"In America people starve because nobody takes care of them," Jonathan said. He was sure Eyvindur wouldn't believe this. He had never met a European willing to give up his idea of rich America.

"Yes! Yes! You have social unrest. We are sheep. Nobody is restless here."

"Do you agree?" Jonathan asked Daniela. He considered putting his hand on her arm, then decided not to.

"It's true that we are not restless. If you are restless, you must leave the country."

"As you did," said Jonathan.

"And I," said Eyvindur. "I left this stupid country where everybody puts their noses in your business, looking over your shoulder to see what you are painting, coming over to see what you are having for dinner, because they have nothing else to do."

"But you came back, both of you."

"It's my home," said Daniela.

Jonathan waited for Eyvindur's reason. Eyvindur stood up.

"A man does not choose his homeland, Jonathan," he said. "Come, we will drink whiskey in the living room and become maudlin." He looked at Jonathan. "I know you think I am already maudlin. You are wondering what I will be like after I drink whiskey."

Jonathan laughed; that was exactly what he had been thinking. He felt a rush of affection for Eyvindur—for understanding him, for understanding himself, for possessing the one thing Americans, with all their freedom, lacked: realism. What Jonathan meant by realism was a fatalism leavened by pleasure in the oddities of this life, which could be amusing on its inexorable downward course. Brushing up against this consciousness had been the charm of his previous trips to Europe, and he was charmed anew to find it here, though he supposed it might be a mainland specialty, imported from Italy by Eyvindur alone. Another cultural trail to follow: Did Faroese happiness lie in this cheerful hopelessness? Was the American conviction that Things Would Improve the source of his—and his country's—miseries?

Daniela and Jonathan followed Eyvindur into the living room, where he pulled the whiskey bottle out from behind some books on a shelf. Not much was left in it. "Two glasses, Anna," he called. "You share one," he said to them. Anna brought the glasses in hands still soapy from washing dishes. When she'd gone back into the kitchen, Eyvindur sat down next to Daniela on the sofa and put his arm across the top of the pillow, so that her head would be under his protection were she to lean back.

Jonathan was on the other side of Daniela. He had to lean over her to see Eyvindur. He didn't like this arrangement, which made him feel that he was in a waiting room and also that he and Eyvindur were competing for Daniela's attention.

Eyvindur poured the whiskey and passed a glass to Jonathan. "I suppose you think I treat Anna in a very chauvinistical manner," he said. He had switched to English.

"Um." Jonathan took a sip and handed the glass to Daniela.

"I get amusement at playing like a Viking with her. She understands. We have a very good marriage."

"Oh," said Jonathan. He didn't want to hear about it. He wanted more whiskey. He put his hand out for the glass. Daniela was staring out the window. He nudged her knee with his. She moved a little farther away from him. "Whiskey," he said.

"Oh," said Daniela. She took a sip before handing it over.

"Marriage is the most important thing in the world," said Eyvindur. Jonathan noticed that Eyvindur had already drunk most of his whiskey. "It is much more important than painting. My babies! My beautiful babies. What painting would ever be as beautiful to me as my babies? They are my inspiration, they are my teachers. Truly, Jonathan"—he leaned across Daniela's lap—"I have learned to see the world again as new, like a baby myself, from them." He subsided back into his spot and finished off his whiskey.

Jonathan disapproved of this concept of the child as teacher, which was common in Cambridge, where all the parents he knew were graduate students who claimed their toddlers had taught them more about psychology, biology, or physics than they had ever learned from books. Any child whose parents pontificated about this had Jonathan for an ally immediately, and he thought now sadly of Marta and little Anna asleep in their beds, burdened by their careers as instructors in seeing. Why didn't people leave children alone? But would he do any better? Wouldn't he see his children as informants from the child world, whom he could pump for data about sensations and emotions lost to him?

"They're just kids, Eyvindur," he said.

" 'Kids,' I love this word for babies. The American language is marvelous." Eyvindur patted Daniela's thigh enthusiastically. She shifted back toward Jonathan.

Jonathan now felt sympathy for everybody washing over him in a whiskey-induced tide: poor Daniela, trapped between two oafs, poor babies the world over, poor Eyvindur, whose marriage probably wasn't as happy as he claimed, poor Anna, who seemed to have finished her washing and shuffled off to bed without saying good night, leaving the "grown-ups" to their drinking and their English, which she couldn't understand. He was lucky. He was free: nobody's child, nobody's father, nobody's husband. He looked at Daniela; he wasn't going to be her husband. Maybe he could be her lover, though.

But did she like him? He found it difficult even to guess what she might be thinking at this moment, holding the whiskey glass in her bitten fingers, drawn into herself so as to be smaller than usual and not brush against the men on either side of her. Jonathan looked at the size of her wrist and compared it to his own and worried: such a thin, frail shaft of bone, how could she manage in the world?

He scolded himself for "chauvinistical" thinking; she clearly could manage well. Nothing about her suggested the helplessness that waited under the surface of many American girls' competence. Quite the opposite: Jonathan was sure that a tough heart beat beneath that frilly blouse. With light-headed, late-night, X-ray vision, he saw through the silk and through the breast so admired by Eyvindur to her organ clenched like a fist. That was the barrier to flirtation, not culture or language or his lack of appeal.

This was sad information. Her wounds—for surely someone guarded was someone wounded—made Daniela familiar and less appealing to Jonathan. She was not after all very different from him. Her methods of expressing her unhappiness were exotic, but the unhappiness was not. Tol-

stoy was wrong: it was unhappiness that was the same the
world over, recognizable and tediously comprehensible.
Happiness—that phantom—varied, and its every manifes-
tation was a mystery, a lure, and a dare: Catch me!

It was time to go, back to the hotel where he would
sleep alone. Jonathan wished he were home in Skopun,
where the foreignness was some kind of comfort. He put
his hand on Daniela's shoulder.

"Shall I walk you home?" he asked.

Eyvindur's head, which had been drooping, bobbed
up. "You're leaving?"

"It's late," said Daniela. "I have to work tomorrow."

"We have not discussed Harvard," said Eyvindur. "I
don't care about it anyhow. Go."

Was he insulted? Jonathan looked at Daniela; she was
smiling at Eyvindur. "You're tired too," she said. She
sounded like a wife. To Jonathan she said, "He gets up
very early, to paint."

"That's what you should do," Eyvindur mumbled. He
lurched to his feet. "Good night, thank you."

"Thank *you*," Jonathan said, standing up as well.
"Thank you for a wonderful dinner—"

"Better than last time, eh?" Eyvindur interrupted. "So.
Back to Skopun tomorrow?"

"Yes."

"You'll come for dinner another night?" He sounded
forlorn.

"Of course," said Jonathan. He suddenly had the feeling that it might be a long time before he saw Eyvindur
again. His year stretched in front of him. He put out his
hand. And Eyvindur did what Jonathan had wanted to do,
pulled him into a hug. He smelled of tobacco and turpentine
and man—warm, slightly sweaty, adult.

"You," said Eyvindur, "take care. Take care."

*   *   *

Daniela lived halfway down the hill from Eyvindur. "Alone?" asked Jonathan, as they stumbled among the cobbles.

"With Marius. Girls don't live alone in the Faroes. It's not Paris."

"That's for sure," said Jonathan. "Why did you come back?"

"I told you." She sounded irritated.

"People do leave their homes."

"Not Faroe people." Daniela turned away from him. "The Greeks had a story about a man who lost all his strength when his feet weren't on the earth."

"Antaeus. He was a giant."

"Because the earth was his mother," Daniela went on. She turned back. "We are like that. Perhaps we are very simple people."

They had reached her house. "But all your education—" Jonathan stopped himself; it really wasn't his business.

"Maybe that's not so important," Daniela said. She didn't sound sure.

Jonathan did the only thing he could: kissed her goodbye. Goodbye to Tórshavn, goodbye to Paris, goodbye to their never-to-be-shared future. It was a lovely kiss, a sad and intelligent kiss, and they both gave themselves over to it. They separated as gently as they had come together, as if aware of each other's fragility. Jonathan put his hand on her cheek for a final farewell. "Good night," he said.

"Yes," said Daniela, and opened the door.

Continuing down the hill, Jonathan came to the spot where weeks before he had sat and surveyed Tórshavn and wished for beer. He stopped. Tórshavn looked the same, or worse, now that he'd learned to see the country as beautiful. He sat again, to consider whether he was also the same.

But instead of thinking about himself, he began to imagine a map of the Faroes, with people marking the important points: Petur and his brothers to the south, in Skopun; Eyvindur and Daniela here in the center; Swithin to the west, on Mykines; Wooley on Fugloy, as far north as he could go. And in the east, Europe, locus of Jonathan's yearnings, which he must now, he realized, subdue.

For he too was a landmark. He existed as a point on all these people's maps. He could be counted on to chase sheep, he could be invited to dinner, he could be considered, and rejected, as a future husband. He had auditioned for the part of the Anthropologist, and he had gotten it. Even his simultaneous billing with Wooley didn't, at the moment, dilute his pleasure or his surprise.

Surprise because his own competence was always a surprise to Jonathan. The pleasure was separate. He didn't dare to take pleasure in competence, which inevitably smacked of chance—a fortuitous achievement when he wasn't looking, so to speak. The pleasure was the odd and marvelous details of this life, which were now the details of *his* life.

Jonathan stood up. He felt big. He felt he could take on anything—whales, winter, Wooley. The ocean boomed below, slapped the shore in loud applause for Jonathan. Jonathan bowed. He agreed with the ocean; he had done something remarkable: he was, finally, here.

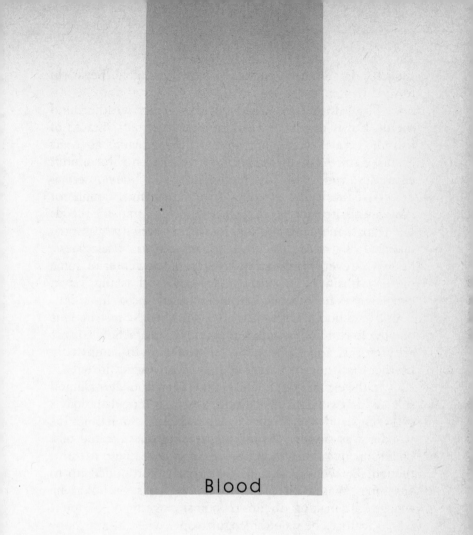

Blood

October, and for weeks the island had lain in an equinoctial calm. Starless, exotic summer had given way to an ordinary autumn, with dawn and dusk at ordinary times. The soft, smooth tundra had turned brittle and brown, and the sea, too, had lost its summer sheen. Dark slow swells broke on the jetty day after day, a steady tide that pulled the world toward winter.

The fishing had picked up with cooler weather, and the dock was now awash in lines and bait pots. Stacks of fish-filled crates waited outside the filleting plant's door. At Sigurd's store captains heaped provisions on the counter: cigarettes, rope and tar, condensed milk, buoys, screwdrivers, batteries. Boats bound for Greenland, bound for Norway, baited for herring, baited for cod, out for blood.

Jonathan's contribution to all this activity was note taking. It began as camouflage for his essential uselessness; he was forever standing four feet from the center of some piece of business he didn't understand and asking for an explanation. In this way he quickly filled one of his spiral-bound notebooks with sketches of fishhooks, instructions on how to coil lines in a pot, diagrams of boats' holds, some salty curses, and a garbled version of a myth common in northern latitudes concerning a seal-woman and love.

In the evenings at home, eating his eight fillets of lemon sole or his two slabs of halibut, Jonathan reread the day's gatherings and wondered what they meant. Sometimes his wonder was simple: writing in pencil against the top of a box or his own knee didn't make for easy reading. Mostly, though, he wondered if all this information added up to anything. Was it on the brink of making sense? Was he engaged in making an impressionist portrait of Skopun, whose features he would recognize only when he was done and stood ten feet away from what, at close range, looked like smears and daubs? Or, the inevitable alternative, was he just wasting time?

But the inevitable seemed to have lost its inevitability. He trotted up and down the village paths, staring and scribbling; he went everywhere and wrote down everything, and by ten o'clock each night he had flopped into bed, dreamless. The occupation he'd invented for himself was a full-time one, and as he did it in public, everybody could see what a good worker he was. The finished notebook on the kitchen windowsill assuaged his remaining doubts. He grew more and more willing to put the question of meaning on hold. He was gathering data—reams of data—and doing it well. Conclusions and assertions would have to wait for Cambridge, where they were hard currency. Hard currency here was how much cod the *Skarvanes* brought in and whether Jens Símun would get a sheepdog.

Within a week or two his cover story had become reality; he had a job, just like everybody else. Jonathan liked having a job. His mission was simple: record. A student's mission was tricky: be wise, be willing to learn; be inventive, remember the facts; be smart, don't be a smart-ass. After seven years on that tightrope, he was daily delighted to click his mechanical-pencil lead out another notch and be ready for work. No extensive mental preparation was needed for curiosity. The more he indulged his curiosity, in fact, the stronger it grew, until Jonathan suspected that his aloofness was only protective coloring. He appeared to have a boundless interest in other people's affairs. Licensed—mandated—to stick his nose into everybody's business, he was happier than he'd been in years.

The villagers too were happy to see him doing his job. A man must have work, and Jonathan out of work, stirring his septic tank and reading his murder mysteries, was a sorry sight. Petur and Jens Símun had decided to offer him a place in the boat if he didn't collect himself; they were relieved to see the notebook in his hands day after day, because it wasn't a very large boat. But now things were as they should be, and Jonathan was going about his proper work, which was playing Boswell to everybody's Johnson. Although nobody had ever thought village life worth chronicling before Jonathan turned up proposing to do it, everyone now agreed that the immortalization of Skopun and its inhabitants in Jonathan's book was fitting and good.

For Jonathan had told them he was writing a book. A

thesis was a sort of book, he reasoned, and his attempt to describe a thesis, and scholarship generally, to Heðin had been a bust. It would be published as a book, he hoped, and so he said it was a book. The Faroese approved of books and read many during the winter; Sigurd the shopkeeper poring over *Gulliver's Travels* was typical. Petur had read *Hamlet*, Jens Símun had cast his bicolored eyes on Ibsen (though he confessed he'd never finished a play, just "looked to see what happened"), all the village children knew Andersen and Grimm. "There's nothing else to do in the winter," Heðin said. "Just read and listen to ship-to-shore radio."

Heðin and Jonathan had become friends. Every third or fourth evening little Jens Símun was sent by his mother to ask Jonathan, "Aren't you coming to eat?" Olí had returned to Vestmanna; it was natural, Jonathan supposed, that Heðin would want to fill his young uncle's absence with Jonathan's presence. Soon he realized he had short-shrifted himself with this analysis. Heðin liked him. Heðin came to visit him, unannounced, on evenings when Jonathan hadn't come for dinner. Jonathan would walk downstairs from the bathroom after dinner and find Heðin making tea or eating an end of bread or leafing through the notebook left on the table. Sometimes he brought a bottle of near-beer, and they sat on the front steps sharing it, watching the stars emerge from the darkness that comforted Jonathan, who had yet to live through a winter without light.

Snaggle-tooth, lanky, green-eyed Heðin had lost no time in turning their private conversations toward his favorite topic, sex. He seemed to have had a great deal of experience for one so young and, to Jonathan's eyes, unprepossessing. He asked Jonathan the English words for acts Jonathan had only contemplated performing; claimed to have fucked a ewe; and added sex to his earlier list of wintertime activities: "There's nothing else to do," he repeated, "so we all get busy in the bed." By matchlight and cigarette glow, Jonathan studied Heðin's face, trying to locate his appeal. Perhaps he had what Jonathan had overheard a woman in a Cambridge café describe as "animal magnetism." His huge hands, swollen from work at sea, were capable of spanning a woman's waist easily, firmly, to hold her in place while he had his way with her. But according to Heðin, they didn't need to be held down.

Jonathan wasn't exactly envious. Plenty of women had nuzzled up to him or sent nuzzlesome glances his way. The difference was that he didn't take advantage of it. Partly because he considered it "taking advantage of," partly because of his distaste for entanglement, mostly, he now decided, because he was a Puritan. He didn't think of lovemaking as a sport. Heðin did, and so did a number of Faroese girls.

All this was bound to make him think of Daniela and, eventually, talk about her, though with trepidation: perhaps Heðin had banged her too? He had not; he didn't even know her. But he knew of her family. He put his nose in the air and sniffed, pan-cultural shorthand for snobbiness.

"Oh, no, she's very friendly," Jonathan said, not wishing to remember that she hadn't been.

"Yah, to an American writing a book." Heðin sniffed again. "What was it like with her?"

"We didn't. . . ."

"Then you must telephone and invite her to come for a visit, so you can have a good fucking. I will find out her telephone for you."

"I don't think that's a good idea," said Jonathan. It appealed to him immensely.

"Why? You are writing your book, you are cousin to my family, you are my friend, all you need is a woman."

Jonathan had to admit to himself that this was true. "She has a job," he said. "It would be hard for her to visit."

"Pah!"

So much for the vaunted equality of the sexes in Scandinavia, babbled about in the Danish guidebook—and at Cambridge dinner parties. But Skopun generally seemed to have one foot in the Bronze Age; Jonathan had thought of calling his book *Viking Village*.

"When the nights get long, you'll call her," said Heðin.

But the nights and the days were still balanced in harmonious intervals of stars and scudding clouds dappling the faraway sky. Jonathan going about his work was sometimes troubled by an image of Daniela, sometimes had an arrow-sharp memory of that kiss, but most of the time he pretended she was Christmas or his birthday: inevitable, possibly fun, and fixed in the future. For he had reached that condition of contentment in which he was aware of being happy, and he wanted nothing to disturb it.

Into this calm, mid-month, something odd intruded.

Though the weather had been generally fair, a little spatter of storms had buffeted Skopun for a weekend and given Jonathan a cold. For a few days he took notes between snorts, but the wet phase passed quickly, leaving stalactites of snot that pricked when he breathed and that could be removed only in private by delicate, persistent excavation. He was at this one evening, flipping through his notes and picking away, when he felt a rush of liquid course down the back of his throat, nearly choking him. He spat: blood. Not a thin, mucusy stream but a dark red glob. Frightened, he blew his nose, gently: more blood, fresh, wet, as if his nose were an open vein. He dashed upstairs to the bathroom to look at himself in the mirror. He was pale, and a steady flow was leaking from his nostril, inching its way toward his lip. His blood tasted sweet and alien. It was coming at him from two points, trailing down inside and out, so he sampled it both hot and cold.

The first rule with blood was to put your feet up, according to Gerda; Jonathan remembered lying on the living room rug with his legs on the sofa after he'd skinned both knees falling off his bike. With toilet paper pressed to his nose, he lay down on the bathroom floor and put his feet on the toilet seat. His floor, he saw, could do with a sweeping: Band-Aid wrappers, strands of hair, a dead spider and a living one were all within an inch of his head. He looked out the window instead, looking at the stars blurred by the pane until he thought it safe to stand up.

The hemorrhage seemed to have stopped. He peered up his nose in the mirror and saw caked, black blood, but he couldn't taste it anymore. Back at the kitchen table, he finished going over his notes and left his nose alone. By ten-thirty, when he was in bed with *Dombey and Son* (ordered by mail from Blackwell's; received only seven weeks later), he'd brushed the episode off.

But in the morning his pillow was soaked, stained brown and crimson, as if he'd been murdered during the night.

Now Jonathan's days and nights were haunted by blood. The pillowcase was an atlas of his sufferings; continents and islands formed nightly and were obscured by new ones rising the next night from the tide of his body's salt water. He told nobody, though his anxiety mounted daily. And he feared a public outpouring almost as much as he feared the blood itself. Exposure, aside from the mess and embarrassment it would cause, would mean a doctor, and a doctor would mean a diagnosis, and Jonathan already knew the diagnosis.

Clearly, he was dying. He had nose cancer; a tumor was pressing on his sinus, or some sort of rot was eating his insides and spitting them out as blood. At the very least, his nose was altered, and his days henceforth would begin with scrubbing his pillowcase and include many deft, furtive checks for blood with his fingers and his tongue—secret movements he'd already perfected.

Thus, Jonathan at his worst. And it went further. He lost no time turning his happiness into the cause of his affliction. He was never meant for this busybody life he'd so enjoyed, therefore nose death was sent to cut it short. Whether he called it divine retribution or psychosomatic illness or his rotten luck—and he called it all of these— nosebleeds had scotched his newfound pleasure in living.

He saw the humor in this black speculation, but that didn't stop him from spinning it out each time he stood at the sink running cold water on his bloody linen. After eight days of this and of walking gingerly on the slick mud roads, with cones of toilet paper wadded into both nostrils, he decided he'd better confide in someone.

Little Jens Símun appeared around seven o'clock with his usual refrain: "Aren't you coming to eat?" Jonathan nodded and went upstairs to unpack his nose. Let his body speak for him. And between the halibut and the tea his nose began to bleed. He knew the sweet taste now and had learned to swallow whole gulps of blood, but soon he felt the warm, thick wriggle coming out his left nostril for all to see. He put his hand up to his face and then, shamed but urgent, held his red fingers out toward Petur.

"Look," he said.

Petur nodded. "Your nose is bleeding."

"It keeps happening," Jonathan said, his voice shaking a little.

"Mmm," said Petur. "I've heard of that."

"Ice is good," Maria said.

"Nah," Petur said, "leave it alone."

"Sometimes it soaks my whole pillow. It's been happening for a week."

"Like a woman, no?" Heðin put in, grinning. He leaned close to Jonathan. "I know what would cure it."

Petur laughed. "Young men," he said. "Maybe it's time you got married, Heðin, so you can pay more attention to your work. You are thinking so hard about women you get the lines tangled up. Soon you'll be courting a codfish. Well"—he sighed—"I was the same."

"Papa," Jens Símun piped up, "take me out in the boat with you. I won't get the lines tangled."

"I only did it once," said Heðin.

"You have to go to school," Maria said.

"Soon," said Petur. "Next summer, I'll take you out."

"It's boring," said Heðin.

"Can be," his father agreed, equably.

"You are not a fisherman," said Jens Símun, fixing a fierce look on Heðin. "I am a fisherman."

"Our conservative party member," Heðin whispered to Jonathan. "Everything traditional for Jens Símun Dahl."

Jonathan checked his nose with his forefinger while pretending to rub his eye. Heðin, astute, said, "Forget about it. It's nothing. I have found her telephone for you."

Jonathan managed a little smile. "Maybe a doctor—" he began.

"You have a nosebleed," said Petur.

And that was the end of it. Named, his nosebleed stopped. His pillow was dry in the morning—and dry the next three mornings. His nose resumed its minor role in life, and life resumed its savor.

For instance, he had the pleasure of going into Sigurd's store and hearing Jón Hendrik's gruff welcome and invitation to "sit here by me," which meant squatting on his heels till his ankles ached and listening to the old man's mumbled gossip about Sigurd's customers. That little toddler Sigrid took care of was Sigrid's big sister Lisabet's baby that she "got" from Páll who lived in Sandur; but Páll was engaged to another girl, in Klaksvík, so Lisabet had gone Down There (to Denmark) to work and find a husband, and her family took care of the baby. But that must have been a while ago, said Jonathan, because the little girl looked about two years old. Yes, Lisabet must be having a hard time finding the husband. Was she going to marry a Danish man? Jonathan wanted to know. Well, if that's all she could get. And didn't the family mind having to take care of a

baby? No, she was a good girl, Petra, always stopped to
say hello to Jón Hendrik, even though she couldn't really
talk yet. But the mother, Jonathan persisted, Sigrid and
Lisabet's mother, wasn't it hard to have a little child around
again? No, it's good to have a baby in the house, said Jón
Hendrik, shaking his head, as he often did, at the wonderful
stupidity of the American.

And that one—bobbing his chin at a roly-poly man
who walked with a swagger and whom Jonathan had often
seen on the dock, chatting with people who were baiting
lines—what a lazy one! Talk and talk. What did he do for
a living? Jonathan asked. Watch other people work, that's
what. Jens-Egg we call him, because he looks like an egg
and because of a story. Do you want to hear the story? Of
course, said Jonathan.

Sigurd coughed and shuffled his feet in the sawdust,
his signal to hold off until the person in question had left
the store. Jón Hendrik obeyed these commands with bad
grace. "Jens-Egg, hah, hah, hah," he said, so that Jens-Egg
would be sure to know he was up for dissection. Spitting,
rearrangement on his box, and new wads of tobacco carried
Jón Hendrik over until he was at liberty to speak again.
Jonathan took advantage of these pauses to stretch his legs
and eat a hunk of cheese. Each time Sigurd had a cheese
order, he cut a piece for Jonathan too, and a row of Tilsit
chunks wilted on the windowsill.

So. The story was this: Jens-Egg was a rich man's son.
His father, Jøgvan, had been the son of the King's farmer
here. He didn't know what that was? That was a person
who had more land, and also his land was all together, not
in a little patch here and a little patch there. So he got more
potatoes and it wasn't so hard to plant and harvest them,
because they weren't all spread around. Jonathan looked
confused. Jón Hendrik spat and explained. When you got
married the woman brought a little land from over here,
where her father had a piece of land, and the man had a

little land over somewhere else, and then those little pieces of land had to be divided up again more for the children later on. But not King's land; that didn't get divided. So. He was son's son of the last King's farmer.

"There aren't any now?" Jonathan asked.

Jón Hendrik growled with irritation; he hated to be interrupted in his stories. "We are independent," he said firmly.

So. Notwithstanding Jens-Egg's wealth—and King's farmer families were always wealthy—he was greedy. Or maybe that was why he was greedy. Anyhow, during the war—

"The Second World War?" asked Jonathan, knowing he risked another growl but intent on facts.

"The English war," Jón Hendrik answered. "When the English came."

Jonathan nodded; that was the Second World War. He scribbled. Jón Hendrik spat. Then they got back to business.

So. During the war he had chickens. He was a young man then, not yet twenty. He had chickens and he had feed for them too. Most others didn't have feed, so they ate their chickens early in the war. Then they didn't have any eggs. Everybody was hungry. Here he paused, scanning his memory of hunger. We ate scallops!

Jonathan didn't know the word. "Draw it." He offered his notebook. Jón Hendrik drew a nice portrait of a scallop shell and made a face of disgust. "In America we like those," Jonathan told him. "We pay a lot of money for them."

Jón Hendrik stared. What a country! "You eat them now, after the war?" Jonathan nodded. Jón Hendrik shook his head. Well. He had eggs. He hoarded them, though. He buried them in a barrel of peat ash in his basement. You can keep an egg that way—but not for as long as Jens-Egg kept them. He waited until everybody was very hungry, then he began to sell those eggs. Some of them were like rocks. But what was there to do? We were sick of those scallops. So he got richer, from selling his eggs. So he's Jens-Egg.

Then there were the more complex and sociable plea-sures of the dock, where Jonathan went after lunch. Small boats that had set out from Skopun before dawn were re-turning then and the fish-plant workers were straggling back in to the briny tables where they sliced four fillets a minute. Those who from age or disinclination did not work were gathering in a line by the railing to watch for the mail boat, due in at three.

Jonathan on the dock was Jonathan at his best. He was a good hand at unloading and stacking; he'd learned to fasten quickly a line thrown at him from a bow and to ask, with the correct offhandedness, "How did you do?" He could stand comfortably alongside the village elders rolling the occasional cigarette and commenting on the color of the sea and the sky, the prospects for storm, the likelihood that today Árni's new toilet would arrive from Tórshavn. He was no longer the nincompoop underfoot or the possible spy from America (two of his earlier assignments). He was not even the Scribe of Skopun anymore, it seemed. Since his reprieve from death, Jonathan saw himself, and felt himself seen, as one of the guys.

An odd guy to be sure, but everybody had quirks. He didn't know everyone's name, but neither did Elin's new husband, Jákup, who was trying to get Jens Símun to buy a boat with him—well, that was a stupid idea, because Jens Símun hated to go fishing and he already had the boat with Petur. But he'd learn. (Jonathan listening to this marveled at the intricacies of language: Jonathan would learn the names, Jákup would learn the names, and Jákup would learn to give up on his boat project.) He was writing that book, but writing that book was a good idea, and maybe you'd have to come from outside of Skopun to have that idea. (Jonathan was pleased to know that America, once as far away as the moon, was now in the same universe as Klaksvík or Vestmanna: that is, the Outside of Skopun universe rather than the Down There universe, which commenced at the Faroes' disputed three-hundred-mile fishing limit and radiated into the depths of the Milky Way.) He wasn't married, but they could fix that. And hadn't he met some pretty girl in Tórshavn? Heðin said—well, Heðin said a lot of things about women—yes, but he'd said that Jonathan had met a pretty girl. (Jonathan blushed.) Anyhow, plenty of young men didn't get married until they weren't so young anymore. He had to finish the book first and get rich, so as to marry a rich pretty girl.

This public discussion of his characteristics was the clearest sign that he'd been accepted. The old men mulled over each other's traits and habits daily, poking each other with their sharp old elbows as they delivered especially insightful comments. That guy walks just like you—poke— like he's two years old with his pants full of shit. And closer to the bone. One rheumy old guy about another who could barely stand up: I think he keeps living just to spite his daughter. He never wanted her to marry Árni, so now he's making their lives miserable by being so sick. Poke.

The day citizenship was thus conferred on him, Jonathan went home in a very good mood. The three-o'clock boat had brought a letter from one of his classmates who was just now heading into the jungle, having spent months preparing his supplies and making his arrangements. Reading about mosquito netting, malaria pills, snake-venom kits, antifungal foot creams, the need to start the day by shaking the scorpions out of your shoes, and the difficulty of getting permission to travel from the torpid bureaucrats at provincial headquarters made Jonathan kick up his heels with pleasure at his own situation. He was in the absolutely perfect place. He looked out his kitchen window to the purple ocean that was the backdrop to the red-roofed church and snug clusters of houses; he leaned against his kerosene stove, dependably pumping warmth into his home; he wriggled his toes in his pest-free shoes; he contemplated his high-protein dinner, his neighbors who cared about him, his bulging notebooks. Somehow, he had lucked out, and he bent his head toward the dusky sky in brief but heartfelt thanks.

When he lifted his head he saw Sigurd coming toward his front steps, tugging a sheep. Another phone call, Jonathan figured. Perhaps Daniela had thought about him as much as he had thought about her? Which wasn't that much, he emphasized to the inhabitant of the sky, in order not to jinx his prospects. Sigurd was trying to coax the sheep to walk up the steps and failing. The sheep had dug itself into the ground with its front feet and lowered its head ominously.

"Hey!" said Sigurd. He had hold of the sheep by its ear.

Jonathan opened the front door.

"Help me with this," Sigurd said.

"What do you want me to do?"

"Pull it up the steps."

Jonathan pulled and Sigurd pushed, and they got the sheep into the kitchen in short order. It stood there shaking with confusion, moving its black, soft nostrils in a frantic but silent effort to understand its circumstances. Jonathan was puzzled too.

"What are you doing with it?" he asked.

"It's yours. It's your sheep." Sigurd sat in a chair and sighed.

"What do you mean?"

"Well, really you're only entitled to half a sheep, but we thought it would be welcoming for you to have a whole one, and then, you don't go out fishing, and we wanted to be sure you had food for the winter. So we decided you'd get a whole one. Jens Símun decided."

Jonathan looked at the sheep. It popped a turd onto
his floor. Sigurd got out of the chair.

"I'm going to get the gun," he said. "I'll be right back."

Jonathan sat down in the chair and put his head in his
hands. The sheep clicked over to him on its sharp, small
hooves and bent its head down to his and sniffed. Then it
said "Ah-ah-ah." Jonathan put his hand on its hard brow
and looked into its black eyes. In a horrible facsimile of a
human movement, the sheep tipped its head to the side to
get a better look at Jonathan. At this, a lump filled Jonathan's throat.

It was completely impossible to have this sheep for
dinner. He was not so sentimental that he would forego
eating lamb altogether, but it was intolerable to eat a sheep
he knew, even if only slightly. He would explain this to
Sigurd and arrange to get half of a different sheep—which
would be better anyhow because he didn't think he should
get special treatment in the village. Resolved, Jonathan
stood up.

Sigurd came in the door after the gun, which he held
at arm's length in front of him. "I hate this," he said. Before
Jonathan could get a word out, he'd pushed the sheep onto
the floor, sat on its back, and shot it in the head. The shot,
muffled by all that thick bone, sounded like the merest thud
in a nearby yard. The sheep's tail twitched once.

"Get a pot," said Sigurd, He stood up and put the gun
on the counter beside the sink.

Jonathan didn't move.

"Hey. Get a pot." Sigurd pulled a wicked-looking
knife from his belt.

Jonathan got a pot and returned to his spot on the
floor, with the pot hanging from his hand.

Sigurd took the pot from him and put it next to the
sheep's head. Then he cut a gash in the neck and lifted the
animal up so that it lay on the pot with its blood pouring

out. The blood was thin, pink, frothy, and quick to flow, and it flowed for more than ten minutes, during which Sigurd raised the sheep's hindparts so all the blood could come out and Jonathan stood in his spot.

"Okay," said Sigurd, finally. The carcass was flat and shrunken. He took up his knife and sawed off the head; the neckbones resisted the blade, and he had to work the knife back and forth, making a scraping noise, to cut through. He put the head on the counter beside the gun. The ears, drained of blood, flopped down like a spaniel's.

Sigurd stood up and flexed his legs. The floor around his feet was a mess: wool, blood, and bits of flesh and bone surrounded the body. "Sorry," he said. "I guess in America you have a special room to slaughter the sheep, no? You don't do it in the kitchen."

"No," Jonathan said. He could barely get the word out.

"Now," Sigurd said, wiping his knife on his pants, "the innards." He slit the belly with one quick move, and the long, pale, complex intestine of an herbivore tumbled onto the floor. Jonathan felt his stomach heave. Steam was rising from the entrails in the cool kitchen, and the smell of shit in its most elemental phase—pre-turd—was mingling with the musk of sheep fear and the heavy, sweet smell of blood.

Jonathan went to his bathroom, where he retched out lunch.

When he got back, Sigurd was detaching a gray baglike item from a pink sacklike item. "Stomachs," he said, holding the gray bag aloft. "Lots of stomachs in sheep. You need them for sausage." He looked at Jonathan, who was pale. "You don't like this, hah?"

"In America, other people slaughter sheep."

Sigurd frowned. "I'm doing that for you."

"No. I mean, there's a place where they do it—it's like the fish factory. All the sheep are taken care of there."

"So, so, so." Sigurd nodded. "Well, here, nobody likes to do it, so each man must kill his own. Nobody would want to spend his days killing sheep for other people. That is," he hastily added, "except as a favor for a friend like you."

"Thank you," said Jonathan humbly. "I really couldn't have done it myself."

"Now you can help," Sigurd said. He picked up the little pile of stomachs and offered them to Jonathan. "Wash these. Turn them inside out. You see all those little bubbles?"

The inner surface of the stomach was dotted with tiny flaps of flesh. "Yes," said Jonathan.

"You must scrub until all the bubbles are clean and the stomach doesn't smell anymore."

Jonathan went to the sink and began his work. The sheep's head rested by his right elbow, its eyes shut, a thin line of foam around its mouth. The stomach was a tough item to clean. It had a rubbery, resistant texture that held in the years' worth of mulched grass. At Jonathan's feet, Sigurd was extracting kidneys and lungs, digging around for the liver, piling the organs by the sheep's shoulder. The pot of blood stood at the sheep's hindquarters.

And so they worked, in the waning light, Jonathan scrubbing and staring out the window, Sigurd now pulling the sheep's skin off with long, heart-stopping rips. He held the pelt up for Jonathan to admire. It had been a handsome white animal.

"This will be your rug. I got it off nicely for you. Tomorrow, I'll show you what to do with it."

Jonathan nodded. The sour odor of the stomachs was nauseating him anew. He glanced at the carcass; without its skin it looked like an embryo—raw, vulnerable flesh that was never meant to be exposed. He turned back to his stomachs. Three remained to be cleaned. He sniffed the two he had worked on; they still smelled of bile.

"I can't get these clean," he said.

Sigurd nodded. "That's women's work. It takes forever." He draped the lambskin over the back of a chair and
took up his knife again. "Maria will help you. She'll help
you make the sausages. You should have a wife." He now
embarked on butchery. Grating noises and grunts of effort
accompanied Jonathan in his scrubbing. A bone cracked
occasionally as Sigurd snapped off a limb. Before Jonathan
had finished his third stomach, Sigurd stood up for the last
time.

The sheep as an integrated unit no longer existed. Its
components were scattered about the room. The four legs
were balanced in a pile beside the bucket of its blood, the
edible organs were on the counter near its head, and a
smaller pile of meat—chops, Jonathan supposed—flanked
the legs. Sigurd had pushed the large intestine under the
chair where the rug-to-be was hanging.

Sigurd sat down in the other chair and began pawing
through the intestine, tearing off yellow, lardy hunks and
stacking them on the table.

"What's that?" asked Jonathan.

"Tallow."

"For candles?"

"Hah? For eating, with meat or in the sausage."

Jonathan shuddered and returned to washing. Despite
his queasy afternoon, he was beginning to feel hungry, but
he couldn't imagine cooking dinner in this war zone of a
kitchen. He had an impulse to telephone Eyvindur and skip
town—but the afternoon boat was long gone. He was ma-
rooned in a slaughterhouse.

"The head," said Sigurd. "Do you like it?"

Jonathan looked at it. The head just made his sorrow
well up again. "I don't know," he mumbled, unsure if Sigurd was asking for an aesthetic or a culinary opinion.

"Have you had it?"

Culinary: "No. But please, take it."

"Yah?" Sigurd smiled. "You don't want it?"

"No. I think you can take the tallow too." Jonathan looked around the room at the other parts. "And the blood."

"No. The blood is important. You need the blood for sausages. But maybe I'll take the tallow. In America, you are not so fond of eating it?"

"Not as fond as you." Jonathan could more easily imagine eating a light bulb.

"Tonight you have lamb lung for dinner," Sigurd announced with vicarious anticipation. "Lung and liver and kidneys—all that for dinner."

Possibly the kidneys, Jonathan decided. "You can take the lungs." Then, not wanting Sigurd to think he was merely getting rid of garbage, he said, "Really, you have been so good to do all this for me. Please take anything you like. Please."

"Well, you know, Jón Hendrik and I only get one sheep between us. . . ."

Jonathan plucked the lungs from the counter and held them out to Sigurd. Sigurd's hands were full of tallow.

"I'll come back for them," he said. "I have to get the head and the gun too." He left, kicking the front door open with his foot.

As soon as Jonathan was alone he went up to his bedroom, where he sat on the bed and looked out at the sea, gray and smooth against the white horizon. The evening stars blinked through the clouds. Petur and Maria's lights cast a mild yellow mist into the yard. Jonathan walked to the window and leaned his forehead against the glass. Sigurd came into view, returning for his booty. But he went into Petur's house. Jonathan waited, his head still on the cool pane.

He was beset by the image of the peeled sheep. Without fur, what had been a carcass shifted in memory into the realm of corpse—a dead being whose skin could no longer protect it, whose eyes' liquid had set into eternal jelly, whose form, made for movement, would not move again. And Jonathan could not stop himself from speculating on its thoughts. A sheep was capable of volition, aversion, curiosity; couldn't it lift its hard head up to sniff the evening air, or yearn for its summer pasture?

Jonathan touched his nose. He too would die. All the force of desire, pride, pleasure, confusion, and every other disembodied feeling that chose *his* body to sing through was not enough to stave off the silence waiting for him. He realized he'd thought it was. But being alive was no guarantee of immortality—quite the opposite.

He had never before considered the facts. His bleeding nose, a bout with measles at thirteen, intestinal paroxysms in Italian villages were mere skirmishes. Jonathan thought of the old men at the dock railing. Their faraway fishermen's eyes looked out to yet further islands and seas. Some were so old they had begun to dry up and cool down; one hand laid on Jonathan's arm had felt as light as papier-mâché, and as bloodless. Time had defeated them, and, if he was lucky, it would defeat him too.

And more sheep would be slaughtered, and fish gutted, and birds snatched from their nests—and what was most amazing about this was that it was the way the world was supposed to be. It wasn't savage or primitive or avoidable; it wasn't even sad.

He lifted his head, opened his window, and put his face into the heavy salt air. The clouds were skimming the sky, frothing at the edges and shredding in the center, and a pie-perfect amber moon was rising above Petur's roof. From Petur's door came Sigurd, with Maria behind him holding a huge pot. Jonathan went downstairs.

Sigurd had the head in hand; Maria was sniffing one of the stomachs.

"We'll make the sausage after dinner," she said. She scooped the stomachs into the pocket of her apron and decanted Jonathan's pot of blood into her pot.

"So, so, so," said Sigurd, looking around the kitchen happily.

"I reckon so," said Jonathan, weary but polite.

The three of them trooped over to Petur's, Jonathan carrying the gun and the armful of innards as directed by Maria, Sigurd stopping to place the sheep's head on the doorstep. Inside, Jón Hendrik sat at the kitchen table, tossing back a cocktail of straight aquavit.

"Ho, the American!" His traditional greeting. "A cowboy," he went on, in English now, "home from the range, where the animals play." Jonathan nodded hello. He wished Sigurd would relieve him of the gun, and Maria of the innards. But for several minutes nothing happened at all. He stood holding these things while Jón Hendrik had another shot of aquavit. Maria was fussing at the stove, Sigurd had vanished, and not even little Jens Símun was around to bother people. After two glasses of liquor, Jón Hendrik offered the bottle to Jonathan. "Drink," he said.

Jonathan laid the gun on the table.

"Don't put it there!" Jón Hendrik shook his head.

"Well, where should I put it?"

"Not there."

Jonathan felt like strangling Jón Hendrik; why was this old man so exasperating? He grimaced with the frustration and embarrassment of ignoble feelings. A harmless old guy, and he wanted to kill him.

Jón Hendrik bared his yellow teeth in a forgiving smile. "Put it outside," he said. "It's not good to have a gun inside."

Jonathan put it outside, leaning against the house next to the head. Then he dumped the kidneys and the liver and the lungs, which Sigurd hadn't taken, on the counter beside the stove. This move gave him a glimpse of what Maria was up to: stirring the pot of blood. He gulped and headed back to the table for aquavit.

But Jón Hendrik had hold of the bottle by the neck

and wasn't offering anymore. Instead, he poured a last shot for himself and shuffled to his feet to put the liquor in its hiding place in another room. Jonathan sat at the table alone, listening to the pot of blood bubbling on the stove and silently cursing Jón Hendrik. For he found that he wanted a drink very much. And he realized this was part of a trend: many events in the Faroes made him want a drink. Nothing in America had ever made him want a drink—at least, his frustration had never surfaced through that particular desire.

In Jonathan's family, "wanting a drink" was the first sign of losing one's grip. Bear Brand, son of Hoosier tee-totalers, had learned to appreciate wine with dinner from Gerda, daughter of a professor (of course! It was like hemophilia, Jonathan supposed, this academic heritage) at the University of Vermont. And a beer in the sultry afternoon on the porch in Maine was okay, too; even Jonathan had sat with a bottle drenching his fifteen-year-old hand with condensation during the dog days. But "I need a Scotch" was danger. Next thing you knew, you'd be hung over at your morning class, or dribble onto your tie at lunch in Kirkland House, or snooze snorily at a faculty meeting. They were far less concerned about drugs; they'd read Huxley, and Gerda had tried what she called "weed" back in the forties, when it was still called "weed." "They drink" was in the Brand household a condemnation as damning as "They're boring."

And here was Jonathan, drumming his blood-encrusted nails on the table because he couldn't get a snort of aquavit.

Oh, but what did they know? They had done library research for their theses. They had not been up against dismemberment and evisceration in their own kitchen, or kettles of blood (they thought these occurred only in *Macbeth*, probably), or Jón Hendrik, mean old Indian giver of aquavit, or case endings of Faroese nouns (four!), or bad weather, with which Jonathan had yet to contend but which would surely come along soon, now.

Making this list of his burdens had a somewhat quieting effect on Jonathan. It also reminded him that he was an anthropologist; he oughtn't to take everything so personally. It was really like being the psychoanalyst of a culture: if the culture chose to "present" lamb lung and crotchety elders, then he would make sense of them, but he was not in any way obliged to like them. Jón Hendrik's behavior was perhaps useful for illuminating attitudes toward liquor? But no, this thought was quite enough to tumble the shaky structure of disinterest. Jonathan still wanted a drink, and Jón Hendrik hadn't let him have one.

His yearning for a little oblivion—at least a slight blurring of things—continued during dinner, over which the story of his barfing at the sight of the opened lamb was told twice, once by Sigurd to Jón Hendrik and once by Jón Hendrik to Heðin and Petur, who came in late from fishing. Jonathan knew that by the time he reached the dock the next afternoon, all the old geezers would have chewed it over among themselves and be ready to tease him with it. He tried to be affable; these were his friends, after all. A little ribbing between friends was nothing.

But they were odd people, his friends, these villagers. So—so mired in blood, he thought, surprised by himself: spatters of it on Maria's apron, a long brown streak of it on Sigurd's forearm. Jonathan thought of incidents he'd paid little attention to at the time, such as a chicken's neck being snapped casually, during conversation, by Jens Símun the elder ("too old to lay," he'd muttered), and the heartlessness with which heaps of cod were allowed to gasp and flutter on deck. He wondered if he was just a city innocent, unused to the easy brutalities of country living. Or maybe he was looking too hard for Viking traces, bloodlines of savagery. After all, hadn't Sigurd announced that he hated what he was about to do before he shot the sheep? And did he,

Jonathan, really expect fishermen to sympathize with fish?

No. And yes, he could admit to a touch of naïveté in his distaste for such graphic lessons in where food comes from. But all the evening Jonathan wondered about something he saw in the faces around the table, something as strange to him as the faraway look in the men's eyes, and not as benign.

After dinner Maria sewed each sheep stomach into a small bag open at one end and told Jonathan to hold them so she could pour in the blood-flour-sugar mixture she'd brewed up. "Raisins or tallow?" she asked.

"In here?" Jonathan peered into the steaming red stomach.

"Give him raisins," said Sigurd. "He says they don't eat tallow in America. It's good with raisins. Many people prefer it that way."

They *were* his friends. They were always looking out for his welfare, protecting him from things he wouldn't want to eat and assuring him that he wasn't peculiar for not wanting to eat them. They were generous and kindly, all the villagers, and this family that had taken him in—this odd assortment of dreamy men clustered around one stout-legged woman who missed the stars in summer.

And yet, he knew that he did not know them, or did not know some important thing about them, and that he had better learn.

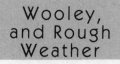

Wooley, and Rough Weather

Wooley arrived on November ninth. Jonathan was sitting at his kitchen table looking at a dismal chart he'd cut out of the newspaper a week before, which gave the times of sunrise and sunset for the month and which he checked daily—as if the experience itself were insufficient. The sun had risen that morning at 8:26 and would be setting at 3:54, twenty minutes after Wooley, ominously large knapsack in hand, opened Jonathan's front door.

The chart's accuracy was flawed by the fact that Skopun lay northwest of a large rise that obscured the sun for a good hour of the morning. This meant that although a sort of light permeated the atmosphere beginning around eight-thirty, the source of that light didn't make an appearance until almost ten. When it did, it looked tired already, rather as it had in Iceland at one in the morning, months earlier. And to make matters worse, drear had set in. Long murky clouds swooped across the sky, trying to erase the sun and frequently succeeding. No day passed without an interlude of rain; many days were entirely rainy, and on these everything in the world—the ocean, the cliffs, the dried, dead tundra, the cement-block houses—was a uniform, steely gray. Even the red roof of the church was soiled and dimmed by the weather.

Jonathan was having quite a bad day. His window frames had swollen from the rain and wouldn't shut properly, so a wet wind was sneaking into his once-cozy kitchen. And the direction this wind was blowing seemed to be down his chimney, for the stove kept rumbling and whooshing in an effort to stay alight. And then, though he'd postponed and postponed, hoping for a clear day, he'd finally had to give in and do his laundry, which was now hanging above the stove on improvised lines, dripping. Each drip hit the stovetop with a hiss and a puff of cooked soap; it was impossible to rinse clothes thoroughly in this cold hard water, but air drying had taken care of that in the summer. Those days were over. Jonathan looked for the thousandth time at the chart. By December twenty-first, the sun would rise at 9:45 (read 11:30 for Skopun) and set at 2:56. The most generous calculation couldn't make much more than three hours out of that day.

But though the laundry and the stove and the windows

were irritations, they were not the cause of Jonathan's bad day. The problem was Daniela.

Heðin's prediction had proved correct. At the end of October, when the nights shifted to "long," Jonathan began to think obsessively about Daniela. His eiderdown puff wasn't warm enough anymore, and he took to sleeping in a long-sleeved shirt and his underpants. As he lay in bed with the coverlet up to his nose, he thought about how warm he'd be if Daniela were under there too, especially if together they were generating a little extra heat. And so he called her.

"Hello, Jonathan," she said in her measured voice. Jonathan remembered just how measured she was and quailed at what he had proposed to do, which was to blurt, "Why don't you come to visit me?" Instead he said, "How are you these days?"

"Oh, I am fine. And you?"

"I'm fine too. I mean—no, I'm fine. Weather's a bit dreary down here in Skopun."

"So," said Daniela.

Was she going to hang up already? He gulped. In the kitchen Sigurd was shuffling about; he'd had to put the call through for Jonathan and now he was hanging around to see what was going to happen with the pretty girl in Tórshavn. English seemed to offer meager protection from Sigurd's eavesdropping.

"Well, so. Daniela, I thought perhaps you'd like to come for a visit here sometime. Would you?" His voice cracked a little, so he cleared his throat and restated his case. "I would really enjoy seeing you again, and I thought you might like to have a weekend away from town. Or something."

"Mmmmm," said Daniela.

What the hell does *mmmmm* mean? Jonathan wondered. But he didn't ask. He said, "So, anyhow, if you'd like to come, I'd be pleased to see you."

"Oh," said Daniela. Then she said, "Someone has just come into the office, Jonathan. I will have to call you again. I will call you soon."

"When is she coming?" Sigurd asked, as Jonathan shut the door to the parlor.

"I don't know," he mumbled. He mumbled the same thing that evening to Heðin, who'd heard about the phone call and come over to get the story.

"What do you mean you don't know? Call her back and say, 'When are you coming?'"

"If she wants to come she can call me."

"No. That's not right, for the woman to call. You must call her tomorrow and ask when." Heðin offered Jonathan the cigarette he'd just rolled, a special treat for the downcast suitor. "You must make the woman feel how much you want her. Then she can't resist."

But Jonathan needed to feel that Daniela wanted him, and so he did not call again.

In the week since their conversation, he'd had too much time to think about what she was likely to do and had worked himself into sad, long fits of doubt and equally long and elaborate happy fantasies: Daniela at the stove cooking their dinner, Daniela reading books while he made his daily gossip rounds, Daniela painting in the guest room while he wrote the first chapter of his thesis. These domestic scenes were as captivating as the sex scenes that followed them in his mind; they seemed a necessary foreplay, in fact. He cautioned himself against them. If she ever did turn up, he would have overloaded their relations so heavily that he would be in danger of acting like the groom in the joke who each day paints part of the horse green in an effort to catch the attention of the pretty rider, and when she finally exclaims, "Why, my horse is green!" he yelps, "Yeah, so let's fuck!" But the issue here was not fucking; it was loving.

Each day that Daniela didn't call, Jonathan said to himself, She didn't call; each night he went to bed thinking

she might call tomorrow. He sustained a tingly condition
of anticipation that made him jump at sudden noises and
lift his head up from his book to stare into space, willing
the telephone at Sigurd's house to ring. So when his door
opened on Friday afternoon, he was utterly surprised to see
a man instead of Daniela, whom he had, in some dogged
way, expected.

It was Wooley, Jonathan was sure of that. And he was
here for a while, judging by the fullness of his knapsack.
And they were not going to get along.

"Hey, bro," said Wooley.

Jonathan just looked at him. There was a lot of him
to look at. He was tall, barrel-chested, and well made, a
perfect specimen of American nutrition. He was wearing
complicated rain gear—a long black slicker with many pockets and metal fastenings, red-topped black galoshes, and a
Maine lobsterman's yellow hat dangling off its string on his
broad back. The slicker had a "designed" aura, as though
it had been made in Paris or Milan: a playboy's fantasy of
foul-weather apparel. Wooley's face atop all this was
friendly and appealing, with even features and healthy skin.
Something about him was unbelievable, though. He looked
like a magazine advertisement for anthropology.

"Jonathan, right?" said Wooley. He put his bag on the
table.

Jonathan nodded. "Jim Wooley?"

"Yup," said Wooley. He sat down.

"Tea?" Jonathan offered.

"Got coffee?"

Jonathan made coffee. He did not ask the question
foremost in his mind, How long are you staying? Instead
he asked the polite version, "What brings you to Skopun?"

"I figured I'd come before the weather made it impossible. I thought you'd be up to Fugloy by now, but this
week I said to myself, He's not coming, so I hopped on the
boat."

Wooley at least had a burning desire to see him. Jonathan tried to make this into a compensation for Daniela's lack of desire. But what good did Wooley do him? Was Wooley going to keep him warm at night? No. He was going to drink a lot of coffee (he'd downed one cup immediately and started on another) and talk, probably about himself, and all the while he would be investigating Jonathan and his progress.

Jonathan felt hemmed in already. The kitchen was steamy from coffee production and laundry, and Wooley took up a lot of room.

"I think I'll get us some fish for dinner," he said. "Halibut okay?"

"Don't you have any lamb left?" Wooley asked.

Jonathan looked up from his sneaker laces. "Left?" He thought of Alice being offered "more" jam by the Mad Hatter. "Left from what?"

"From the slaughter."

A momentary jolt of paranoia subsided as Jonathan realized that probably sheep were slaughtered at the same time on all the islands. "No. I've just got legs, and they're drying in the shed." In Petur's shed, to be accurate; without Petur, Sigurd, and Maria, his sheep would be tethered to his stove gnawing on a shoe. But they had provided him with chops (it was these Wooley was after; Jonathan had finished them), with a rug (at his bedside now), with a shed wherein the magical transformation of lamb leg into compacted, sweet meat candy would take place, and with five blood sausages. He wasn't wild about these, and so he offered them to Wooley. "How about blood sausages?"

"You make those?" Wooley sounded impressed.

"Do you like them?" Jonathan didn't want to admit he hadn't made them.

"Sure. But get some fish too."

On the dock negotiating for fish, Jonathan breathed a

little easier. Never mind the rain that was rushing off his short slicker (yellow, purchased at Sigurd's store, and a far cry from Wooley's Armani creation) and soaking his blue jeans; never mind that there wasn't any halibut and he had to take lemon sole instead; Jonathan was happier not being in the kitchen with Wooley. And if the weather kept up, he could be spending a lot of time in the kitchen with Wooley.

"Do you think the weather will shift?" he asked the man who was selling him fish, counting out one-kroner coins in his sea-worn palm.

"Hah?" he responded with disbelief. "Sure. It'll shift in April, I reckon."

Jonathan walked over to Sigurd's to get some potatoes. He had decided that the time had come to negotiate as well for some aquavit, and Sigurd seemed a likely prospect, given that he must have access to an unending supply of it for Jón Hendrik's needs.

"Your friend came," Sigurd announced.

This was a good lead-in. "Yes, and I want some aquavit to celebrate." Sigurd's face went blank. "I'll pay whatever it costs." Sigurd's face darkened. "What I mean, I mean of course I will pay for it." Jonathan was astonished at how quickly he had created a muddle.

"You can't get aquavit," said Sigurd. He fingered the potatoes Jonathan had heaped on the counter. "Two kroner."

This looked to be the shortest transaction ever to take place in Sigurd's store. He must be deeply offended. Jonathan played an ace he'd sworn he'd never use. "Sigurd, please forgive me if I said something wrong. I am a stranger here and I don't know all your customs."

But Sigurd was much too smart to go for that. "Pah," he said. He looked out the window. Then he looked at Jonathan and said, "You don't want to understand. In America, you have everything."

Jonathan thought Sigurd was being unfair. He shook his head.

Sigurd shook *his* head. "Okay. Listen. We need it. You don't need it. We need it here. It is part of living here in the Faroes. You are visiting, and we will give you aquavit when you come for a *temun*, but that is all."

"But why can't I buy some?"

"Because there isn't enough!" Sigurd was exasperated. "There's plenty of sheep and fish and potatoes. Have those!" He put Jonathan's potatoes into an old paper bag and pushed it toward him. "Two kroner," he repeated.

Jonathan grinned at Sigurd, trying to convey with his grin that he knew—and knew that Sigurd knew—that potatoes and aquavit were hardly equivalent. Charm had no more effect than forthrightness. Sigurd was implacable.

"He's got some anyhow," Sigurd said suddenly.

"Who?"

"The Other American. He has a metal bottle. He was drinking on the boat." Sigurd relaxed and put his hands on the counter, his usual pose. "He's an idiot. It's stupid to drink on a boat."

"Why's that?"

"Bad luck," said Sigurd. "Also, it makes you sick."

"Oh," Jonathan said. "He's not my friend," he added.

Surprise crossed Sigurd's face. "He is your countryman."

Jonathan wished he lived in such a simple world. He had—or was approaching living there—until this Wooley arrived to drag him back to America. Now his efforts to be just another village oddball would be undone by foreignness-by-association with Wooley. And he had started the process himself with his ill-advised plea for Sigurd's tolerance.

"Jo-Na-Than," Sigurd said, shaking his head affectionately. "Don't you get homesick? Don't you want to talk about home with the Other American?"

"No. I like it here."

This pleased Sigurd. "Yah, life is good here, isn't it?" He beamed. "In the Faroes, we are free."

Jonathan looked around Sigurd's store. It was about the same size as his parents' living room, lighted by one large, fly-dotted bulb that hung three feet above Sigurd's head. The stock was haphazardly arranged on the shelves, with a few examples of motor oil beside a few examples of canned cabbage. At the end of the counter was the milk bucket, containing at this hour of the afternoon only the skim-milk dregs. A day-old newspaper and a cardboard display case of rolling tobacco were at Sigurd's left elbow; at his right, the adding machine with its green keys, never used (Sigurd totted up prices on paper bags). Tacked to the wall behind Sigurd, a full suit of rain gear— hat, slicker, overalls, waders—arranged in human shape had faded over the years from yellow to beige: the ghostly guardian of the store. Jonathan thought of Eyvindur saying "We are not free" and thought also of the missile watchtower across the fjord—that third countryman who, like Jonathan and Wooley, was a trained observer from the land of the free.

America: what a paradoxical homeland! Jonathan on previous trips to Europe had tucked his passport deep into his pocket, not to protect it but to protect himself, and relied on his excellent French to screen his origins. There was no virtue, this late in the century, in being an American. Jonathan knew he'd missed the era when his citizenship might have been something other than a juggling act. Freedom was no longer a major U.S. export; even domestic production seemed to be falling off. Jonathan's freedom at home, like that of many city dwellers, was burdensome because he saw so many who lacked it. He could feel guilty or he could feel threatened, but he could not feel easy. Like the generation before his that had sat in, marched, burned, and bombed, he and his peers were permanently disenchanted with the government; unlike them, they had no ideal of a more perfect union.

And so, in the matter of love of one's country, as in the matter of love in general, Jonathan was an emotional virgin. Nationality was to him akin to an arranged marriage or being saddled with difficult parents. He thought of another of Eyvindur's pronouncements: A man does not choose his homeland. In Eyvindur's case, an explanation for attachment; in his own, an excuse for detachment.

But the drive to love is strong. Jonathan in Sigurd's store could—and did now, in the twilight—shut his eyes and know his visceral connection to the fine Georgian wood-frame houses (pre-Revolutionary, but still American) that fronted Brattle Street, to the joy of driving too fast down an interstate in one of his country's homegrown oversized cars, and, most profoundly, to the comfort of feeling the entire continent at his back when he stood wind-buffeted on the rocks of Acadia, looking out to the ocean that had all the while, unknown to him, cradled these islands.

He opened his eyes. Was this Arcadia? Had he reached Paradise—a fishy, rainy, circumscribed yet charmed universe where only nature demanded obedience, where intimacy performed the function of law, where patriotism was as easy as—or equivalent to—admiring the landscape? In all its dreary, disorganized splendor, the Faroes was a place Jonathan would be proud to call his home. What good was three thousand miles of country if he didn't feel that it was his? Wasn't home the place where you recognize yourself? Perhaps these two hundred square miles of peat and stone were a more congenial vantage point on the world. Perhaps he'd come not from but to the land of the free.

Jonathan realized that Sigurd was watching him, waiting for his two kroner and a rejoinder to "we are free."

"I think you're right," he said. Sigurd cocked his head. Had he been expecting a quarrel? Probably; he looked prepared to argue into the night for the existence of perfect

freedom in the Faroes and surprised at Jonathan's unwillingness to stick up for his own side.

"How many people do you have there?" Sigurd asked.
He was squinting, anticipatory, as if the answer would
clarify why Jonathan didn't love his country.

"Eight million." No, that was New York City. "Five
hundred million." That was implausible. Sigurd was bug-
eyed. "Lots." Jonathan finally settled it. "We have lots and
lots."

"Soon you'll have to move to the moon." Sigurd
laughed. "Where do they fit?"

"It's bigger than here." Jonathan pushed his arm
against the chilly, damp air, expanding Sigurd's store.

"I reckon so." Sigurd nodded to himself over the size
of America, then asked, "So, the Other American, you don't
know his family?"

Jonathan put two kroner on the counter; how could
he hope to be a member of this world? "I don't," he said
gently, and went off to make dinner for Wooley.

What an evening! Jonathan shivered with ire and chill under
his coverlet, listening to Wooley banging drawers in the
room where Daniela was supposed to have whiled away the
afternoon painting.

What it boiled down to was that Wooley took what
Jonathan thought of as the "masculine" approach to life and
anthropology. Some people became anthropologists because
they already felt themselves outside of culture: this was
Jonathan's position. Others believed themselves so versatile
and appealing that they would be accepted by any culture:
this was Wooley's position. Wooley was not one to worry
that he'd overstayed his welcome, eaten too much, said the
wrong thing, misunderstood someone's intention. And Jonathan had to admit that this heedlessness was useful.
Wooley had steamrolled his way into life on Fugloy with
his bulk, his terrible pidgin Faroese, his daring that took

him down cliffs on ropes to hunt puffins and earned him admiration from taciturn villagers (or so Wooley told it; but Jonathan believed him). Wooley would eat anything, provoking more native admiration. And Wooley blissfully enjoyed every rain-soaked, blundered-through moment of his Faroese existence; that was clear. No sulking in the kitchen for him.

Was he at all intimidatable? Jonathan had tried: Harvard, literary references, French, even—desperately—Daniela and her fictional visit. Wooley didn't bother countering any of these, except Daniela. He claimed to be engaged to a girl in Klaksvík. Jonathan prodded. Well, they were probably going to get engaged. They were sleeping together, and in the Faroes that was considered engaged. Wouldn't he feel badly when he left and didn't take her? Jonathan wanted to know. Wooley shook his head. No, she'll understand. She's a great girl.

"Anyhow," he added, "I might stay."

Jonathan's ire bubbled again at the memory of this. It was worse than if Wooley had been writing his thesis on the same topic; it was grand larceny, emotional plagiarism: How dare he be as captivated as Jonathan?

Going bush. Like many anthropological ideas, this one had been born in jungles and savannahs and gave off a tropical scent. Some old-timers called it "troppo," an occupational hazard that began with lassitude and ended by destroying your objectivity. Stories that went, When we got there, two years later, he was living in a hut with three wives. The trouble was, anthropologists were supposed to be living in huts. The three wives were optional but not exceptional. The line between observer and participant was so fine as to defy detection much of the time. It started easily enough. When members of "your" tribe are going on a journey or planning to get married, they slaughter a chicken and read the blood for omens. They offer to read omens for you before your trip back down the river for supplies. What harm can it do? It will certainly give you a better sense of their worldview, and it might give you a little useful information. Pretty soon you have recourse to chicken slaughter every time you have to make a decision.

Was that what was happening to both of them? Screwing around with Faroese girls (even if only in the mind), scrambling down cliff faces, eating rotten meat? Wooley had been extolling *ræst* meat after dinner. *Ræst* meat was in the first stages of corruption, with maggots crawling in it. "You pick them out, and then you boil it," he explained. Further proof of Wooley's effective insinuation of himself into society, for the villagers had so far protected Jonathan from knowing about this practice.

Wooley had long since stopped fussing with drawers and fallen into a hearty sleep complete with snore. Jonathan was awake, chasing his thoughts all over the map.

There was an important difference, he told himself, between thinking you could be an Amazon chieftain and thinking you could fit in with the Faroese. They had a common heritage, after all. His ancestors were northern Europeans just like theirs. The leap he'd made was more through time than culture: as life was here, so had all life north of France been two, or five, centuries ago. Perhaps racial memory explained his comfort? They were not foreigners, really. The anthropology department agreed with him on this; they had certainly beaten that point to a pulp before granting him permission to do fieldwork in what they said was "not a foreign culture."

But he was here now. Jonathan turned over in bed, wishing he could go to sleep. He punched the pillow and began grinding through the evening with Wooley again.

Of all Jonathan's faults and quirks, the one that gave him the most trouble was his compulsive comparative thinking. A screen of *He's like that but I'm like this* obscured his perceptions of people. Each personality he encountered was a new yardstick by which to measure himself—and frequently he came up short. The Faroes offered some relief from all this. Though a master at self-laceration, Jonathan was unable to pull off the feat of faulting himself for not being, say, a good fisherman, or for not being in a general sense someone who'd spent his life in a village of four hundred on a rock in the middle of the Atlantic. Here he saw clearly how much culture determines character: noisy, agitated, superpower America could never produce a calm, ocean-eyed Petur. These people lived in a comprehensible world; he'd grown up in chaos.

With Wooley, this excuse didn't hold.

Equal opportunity. Not quite equal. Wooley seemed to come from money. He'd mentioned his father's "companies." Jonathan had noted the plural, and also that Wooley had said he'd gone to high school in Beverly Hills. His carefree attitude might be explained by privilege. But Jonathan knew they were both children of privilege, coddled and pushed to success. Wooley was more of a rebel than Jonathan; his father had expected him to go to work in one of the companies.

"But hey," Wooley said, "I had a real great time at college, so I thought, You'd be fucking nuts to trade this for a boardroom."

Jonathan found Wooley's flat California delivery of flat California-style sentences disconcerting, because it gave the impression that he was stupid, and he was not. Stupid people were not accepted into the doctoral program in anthropology at Berkeley, nor were they given large traveling fellowships.

"What got you into anthropology?" Jonathan asked. He didn't want to know, but there was no way to deflect the conversation from Wooley's accomplishments.

"I was in soc"—pronounced *soash*, making Jonathan wince; he was used to the staid Harvard term *soc rel*, for social relations—"and I did a study of Chicano gangs in LA for my senior thesis. They were *bad*." What a posturer, thought Jonathan. "Man, they had these amazing jackets. They had like jacket art. It was fantastic. Anyhow, my professor said I ought to go into anthro. He said I had the perfect observational distance for it. I don't know what the fuck he meant, but I did it."

So he was a braggart, and an insensitively flagrant one. Jonathan had met plenty, though most were the sort who weave their braggadocio into conversation subtly. Still, *he* was sensitive enough to see there wasn't much difference in the end. But here came the trouble spot. Wooley was crass, self-important, a blunderbuss of a guy, and Jonathan could only wonder why he too didn't possess these qualities, even though he found them distasteful. Because Wooley didn't find himself distasteful, and he seemed to be having an easier time living than Jonathan.

Possibly Wooley had doubts invisible to the naked eye—to Jonathan's naked eye, anyhow? He didn't think so. Jonathan believed himself to be the only person in the world with a large discrepancy between inner and outer self, and his uniqueness in misery was dear to him. It was a loophole through which he could escape from failure, loneliness— even his own incessant measuring. For at the heart of his belief was this spectacular disavowal: It wasn't really me, you have never known me.

But what had been a comfort, a plumb line to a private reality, seemed now, at three o'clock in the morning in his chilly, foreign bed, odd and not comforting. A terrible question, which had never occurred to him before, presented itself: If his actions, words, and "self" were not the real Jonathan, then where was that Jonathan? For years he'd assumed that a finer, smarter, more capable Jonathan lurked in the wings waiting for his cue. But what was the cue? And what evidence did he have that the Other Jonathan was going to make an appearance?

Jonathan sat up in bed, transfixed by a new possibility: the Other Jonathan didn't exist. That would certainly explain his failure to show up. Jonathan's eyes widened; he realized he couldn't imagine living without this shadow self, though he knew that he did, in the sense that it was everyday Jonathan who spoke and ate and made dinner for Wooley. Nothing, not Harvard, not the Faroes, not Daniela, had ever conjured this better Jonathan, and still Jonathan had believed in him.

Oh, if there was no Jonathan-Messiah, to save him from himself! Then this was life. As it was, it would be. He would envy Wooley and disdain him, and no wise, skillful Jonathan would rise from the ashes of those base emotions to command Wooley's respect; he would wait for Daniela to call, and she would or wouldn't do so according to her inclination, and no magic dance performed by the delicious Other Jonathan could fix her inclination toward him. Worst of all, he would have no excuse for his incapacities and reluctances—not that he'd ever used it with anyone except himself. But it had been there, a chant that sounded, now, like something from first grade: You'll see, you'll see. What would they see? They would see more of what they saw. Which was? Him. Plain old everyday Jonathan.

He sank back under his eiderdown. The whole business was fundamentally embarrassing. He'd spent years deluding himself. Memories—little barbs of shame— popped into his mind: the papers whose mediocre grades he'd dismissed by dismissing the intelligence of his teachers, who after all didn't have the wit to detect the brilliance of the Other Jonathan; the high-school debating team that didn't include him because he was "above" such sophomoric intellectual activity; the parties where he'd been ignored by people too ignorant to notice how interesting he was. But hadn't he thought his paper rather good, hadn't he tried out for the debating team, and hadn't he spent too much time at parties watching others enjoy themselves?

Two-thirty in the morning on an island far from home

was an odd time and place to get the news that he, his parents, and his elite schools had all been wrong. He was not brilliant or unusual; he—and they—had merely assumed that he was. Everybody in Cambridge assumed this of himself, but surely not everybody could be right. Despite his shock, Jonathan broke into a grin at the thought of an entire city obsessed with intellectual glamour, each citizen returning home at night to explain to his mate or his mirror why he was more insightful, better informed, or just plain smarter than everybody he'd spent the day with.

What a world. Jonathan was a veteran of many such fervent self-promotion campaigns (usually involving the mirror), but he'd never before questioned the justice of meritocracy. He'd never had to, he saw, because he'd thought he was at the top of the heap or bound to get there eventually. And it is the losers in any system who are the grumblers, the visionaries. Jonathan bereft of his perfect phantom and cut off from a place at the top was not so keen on survival of the smartest as he'd been even three hours earlier, when he'd smugly noted Wooley's unsophisticated speech patterns.

But if King Brain were deposed, what would the world be like? Jonathan couldn't imagine. Though, he supposed, he was at the moment living in such a world. The Faroese didn't use their brains as weapons (this seemed the most accurate description of the Cambridge usage); the Faroese seemed to take people as they came—maybe. He couldn't tell, really, if they did. They seemed to take him as he came, but perhaps he wasn't a conclusive example. And even if they did, wouldn't that mean he'd have to stay here forever to avoid a confrontation with the second-rateness that awaited him at home?

Jonathan pulled the eiderdown over his head and sighed into the warm darkness. It was a lot to lose, the promise of greatness. And was his next task to learn the rankings on some diminished scale of ambitions? Adequate,

well done, rather interesting—such terms had seemed the
very equivalent of failure; they might now encompass his
shrunken future.

Sobered, exhausted, and still quantifying, he fell
asleep completely covered, like a corpse.

Wooley had brought terrible weather with him. It was rain-
ing hard the afternoon he arrived, and by the next morning
the wind had risen to a near gale, blowing the rain in bands
across the horizon and stirring the sea to a black-and-white
fury. From the kitchen window Jonathan could see great
towers of foam and spray shooting up from the jetty where
the waves broke. He stood at the sink looking at these
formations of water—they were as transient and suggestive
as clouds—and drinking his coffee, while Wooley sat at the
table drinking his.

Ten-thirty, coffee finished, and Jonathan felt a knot
of tension: What were they going to do today? Telepathic
Wooley suddenly said, "How about a walk?"

"In this weather?"

"Yeah. Let's go out to the cliffs and watch the storm."

It sounded better than festering in the kitchen.
"Okay," said Jonathan. He wished he had a long slicker like
Wooley's. Then when Wooley was all suited up, he was
glad he didn't; he might get wet, but he wouldn't look like
a male model.

Their progress through town drew many a face to
many a rain-streaked window. Sigurd made the unprece-
dented move of leaving his spot behind the counter and
putting his head out the door to say good morning.

"Terrible weather," he called.

"I reckon so," said Jonathan.

"My name is Jim Wooley," said Wooley, moving on
Sigurd with his hand out.

"Well, good day to you," Sigurd said. He looked astonished.

"We're going for a walk," Wooley continued. His accent was atrocious.

"Eh?" Sigurd looked at Jonathan.

"A walk," Jonathan translated, "out to the cliffs."

"Don't get blown over," Sigurd said. Then he laughed. "Even a man as big as you"—he tipped his head toward Wooley—"can get blown over."

"So, so, so," said Wooley. He had that part down all right, Jonathan noted. "Where's the best spot to see the spray?"

"Eh?" said Sigurd. He squinted.

"The *spray*," said Wooley, louder than before.

"Oh. The spray." Sigurd nodded.

"We want to see the big sprays," Wooley said.

Sigurd understood this time and launched into a detailed description of where to see big sprays, which Jonathan had trouble following. The gist of it seemed to be that there was a big rock out west near the "troll house," where there was good spray when the storm came from the north, as this one did. The troll house was a new landmark, though. Jonathan didn't think he'd recognize it.

"The troll house—" he started.

"I know it," Wooley interrupted, in English.

"How can you know it?" Jonathan protested. "You've never been here before."

"It's a kind of rock. I'll show you."

Sigurd was watching this exchange closely. "Jo-Na-Than," he said. "You bring this American for a *temun* tonight. Okay? We'll have a nice after-dinner *temun*." He winked, so Jonathan would know just what he meant.

"Thanks," Jonathan said. He remembered Sigurd's assertion that Wooley had a flask of something. Maybe he could get Wooley to bring it out before dinner and spend the entire evening soaked in aquavit.

A troll house, Wooley explained as they left town, heads down against the wind, was any large boulder sitting alone on land in the *bøur*—near the village. "They think that's where trolls live," he added.

"I got that," said Jonathan.

Sarcasm rolled off Wooley as easily as rain off his fancy slicker. He began to whistle. He had a true and melodious whistle, and he was doing an old favorite of Jonathan's, "Loch Lomond." Bear long ago had sung Jonathan to sleep with it. "I'll be in Scotland before you," whistled Wooley.

"But me and my true love," Jonathan joined in, singing.

"We'll never meet again," Wooley whistled.

"On the bonny, bonny banks of Loch Lomond," they ended together. And it sounded so nicely mournful, singing and whistling this sad song in the rain, that they went through the verses again, Wooley weaving a pattern of trill and quaver with his really quite marvelous whistle.

"Here's the troll house." Wooley broke off the music. "The big rock should be right down there." They peered carefully over the cliff, which at this point on the island rose more than three hundred feet straight up from the sea.

There were several big rocks, one of those strange strings of stone droppings that occasionally decorated these shores. Tides had carved out a cave in one, and into this hole the sea poured and swirled, roaring. Huge white sheets of water rose from the impact of ocean on the other rocks, and a pale salt mist rose even higher than the waves, spreading up and across the cliffs to add its moisture to their already wet faces.

"Great, hunh?" Wooley yelled.

Jonathan could only see his mouth moving, the noise of the water was so deafening. But he nodded.

"Louder than Niagara," Wooley yelled. "God," he spread his wet arms wide, "what a great country!"

Jonathan found Wooley's enthusiasm embarrassing. He busied himself with leaning forward so that some of the rain collected in the folds of his slicker would run onto the turf instead of onto his jeans.

"Wet." Wooley offered this comment at high volume. Jonathan nodded. "Go?" asked Wooley, moving inland ten feet.

The wind was at their backs as they walked home, shortening the journey considerably and soaking the parts of them that had managed to stay dry on the way out.

"Let's stop at the dock and get some fish," Jonathan said. "That way we won't have to go out again."

"We need milk too," said Wooley.

Jonathan was struck by that *we need;* he had never shared a household, and in his fantasies of doing so, it was always a woman's voice saying *we need.* Still, he liked hearing it, even though Wooley was speaking. Something about the phrase was comforting and conjured images of coziness in a warm, well-supplied home.

But the reality of supply, that day in Skopun, did not meet demand. The milk bucket at Sigurd's was down to the dregs already, though usually the whole milk lasted until after lunch. "Everybody's coming in for milk because to-morrow maybe it won't arrive," Sigurd explained.

"Why?" Jonathan asked.

"Weather," said Sigurd, terse.

"Where does it come from?"

"From Sandur." Sigurd gestured south, toward that other country ten miles across the island. "Milk from San-dur."

"Why couldn't it arrive? Doesn't it come on a truck?" Sigurd didn't answer this. "Cheese?" he suggested.

Jonathan bought half a liter of watery milk, some cheese, and a few potatoes. Wooley didn't offer to pay. As Jonathan was digging coins out of his wet pocket, Sigurd added a box of eggs to the pile.

"Get these," he ordered.

"Why?"

Sigurd ducked this question too. "See you tonight," he said, with his theatrical wink.

The dock was nearly deserted. All the boats were fastened down and empty, and they banged against each other with dull, water-muffled thuds. Two young men were sheltering beneath the overhang of the fish factory's loading platform. Jonathan was glad to see that Heðin was one of them.

"Eh," said Heðin, through his wet cigarette. He waved Jonathan over.

Jonathan was nervous about introducing Wooley, but Heðin took the situation in hand. "My friend Jonathan," he announced, "and his friend from America."

"Wooley," said Wooley.

The other young man nodded shyly. Then nobody knew what to say.

"So, so, so," said Heðin. "Terrible weather."

"I reckon so," said Jonathan.

"So, so, so," said Wooley.

This was getting nowhere. "I want some fish," said Jonathan.

"No fish," said Heðin.

"Because of the weather?"

"Yah."

"I reckon so," said Wooley. That wasn't his cue; both Jonathan and Heðin looked at him. He smiled.

Heðin became loquacious. "No fish, Jonathan, no fish today, no fish tomorrow, maybe no fish for a week!" He shook his head. "Winter," he said, as if this explained it.

"No fish all winter?" Jonathan asked.

"Can't fish in a storm like this," said Heðin's friend.

"And does it storm like this all winter?" Jonathan was fearful of the answer.

The village boys laughed. "Most of the time," said the friend.

"But not all the time," Heðin added. "And you get good fat cod after a storm like this. They get fat from eating so much during the storm."

"So, so, so," said Heðin's friend.

The conversation was over, that meant. "I reckon so," said Jonathan. They could have omelets; he was glad Sigurd had insisted on the eggs. But that left lunch up in the air, and he was hungry. "Let's go back to the store and get something for lunch," Jonathan said to Wooley in English.

"Lunch, dinner, breakfast," said Heðin, also in English. "Morning, nighting—"

"Night," said Jonathan.

"Okay," said Wooley.

Sigurd wasn't surprised to see them. "No fish, hah?" He grinned. "Here." Jonathan was touched to see that he had made a pile of things they might want: cabbage in a can, a wizened hard salami, a package of crackers, some dehydrated vegetable soup, and some more potatoes. Jonathan bought them all.

"See you tonight," said Sigurd.

"One last stop," Jonathan said as they set off again, gripping their paper bags tightly because the rain was turning them to pulp. But at the post office, where all the old men had gathered for their morning meeting, usually held on the dock, the slow, careful postmaster said, "No mail today."

"No boat?" Jonathan asked. He knew the answer already.

"No boat tomorrow, either," snapped Jón Hendrik. "You two are going to have a nice long visit."

"How long?" Jonathan ventured.

"This storm?" Jón Hendrik sniffed the air.

"Three days," said one of the other old men.

"No. Four days," said Jón Hendrik. "Four days." He nodded sagely.

"But the boat—the boat will come, won't it?"

"How can it?" Jón Hendrik asked.

Indeed, as they walked back out into the storm, Jonathan did not see how the boat could come. The harbor was a mass of yellow-flecked, roiling foam, and the sea beyond had gone black. "Hmm," he said, looking at this hopeless scene.

"Happens all the time on Fugloy," Wooley said. "Sometimes the boat doesn't come for a week."

"I reckon so," said Jonathan. It seemed to be the most appropriate response.

A full bottle of Aalborg aquavit, its seal unbroken, was standing on Sigurd's kitchen table when they arrived. Jón Hendrik had a glass of something else, probably his bad brandy. A newer version of the terrible cake Jonathan remembered from the summer sat on a plate, already impaled by a knife.

Jonathan got drunk quickly. He was used to eating more than he had eaten that day, and the liquor went right to his head. More than that, he wanted to get drunk, had been wanting to get drunk for several days. It was compensation for everything—the weather, the lack of fish, Wooley snoring in the guest room, Daniela's damned silence, his long night's brooding. He put back two stiff shots and skidded into the now-familiar condition of blur.

Blurred, Wooley was no longer his responsibility. As they'd walked through town in the windy night, Jonathan had worried that Wooley would galumph over Sigurd's delicate sensibilities or not give Jón Hendrik the proper amount of respect, and that he would have to trail Wooley all evening, mending the fences he broke. This now seemed ridiculous. Wooley was a phenomenon; Sigurd and Jón Hendrik would have to contend with him—just as Jonathan had been doing for the last twenty-four hours.

Wooley and Sigurd were trading names of people on Fugloy.

"Jørgen? Jørgen *hjá* Jákup, who married Anna, the one with the sister who moved to Iceland?"

"Yes. Now he's got a big boat, goes out to Spitzbergen."

"So, so, so. I was at his wedding."

"Now he's got a little grandson, born this winter."

"So, so, so." Sigurd chewed this over and began on another cud of information. "How about that old Johannes, whose father came from Nolsoy?"

"He's still alive, but he's too old to walk now."

Jonathan was bored by this, so turned his foggy attention to Jón Hendrik.

"So. Jón Hendrik," he said.

"Is this your kinsman?" Jón Hendrik asked.

"No. He's just another American."

"He's a strong man," said Jón Hendrik. He looked at Jonathan, then back at Wooley. He leaned close to Jonathan and, breathing liquor-laced tobacco on his cheek, said, "He doesn't speak very good Faroese. You should teach him."

"He won't be here long," Jonathan said. He put more aquavit in his glass.

"But you learned fast," said Jón Hendrik.

"I've been here six months." Could it be true? Had he gotten anything done? He took a drink.

"You speak good Faroese," Jón Hendrik said. "You don't use Danish words. Pure."

"Do you listen to that radio show about the language?"

"Pah!" Jón Hendrik made a face. "I don't need to be told how to talk." Then, with a grin, "Do *you* listen to it?"

"No. I had a good teacher, in America."

"A Faroe man?"

"No. He was Norwegian."

"The Norwegians are the best," said Jón Hendrik. "Not like those terrible Danes."

"How about the Icelanders?" asked Jonathan.

"They lisp," said Jón Hendrik. He fell into silent admiration of his brandy glass.

Sigurd and Wooley had run out of steam too. Jonathan yawned. Then everybody else yawned. In the silence the rain beat on the tin roof. Wooley smiled at Jonathan, a conspiratorial, quick smile.

"So, so, so," Sigurd said. "Two Americans in Skopun. Will you miss us, when you go home?"

The storm was worse in the morning, when Jonathan woke with a hangover. He stumbled downstairs. Wooley was drinking coffee in the rain-dark kitchen. Thunder rang out from the mountain behind the village, and long sharp trails of lightning split the black sky above the sea.

"Wow," said Jonathan. Here was bad weather with a vengeance.

"This could be the worst of it," Wooley said. "Coffee?" He raised the pot. "Or I could make a fresh one."

Jonathan had the sensation of being Wooley's guest, which he did not like. "I'll do it." He turned on the lamp above the table and bustled about, rinsing the pot, wiping the counter, claiming his kitchen.

"I bet this breaks tomorrow." Wooley nodded as he spoke.

"I hope so." Jonathan looked to see if Wooley had been insulted by the hidden hope for his departure; he was guzzling his coffee contentedly. Jonathan was eager for coffee. His head felt spiked, as if a stake had been pounded through his temple.

A new fusillade of thunder shook the windows and doors in their frames. Something heavy and made of metal was blowing about outside, crashing into concrete and thudding along the wet ground. This noise set Jonathan's teeth on edge. He peered into the pot to see when the coffee would be ready. And then the lamp started to flicker. The power ebbed and surged a few times and vanished, taking with it the hot plate and Jonathan's hopes for coffee.

"Shit." He dropped into a chair and put his head in his hands. "That's it for cooking." He glared at the hot plate.

"That may be it for heat, too," said Wooley. "I think your kerosene pump is electric."

"No. I have to do it by hand."

"Right, you fill it by hand. But I think then the fuel is pumped in by a motor."

Wooley was, of course, correct. The temperature of the hallway was a frigid preview of the temperature of the kitchen by evening, and in the time it took to find the now-silent motor, Jonathan's hands and feet began to tingle with cold.

"We'll have to keep the kitchen doors shut," Wooley said. "It'll stay warm for a while, and maybe the power will come back." He opened the refrigerator. "Let's eat everything we don't have to cook."

"I'm not hungry," said Jonathan. His head was throbbing.

"We need to eat, to stay warm." Wooley was piling cheese and butter and jam and bread on the table. "How about raw eggs? You like those? We could shake them up in some milk."

"Don't," Jonathan said, "please don't." He sat down. "Can I finish your coffee?"

"Sure." Wooley was rooting in the refrigerator. "Blood sausage?"

"Go ahead." Jonathan swirled the last of the coffee in his mouth, trying to negate the taste of bile and aquavit. He noted a slight improvement—but how much better he would feel with a whole cup of coffee, and without the prospect of a heatless, lightless, endless day with Wooley. He lurched to the window and scanned the houses around his; there wasn't a light in any of them. Smoke, however, plumed into the air above Petur's roof. Heðin's characterization of his little brother as "conservative" applied to the whole family: they had kept their peat-burning stove. Jonathan splashed some water on his face. "I'm going next door for a minute," he said.

"I'll come with you," Wooley said, with his mouth full of cheese.

"That's okay." Jonathan rushed into his clogs and slicker. "I'll be back in a second."

Crossing the twenty feet between his door and Petur's, Jonathan got chilled through and wet. He walked in without knocking, a true Faroese visitor, and kicked his clogs off in the hall. Little Jens Símun sat at the table working on a coloring book while Maria tended to a pot that put forth the worst smell Jonathan had yet encountered in these islands.

"So, so, so," said Maria. "Sit down and have a *temun*."

"Are the stems of trees green?" Jens Símun asked.

Desire for coffee and company other than Wooley's warred with nausea from the smell. "What are you cooking?" asked Jonathan.

"*Ræst kjøt*. Meat before it gets hard rotten. It smells bad but it tastes good." Maria covered the pot. "We are used to the smell, but I know visitors don't like it." She pointed the coffeepot at Jonathan. He nodded.

"It's lucky you kept your peat stove," he said.

"*Are* they green?" Jens Símun held up a green crayon and waved it.

"No, they're brown." He took a wonderful gulp of coffee. "We've got no heat or light."

"Yes. Petur went out with Jens Símun to try to fix the power. Come for dinner. I can make you an egg again, if you don't like the meat."

"The American who's staying with me likes *ræst* meat."

"What's his name?" asked Jens Símun. "He's very tall. Also, he's got a stupid coat."

"Shh," said Maria, but she smiled.

"His name is Jim," said Jonathan. "I think his coat's stupid too." He'd almost gotten used to the smell, and the coffee had changed his mood entirely.

"What are these?" Jens Símun pushed his book toward Jonathan and pointed to the bottom of the page.

"Those are a flower we call tulips. They can be white or red or yellow."

"And are the stems brown?"

"Green." Jonathan turned to the front of the book. "Where did you get this?"

"It's a Danish book. My cousin Lisabet sent it from Down There."

"Lisabet who's the mother of the baby, Petra?"

Maria nodded. "She's getting another baby, from a Danish man this time. So she'll come home soon, I think."

Jonathan had a quick, intense vision of the unknown Lisabet's white and swollen body beneath him; maybe, after this baby was born, she'd like a baby from an American man. Featureless, fecund Lisabet dissolved into Daniela with her mocking gaze. When was this storm going to end, so that Wooley could leave and Daniela could arrive? "Where's Heðin?" he asked; he was now ready to enlist Heðin's help in luring Daniela across the fjord that separated them.

"On the dock. They are taking the small boats out of the water." Maria lifted the lid off the pot.

"I'd better go home," said Jonathan. The smell was remarkable. This fresh whiff of it was overpowering—like a combination of boiled sweaty feet and singed hair. "I have some eggs I could bring," he offered. "In case," he said quickly, "I don't like the meat."

"I have eggs," said Maria.

"What time is dinner?"

"When you come. It's always when you come. In America, do people eat at a special time?"

"No, not exactly. They tell you to come at a special time, though."

"Why?" Maria asked.

"I'm not sure," said Jonathan. "It probably has to do with the kind of food we eat." He was floundering around. "Food that's ready at a particular time—I mean, that takes a particular amount of time to cook."

"All food is like that," Maria said. "You just make it ready by evening."

Jonathan thought of a few things that would not do well just being "ready by evening," such as fettucini Alfredo and trout poached in white wine, but he decided not to go further into the matter. The details of American dinner invitations—come at seven-thirty, bring red wine, wear a jacket because Professor Hoopla will be there—seemed at this moment complicated and fundamentally unfriendly. "Different customs," he said to Maria, but saying this underscored his growing sense of having entered a limbo where America and the Faroes were equally foreign. It was like trying to give Sigurd population statistics. He kept seeing the information about his own country from their point of view—and finding it crazy. He would take refuge in a homey understanding of Faroese ways only to be slapped back to an uncomfortable position as an American by some terrible smell: uncomfortable because he could no more now imagine himself standing at an oak door with a brass knocker, wearing a tie and holding a bottle of Médoc, than he could picture eating rotten meat. He was floating around in cultural hyperspace; nothing felt right.

And now, back to Wooley. Jonathan put on his clogs and dashed home.

"We're invited for dinner," he said. "They've got an old-fashioned stove."

"Who's this family?"

"Brother of Sigurd, where we were last night. Petur and his wife, Maria—who's also the granddaughter of Jón Hendrik, the grandfather of Sigurd and Petur, the old man last night."

"First-cousin marriage?"

"Second. Different grandmothers. I don't quite follow it." Jonathan didn't like the sound of that. "I've got it written down," he added, "in a notebook."

"Yeah, I've got all sorts of shit written down too. I never look at it." Wooley laughed.

Jonathan saw himself eight months from now on a hot Cambridge afternoon, with a stack of notes beside him and a blank sheet in the typewriter. "Oh, God," he said, dropping into the chair next to Wooley. "What are we doing here?"

"Fieldwork," said Wooley promptly. "Going nuts in a kitchen during a gale is just a typical fieldwork routine. You think Evans-Pritchard and all those other hyphenated guys didn't lie around in their hammocks and wonder what the fuck they were doing?"

Jonathan laughed for the first time since Wooley's arrival. "I suppose they did. They never write about it, though."

"He lost all his notes, I think. Didn't they fall out of a canoe and sink to the bottom of the Nile?"

Jonathan shook his head. "What would you do if that happened? I can't imagine it."

"Well, I'd just wing it. I think he went back and repeated his study. The English are compulsive." Wooley drummed on the table with the butter knife. "Maybe he just wasn't ready to go home."

"How could you ever be ready?"

"You mean, like, finished?"

"Partly that." Jonathan took a breath. He had an urge to confide in Wooley. After all, he was an anthropologist too. Maybe Jonathan's trouble was a standard professional one. "I think I have a case of advance culture shock," he announced. Wooley looked puzzled. "When I think of Cambridge, it seems even stranger than this place. I feel so far away from it I might as well just stay here."

"Everyone always thinks they can stay," Wooley said.

"You said you might." Jonathan spoke sharply; that *everyone* sounded patronizing.

"I'm just kidding myself, I guess." Wooley appeared unperturbed admitting this. "In the end—"

"You're always an outsider, right?" Jonathan broke in.

"No." He held the knife straight up for emphasis. "I think in the end you become one of them. And that isn't what I'm after. I like being an outsider. I like that distance— that sort of queasiness. So I figure, when I get home, I'll feel like an outsider there for a while."

"And then you'll go off into the field again so you can maintain your outsider status indefinitely?" Jonathan intended this as sarcasm, but Wooley received it as a reasonable suggestion.

"That's a thought," he said.

"You're right, though," Jonathan went on. "We will fit in again at home, eventually. Whatever this is, it'll wear off. But I don't think it works the other way. I think you're wrong. I'd never fit in here."

"Sure you could," said Wooley. "I do."

"Oh, come on." Jonathan leaned toward Wooley. "Do you really believe the people on Fugloy consider you one of them?"

"I'm their American. I'm an institutionalized deviant. I'm like a movie-star neighbor in Beverly Hills. This is a very loosely organized society, fluid roles, high tolerance for eccentricity—"

"I know, I know." Jonathan balked at being lectured on Faroese society. "What you're kidding yourself about is fitting in." He crossed his arms and waited for Wooley's response.

It was not at all what he expected. Wooley smiled at him—a more genuine, less stagey smile than most of his— and said, "You know, Jonathan, it's really about where you want to be. Where your heart is."

"Home is where the heart is?"

"Clichés are interesting," said Wooley. This also surprised Jonathan; it sounded like a remark he would make. "They get to be clichés because they're true."

"I think they just express the norms society is trying to enforce."

"Oh, give me a break. You don't believe that—it doesn't even mean anything."

Jonathan had to admit to himself that this was true: a point to Wooley for knowing it, another for saying it. To even up the score, he said, "I know. It's the sort of bullshit people spout at each other at Harvard."

"They do it everywhere. I mean, we all have to do it, right? Except we don't now. Vacation from bullshit."

"Sometimes," said Jonathan. "Sometimes it is."

Wooley leaned back in his chair. "Man, I feel so free here. Don't you?"

"I guess so." Jonathan thought of his happy days on the dock. "I used to."

"What happened?"

"I don't know," said Jonathan. But he had an idea: it was something to do with the blood. He tried to articulate it. "There's a barrier between us, a line I can't cross. I wouldn't be surprised by that if they were primitive—if we were in the jungle."

"You're not supposed to say that," Wooley joked.

"It's true, though. They're so much like us, the differences are more shocking." He went over to the window. The heat of the kitchen had begun to dissipate, and the

house without the hum and burble of the stove was too
quiet, as if it had stopped breathing. In front of his door
some sheep stood with their wet faces turned toward the
wind, enduring the weather. "For instance, all this blood,"
he ventured. He kept his back to Wooley.

"Oh, yeah, the *grind*."

"No, I haven't seen one yet."

"If you've got some thing about blood, you're not going
to be too happy at a *grindadráp*."

"It's not the blood itself, really. After Sigurd slaughtered the sheep here, in the kitchen—" Jonathan paused.
"I think they are truly innocent," he said, turning around,
"and I know I'm not."

"Innocent," Wooley repeated. He walked over to Jonathan's side and put a heavy, friendly arm around Jonathan's
shoulder. "You seem pretty innocent to me."

Jonathan shook his head. The simplicity of being
touched, the heat and weight of Wooley's arm, made him,
briefly, speechless. "I'm not," he mumbled, "I'm self-con-
scious."

Wooley laughed and leaned harder on Jonathan.
"That's for sure. But that doesn't make you corrupt—or
whatever the opposite of innocent is."

"The opposite of innocent is unhappy."

Wooley took his arm off Jonathan's shoulder. "I don't
get what's bothering you," he said. "Maybe I don't understand exactly what you mean by *innocent*."

Jonathan sighed; he felt creeping over him the alien-
ation that always followed requests to define his terms.
Classmates and teachers were forever asking him to do this,
as though he spoke a foreign language they didn't understand. And he knew from experience that "define your
terms" was a polite warning that he was talking drivel and
was about to get into an argument. He didn't want to get
into an argument with Wooley. They had a long, cold, dark

day to get through together—possibly several. The best thing was to lie low.

"Never mind," said Jonathan bravely.

"Do you mean unpremeditated or instinctive? Something like that?" Wooley had moved a few steps away from Jonathan and was looking at him. "Untrammeled, like?"

"It doesn't matter." Jonathan turned on the water to fill a pot for coffee, then remembered that the hot plate was out of commission. Buoyed by his surge of irritation, he said, "What I mean is that they just live, while all I do is think about living."

"Instinctive." Wooley nodded.

"It's not that simple," snapped Jonathan. Wooley looked expectant, but Jonathan didn't know what to say next. If he said nothing, they could avoid the argument; his mind emptied obligingly.

"Is that all you're going to say?" Wooley sat down at the table again. "Come on, Jonathan. What else have we got to do? Let's discuss Faroese character."

Jonathan had thought they were discussing *his* character. Confused, he joined Wooley at the table and cut himself a piece of Tilsit from the heap of food in front of them.

"Your idea is that they're noble savages, right?" Wooley had hold of the butter knife again and was sketching imaginary columns with it on the table. "And my idea is that they're modern men in particularly inhospitable circumstances." He looked up from his columns. "See, my theory is that if you took these people and put them in Baltimore or some provincial capital in France, they'd fit right in. They're gossipy, bourgeois, family-oriented—"

"Twenty minutes ago you were telling me how anarchic the society is." Jonathan was startled by how much he disliked Wooley at this moment. "And my idea is not that they're noble savages—that's your idea of my idea."

"Okay. What is your idea, then?"

Many responses flashed through Jonathan's mind, ranging from a mild *I'm not sure yet* to a wild *None of your business*. Put on the spot, he couldn't come up with anything meriting the label *idea*, yet he'd felt himself coming closer, this last month, to a way of seeing the Faroes: a pattern deeper than the web of social ties, which was complicated enough but was not the whole story. He'd had visions in which the islands and their surrounding waters were transparent, revealing every dart of life within (worms, ants, mussels clamped to rocks), and all this life was transparent too, so that he saw the heart of each bird, fish, sheep, and person beating in unison—as though together rock, water, fin, feather, and bone made one breathing organism, one body that constituted the Faroes. It was not a metaphor; Jonathan seeing this vision (it was infrequent but clear) knew he was seeing the truth—some kind of truth. But he was not about to say this to Wooley.

The most he was willing to say was, "I really don't think they are modern, not in any meaningful sense."

"Yes?" Wooley was waiting for more.

"Peasants. You don't consider peasants modern, do you?"

"There are no more peasants, Jonathan. There's nobody left in the world with a small, integrated universe. People know too much—except really isolated tribes."

"Is that the line out at Berkeley? No more peasants?"

"Hey, look," said Wooley, "I'm not trying to have a fight."

"Oh," said Jonathan.

"I'm just trying to find out what you're thinking."

"I'm thinking they're peasants, with just the sort of small, integrated universe you say people don't have anymore. They're positively medieval, is what I'm thinking. And I'm also thinking that you think my ideas are half-baked." Jonathan delivered this speech in a series of angry bursts that were satisfying to produce and left him feeling exposed and uncomfortable. He wished his words back— or at least his tone. Couldn't he have said the same thing with self-assurance or humor?

"Give yourself a break, Jonathan," said Wooley. "You're not the first person with a half-baked idea. Maybe it'll turn out to be a good idea, when you finish with it. And maybe it won't. It's not such a big deal. Don't be so hard on yourself. I mean, you know, we're all just assholes, trying to get by the best we can."

The We're All Assholes Theory: Jonathan had heard it before and he wasn't surprised to hear it now. He'd set himself up for it with his insecure little tirade. Along with "define your terms," this theory was an important weapon in the Cambridge intelligence war. Nobody who said *We're all assholes* included himself in the diagnosis. Jonathan knew the real message was *You are an asshole*. And that wasn't the only insult being offered; the deeper insult was to people's dreams.

This theory was directed at discrepancies between ambition and capacity, at those too blind to make reasonable assessments of their own abilities, at those who, despite failure, still hoped to succeed. Simple arrogance wouldn't trigger it; Jonathan had watched the brilliant be as arrogant as they pleased without anybody telling them they were assholes. And in a weird attempt at chumminess, the brilliant would sometimes spout this theory as if they were taken in by its masquerade of democracy, as if they didn't see into its vicious heart.

But Jonathan was not taken in; at least, he knew what was really being said. He'd certainly had enough opportunities to try his hand at translating it. His parents, his teachers, and many of his friends had told him that everybody was an asshole and that he shouldn't be so hard on himself. What made it insulting were the standards to which these same people held him and the assurances they'd given him that he was a brilliant lad bound for glory. Which was true? They couldn't both be true, Jonathan knew that much. Did he or did he not have a right to his ambitions?

According to Wooley, he did not. And the worst part about hearing this from Wooley was hearing the echoes of his own exhortations to himself two nights before, during his struggle to abandon the Other Jonathan—that being whose desires matched his endowments. Hadn't he told himself to regulate his hopes? Hadn't he told himself to forget about being the best and get used to being merely okay?

It is a universal truth that what we may say to ourselves we do not want to hear from others, and Jonathan wasn't surprised to feel his throat burning with anger at Wooley. He was again tempted to say a number of nasty things and again bit them back in the interests of peace—and maturity. It wasn't Wooley's fault that Jonathan was disappointed in himself; he couldn't even blame Wooley for the ancient crime of being the bearer of bad news, since he'd got the news already. Explaining this to himself did nothing for Jonathan's anger, which was now charring his stomach as well as his mouth.

Jonathan jumped up from the table and began pacing the room, trying to work off some of his agitation. Movement helped. With each circuit of the kitchen his thoughts grew clearer. Up to the window, which framed the ragged, stormy view: Was he going to be judged and judge himself by standards he questioned? Back to the stove, cold and quiet: He did question them, didn't he? Over to the hall door, where bursts of air whistled around the hinges: Maybe questioning wasn't enough; he'd been willing to ditch the Other Jonathan, who after all embodied hope, however awkwardly. Into the hall, where the cold stairway rose to the obscured second floor and appeared to go nowhere: Why not ditch the whole world he'd been brought up to see—

which was exactly that, the visible, evident, proof-is-in-the-pudding universe?

Jonathan stood in the hall, looking up the stairs into darkness. There was another world, he was sure of it. It couldn't be true that the unsuccessful weren't entitled to their dreams, that the mediocre life wasn't worth living. And it couldn't be true that people were known by their accomplishments or that the past was an accurate predictor of the future.

He thought of his parents' enlightened pessimism that had cast its shadow over him for as long as he could remember: the sober assessments of his third-grade paintings, the reasoned criticisms of his fourth-grade classmates, the guarded encouragement given his early passion for novels (guarded because where, exactly, would this lead?). They were convinced they saw the seeds of the end in every beginning.

Suddenly he understood what he meant by *innocence*— that is, he knew how to say it: no expectations of the future, no claim to know what it would be. Put more simply: belief in chance and transformation. And only a heart that had forsworn the whole idea of *knowing* on a grand scale could beat comfortably to that unpredictable rhythm.

Jonathan's head was light and clear, and he was breathing deeply, as if after a long winter he stood outside in sunshine. He went back into the kitchen. He was not an asshole, and he was going to tell that to Wooley.

He sat down at the table.

"Did you figure it out?" Wooley asked.

"Figure what out?"

"Whatever you went back there to figure out."

"Yes," said Jonathan. Then he completely surprised himself by saying, "We *are* all assholes."

"That's what I said," said Wooley, with his inevitable grin.

"I mean, I mean—" Jonathan was carried away by how everything seemed to have flipped around. "We are. People—we're just confused and worried about ourselves, aren't we?"

"Everybody I've ever met seemed to be. At least, basically they were, even if they looked okay. About something." Wooley leaned toward Jonathan. "Everybody's worried about something, you can bet on it."

"Why don't they admit it?" Jonathan was really puzzled by this.

"Why should they admit it? They figure everybody knows it already."

"I didn't know." Jonathan sighed.

"Well, if that isn't innocence, I don't know what is." Wooley punched him in the shoulder, a locker-room gesture.

Jonathan looked at Wooley. He didn't like being punched—the assumption of intimacy, the heartiness that passed as affection between men—and he didn't like Wooley any better than he had yesterday. But these dislikes didn't seem so important anymore. It was as though he'd been granted a present tense, in which people and events could come and go without setting off shock waves that reverberated into the past. This was an unforeseen balm. Jonathan had always figured that if relief from misery existed, it would take the form of insight into the deeper connections between Now and Then: that was how he imagined psychoanalysis worked. Instead, the conduit that had led inexorably back to all his failings and disappointments, so that each new episode was poured, so to speak, into an old mold, seemed to have closed. He didn't want Wooley for a friend: so what? He couldn't generate any more feeling about it than that.

"You'll have to come visit me on Fugloy," said Wooley.

"It doesn't look like you're ever going to get back to Fugloy."

"This storm will break tomorrow." Wooley ambled to

the front door and put his head out. "I bet you. I bet you a bottle of aquavit that I'm on the afternoon boat."

"Can you get aquavit?"

Wooley winked.

"I can't get any," Jonathan said. "I tried the day you came." He remembered Wooley's alleged flask. "You have some with you, don't you?"

Wooley winked again.

"Let's drink it." Wooley didn't answer. Jonathan took another tack. "Let's take it next door as a thank-you for dinner."

"I need it," said Wooley.

"That's what Sigurd said to me when I tried to buy some. What do you mean, need it?"

"I need it for the boat." Wooley came back to the table. "I hate boats," he said.

"You hate boats! How can you manage here?"

"That's why I need the aquavit." Wooley came back to the table. "How about that for a ridiculous problem?"

"Well," Jonathan made an effort to be sympathetic, "it's a difficult problem to have in the Faroes." Then he couldn't resist asking, "How did you get the aquavit?"

"I told a friend on Fugloy that I was scared of boats, and he got me a bottle."

Could life be so simple? Was announcing fear part of living in the muddled new world? Jonathan began to slip into a sad reverie, thinking of how he'd never trusted (or even believed) in people's goodwill, and was pleased to be interrupted by a commotion at the front door, which culminated in the entrance of Heðin, dripping, wind-whipped, and full of instructions.

"Get dressed. It's too cold in here. You have to come to my house. We'll play cards. Put the food back in the refrigerator. Tomorrow the power will be fixed. Turn the light switches off so that when it comes back you don't blow a fuse. Come on."

He was outside again before either of them had as much as stood up.

Many hours later, full of eggs (Jonathan) and *ræst* meat (Wooley), tea, and talk, heavy-headed from the hot, moist air of the Dahls' kitchen, and quite a number of kroner poorer from playing a whistlike card game whose rules Heðin had barely explained, assuring them that they'd "figure it out," they stood on the dark road watching the wind blow the white storm clouds south toward the Continent. Stars blinked in the sky above the harbor, and a Turkish crescent of a moon pointed its horns west.

"You were right," said Jonathan. "The storm's over."

Wooley kicked a stone back and forth. "Home to Fugloy," he said. He kicked the stone to Jonathan, who let it lie. "Maybe I'll stop in Klaksvík."

"For your girl?"

Wooley nodded. "How about yours?"

Jonathan shivered. "It's cold," he said, turning back to the house.

"Hey, Jonathan," Wooley said.

Jonathan turned around. But Wooley didn't say anything. "Yes?"

"Oh, I don't know. Thanks for the visit."

"You're welcome." Jonathan waited; Wooley seemed to have more to say.

"I know you're not going to come up to Fugloy, but if you're ever in Berkeley—"

"Sure," said Jonathan.

"We could drive up the coast—sort of looks like this. It's beautiful." Wooley stopped for a minute. "Well, it was a weird couple of days." He laughed dryly.

"Come on," Jonathan said, walking back to Wooley. "It's late." He regretted, suddenly, all the bad things he'd thought about Wooley. He touched Wooley's arm. "Maybe I will come see you in Berkeley."

"Shake?" Wooley put out his hand.

Jonathan shook hands with him, unsure exactly what deal he was confirming: something less specific than a visit to Berkeley, he guessed.

"So, I'll be on that morning boat." Wooley nudged Jonathan.

"I owe you a bottle of aquavit, then." Jonathan started back to the house a second time.

"Oh, don't worry about that." Wooley followed him into the kitchen, which was as dark and cold as the road. "What's a bottle of aquavit between friends?"

That was what the handshake signified: Wooley wanted to be friends. Could they be? Jonathan reconsidered his classification of Wooley as not-a-friend. Though the competitiveness that had skewed their relations had abated somewhat, Jonathan still found Wooley brash, slick, unfamiliar in an irritating way. Added to that was the burden of all the nasty comments Jonathan had made to him; he couldn't understand how Wooley had been able to disregard them. The blitheness that didn't register Jonathan's dislike was the fundamental reason they couldn't be friends.

But they didn't have to be enemies. Jonathan made a stab at a peace offering. "Maybe I'll bring you a bottle of Jack Daniel's a year from now in Berkeley," he said. "Who knows?"

"Right," said Wooley. He turned to go upstairs.

Resignation and anger were in his voice—Jonathan heard them clearly. Wooley knew his overture had been rejected. Jonathan flushed with shame in the darkness: maybe Wooley was aware of every little dig he'd endured these last three days. If that was true, Jonathan, not Wooley, was the blithe one, eager to take affability at face value, to construe tolerance as insensitivity. He thought of Wooley saying, I know you won't come to Fugloy, and cringed; Wooley knew plenty. It was only because he hadn't responded in kind that Jonathan assumed he was unaware.

"Jim," he said, taking a step toward Wooley.

"It's late," said Wooley, pausing at the door to the hall. "See you tomorrow."

Jonathan listened to Wooley walking up the stairs. He had a light tread for a big fellow. And how lightly he'd trod with Jonathan! He'd had countless opportunities to pay back scorn and intimidation in the same coin, and the worst he'd done was to be a bore.

Jonathan put his hands to his face and wished he were a better person. And it struck him that he could actually become one. Unlike a higher IQ, which he'd wished for thousands of times and which no amount of wishing could give him, tolerance and forbearance were available, if he wanted them enough. How much did he want them? Wasn't there in every fairy tale a moment when the genie said, Choose carefully, for your wishes will be granted?

The Herald

Three rings band this tipped earth, and the Faroes lie just below the first. Latitude and light are its coordinates: the northernmost reach of daylight in December, and in June the southernmost reach of the midnight sun. Perched on the rim of the Arctic Circle with a view into perpetual night, the islands at midwinter seem to be drifting north, loosed from their basalt moorings and drawn by every shard of iron buried in the hills toward the magnetic pole.

That minimal landscape—wave crests echoing the rise and fall of rocky earth—recedes to nothingness under the winter sky, whose vast and glittering territory is full of wonders. At these latitudes almost every star of the northern hemisphere is circumpolar, from Arcturus to Mintaka, the smallest piece of Orion's belt. Each night the entire zodiac wheels round the horizon: Aries gives way to Taurus, Taurus to Gemini, Gemini to Cancer—a year's worth of phases compressed into twenty-four hours.

And stars—such density, such numerosity rainbowed from translucent shadow-glow to heavy carmine, the pearl-spill of the Milky Way, implacable blue Polaris pointing north, though there is no farther north to go. These are the heavens as a child draws them: full-bodied planets, coronaed moon, the jet trails of meteors, and all the known constellations visible at once.

But a great silence and a great sorrow suffuse the night. The sky is a graveyard incalculably wide, dense with dead who never rest. Cold burnt-out husks still trace their sad trajectories above our heads, with endless movement but no vitality.

This clockwork universe has been for centuries a cause of wonder that tends to shift to gloom: too big to comprehend, immutable as nothing else in life, dazzling, distant, charted but unexplored, it is our only portion of eternity, and who can bear to contemplate eternity?

A boom and crackle woke Jonathan from a deep sleep one mid-December night. At first he thought he'd dreamed it. He got out of bed and opened the window. The night was clear black, cloudless, arched over the dark, sleeping village; the stars winked their unbreakable codes across the sky. He shut the window. A dream. But as he turned to get back

into bed, a movement flashed past his eye and the sound
came again.

It was an enormous thunder that encompassed the
night in a surround of rumbling, followed by a shredding
noise—as though a piece of fabric miles long were being
torn by giant hands. Above the village a patch of sky lightened briefly, pulsed yellow, then faded into dark.

Jonathan shivered, not only from cold. He felt queasy.
Once in Italy he'd sat in a café while the earth quivered
beneath his chair and his coffee cup rattled gently against
its saucer; a similar uneasiness had gripped him then. It
wasn't fear exactly, more a sense of inconsequentiality, the
nausea of having one's limits so brutally pointed out.

Another boom, and this time the shredding took place
within the booming. Jonathan got dressed and pulled a chair
up to the window. Ringside seat at the great light show: he
might as well be comfortable.

For the next ten minutes—which seemed a long time
in his queasy, sleepy state—nothing happened. He sat there
growing cold and disheartened, wondering if those three
booms had signaled the end rather than the beginning of
the performance. One pale glimmer: not an impressive display for a phenomenon whose very name had an aura of
magic.

Jonathan had never seen the northern lights. The over-
illuminated urban sky of Boston, the winter cloud cover of
New England, the warm air of Mount Desert in August—
all these had blocked his view or impeded their occurrence.
He wanted to see them, and his desire had been fed by the
fact that nobody who'd seen them could offer a good description. Not only that, the descriptions, lame as they
were, contradicted each other. From a skier in his high-
school class: *Real bright flat lightning;* from a skier in his
Harvard class: *Orange lines up and down, with white dots in
between;* from his father, who'd seen them from a troopship
heading to England during the war: *Flashes, like flares, red,*

all over the sky. Only his father had mentioned noise, and
the noise he'd heard had been more like cannon shot than
thunder. Each report concluded with the reporter shaking
his head and saying, *I can't describe them.*

So Jonathan perched on his chair, scanning the night
for flashes, orange lines, and flat lightning. The night continued to be starry, silent, and immobile. And the longer
he stared out, the flatter the sky seemed, until the stars were
mere dabs of bright on an endless bolt of black cloth
stretched taut, like a screen placed there to hide a living
mystery that danced behind.

Without warning the sky moved—*shrugged* was the
word that occurred to him, as though a person shook a
heavy garment off his shoulders. What had been flat now
buckled and rippled, and waves of noise cascaded across
these movements: an anunciatory drumroll. The hair on
his arms stood to attention. He put his head out the window; the air had a strange charge to it, a tang and siz-
zle that made him queasy again but also woke him thoroughly.

Then it began. The first vision brought him to his feet
with amazement. A huge pale green curtain appeared above
the village, billowing out and shimmering with yellow
threads. Then the curtain was pulled eastward, revealing
another, greener curtain beneath—and this went on an un-
countable number of times, faster and faster. Simultaneously, to the west, a lozenge of white light pulsed and
disappeared and at each reappearance grew larger and more
detailed, until it had taken the form of an outstretched palm
the color of a moon. The sounds accompanying all this
ranged from whistling to popping to outright banging—as
if the palm were smashing its way through a wall.

As suddenly as these sights had materialized they were
gone, but the atmosphere remained peculiarly energetic.
Jonathan was sure there was more to come. And as he sat
down again to wait for the next event, a milky band drifted

across the sky, a cloud of light that mimicked dawn and put out the stars.

The band widened as it moved, until it was a ghostly valance above the entire sky. Soundless winds fluttered it, creased and released its pleats, gathered it into thicker folds. The night vibrated with a hiss that Jonathan could feel but not hear; when he concentrated on the noise it vanished or seemed to translate itself into an airy trembling.

Then the whole sky moved again and burst into brightness. Molten ice-white light scattered and rebounded off inert roofs, stones, windowpanes. The world beneath this glare was rigid, as sometimes it will clench under a bolt of lightning, braced against so much energy. And in the air, what had been insubstantial took on volume and depth. The filmy pale fringe high aloft lengthened and shuddered into three dimensions. Seconds before it had been a transparency laid on the dense dark background. Now energy gathered what it had dispersed as light and collected it into a sky-wide swag of sculpted drapery as smooth as marble yet rushing like a river—and that became reality. The stars, the village, the bowl of ocean were shadows and wraiths.

Then this drapery parted, pulled from both east and west, and there were whiter, more luminous spills parting already beneath, sweeping back from a foaming white heart that roiled in the center.

Jonathan looking into this pale vortex felt himself looking into the heart of space—a white core that receded back and back and commanded his eyes to follow. And the longer he looked into that cauldron of light the more convinced he became that he was looking at something—the one thing in the universe, probably—that was freed from time.

How else explain its contradictions? How could it be both fixed and moving? How could it simultaneously span the sky and blast a hole in the sky's center? How drift dreamy white and cool across the world while boiling so fiercely that it devoured night?

It came to him first as a wisp of thought, as the aurora had first come, this notion that he was witnessing a dissolution of time. And then a jumble of ideas crowded his head, their clamor mirroring what he suddenly understood was going on above him.

This billowing, parting, drifting, closing, glowing, shining, deepening, and widening was not only out of sequence, it was out of the realm of sequence. This drapery was at every moment in all the conditions it could be, had been, or would be at all points in time—and time was no longer a chain of discrete states, one following another. It was a medium, like water or air, in which past, present, and future existed together.

And with a shock he realized he was as good as gone from here: from his seat by the window, from his sojourn in the Faroes, from his time on earth. For he would be leaving, that was certain. As even the northern lights were leaving; he saw them bleaching out under the stiff glitter of starlight. Were they disbanded, or had they just moved behind the shield of night?

He leaned out the window, straining his eyes to see around or past the stars and catch one more glimpse of incandescence. Nothing; the sky arched away into forever. But back of that night was light, he knew it; back of that silence, shards of bang and boom. And back of this life, this body—Jonathan shuddered. He was not prepared to go further.

Red Sky
at Morning

Solstice midnight, dawn still ten hours away, and the sea in cold unbroken swells left trails of rime along the shores of Sandoy, where everyone was sleeping. The twenty milch cows of Sandur snored in their stalls, Jens Símun's rooster settled deeper in his hay, sheepdogs on the thresholds of bedrooms in Húsavík curled their tails over their noses; even the island's hundred cats had left off late-night wandering to nestle underneath the stoves. And in their beds, dug into sleep like bears, the villagers dreamed of light as of another country, not knowing they had just crossed its border.

Out beyond the Faroe Bank, past Bailey's Bank and Lousy Bank, where the sea floor drops and the North Atlantic Drift draws the Gulf Stream up to warm the Faroes' feet, the whales were gathering. They shot their sweet call through the deeps until they were forty strong, then fanned out like geese behind their leader, headed north to feed. At the arctic waters of the Norwegian Sea they turned west; by the time they reached the ridge the Faroes ride, their school had doubled. And when they broke through the waves at the mouth of Húsavík Fjord, a hundred whales were spouting in the air.

"East off Húsavík." Sigurd was huffing. "A two-man boat saw them." He sat briefly in the chair opposite Jonathan and popped up again, circling the linoleum in his heavy boots. "An hour ago—they saw them an hour ago!" He was as near to frantic as Jonathan had ever seen anyone in these islands.

"You're sure you don't want coffee?" He lifted the pot a second time.

"There's no time for coffee." Sigurd snatched the pot from Jonathan's hands and clanked it in the sink. "Get your boots."

"Can I just finish this cup?"

"I'll get them." Sigurd ducked into the hall closet and clattered around.

"They're here," Jonathan called. "They're by the stove." Trying to enter into the spirit of the moment, he gulped his coffee and grabbed his boots. "I've got them," he reported to Sigurd, who was still tangled up in the closet. "They're on," he added. Getting no response, he stepped into the hall; no sign of Sigurd. He opened the front door in time to see Sigurd bounding up Petur's steps. He took the coffeepot out of the sink and poured himself another cup.

He hadn't drunk half of it before Sigurd blasted back into the kitchen with Heðin behind him.

"Hah," said Heðin. "No time for coffee. Let's go."

Jonathan stood up.

"Bring your slicker," said Heðin. And to Sigurd, "Have you got the knives?"

Sigurd nodded and made a last circle around the kitchen while Jonathan tugged the slicker over his heaviest sweater. "Are we ready?" Sigurd asked. Heðin, scuffing the floor like a horse pawing the dirt, watched Jonathan fumble with his snaps. "Leave it, leave it," he said. He flung the door open and led them out.

They piled into a rusted-out Dodge Dart that sat idling a few feet from Petur's door: Sigurd in the driver's seat, Jonathan squeezed in the middle, knocking into the gear-shift, Heðin holding on to the roof through the open window.

"Can you shut that window?" Jonathan asked. It was early still, about nine-thirty, and dark and cold.

"Can't," Sigurd said. "Door opens."

"What?"

"I've got to hold the door shut like this," said Heðin.

Jonathan sighed and finished snapping his slicker.

They were heading out the eastern road that crossed the mountain separating Skopun and Húsavík. As they neared the crest of the hill, the car slowed to a heaving, whining pace. Up at this height, the land was barren; it lay in gray, frost-edged slabs around them, drained of even the brown that tinged the turf around the village. And then they drove into a cloud, so dense Sigurd turned on the wipers. Heðin began to sing, "*Noregis menn, dansið væl.*"

Norsemen, dance well, Jonathan translated to himself, then asked, "What's that song?"

"*Sigmund's Kvæði*. We sing it after the *grind*."

"Don't sing it yet," said Sigurd. "Ah, look." He stopped the car.

They had cleared the cloud and reached the top, and below stretched the long finger of Húsavík Fjord. Staining the sky all around the horizon, the sun rose tomato red out of the ocean. All three men smiled. It was the time of year when the mountain obscured the sun till nearly noon in Skopun, and for weeks they had seen only an exhausted star already on the wane.

"Good, a red sun," said Sigurd.

"Why is that good?" Jonathan asked.

"Much blood," said Sigurd.

Jonathan gulped. He had so far put out of his mind what was awaiting them in Húsavík. He decided to change the topic. "We have a saying in America: Red sky at night, sailor's delight, red sky at morning, sailors take warning."

"We have it too," said Heðin. "It's about fish, though, not whales."

"Fish? I thought it was about weather."

"Fish, weather, what's the difference?" Sigurd snapped the car on again, popped into neutral, and began coasting down the hairpin turns.

Sigurd was a remarkably bad driver, jamming the brakes on in the middle of curves, grabbing at the wheel and wrenching the car dangerously close to the boulders and cliffs that edged the road. He seemed, though, to be having fun, smiling and drumming his hand on the dashboard in time with Heðin, who was still humming the dirge-like tune of the *kvæði*. Jonathan was cold, getting hungry, and nagged by a sense of having forgotten something important. As they reached the outskirts of Húsavík, he realized what it was: his notebook.

"Oh, Jesus Christ," he said.

"Yah, we're going to have a good Christmas this year," Sigurd said. "A Christmas *grind*—that's very nice. Whale and *spik* on Christmas eve."

"I forgot my notebook," Jonathan couldn't believe he'd done this.

"There's no time to write at a *grind*," said Heðin.

"You write too much anyhow," Sigurd put in. "You're always walking around writing. You could make the Encyclopedia Britannica of the Faroes by now."

Jonathan wondered where Sigurd came up with all his literary references: Swift, encyclopedias; soon he'd be quoting Milton. He looked at his boots and shook his head. Without the notebook, he felt unprotected. Without the notebook, he would have to participate in what was probably going to be mayhem. And now, worrying him further, Heðin opened the glove compartment and drew out three knives with blades about eight inches long and yellowed bone handles.

"Here," he said, handing one to Jonathan, who took the knife and held it, blade up, between his knees.

"Hold it down, it's sharp," Heðin said.

"I know," said Jonathan. "I know knives are sharp."

Heðin leaned over, lifted a lock of Jonathan's hair, and sliced through it without a sound. He held the clippings in front of Jonathan's nose. "Really sharp," he said. Then he laughed.

Jonathan did not laugh. Heðin slapped him on the knee. "*Mokka*, you know what that means?"

"To cut with a knife," Jonathan answered.

Sigurd laughed. "We do that later, after we sing," he said, leaning toward Jonathan.

"Do what?" Jonathan didn't like being leaned on by these people who, at the moment, seemed like strangers, rather coarse strangers.

Heðin slid his right index finger back and forth across his left palm: "*Mokka*," he explained, and winked.

"Oh." Jonathan braced himself for a comment about Daniela, and sure enough, Heðin said, "Your girl in Tórshavn, we'll call her from the post office. She could be here for tonight."

"No," said Sigurd. "He'll get a new girl. A Húsavík girl."

"Two girls," said Heðin, "one for Sandoy, one for Streymoy. That way, you don't have to wait for the fucking boat."

"Very practical," said Jonathan. He'd intended this to end the conversation, but it only set them both laughing.

"You like them fat?" asked Sigurd. Without waiting for an answer, he said, "I like a fat one. Like a nice little puffin. Keeps you warm."

"Nah." Heðin waved away the fat girls. "I don't like them fat."

Jonathan did not like the discussion. Talking about girls with Heðin was one thing; talking about girls with Sigurd was something else. Jonathan was young enough to find a middle-aged man's lust embarrassing. And thinking about Daniela, even in private, was embarrassing. A number of times since Wooley's visit he'd caught himself shaking his head and blushing as he cooked dinner or walked around town—discomfited by the awkwardness of the Daniela episode, which had been in some way compounded and amplified by Wooley. He'd missed the mark with both of them, and had watched his love darts and his barbs fall equally unheeded on the ground. Jonathan these days felt constantly cut down to size, and the size he was trimmed to seemed too small. But every time he tried to stretch out a bit, the thought of Daniela or Wooley nipped him, pinched him back. As for his resolve to be a better person, buying potatoes from Sigurd or fish from toothless Gregor on the dock didn't offer much scope for experiments with a new personality.

But today, the whale hunt, where there would be new people and new events—startling events, he was sure— offered scope: more scope than he wanted, in fact. Jonathan sensed himself shrinking from opportunity, not being a better person. What would it be, that betterness? He looked at the black-streaked, whorled handle of his knife: courage, at any rate. Maybe Sigurd was right; maybe it was good he hadn't brought his notebook. He couldn't play the innocent bystander anymore.

Sigurd pulled over to the side of the road and parked with one front wheel on some rocks, making it difficult to get out of the car, which swayed and teetered as first Heðin, then Jonathan, jumped to the ground. Heðin put his knife under his belt and handed a knife to Sigurd, who did the same. They looked to Jonathan like mild-mannered pirates, the fierceness of their weapons belied by their muddy rubber boots and homemade sweaters. Jonathan smiled, anticipating, suddenly, an adventure.

But now Heðin and Sigurd were serious and didn't smile back. Sigurd was digging around in the trunk of the car and Heðin was rolling a cigarette, staring out to sea. He squinted, then pointed. *"Grindahvalur,"* he said. "That's him."

Jonathan looked, squinted, didn't see anything. "Where?"

"Out east." Heðin pointed again. "See the boats?"

Jonathan did, barely, see some dots that might have been boats at the mouth of the fjord. He nodded.

"See off east of them, something cuts through the water?"

Although Jonathan did not see this, he nodded again. "That's him."

"Who?"

"The leader." Heðin lighted his cigarette.

"And now they kill the leader?" Wasn't that what the Danish guidebook had said?

"No. Why would they do that?" Heðin scowled. "They drive him in."

"Oh. Into the fjord?" Heðin nodded. "And how do they do that?"

"Throw rocks."

"Like herding sheep." Jonathan laughed.

Heðin scowled again. "This is not a game, Jonathan," he said.

"Hah," said Sigurd, from within the trunk. "I knew I had it." He pulled out a long, thick, greasy rope, which he wound around his waist. "Let's go."

The walk to the harbor was conducted in total silence. Just as well, Jonathan decided. He urged himself into a different frame of mind. He would be alert, awake, collecting every shred of information about this sacred Faroese ritual, this Corn Dance of the north or whatever it was. He put his knife under his belt and strode down the road in step with Sigurd and Heðin, armed, ready for anything.

A vigilant calm hung over the harbor when they arrived. Jonathan had expected bustle. Instead, the few people who were about had the look of an audience waiting for the curtain to rise. Ten or a dozen children perched on the end of the jetty looking silently out to sea. Down on the barren gray shingle, a line of men stood knee-deep in the yellow foam. The dock was empty of boats and looked naked and sad, its walls lined with peeling tires and barnacles waiting for high tide.

"There aren't many people here," he said to Heðin.

Heðin lifted his chin slightly toward the horizon. "Out on boats," he growled.

Turning to Sigurd, Jonathan asked, "What's that rope for?"

"Pulling," said Sigurd.

Maybe the point they were trying to make was that he shouldn't ask questions. Well, then, Jonathan resolved, he would not. He would watch what they did and do it too, without calling attention to himself. He would be one of them, and they would be impressed; or perhaps he would succeed so well that they would forget he was an idiot foreigner. And then he could forget it too.

For the moment, though, all Heðin and Sigurd were doing was standing at the top of the jetty with their hands in their pockets, something they did every day in Skopun and which Jonathan had long ago mastered.

"Where's Petur?" Jonathan asked, and cursed himself: a question! Hadn't he just determined not to ask questions? But this seemed to be an acceptable one. Sigurd and Heðin moved their heads right and left, conferring.

Sigurd pointed out into the fjord. "See how there are two lines of boats there?" Jonathan saw only waves and dots; squinting, concentrating, he convinced himself he saw two lines of boats and nodded. "Petur is in the northern line"—the northern line must be the one to the left, Jonathan figured—"and he's the second boat."

"Ah. I see." Could he pull this off? Jonathan could no more pick out Petur's boat in the water than he could see the dark side of the moon: not an auspicious first move in his game of Be the Native. He heard Heðin's words again, *This is not a game.* A warning of some sort? A raw wind gusted off the ocean and gave him a chill. And then suddenly his vision resolved the blurs into boats, two long processions of boats that like pincers grasped between them a frothing mass of water sliced and scored by the fins of whales.

The line of men on the beach shifted, stretched out to cover more territory, and a murmur rose up from it. Then, as if this sound had triggered them, other sounds began: the kids on the jetty scuffled their feet against the cement, a few elders who'd joined Heðin, Sigurd, and Jonathan

coughed and whispered, Heðin and Sigurd bent their heads
together for another mumbled conference. And swelling up
behind these sounds, overtaking them within minutes, was
a roaring compounded of the screams of gulls, the yells of
men, the slapping of water on wooden hulls, and a high
thin keening that seemed to be the voice of the ocean itself.
The collective agitation that was the *grind* was moving closer
to land, bringing its halo of sound with it. It was a living
vortex, whirling and rushing to swallow everything within
reach and to fix all eyes on its splendid voracity.

The sky above the water had gone flat white and was
glazed with sea fog. Twenty degrees up from the horizon,
the pale sun overlooked the fjord and its activities, casting
toward land the huge shadows of men and birds, so that
they moved in a mottled darkness.

They were close enough for Jonathan to distinguish
words and faces: Petur yelling "Faster, faster!," Jens Símun
flailing the sea with a length of wood, Jón Hendrik perched
at the bow of a six-man boat, teetering as they rode the
swells but directing the crew and their oars with his thin
arms. And over, under, through all of this, the keening ran
like a silver thread, pure and ceaseless. One whale heaved
up in a great black arc, and Jonathan saw his dark eye
rolling, his dark mouth gaping. Water flashed off his flanks
as he crested, soaring on the wing of his fin. And at that
perfect moment, when in his black entirety he floated in
the air, Petur speared him, and the ocean bloomed in blood.

Jonathan gasped. The men on the beach and on the
dock drew in a breath as well, and for a few moments
everyone stood in silence watching the red streamers spread.
Petur was poised at the side of his boat, dark-tipped spear
in hand. Then the wounded whale crested again, and the
glare of the gash in his side, so bright against his skin, broke
whatever spell had stilled them all.

One of the men on shore waded out to sea holding an
iron prong and hooked the whale on his second try. At this,

Heðin and Sigurd rushed down to the beach, bumping Jonathan along with them. The rope attached to the prong was already thick with hands, but they took the last three feet of it and joined the pulling. Jonathan stood staring. On the fjord, dozens of spears were being stabbed into the sea, jets of blood combining with the watery exhalations of the animals.

"You can't stand there!" Sigurd yelled at him. "Get on the rope!" He was red in the face and looked furious. Jonathan took a few steps toward the crowd and faltered. Sigurd dropped his portion of rope and went to Jonathan's side.

"It's illegal just to watch." He stood with his hands on his hips. "You must either help or get out of the way."

A second whale had been hooked, and half the men were heaving on a new rope. This whale was bigger than the first and fought more. His tail smacked the water, jolting the boats around him and shooting up curtains of spray. He cried, too, with a powerful high voice that cut through the din of waves and yells.

Jonathan looked at Sigurd, who was silhouetted against the dark, churning sea and whose face, though shadowed, shone with an intensity Jonathan hadn't seen there before. The lines around his mouth—the remnants of thirty-odd years of a shopkeeper's smiles and frowns—had been transformed to sharp slashes in his flesh, so that his face seemed like a mask of itself. His eyes were open wide, showing white all around the blue, and they fixed Jonathan with a stare he could not duck. Then something shifted, and this new Sigurd relaxed enough to resemble the old, affectionate Sigurd; he put his hand on Jonathan's shoulder. "This is why you came here, isn't it?" he said. "So, come now."

Heðin didn't even grunt a greeting as Jonathan took a place beside him on the rope. They were still hauling in the first whale, and though he was weak from the spearing and didn't resist, he was heavy: the heaviest thing Jonathan had ever tried to move. Eight men pulling had brought him only twenty feet in from where he'd been hit. A spurt came out of his blowhole now and then, but otherwise he seemed to be playing dead, lolling in the water as if trying by his very density to thwart their efforts.

"Ooof." Heðin sighed. To Sigurd he said, "Maybe we should leave him until later."

Sigurd shook his head. "I think we can get him on the beach easier than the other one."

Jonathan glanced over at the second rope. The men on it were having a hard time just holding their ground while the whale bucked and thrashed at the other end.

Sigurd leaned to Jonathan. "Once we get one on the beach, you see, the others follow."

Jonathan's view of the ocean was blocked by Heðin's back. His hands were chilled and sore from the rope, and the sound of rubber boots grinding in cold, wet sand grated on his ears. The whole business of killing whales, which from the sidelines had seemed vicious and awful, was now nothing more than the usual hard work. Running after sheep, baiting barbed lines for fishing, unloading dank holds reeking of cod: everyday life in the Faroes was composed of hundreds of unpleasant tasks, and this was no different. Putting his back behind another big pull, Jonathan figured there was a benefit to this realization. If whale killing was just work, he could do it.

The resistance at the end of the rope changed its character all of a sudden, and a new noise, of scraping and dragging, began. Peering around Heðin's shoulder, Jonathan saw the first few feet of whale emerging from the spume onto the sand. Then they were all pulling again, stumbling backward up the beach. At a yell from the men in front, Heðin and Sigurd dropped the rope, leaving only Jonathan grasping its oily, thick coils. He let it go and ran down to the shore behind the others.

Twice as long as a man, panting in huge heaves, and

with his gashed side rubbed raw from the dragging, the whale lay surrounded by people. In his distress he lifted his head up from the beach and moved it from side to side. His tapered, forked tail sketched a delicate tracery of pain in the sand. He was no longer making his thin cry, only pushing out ragged puffs. Jonathan was close enough to see his blowhole open and then contract. With a shock he understood that this was breathing—the whale breathed air just as men do. This was not a fish struggling for water, a haddock writhing on a deck to provoke in Jonathan an almost shameful pity, but a breathing, bleeding creature, trapped, terrified, more kin to him in its complexity than any lamb or ewe. Jonathan reached out his hand and placed it on the whale's back, which was cool but radiated warmth and quivered under his palm. What comfort could he offer? He drew his hand away, defeated.

People were moving back from the whale's head, parting to make room for a barrel-chested old man Jonathan had noticed standing up on the jetty before the whale was speared. "That's Klæmint, the sheriff," Sigurd whispered. "Now, watch."

Klæmint stood with a leg on either side of the whale, pressing his calves against the head, and drew from his belt a knife even longer and more wicked looking than the ones Sigurd had supplied. Then he bent down, clamping the animal between his knees, pressed his left hand just below the blowhole, and with one quick stroke sliced the neck open. Black popped back to reveal the dense, pale inches of blubber, and then blood welled up. Klæmint made another swipe across the neck; this time the bone cracked. The whale's tail fluttered once. Blood seeped into his still-open eye, which didn't blink.

Jonathan passed a hand over his face and felt his fingers cold against his cheeks.

"That's how you do it," Sigurd said. "You cut the spinal cord. Quick, you see, so they don't suffer."

Blood dripped down the whale's head. The gash in his side had begun to clot before he died; half-coagulated lumps lay dark against the red. The obsidian gleam of his skin was fading already and marred by sand and small wounds. Jonathan could bear neither to look at all this nor to look away, so he kept turning his head aside and then finding himself staring, darting from the lacerated body to the rigid, reddened eye.

Then Klæmint made a cut in the whale's belly, and in a cloud of steam the guts slid onto the sand.

Jonathan looked out to sea, where dozens of whales milled and circled in rose-tinted water. The boats were closing in, oars thudding on fins and tails as the chase funneled toward the beach. Was he going to have to watch a hundred dark eyes blinded, a hundred smooth dark cheeks laid to rest on beds of sand? He put his hand on Sigurd's arm. "I don't know if I can do this," he said, and braced himself for Sigurd's scorn or insistence. Heðin, who'd overheard, turned away. But Sigurd drew Jonathan a few feet back from the crowd, where they could speak in private.

"We will eat all winter from this, do you understand?" He gave Jonathan a hard look, then continued, more gently, "We kill fish and birds and sheep. It's no different."

"They're so big," Jonathan said.

Sigurd nodded. "And they're smart, too. They can get away from us, you know, out on the water. And often they do. But when they don't—" He fell silent. "They come to us," he said abruptly. "They come up to us. Look."

All along the curve of the shore whales were hurling themselves out of the ocean and onto the land. The big one, who'd fought hard against the rope, had been hauled in finally and lay heaving near the first, dead one. The pod seemed to be trying to surround him, this fighter, to make a living shield about him. Those who could not get close to him beached themselves anyhow, a huge black infantry following their general into enemy territory. Waves and

waves of whales broke over each other, until they lined the
beach two and three deep. Some lay in the foam letting the
tide shift their long, slim bodies back and forth, as if hesitant
to say goodbye to their element. All of them were calling
their strange thin sound that had no character but was just
a tone and that seemed too delicate for such large beasts.

"But they're not coming up so that you can kill them,"
Jonathan said. It was obvious to him that the whales were
rallying around their leader.

Sigurd grunted. "Yah, but we do. They won't go back,
you see."

"What do you mean?"

"Once they're up they won't go back. I knew a man
once who tried to get one to go back. It came up alone,
after a big *grind* had come a few days before. He felt sorry
for it, like you do, and he roped it to his boat and towed
it out. It came right back." He shrugged. "So. We kill
them." He looked at Jonathan again. "You'll kill one. You'll
feel better then."

"I don't think it's that simple," said Jonathan. "And
after all, this is your business, not mine."

"You don't need to eat?" Sigurd shook his head. "It's
not like the sheep, you know. Other people divide it. It's
just one cut, maybe two."

"You said you hated killing the sheep." Jonathan was
pleased to have remembered this.

Sigurd shifted from foot to foot and cleared his throat.
"You don't hunt sheep." He looked down the beach at the
ranks of whales. "Hunting is good." His expression and
stance changed as he said this, streamlined to the intensity
of the Sigurd who'd yelled at Jonathan earlier.

The discussion was over, Jonathan could see that. He
could see also that Sigurd was itching to get to work on the
whales, that his continued presence was a mark of his affection; even in his hunter incarnation, Sigurd had time for
Jonathan and his worries. Had made time, rather, for now

he took a few steps toward the shore, where the slaughter was beginning. Then he turned back, put a thick arm around Jonathan's waist, and pulled him bodily down the beach.

Sigurd was stronger than he looked, and surprise weakened Jonathan's resistance. Within minutes they were wading among the flailing bodies. Jonathan felt his heart pounding in time with the crash of the surf and the blood singing in his ears with the calls of the whales. Whales, men, children were everywhere, all spattered with sea-foam flecks. They had to walk farther into the sea to avoid getting hit by thrashing tails. Then Sigurd pushed him up, to where the press wasn't so thick and the animals lay unattended in a single line.

"Here," Sigurd said, straddling a medium-sized whale who had beached somewhat apart from the others, "this is a good one. Come here." Jonathan approached, slowly but without stopping, as if a rope drew him. Sigurd moved off the whale and waited for Jonathan to take his place.

This whale was silent and still, and Jonathan managed to fit himself around it. Again that sensation of heat seeping through the chill surface; his blue jeans were wet from the whale's wet skin, but his legs were warmed by contact with the huge, warm body. "Clamp him," Sigurd said, and Jonathan pressed his knees against the dense flanks. At this the whale began to wriggle and twist. The power was unlike anything Jonathan had ever felt, much stronger than a horse and more impersonal. A horse knows a man, bucks a man off because it refuses to be ridden; this animal had never known subjugation or fear. And Jonathan was to show him both? He loosed his legs somewhat. He began to slide backward toward the tail, which was thumping on the sand.

"Don't let go!" Sigurd yelled. "Watch out!"

Jonathan put his hands on the whale's forehead to steady himself.

"You have to do it now." Sigurd had drawn his knife and was brandishing it at Jonathan. "He'll hurt you with his tail. Get your knife out." But as soon as Jonathan lifted his hands to his belt, he started sliding again. "Stop," said Sigurd. "Use mine." He extended it to Jonathan.

Jonathan clasped the knife: a cold handshake with bone and steel. Between his legs, the whale's muscles rippled and tensed; he had to put his knife hand back on the whale's head for balance, and in doing this he nicked an opening in the neck: the glimmer of pearly blubber, and then, slowly, beads of blood seeping up through the tear in the black sheath of skin. Jonathan gulped. A hopeless shock, as if he'd shattered a precious object, gripped him at this inadvertent wounding.

"You have to do it now," Sigurd repeated.

"I don't know how," Jonathan said.

"You saw it." Sigurd was firm. "Put your hand below the blowhole and make a long cut across the spine. And do it hard. You want to do it quickly, no more than two cuts."

Jonathan looked at Sigurd, implacable in his boots and his Viking stance, legs apart on the wet sand. Then he looked down at the whale's neck, as big as two men's torsos, as black and glittering as December midnight, and raised his arm.

How easy it was! How smoothly the knife bit through the skin and into the creamy blubber. It sailed across the neck, trailing its wake of blood, and at the slightest pressure from Jonathan plumbed deeper into the whale, so that the ping of metal on bone rang in the air. Jonathan felt the body beneath him jolt and subside, almost deflate. He pulled the knife out and then, drawn by that red arc he'd engraved in the skin, plunged the blade back in for the second cut.

"No!" Sigurd took a step toward him. "No more. He's dead."

But Jonathan could not stop himself from finishing

what he'd begun, and when he stepped down onto the sand, what lay dead at his feet was far larger and weightier than a whale.

He held his bloody hand out to Sigurd. "Here's your knife."

"I think you should keep it." Sigurd looked Jonathan over and nodded. "Yes. You keep that knife. But give me yours."

Jonathan shifted Sigurd's knife from one sticky hand to the other and wiped his palm against his thigh before pulling the clean knife from his belt, but the blood was hard to get off and the hilt he offered Sigurd was tacky. Sigurd dipped it in the ocean and dried it carefully on his sweater. Jonathan did the same with his knife, then kneeled to clean his hands. He had to rub sand between his fingers to loosen the caked blood. The tide was rising, slowly swamping his boots and lapping at the dead tail, swaying it back and forth.

"Do you want to open the stomach?" Sigurd asked. Before Jonathan could answer, he said, "I'll do it."

Jonathan stood up. "I can," he said. He leaned over the whale and drove the knife in below the front fins, as he'd seen Klæmint do. No bones resisted him when he dragged the knife down. A strange smell came out of the cut, the freshness of an opened oyster combined with the dark, intimate air of a body's interior. The entrails slithered out—white loops of intestine, the flopping red liver. Jonathan stepped back.

"Done," said Sigurd. "Not so bad, eh?"

Jonathan looked down at his hands, which were bloody again, and then along the shore, which was studded with still-living whales. "What about those?" he asked.

Sigurd laughed. "You want to kill all of them?" He started walking back toward the center of activity, where most of the pod had beached. Jonathan followed. They walked higher up the sand this time, out of tail range.

"These are safe," Sigurd explained. "They won't get

away. It's more important to kill the ones that are still in
the water."

"You said they wouldn't leave."

"They might drift out on the tide."

Jonathan nodded. "So you do kill these too?" He
pointed at the stranded whales they were passing.

"Later," said Sigurd.

The sun had passed its zenith and was rolling slowly
down the slope of the sky, enlarging as it declined. It seemed
not to radiate light but rather to reflect it, as if it had become
the moon; Jonathan found he could look straight at it. And
everything he saw had taken on the color and texture of
mercury. Opaque, dense silver waves slapped the jetty's
gray concrete pilings and divided, foamless, contained in
silver skin. The dead whales were fading to pewter. The
black skins of those that were still alive glimmered with
reflections of the leaden sky. The men who moved among
the animals and splashed in the tide were silvered with
sweat—but at the same time they were matte and muted,
gray shades flickering on a gray background.

A shadow world, a gray otherworld—these were the
huldufólk, the gray people who lived in the rocks and demanded their due from the sea and the sheep. They *were*
the villagers, he saw it now, they were all the violent, terrible impulses that village life could not contain, banished
to the outfield to wait for this moment, when they were
needed. Looking at the havoc they were wreaking with their
silent gray movements, Jonathan could understand why
Heðin, months ago on a rock at the edge of their territory,
had cautioned him to treat them with respect. He glanced
at Sigurd to see if he too was a silver shade, but Sigurd
was not even the Viking; he was plodding down the strand
leaving huge footprints that filled with seawater immediately, and he looked tired.

Jonathan picked out Petur and Jens Símun from the
crowd of men straddling bodies and wielding knives. The

whales were so thick here that finding a foothold on sand
was difficult; some kids were hopping from one felled back
to another, the way kids in America hopped along logs.
The smaller boats had been dragged up onto the beach as
well and lay like pale, short versions of whales among them.
Petur and Jens Símun were wrestling with a very big whale,
at least fifteen feet long. Petur was sitting at his neck and
Jens Símun down closer to his tail, but the weight of two
men was not enough to still his thrashing.

"Eh," Petur grunted in their direction. He beckoned
them over. "Sit on him," he said.

Sigurd plopped himself down just above the dorsal fin.
Then all three of them looked expectantly at Jonathan.

"Hurry up," said Jens Símun.

The resistance, then the pop of punctured flesh, the
scarlet gash, the crack of the vertebrae: it was all the same,
all known and simple. Looking around him, Jonathan saw
in the dozens of animals strewn on the sand potential moments like this: each living creature held the moment of its
death within it, and one simple movement could bring that
moment out into being. The distance between life and death
was short—as short as the length of his own arm. Jonathan
shut his eyes and imagined that every slaughtered body
here about him was a man's, not a whale's. He could imagine
it easily. Whiter corpses, but the same bloody sheen on the
sand and the same quickening in the air, the rush of the
wind of life passing overhead. And could he kill a man?
Jonathan didn't know; he hoped not. But his feet and fingers, stained, muddy, and throbbing, and his chest that
clattered from his busy heart, told him something unde-
niable: killing makes the killer feel alive.

Admitting this changed the look of things again. Substantiality returned to objects and people, and the peculiar
metallic shroud lifted off the sea and sky—making him
doubt his notion that he'd seen the *huldufólk* in action. After
all, he was the one who constantly banished feelings and

maintained an internal shadow government of the emotions.

Jonathan bent down to the water to rinse his knife. Behind him, the three men were sliding off the whale, opening its abdomen, chatting together. As he rubbed sand over the hilt, he consigned to the sea his doubt, his second-guessing, his analyses. He imagined them wrapped in a bundle and bobbing on the waves. Oddly enough, this trick seemed to work. His unpleasant cargo was anchored out there, mute for the moment.

Thus lightened, Jonathan strode through the short, bloody afternoon beside his fellow villagers. They trod spilled innards into the sand as they moved up and down the shore, here helping to pull a whale beyond the high-tide line, there adding their weight to a bucking back. The day was fading, and all the men of Húsavík—even young boys—were working fast to finish before dark. The animals had to be gutted and tugged out of the sea's reach, and then counted and apportioned between the two villages. Some still had to be killed. Jonathan had a bad minute when they came on a calf, about the size of a human being, that was sighing and whimpering beside its dead mother; it had a cow-brown eye, which it blinked rapidly at their approach. Jens Símun killed it.

The dark came down at about three, compressing the daylight to a pale pink streak around the horizon and a few rosy streamers shooting into the sky. In the quarter hour of tinted gloom that was all the Faroes got of twilight in winter, the ocean was purple, the sand black. Men now were as dark as whales and almost as big, looming out of the murk. Wind came up and whipped a lavender foam on the sea, and the waves that with each retreat washed the beach clean of blood broke red again at each advance of the tide.

It was over. Up and down the beach red dots of cig-arettes signaled the end of work. People began leaving, tramping uphill through thick cold sand. Heðin appeared out of the darkness to offer Jonathan a welcome cigarette. Their little Skopun group seemed a bit forlorn, still standing in the breakers while others were on their way home to warmth and food.

"So, so, so," said Petur.

"I reckon so," said Heðin. He sat down on a convenient whale. "Yah, I reckon so." He looked up at Jonathan. "How did you like it?"

"I liked it," Jonathan heard himself say.

"Yes," Jens Símun put in, "killing whales is a good sport."

Sigurd shuffled his feet in the clumpy, clotted sand. Heðin tossed his cigarette end into the sea and said, "It's not only for sport—"

"Let's go," Petur interrupted.

Jens Símun scowled at Heðin, who refused to look at him. Petur put his heavy gentle hand on Jens Símun's shoulder. "Let's go," he repeated. "We'll go find Grandpapa."

Jonathan contrived to fall behind and walk with sulky Heðin, hoping for an explanation of that interchange. Heðin was chewing on a matchstick and noisily spitting out splinters.

"What was that, about sport? What did you mean?"

Heðin ejected the matchstick onto the sand. "My uncle is a brute," he said. Five paces ahead, Jens Símun plodded along unheeding, though Heðin hadn't taken the trouble to whisper. But Petur stopped and waited for Heðin and Jonathan to come abreast.

"I know, I know," said Heðin to his father.

Petur just grunted. After a minute he caught Jonathan's eye; he pointed at Jens Símun's back, then at his own head, and moved his hand from side to side, seeming to indicate that not everything in Jens Símun's head was as it should be. This made Heðin mad.

"There's nothing wrong with him," he growled.

Petur shrugged his shoulders and speeded up to his brothers, the brute and the merchant.

Heðin stopped walking and began to roll another cigarette. He lifted one thick, blood-blackened finger and beckoned Jonathan closer. "He's stupid, that's all, and he's mean. You watch tonight, at the dancing. He gets mean when he's drunk. Then we have to take him home. You'll see." He jammed the cigarette into his mouth, then removed it to say, "Sometimes I wish I could leave this goddamned place."

Jonathan was amazed. He thought of Heðin as the perfect inhabitant of the Faroes: young, strong, well versed in the arcana of sheep driving, whale killing, womanizing, fishing—not only how to do these things, but how to do them in the proper Faroese way. "Where would you go?" he asked.

"Yah," said Heðin, lighting his cigarette. "Exactly."

They were on the dark village streets now, and the men ahead were peering in windows looking, Jonathan supposed, for Jón Hendrik. He felt tired, cold, hungry, and dirty. "I'd like to take a bath," he said. Heðin laughed.

"You can forget that," he said.

Sigurd beckoned to them from a lighted doorway. Jonathan and Heðin added their boots to a great black heap in the hallway and stepped into the kitchen, where Jón Hendrik presided over a bottle at the table, flanked by Petur and Jens Símun. A blonde girl with a short nose and dimpled arms stood at the stove pouring hot water into a teapot.

Heðin approached her with his hand out. "Heðin," he told her.

"That's Kristina, that's Klæmint's granddaughter," Jón Hendrik said. "She keeps house for him. She's living here all alone with her grandfather." He tittered.

"Okay, okay," said Heðin, but he gave his crazy-tooth grin to Kristina, who turned quickly back to her kettle without shaking hands.

Jonathan didn't want to be left out. He moved toward the stove too, hoping Heðin would introduce him. Heðin was staring at Kristina's back as she fussed over the tea; every now and then she'd glance over her shoulder at him, and when she did, he'd show his strange teeth for a moment. Jonathan cleared his throat.

"I'm Jonathan," he said.

"Jo-Na-Than," chanted Sigurd, who'd settled himself in at the bottle. "Have some brandy."

Jonathan waited another few seconds for a response from Kristina, then retreated to the table.

Each man had a tumbler of brandy—filled, as if the contents were orange juice, not liquor. Jón Hendrik was grinning and squinting, so probably he'd got a head start on the others. Sigurd poured Jonathan a glass and pushed it toward him. Some spilled. Jonathan looked at the glass and then over at the stove; he was more in the mood for tea. But tea was being held up by Heðin. He was leaning against the wall next to the stove watching Kristina, and though she made several moves to bring the teapot to the table, her attention to what she was doing kept faltering. They ended up just staring at each other, Heðin with his arms crossed, Kristina holding the teapot in both hands, her mouth slightly open.

Jens Símun saved the day. "Tea!" he roared suddenly, banging his empty glass on the table.

Kristina closed her mouth and made it to the table, with tea, cups, a plate of cookies, a half-moon of cake. Everybody fell to in a shower of crumbs and dribbles. Even Heðin abandoned his predatory position at the wall and slid in beside Jonathan to eat.

Ten minutes later the drinking started. Jonathan had never seen anything like it. The brandy glasses were downed in two big gulps—he shuddered as he watched Jens Símun's throat moving snakelike over what in America would be four shots. Stolid Petur, clever Sigurd, ancient

Jón Hendrik, besotted Heðin: all of them were tossing it back like professional winos. When they'd finished a glass they poured another and did it again. Kristina washed dishes with her back to this bad behavior. The bottle was empty after half an hour.

Petur lurched to his feet and into the hall, fell over the pile of boots, and came back with a new bottle, aquavit this time.

Jonathan blurted, "You can't mix aquavit and brandy. You'll go crazy! You'll get sick!"

They slowly swiveled their heads to look at him.

"That's the idea," said Heðin. He poured aquavit for everyone, concentrating hard. Then he stuck his face up to Jonathan's and pointed the bottle at his glass, which was still three quarters full of brandy. "You're not drinking," he said.

"I can't drink like this."

"Jonathan." Heðin dropped his head onto Jonathan's shoulder and talked sweetly into his neck. "You must drink. Drink. We have to dance."

"Can't I dance without drinking?"

"You wouldn't want to," Heðin said. "Drink," he whispered, then jerked himself off Jonathan into a semi-upright position.

Jonathan steeled himself and drank his brandy, which wasn't very good and left a hot line from his throat to his stomach. His next assignment, the aquavit, appeared in his glass courtesy of Heðin. Jonathan decided he couldn't continue without a breather. He stood up, holding onto the table for balance. "Toilet," he said.

Kristina pointed upstairs without turning around.

"Stairs in the hall," mumbled Petur.

The toilet was much better equipped than his own: hot water. Jonathan found a pink nailbrush in the shape of an elephant and scrubbed his hands with it until all the mire and blood was off. Then he washed his face. Then he thought he might as well do something about his hair, so he took the yellow toothbrushes out of the yellow plastic cup and used it to pour hot water all over his head. Drying off with a pink towel, he considered taking a bath. The idea was seductive but seemed like trespassing. He looked at himself in the mirror: improved, though his eyes were red. They would be redder before this day was over, he figured. Thinking of his glass full of aquavit made him queasy. He simply would not drink it—they couldn't force him to. A brandy burp rose out of him and cleared his head a little.

Things had changed when he returned to the kitchen. Jón Hendrik was asleep. Heðin was back on the prowl by the stove, and Kristina had thawed a bit; they were smiling at each other. Petur and Sigurd were having a hard time sitting up and kept tipping right and left. Only Jens Símun maintained equanimity, though his brown eye was shut and his blue eye rolled around in its socket. Still, he sat straight in his chair with his head high. He was drinking something new: a bottle of near-beer.

"You're drinking beer?" Jonathan asked.

Jens Símun nodded gravely. He lifted the beer bottle and set it down again with care. Making an obvious effort to organize his tongue, he said, "If you have it with an aspirin, you can get drunk." He looked at Jonathan and added, "You can get more drunk."

Jonathan took an experimental sip of aquavit. It wasn't too bad. Aquavit was easier, somehow, than brandy. He took another sip, but this was a mistake. Immediately he was jolted by a loud ringing in his ears and the sensation of his head being split apart, perhaps by a knife. He put his head into his hands: another error. He understood why everybody was taking pains to stay upright. How long, he wondered, were they going to sit in the kitchen getting drunk? He sat absolutely still and tried to guess the time. Six o'clock, he decided, after rejecting four o'clock and midnight.

"What time is it?" he asked. When nobody answered, he leaned across the table to Petur and repeated the question.

"I don't care," said Petur slowly.

"I care," Jonathan said. "Heðin, what time is it?"

Heðin wasn't there. Neither was Kristina. Jonathan took another sip of aquavit.

If it had been in fact six o'clock when Jonathan asked, it was at least eight and possibly ten by the time they were all trying to put their boots on again. On the other hand, he thought, as he intently worked his right foot into Sigurd's left boot, probably it had been only four o'clock, so now it was maybe nine? Jonathan was convinced he would feel better if he knew the time. He'd made another trip to the toilet that was actually a search for a clock, and a search for Heðin and Kristina. He'd found a closed door, evidence of them, but no clock. And now everybody was back in the kitchen surveying the pile of boots, which Petur had dragged in and which looked like a nest of snakes. Kristina was washing glasses, finally empty, and wearing a pretty red kerchief on her fair head. Heðin was making up for lost time by swigging down the dregs in the aquavit and beer bottles.

"Goddamned boot," snarled Sigurd, waving his foot aloft.

"I think that might be my boot," Jonathan said. They traded; things went better after that.

Jonathan had never been anywhere near as drunk as he currently was. He was beyond drunk—he felt he'd been put into a bottle of liquor and was marinating in it. His limbs were squishy and his insides seemed to have evaporated. It was rather nice. But it was confusing. For instance, he was out on the street walking next to Petur, and not doing too bad a job of walking, he was pleased to see, but he didn't remember leaving the house.

"Did we leave the house?" he asked Petur.

"I think so," Petur looked around. "Yes. Here's the street."

Sigurd and Jens Símun were walking arm in arm ahead, singing about birds.

The next thing he knew he was in a big room with wooden rafters and a lot of other people, most of whom were yelling. The room was hot, and the change in temperature made him dizzy. Jonathan sat down on a bench.

Now he did not feel good. He was cold and hot. His stomach was jumpy. His hands hurt, and when he held them up to his face to wonder why they hurt, he saw cuts in his palm and a gash along his wrist. His knees were not working; when he tried to keep them together they flew apart, so that he sprawled on the bench and started falling backward. Then an earthquake began, rattling the floor and making it nearly impossible to stay on the bench. Jonathan was surprised by the earthquake. He didn't remember the Danish guidebook talking about seismic instability. Luckily, Heðin was on the bench too.

"It's an earthquake," Jonathan said. He didn't know how to say *earthquake* in Faroese, so he said it in English.

"Now we dance," announced Heðin, standing up and dragging Jonathan to his feet.

"I think we have to get into a hole," Jonathan protested.

Heðin wasn't listening. He pulled Jonathan into a line of people who were stamping their feet and yelling. "Right foot over left foot," he said, demonstrating.

Jonathan moved to the left in order to avoid being knocked over by Heðin.

"Good, good," said Heðin, "again."

"Oh," said Jonathan, "we're dancing." He took two more steps left.

"No!" Heðin tugged on his hand. "Two left, one right."

Soon Jonathan was dancing: two to the left, one to the

right, then a stomp. It was the stomps that accounted for
the earthquake. He was pleased to have figured this out.
And he liked dancing. It was a stylized version of a drunken
lurch and therefore came naturally to him and all the other
drunks in the room. Singing was harder. The tune—it was
more of a drone—wasn't too difficult to learn, but the words
were beyond him. He had a vague memory of Heðin singing
some of them years ago, this morning: Norsemen, dance
well. But that was only the refrain. The rest of it, and there
were several hundred verses, concerned two chieftains,
Tróndur and Sigmundur, and some sort of fight.

"What's this *kvæði* about?" he asked Heðin.

"They're fighting over whether to become Christian."

"This is a very old one, then?"

Heðin whispered, "The Icelanders wrote it."

"But it's in Faroese."

"We stole it." Heðin resumed yelling out the *kvæði*.

Moving, yelling, and stomping were sobering Jonathan
up, and he was able to take in the scene around him. They
were in some sort of meeting hall: benches all around the
walls, a raised platform at one end, high, small-paned windows. The room contained an extraordinary amount of
wood for a Faroese building—not only the rafters he'd noticed earlier, but framing around the windows and tongue-
in-groove wainscoting. Most Faroese windows were simply
cut into the plaster, as wood was too precious to use for
decoration.

"Where'd all this wood come from?" he asked Heðin.

"What wood?"

"Here." Jonathan tipped his head toward the walls,
creating a bout of dizziness.

"It's an old building," Heðin said.

This wasn't an explanation. "Yes?"

"Just dance, will you?" snapped Heðin. "Questions all
the time," he mumbled.

It was true; questions all the time. Jonathan sighed.

Well, he would save up his questions. Maybe somebody would answer them another day. He was sober enough now to remember his notebook resting idle on his kitchen table, and this provoked a second sigh. Then, conjuring the image of his worries bobbing offshore in the gray sea, he tossed the desire for his notebook onto the waves and resumed looking around.

He and Heðin were at the outer arc of a line of dancers that spiraled in to a knot in the middle of the room. Parts of the line were straight and well formed, but most of it was pretty ragged, because so many of the dancers were drunk beyond standing. At least two hundred people were dancing, and more than half of them were completely looped. The women scattered here and there propped up the men on either side of them. Some of the village elders looked sober too, holding their white heads high and chanting every word to every verse. Klæmint the sheriff looked particularly dignified, dancing next to Jón Hendrik, who looked particularly blotto. Jonathan couldn't find the others from Skopun. And Kristina, where was she? He peered around Heðin and found her, cheeks flushed, red kerchief awry, holding tight to Heðin's hand. He leaned toward Heðin.

"*Mokka*," he said, and winked.

Heðin punched Jonathan in the stomach.

"Hey!" Jonathan yelped, and fell to the floor. He bent over his knees and gasped. "Jesus Christ," he said. "Fuck you," he went on, in English. "I don't know how to get along with you people."

A thin young man from Húsavík who'd been dancing a few feet down the line from Heðin and Jonathan darted up to Heðin, took a swipe at his head, and missed. Heðin swiped back and connected on his shoulder. Jens Símun and Petur appeared, waving their hands. Kristina, cause of all this, had meanwhile danced out of sight, swallowed by the line that continued to take two steps left, one step right, swerving around Jonathan on the floor and the clutch of men standing near him, all with their arms raised.

"So, so, so," said Petur.

"Goddamned American," said Heðin.

Jonathan retched.

Petur took two steps toward Heðin and pushed him hard on the chest. "Crazy kid!" he yelled. He pointed at Jonathan, curled up on the floor. "That's your friend."

The thin guy from Húsavík had been joined by another with straw-colored hair and bad skin. "These assholes from Skopun," said the new arrival, "they're always fighting in that village."

"Is that so?" Heðin delivered another shoulder punch to the thin one. "Hicks," he said, and punched Bad Skin too for good measure.

Jonathan looked up just in time to see both Húsavík boys draw their *grind* knives from their belts.

Petur grabbed Heðin before he could get his own knife out and pushed him toward a bench on the wall. Heðin let himself be pushed for a few feet, then pushed back. "Come on, come on," said Petur, but Heðin pushed him aside. Now, however, Jens Símun was standing in front of the two from Húsavík, blocking Heðin's access.

"Goddamn you, get out of my way!" Heðin charged Jens Símun. Jens Símun, who was considerably bigger than Heðin, stayed put. Heðin ran into his chest and rebounded. Then he drew his knife.

"I swear I'm going to kill you," he said.

Jonathan scuttled back toward the wall, where Petur was sitting on a bench not doing anything. "Can't you stop them?" Jonathan asked him.

"Nothing will happen," Petur said.

Jonathan didn't believe that. And now Jens Símun did something dangerous: he laughed at Heðin and his upraised knife. Jonathan shut his eyes.

"You want to have a fight?" Jens Símun said. "Okay."

Jonathan couldn't resist opening his eyes. He saw Jens Símun move away, so that Heðin was face to face with the guys from Húsavík. But they had dropped their hands. The one with bad skin had even put his knife back in his belt.

"These people are crazy," he said to his friend, and they both slipped into the line of dancers.

Jonathan hoisted himself up onto the bench beside Petur, which made him retch again; nothing was coming up except bile. Petur took a pint bottle of aquavit out of his pants and offered it. Jonathan took a swig. What the hell, he thought. Maybe it would help. Petur took a swig too, then waved it at Heðin. Jonathan thought this unwise. Heðin was standing on flexed, taut legs, his knife still threatening someone—anyone. Jens Símun had melted into the crowd.

"Eh, Heðin." Petur waved the bottle again.

Jonathan hoped he wouldn't come over. But he did, and he flopped down right next to Jonathan and draped a strong, knife-wielding arm over his neck.

"Going after my girlfriend, hah," he said. Then he laughed. "Tricky. Tricky American."

"I wasn't." Jonathan spoke softly. The knife was near his ear.

"Have a drink," said Petur. He sounded bored. "When's the wedding?"

Heðin took a pull from the bottle. "Summer. A summer wedding is nice, don't you think?" He beamed his best smile at Jonathan.

"Okay," said Petur. He got up and began dancing again.

Jonathan felt vulnerable sitting by himself with Heðin and his knife. "Want to dance?" he asked.

"You're afraid of me." Heðin tightened his grip on Jonathan's neck. "Don't be afraid of me. I'm just drunk."

"I know," said Jonathan. He felt nervous.

"Don't you get drunk in America?"

"Not this drunk," said Jonathan.

"Drunk!" Heðin yelled. "This *is* drunk. Either you're drunk or you're not drunk."

"Okay." Jonathan looked around for Petur.

Heðin dropped his knife all of a sudden, and it clattered on the floor. "My head," he said. He put it on Jonathan's chest. "I'm so goddamned tired," he said.

Jonathan patted Heðin's head tentatively. He moved his foot as quietly as he could until he had the blade of the knife under his heel. Then he said, "Maybe we should go home."

Heðin banged his head against Jonathan's chest, indicating no. Doing this got him off-balance, and he began sliding down, until he came to rest with his head in Jonathan's lap and his knees on the floor. "Jonathan," he mumbled, into Jonathan's thighs.

"What?" Jonathan checked that the knife was still safe.

"You are my friend." Heðin looked up and widened his big, red-streaked green eyes. "My friend."

"Yes," said Jonathan. And they drank to their friendship with the aquavit that Petur had kindly left behind.

More dancing; standing outside in a windy drizzle with Jón Hendrik, who'd got hold of some vodka; sitting on a bench with Sigurd not listening to him explain how to cure whale meat in salt: the night seemed to Jonathan to have been going on for weeks and to have no end in sight. The noisy room and his aching head were eternal conditions, a benign but boring Faroese hell to which he'd been condemned. He wasn't too drunk, though, to realize that everybody else was in heaven. They loved dancing around yelling with bottles sloshing in their pockets and picking fights and collapsing onto benches for restorative snoozes that enabled them to keep it up for another two hours.

His obsession with time had recurred, and Jonathan whiled away part of the night by trying to catch a glimpse of a watch on some passing wrist. Though the crowd had thinned a little, there were still at least a hundred people whirling by him; not one of them had a watch. He tried to tell himself that his interest was anthropological, that the accuracy of his report on the *grind* would be compromised if he couldn't supply a schedule of activities. But this attempt to diminish the space between Jonathan tipsy on a bench and Jonathan maintaining the perfect observational distance failed: he'd left that position behind hours ago— how many hours ago, he had no idea—when he'd killed the first whale. He knew that, and he knew as well that the only reason he wanted to find out the time was to estimate when he'd be back in Skopun, sleeping off the effects of this interminable experience.

So he sat against the wall, head cocked slightly, on the lookout for timepieces, lapsing now and then into a sort of sleep during which he dreamed passionately of his pillow and his eiderdown. He was in a stupor when he was roused by Petur patting his hand, saying his name softly over and over.

They were all standing in front of him, Sigurd and Jens Símun, Heðin, Jón Hendrik, all looking gray and gaunt and in need of a shave. Jonathan touched his own cheek: a slow-moving timepiece, but it told him that at least twenty-four hours had passed.

"Hoopla," said Petur, as if talking to a child. "Off we go. Let's go."

Jonathan stood on tired, spongy feet. "Where now?"

"Time to divide the whales," said Petur.

They straggled through the dim wet streets, sliding on muddy stones down to the harbor. The sun was just coming up as they arrived, a red smear at the juncture of sea and sky.

"Storms are coming," muttered Heðin.

"Good thing we have all this *grind*," said Petur briskly. He alone had survived the night intact; his brothers were slipping and stumbling, Jón Hendrik looked near death, Heðin kept stopping in his tracks and closing his eyes. "We won't be out fishing for a while," Petur went on.

"Papa, don't talk so loud," said Heðin, shutting his eyes.

Jón Hendrik wove his way over to Jonathan. "So, so, so," he said. "Now you are a Faroese man." Jonathan looked at him blankly. "Now you are a Faroese man," said Jón Hendrik again. He teetered and lost his footing in the sand, then fell against Jonathan. He was all bones, rattly, sharp, gnarled bones, and Jonathan gripping him around the shoulders felt he was holding a bird of prey, light yet intense with the desire to sink his talons into something.

"Why do you say that?" Jonathan asked, putting him back into a standing position.

Jón Hendrik just said it again, like a bird with only one call.

"He wants to know why, Great-Grandpa," said Heðin. Then he covered his eyes with both hands and said, "Oh, God." He sat down on the sand.

Petur came into view, lugging a sack of whale meat. "Go get your meat," he told them.

Heðin stood up again. "Come on," he said to Jonathan. "We'll get Grandpa's meat too." He put his hand on Jonathan's back for support. "I feel terrible," he confided.

Jonathan felt terrible too, and the sight of dozens of butchered whales didn't help. Nor was he especially eager for a sack of whale meat; one steak would be enough for his taste. But because Petur had speared the first whale, and because the *grind* was a large one, and because Jonathan was considered an honorary member of the Dahl family, he got a sack so full he had to drag it behind him on the sand. Heðin was dragging two. Jonathan was glad to see Sigurd standing beside the car on the road above the harbor; at least they wouldn't have to haul a hundred pounds of whale through the whole village.

It all went into the trunk, and Jón Hendrik was coaxed into the back seat with Heðin. Jonathan was about to get into the front when Petur said, "No, no, you come back on the boat with us."

"I don't want to go back on the boat." Jonathan was too tired to mince words.

"It'll be good for you," said Petur.

Jonathan looked wistfully into the car, where Heðin and Jón Hendrik were already settled in, napping. Then he watched Sigurd try to start the car with the skeleton key that opened his shop and figured he might be better off with Petur.

Jens Símun was bailing out the boat with an empty red-cabbage can, rather small for the job. But he had another one, which he thrust into Jonathan's hands. They bailed while Petur checked over the oars, looking for damage from yesterday's battle. "Okay," he said after about ten minutes. They cast off into the fjord.

The ocean was calm and their progress easy. Peter and Jens Símun, intent on their work, rowed without speaking. Jonathan sat shivering in the stern; he slid his hands up in his sleeves and huddled into his slicker.

Silence: even the oars slicing the water and the water breaking on land were silent. The boat slipped along the sea between the gray cliffs of Húsavík, leaving far behind the beach where kittiwakes and gulls reeled above the carcasses. Dead ahead, the sun loomed at the mouth of the fjord, clear of the water now but still blurred by sea fog. On they went, a dot in all that gray vastness, the hooked prow of the boat cutting straight through the chill swirls of mist and murk.

Jonathan's head was heavy, and despite the cold he felt himself drifting into sleep. He had the rare sensation of falling—as if "falling asleep" were a simple description of an action. He was tumbling down a long dark shaft, sometimes floating, sometimes plummeting, and the deeper he fell, the lighter grew his hold on consciousness. And then, in a peculiar reversal, he seemed to be rising, or, rather, rising and falling simultaneously. His body dropped down deeper—he could actually see it sinking—and his mind, reawakened, shot up to the top of the shaft, where a circle of light beckoned. With a rush he popped out into the sky.

Below him the boat lay in the water with three forms in it, two rowing, one still. That still one was himself, but he had no feeling for it. Whatever his essential self was, it was in the sky and rising higher with gusts of speed that made him dizzy but thrilled him. He soared into darkness, above the range of the sun. The whole fjord ran silver under his eyes, flanked and banked by rock that pressed the water out to sea. He could see the tug of the tide below the waves, the shoals where cod lay sleeping. He rose another notch, up to the clouds, through whose veils islands glimmered brown and gray, long Streymoy, tiny Mykines, and his home, Sandoy.

Jonathan knew he had seen this before. The effort he made to remember when dislodged him from his vantage point, and with sickening suddenness he was back in the boat, jerking awake on the wooden seat.

"Fell asleep, didn't you," said Petur. "That's good."

He had seen it from the airplane, when he'd first arrived: the patchwork of land and sea, the dot of a boat on a fjord. But then the scene had been static and impenetrable, like a painting, and like a painting, too, provoking sorrow, almost nostalgia, for a world he could not enter. Now it was not a painting, it was real and he was in it—deep in it: wet with its water, cold with its wind, stained with its blood.

The Cat King

January produced snow, a rarity in this maritime climate. The kids went out on flattened cardboard boxes, screaming past Jonathan's house down to the harbor, where they smashed into barrels and lay laughing on the concrete. Jonathan made a short but elegant snowman in his front yard, which was visited and commented on by all the villagers as if it were a wonder of nature. Lacking a carrot, he'd used a potato for the nose; he was particularly happy with the eyes, which were fish eyes still in fish faces, embedded in the snowman so artfully that they seemed to be returning the stares of the admirers.

The entire fall was gone after three days, melted down by the usual torrent of winter rain. And most of February was the epitome of drear: gale-force winds kept the mail boat away for several days at a time, and the calms between the storms were tentative, overcast, mere brewing periods for more bad weather. As Petur had predicted, everybody was eating a lot of whale meat. Only the biggest boats were out—and they were far out, gone for weeks. When the *Skarvanes* returned late in the month, Jonathan went over to the Dahls' to gorge on halibut and cod. But soon they were back to *grind*, digging around in their buckets of salt for yet another slab of overrich steak. If Jonathan had been less finicky, he could have varied this with half-rotted cod, braces of which hung from Maria's clothesline. Instead he reminisced about a sausage—it almost qualified as a hot dog—he'd eaten in Tórshavn when he first arrived in the Faroes, and made omelets twice a week.

From the sausage to Daniela was not a big leap. Jonathan decided to take a trip to Tórshavn. Easy enough to decide in his snug kitchen, with *Tom Jones* lying open on the table in front of him (he was reading his way through the large classics, ordering from Blackwell's only fiction of over four hundred pages); the season was against him. Reconnoitering on the dock one dark morning near the end of the month, he got many pessimistic assessments of when the next boat trip would take place, ranging from "tomorrow" to "March." He called Eyvindur.

"Bah," said Eyvindur, disgusted. "They use the weather as an excuse to stay on their godforsaken little island. Come immediately."

"Well, I can't, if the boat doesn't go."

Eyvindur snorted at the irrefutability of this. "Come in a fishing boat, then. We'll send the helicopter."

"I'll do what I can. I just wanted to let you know I'm hoping to get over there."

"We'll have a special treat when you come. Fresh whale steak."

Jonathan sighed. "How about puffins? I like them so much."

"There are no puffins now. Puffins are in summer."

"Frozen puffins?"

"Jonathan, you get here, then we'll discuss dinner. Dinner is not important; social intercourse is important." With this piece of arch-Eyvindur wisdom, he hung up.

He called back just as Jonathan was going out Sigurd's door. "We'll have frozen puffins for you," he yelled, and hung up again.

Jón Hendrik was manning the phone that day, and unlike Sigurd he had no interest in people's calls. He contented himself with saying "Eyvindur, hah," as Jonathan left.

When he got home, Jonathan noticed an odd smell. He'd got a whiff of it the day before, but it had gone away. Now it was back: sweet, thick, sneaky. He poked in his whale bucket, but that smelled only of salt water. Some ancient potatoes in the refrigerator might be the culprits; although they smelled clean when he sniffed them, he threw them out. No leak in the kerosene line, nothing objectionable about a small pile of socks in the bedroom closet. He would ignore it, he figured.

By morning it was unignorable, or perhaps it was because his plans for a trip were still frustrated—for whatever reason, Jonathan focused on the smell. It had an undertone that made him gag, and it seemed to be getting stronger. He called Petur in for a diagnosis.

"Mice," said Petur, standing in the middle of the bedroom, where the smell was worst. "Could be dead ones. You need a cat."

"I don't want a cat. In fact, I want to go to Tórshavn tomorrow."

"In this weather?" Petur shook his head. "Jens Símun has cats. He'll lend you one."

Jonathan didn't like cats. "What good will the cat do?"

"Find the mice." Petur looked at him strangely.

"I know, but then what?"

"Eat 'em."

"Even the dead ones?" Jonathan was now sure that dead mice—flocks of them—were causing the smell.

Petur shrugged his shoulders. "Go get a cat," he advised.

Jens Símun's extra cat was a svelte little creature, speckled brown and gray. Sigrid offered to carry it over to his house.

"What should I feed it?" Jonathan asked her as they paraded through town.

"Don't feed it anything," she said, "or it won't look for the mice."

The cat yowled when Sigrid left it in Jonathan's kitchen. "Shh," said Jonathan. The cat stared at him with yellow eyes. Jonathan had to look away. This was one of the reasons he didn't like cats; they enjoyed staring people down. "I'm not playing that game," he told it, and took up his book. But he felt uneasy with the cat in the room.

He stood up. "C'mon," he said, "let's go upstairs." He had little hope that the cat would follow, and it didn't. He waited in the hall for a minute, then poured a bowl of milk and, waving it under the cat's nose, tried to lure the animal up the stairs. The cat ignored the milk. Jonathan left the bowl near the bedroom door and went back to his book. When next he looked, the cat was asleep on the bench by the stove.

Heðin came over after dinner. Jonathan was glad to

see him. Dinner with the cat had been a trial. It was whale night, and the cat had wanted some whale for itself and had rubbed incessantly on Jonathan's leg while he cooked. Then it had stared at him all through dinner from its perch by the stove, tracking the movements of his fork from plate to mouth with its yellow eyes.

"Hey, what a nice little cat," said Heðin.

"What's nice about it? I'm borrowing it from Jens Símun and it's a terrible cat. It's supposed to find mice but all it does is watch me."

Heðin picked up the cat and tickled it under the chin. "You have to make friends with a cat, Jonathan."

"I don't like cats," Jonathan whispered. The cat heard and stared at him.

"What's its name?" Heðin asked.

"I don't know."

Heðin dumped the cat into Jonathan's arms. "Tickle it," he said, "and give it a name."

"It's just borrowed," Jonathan protested. The cat settled into his arms and started to purr. Unthinking, Jonathan stroked it. "I'm not going to bother with a name." He put the cat on the floor. It hopped back into his lap.

"See, now he likes you," Heðin said. "See how easy it is?"

"How about getting to Tórshavn? How easy is that?"

"Did you call her?" Heðin grinned.

Jonathan shook his head. "I will, though. I'll call her as soon as I know I can get over there. But everyone keeps telling me I can't."

"Well, you *could* get there." Heðin seemed doubtful. "I don't think you'd want to get there." He leaned over the table. "It's that boat, you know. It's so horrible in bad weather."

"I've been on it," said Jonathan.

"That was in summer." Heðin leaned back. "In

winter . . ." He didn't bother finishing, just rolled his eyes.
"But maybe you don't get seasick?"

"I do. At least, I did."

"If you *had* to go . . ." Heðin trailed off again.

"Wouldn't you go, if Kristina were in Tórshavn?"

"Nah," said Heðin. "I'd make her wait." Then he
winked. "Lucky I don't have to worry about that."

"Are you really going to get married?"

"Of course." Heðin nodded. "Of course we are. So
will you. We'll have a double wedding."

"Not if I don't get over to Tórshavn," said Jonathan
grimly.

The cat slept at his feet. The day dawned dark, windy,
and more redolent of the smell. Jonathan shut all the doors
to the kitchen, shutting out the smell, and made a lot of
progress in *Tom Jones*. He had an omelet for dinner. The
cat wanted omelet just as much as it had wanted whale.

"No," Jonathan said to the cat, as it yowled at the
frying pan. But when it jumped into his lap and began
licking forlornly at the edge of the plate, Jonathan felt too
sorry for it to protest. They finished the omelet together.
Then the cat curled up in Jonathan's lap.

The next morning he hardened his heart, shut the cat
into the bedroom, probable home of the mice, and went
down to the harbor. Jens Símun was standing on the dock
looking mournful.

"Terrible weather," he said. Jonathan agreed. "How's
Tróndur doing?"

"Tróndur?"

"The cat."

Knowing the cat was named for the hero of a saga
changed Jonathan's feelings about him. Perhaps at this moment Tróndur was tearing into mice. "I left him near the
mice," Jonathan said.

"He'll get them. He's a good cat." Jens Símun relapsed into gloom. "What a terrible winter," he said.

"Do you think I can get over to Tórshavn this week?"

"Maybe next week." Jens Símun brightened a little and added, "Maybe tomorrow."

"Really?" Jonathan was eager.

Jens Símun looked up at the impenetrable sky. "No, I reckon not."

Jonathan went home to check on Tróndur's progress. He was asleep on the bed. The smell had overtaken the entire atmosphere of the room.

"That does it," Jonathan said out loud. He set off again, to complain to Sigurd.

"I have mice," he began. Sigurd pulled a mouse-trap from under the counter. "No," said Jonathan. Frustration seized him. "No, listen. I've got this cat of Jens Símun's, Tróndur, and it doesn't do a damned thing, and the mice are rotting in my bedroom somewhere, I can smell them—"

"So, so, so," Sigurd cut in. He put the mousetrap away. "That's a problem, I reckon." Jonathan was momentarily soothed. "That's a good cat, though."

"Sigurd," Jonathan banged his hands on the counter. "Please. The cat isn't working. I have to do something else. I want to go to Tórshavn."

"You won't find a better cat in Tórshavn. That's a good cat."

"I'm not looking for a better cat," Jonathan said slowly. "I want to go to Tórshavn for a visit."

Sigurd smiled. "To see your fiancée?"

Jonathan ignored this. "Can you help me?"

Sigurd looked out the window. "You might have to take up the floor," he said dreamily. "Sometimes they get under the floor." He looked back at Jonathan. "The cat can't get under there, you see."

"Can we do that today?"

"You could do it right now," Sigurd said.

"Couldn't you help me?" Jonathan was reduced to pleading.

"Jens Símun. He's good at that."

Jonathan bought a raisin cake for Jens Símun and went back to the dock.

"A good day for raisin cake," said Jens Símun, eyeing the box Jonathan held.

Jonathan's frustration abruptly funneled into hatred of the smallness of Skopun, where everybody could tell that you'd bought raisin cake from Sigurd by the shape of the box you carried. Anonymity, privacy, solitude—forget it! But did that mean they rushed to help out with the vermin they knew were in the house, or the cesspool they knew was clogged? No. Jonathan tried calming himself down by seeing this reluctance to help as their version of privacy: Do nothing unless asked. Well, here he was asking—and asking Jens Símun again.

"Would you like to come over for a *temun* with me?" he said. "I've got a problem."

Without a word Jens Símun turned from his sad contemplation of the weather and walked home with Jonathan.

"Puuh," he said when they were inside. "What a stink!"

Hearing his master's voice, Tróndur dashed down the stairs and into the kitchen, where he yowled loudly, complaining, Jonathan supposed, about his bad treatment over the past two days. Jens Símun paid no attention. "Got a hammer?" he asked.

Jonathan found a hammer and a screwdriver under the sink.

"Bring them both," said Jens Símun. They went upstairs, Tróndur accompanying them. Jens Símun lay down on the bedroom floor and wriggled along it, nose to the boards. "Aha," he said after a while. He sat up and attacked the floor with the claws of the hammer, which had no effect.

Then he began hammering the screwdriver in between the planks. Jonathan sat on the bed and watched. Tróndur hid in a corner.

Soon Jens Símun had destroyed a foot or so of flooring. "Come here," he ordered. Together, he and Jonathan pulled up several boards, revealing a dark, dust-ball ridden landscape. "Got a broom?" Jens Símun demanded. Jonathan produced a broom from the closet.

After ten minutes' poking, Jens Símun fished out a tiny gray lump about the size of a man's thumb, which he held aloft by its thread-thin tail. Tróndur came out of hiding to stare up at it. The sweet smell of rot was overpowering.

"A little thing, a lot of trouble," said Jens Símun.

"You think there's only that one?"

"We'll leave the floor like this for a couple days, in case we need to get in again, but I reckon that's it." Jens Símun opened the window and threw the mouse into the yard.

As Jonathan put a cup of tea and a slice of cake in front of him, Jens Símun said, "Poison."

"What? The cake?"

"That mouse was poisoned. That's why it smelled so bad."

"I didn't put poison out." Jonathan took a piece of cake for himself.

"Somebody did. It came to your house to die. That's why Tróndur didn't go after it. He could smell the poison."

Jonathan was unwilling to credit Tróndur with so much logic, but he nodded anyhow, happy to agree with almost anything Jens Símun said.

"That's a good cat," said Jens Símun.

And Jonathan, grateful, said, "Yes, very good."

Jens Símun was gone, leaving a trail of crumbs and Tróndur—"In case there are more mice." Tróndur ate the crumbs but showed no interest in the world beneath the floor. Jonathan wondered if he should spend the night at the Dahls'; his bedroom stank more than ever, even with the window open. When Heðin came over after dinner (whale night again; rubbing and complaints again), Jonathan took him upstairs.

"Do you think I ought to sleep in here?"

Heðin was more interested in Jonathan's things than in his predicament. He poked around on the bedside table, looking at the books and the alarm clock, opened the door to the closet and the top drawer of the bureau, examined Jonathan's hairbrush. "A wooden hairbrush," he said. "I've never seen that. We have plastic."

"Well? What do you think?"

"It's a nice bedroom." Heðin nodded at the furniture. "And you have two beds." He grinned and sat down on the one Jonathan used. "Good for guests." He winked.

"What about the poison, and the smell?"

"That'll go away." Heðin stretched out on Jonathan's bed. "You want to trade for the night? I'll stay here, you can sleep at my house? I could go get Kristina."

"You don't think it's dangerous?"

Heðin shut his eyes. "I would like to have a nice big bedroom like this." He sat up. "I'll build one. Next spring. I'll be building a house next spring."

"Oh." For politeness, Jonathan asked, "Where?"

Heðin went over to the window and pointed at a muddy stretch that lay between the house opposite and a small drying shed. "That's our land."

"It won't be a big house," Jonathan said.

"That's our shed, too. We can get rid of that. You'll help us."

"Mmm." Jonathan grunted. "Want some cake?"

Heðin stayed late, drawing possible floor plans in Jonathan's notebook and eating up the cake. Watching Heðin debate whether two extra bedrooms for children were enough made Jonathan feel like a teenager; he was just hoping to get a date—and with a girl whose interest in him was uncertain.

"Two will do," Heðin concluded as midnight approached. "We can have four babies, then."

Jonathan yawned. "What will you name them?"

"Petur, Jens Símun, Sigurd, and Heðin. Or Kristina, if it's a girl."

"Suppose they're all girls?"

"They won't be. We have many sons in my family."

Huddled under his eiderdown trying not to breathe in too much of the foul air in his bedroom, Jonathan was haunted by this sentence of Heðin's. In its cockiness, reverence for lineage, and quasi-magical reliance on the past as a predictor, it exemplified Faroese pretensions to a primitive life. Maybe "pretensions" was too strong, although, like the crushing intimacy of Skopun, this quality had begun to bother Jonathan. Behavior that two months ago he would have seen as expressions of culture he now saw as poses—the favored pose, naturally, being the Viking. Long, meditative examinations of the pattern of waves, head held high, chest braced against the wind: just a dramatic way of passing a few hours on a rainy afternoon. If he chanced to observe them at this, so much the better for Jens Símun, or Petur, or whoever was playing out the charade with himself. They were all entertaining themselves by pretending to be their ancestors. Jonathan suspected they had romanticized their origins even more than he had.

This line of thought was depressing. Rolling around in his bed, Jonathan wished for it not to be true, to be rather a product of his grumpiness that would evaporate if he could get a breather in Tórshavn. He imagined the concrete arms of Skopun's harbor open to him on his return, the familiarity of the muddy street, the pleasure of seeing Jón Hendrik on his box in the store—all the subtle and comforting delights of coming home that make the everyday rewarding. In the middle of trying to project himself into this future, he fell asleep.

The clouds blew away while he slept, and though the wind was still fierce, the bustle on the dock the next morning was evidence that a change was in the offing. Gregor the fishmonger perched hopefully on a crate, awaiting something to sell; Jens Símun sat in his boat scraping at the paint; Heðin and his cronies were smoking and baiting a pot of lines.

Jonathan's clouds too had blown off, and he felt vigorous and well organized. He nailed the broken floor boards back into place, put Tróndur into an old pillowcase, and went over to Jens Símun's to give him back. Tróndur didn't like traveling in the pillowcase. He bit and scratched and tore his way through it so that when they arrived, Jonathan was holding in his arms a cat cloaked in tattered strips of muslin. He seemed delighted to be home and jumped out of Jonathan's grasp, running around the kitchen sniffing every inch of floor and dragging his white train behind him.

Sigrid laughed. "What a funny cat," she said. "I guess he didn't get the mice—but he would have, you know."

"Oh, yes," said Jonathan. And though he didn't believe Tróndur would ever have done anything, he was surprised to find that he regretted giving him back. He was a weird sort of company. "Thanks anyhow," he said to Sigrid. "Thank Jens Símun again for me."

"Sit, have a *temun*."

Jonathan debated this. A homemade cake on the table looked inviting, but he was determined to get organized for his trip. "I can't today," he said.

"Oh, yes, you're going to Tórshavn." Sigrid nodded. "Well, you will go tomorrow, I reckon."

"I reckon so." Jonathan decided that "I reckon so" was preferable to "I hope so": it was positive thinking, and it signaled his departure from the kitchen.

"So, so, so," said Sigrid.

*　　*　　*

Jonathan washed some socks and pawed around in his bureau, dissatisfied with all his clothes, even the new ones he'd bought in the fall in Tórshavn, which had taken a beating and now looked as shabby as the rest. All his trousers were stained with fish offal and mud, his underwear was gray, his socks were full of holes, his gloves were splitting on the thumbs. Examination of himself in the mirror was no more rewarding: too much hair and skin as pale as a boiled potato.

He devoted the rest of the afternoon to self-improvement: a bath, a close shave, nail-cutting; basting of the gloves; disposal of the most tattered underpants; removal of the mud encrusted on his clogs. Flushed from the bath and his efforts, he was much more pleased the next time he looked in the mirror. A haircut would really do the trick, though, and Jonathan decided to pay a visit to the Dahls. Maybe he could get an after-dinner trim from Maria.

It was Petur, however, who was the family barber. He draped Jonathan in an old dish towel and centered him under the kitchen light; little Jens Símun and Heðin rode shotgun at the table. "Watch out, Papa! You're cutting too much on that side," from Jens Símun; then from Heðin, "Not enough! Make it shorter!" Petur's nervous trick of snapping the scissors in the air while planning his next move made Jonathan edgy.

As he sat trying not to wriggle, Jonathan wished he'd been less impetuous about sprucing himself up. Any Tórshavn barber would have more confidence than Petur, who kept darting in at Jonathan's head and then reconsidering, backing off, and taking a slice of oxygen instead. After a particularly long pause in the action, Jonathan asked, "Is anything wrong?"

"I seem to have made it a little lopsided," Petur confessed.

"Even it out, then."

"It's more—well, I'd say it's more, ah, uneven all around, if you see what I mean."

Jonathan went up to the bathroom to see what he meant.

Petur had managed to get a zigzag effect all around his head. It was so amazing that Jonathan started to laugh.

"You like it?" Petur had followed him and was lurking in the hall.

Jonathan looked at him and then looked in the mirror again.

"You don't like it." Petur sighed.

They went back to the kitchen. Jonathan held a small mirror of Maria's and directed Petur. As more and more of his hair fell to the floor, Jonathan's spirits sank; he was not going to be looking good for his trip.

In the end, though, it wasn't too bad, at least Jonathan kept telling himself it wasn't too bad. It was too short, especially around the ears, but the zigzags were gone. He put the mirror face down on the table; he knew how it looked.

"Thank you, Petur," he said. "It's not too bad."

"You look like a chicken," said little Jens Símun.

"She'll like you anyhow, Jonathan," said Heðin. And Maria came over to pat him on the head. "It's not too bad," she said.

Jonathan was drinking coffee and chewing on a hard cardamom biscuit, wondering how much his hair could grow in a week and whether it was enough to make postponing the trip worthwhile, when Sigurd clattered into the kitchen announcing a telephone call. He stopped midsentence to stare at Jonathan.

"I got a haircut," Jonathan said firmly.

"Aha," said Sigurd. "You got a phone call, too." He moved around Jonathan as he spoke, viewing the haircut from different angles. "You got a phone call. You better come and take your phone call."

"Maybe it's your mama and papa calling from America," said Maria.

"Maybe," said Jonathan. He was sure it was Eyvindur calling to update the menu.

But, as Sigurd couldn't restrain himself from blurting out the moment they left the house, it was Daniela.

"She has called you, Jonathan. She's a very nice girl, she speaks very good Faroese, very proper." Sigurd babbled on in his excitement. "She asked for you by name."

"What else would she do?"

"When Eyvindur Poulsen calls, he just yells that he wants the American. Well, he's crazy, everybody knows that." Sigurd stole a glance at Jonathan's hair. "Why did you get that haircut?"

Jonathan didn't answer. His body was almost devoid of sensation, except for a delicate tingling in his limbs as he walked. And his mind was a blank. He surveyed it for hopes, fantasies, worries: it contained nothing, it was simply a receptor.

So in an almost meditative state he picked up the receiver and motioned Sigurd out of the room. Sigurd pretended to go away, but Jonathan saw him lingering outside the half-open door. Jonathan turned his back and said, "Hello."

"Jonathan."

"Daniela."

He heard her draw a breath. "Jonathan, I know it was a long time ago that you invited me to visit, but I would like to come now."

"Good." said Jonathan. He couldn't think of anything else to say.

"I will come the day after tomorrow."

"Good."

"On the afternoon boat."

Jonathan tried a variation. "Great." Then, inspired, he added, "I'll be there."

"Then I will see you the day after tomorrow."

Now that she was about to hang up, Jonathan wanted to talk. "It's cold here," he said. "The weather's been bad. Bring lots of socks."

"I know."

"And—" Jonathan wanted to warn her about the haircut, but he didn't know how to phrase it: I have a horrible haircut? I have a haircut that you might think is horrible?

"Yes?" said Daniela.

"Oh, just—bring socks."

"Okay. Goodbye."

"Daniela!"

"Yes?"

"I'll see you," said Jonathan.

He went into the kitchen, where Sigurd and Jón Hendrick were pretending to play cards.

"She's coming," he told them. They didn't look up. "I just thought you'd like to know."

"Who?" asked Jón Hendrik.

"His fiancée, from Tórshavn," Sigurd said.

Jón Hendrik nodded. Sigurd made a big show of trumping some cards of Jón Hendrik's. Jonathan could tell it was an act because about half the deck was on the floor under Sigurd's chair. Obligingly, he waited for Sigurd to start pumping him for information. But Sigurd neither asked a question nor asked him to sit down. In fact, after about five minutes, he said, "It's late, isn't it?"

Jonathan could take a hint; he left. The sky was a patchwork of stars and clouds, and the air gusty with fresh winds. A burst of excitement shot through him: she was coming! He made a detour down to the deserted dock, unwilling to go straight home, and stood looking at the waves that would bring her to him. What had changed her mind? What was in her mind? He couldn't imagine—and soon he stopped trying. She was coming,

she wanted to come, she would be here with him, and
he could spend an entire day and night in delicious anticipation of her.

No sensation of pleasure is closer to pain than waiting for
the arrival of a beloved, especially an unfamiliar one. In the
midst of turning the mattress, airing the pillows, sweeping
the stairs, Jonathan would stop from a pang of thrilling
anxiety: maybe she was just coming on a friendly visit. But
no, shaking the eiderdown to fluff up the feathers, she was
coming to stay here, with him, where there were bedrooms.
The fact that there was more than one caused him hours
of confusion. He didn't want to assume too much by putting
her in his bedroom; on the other hand, if he gave her a
separate room, wouldn't that communicate a lack of interest
on his part? He made up the guest room and trusted Fate
to keep her out of it. Scrubbing his bathroom floor, he
worried that they wouldn't have anything to say to each
other. And he became convinced while washing the kitchen
table that her visit was prompted by nothing more than a
Tórshavn strain of the cabin fever he'd been experiencing
these last weeks: she wasn't really coming to see him, just
to have a change. But in between these seizures of doubt
were whole hours of bliss, in which the fact of her arrival
sweetened every minute. And the uncertainty of what
would happen was, at these times, an added pleasure. He
enjoyed scripting their first kiss, now in the kitchen, now
in the hallway, now at the door to her bedroom—which
she would never enter.

It was exhausting work, cleaning the house and waiting
for her to arrive. The cleaning was finished first, leaving
him like a guest in his own home, fearful of making a mess.
One errand he'd better undertake, Jonathan realized, was
to call Eyvindur and tell him he wasn't coming. He ate a
piece of bread while standing at the sink and then went
over to Sigurd's.

Eyvindur was not in a good mood. "Yah, yah, I know you aren't coming. Okay, goodbye."

"Wait a minute," Jonathan protested.

"What?"

Jonathan didn't know what, exactly. He'd thought Eyvindur would be pleased with this turn of events. "Daniela's coming here," he said, repeating his opening line of the conversation.

"You told me. Okay, goodbye."

"Eyvindur, is something wrong?"

"Good-weather friend. Hah! Bad-weather friend."

"Do you mean 'fair-weather friend'?"

"You know what I mean."

Jonathan could imagine the dark, dour expression on Eyvindur's face. "I'm not trying to insult you," he said.

But now Eyvindur laughed. "When the weather's bad you say you'll come, but when it's good you don't. That's a bad-weather friend." He laughed again. "It's a joke. Hah."

"Hah," said Jonathan, trying to please.

"Okay, goodbye," said Eyvindur, and this time he hung up.

Jonathan spent a few minutes brooding about what could be ailing Eyvindur, but he was too cheery to sustain interest in it. By the time he reached Sigurd's store, the only thing on his mind was a list of wonderful foods he was going to buy for Daniela. Tinned Danish pâté, an extra-large portion of Tilsit, a whole dozen eggs, a bottle of pickles: Sigurd obediently fetched these items and stacked them on the counter, maintaining silence on the topic of Jonathan's visitor. Jonathan was disappointed; he wanted the opportunity to talk about her.

"You know, my friend from Tórshavn's coming," he said.

Sigurd grunted. "Anything else?" he asked. "Potatoes?"

"Okay, potatoes." Even Sigurd's refusal to talk couldn't dampen his spirits. "Lots of potatoes."

Jonathan dumped his groceries on his clean kitchen table and went back out to the dock.

For the first time in days the mail boat was in. Jonathan's heart jumped at the sight of it. This time tomorrow, he'd be looking for Daniela's tidy head in the crowd. Gregor was doing a brisk business in fish. Jonathan bought six dab for his dinner and asked if there was halibut.

"Maybe tomorrow," said Gregor.

This was just what Jonathan wanted to hear. He'd been hoping to give Daniela a halibut feast. He smiled at Gregor, at the smooth ocean sparkling between Skopun and Tórshavn, at the sky that today was an enameled blue bowl above him, and, jauntily swinging his string of fish, headed home.

He was filleting the dab in the sink when a tremendous commotion arose out on the street: yelling, banging, clattering. He craned his neck out the window but couldn't see anything. It got louder. He went out to investigate.

It was just a bunch of boys destroying a barrel. Little Jens Símun was directing a group of about ten. Everybody was throwing stones at the barrel, which had been suspended on a rope between the Dahls' old shed and the corner house.

"What are you doing?" Jonathan asked little Jens Símun, more from friendliness than from curiosity.

"Throw!" yelled Jens Símun. Then he turned to Jonathan. "It's the Cat King," he said. He picked up a stone and threw it.

"The what?"

"Throw!"

"Is there something in there?" Jonathan felt a bit uneasy.

"The Cat King." Jens Símun gave Jonathan one of the

withering looks that were his specialty. "The Cat King is in there, and we are killing him."

"Hold on a minute." Jonathan grabbed Jens Símun's arm, which was braced for the next throw. "There's a cat in there?"

Jens Símun wrested his arm away and got his shot off. "That's what I said."

"You can't do that." Jonathan stepped in front of the line of boys. "Stop that." He held his hand up.

"Get out of the way," one of them yelled. "Get out of the way or you'll get hit."

Jonathan looked at Jens Símun. "Tell them to stop for a minute."

"Wait," Jens Símun growled at his troops.

Jonathan went over to the barrel and looked into it. Huddled at the bottom, his fur fluffed out in fear, his back arched to the limit, was Tróndur. His open, panting mouth oozed white bubbles. Jonathan reached in a hand to remove him and pulled it out immediately, deeply scratched and bleeding.

"Move!" yelled Jens Símun.

"That's your uncle's cat," Jonathan said. He didn't move.

"Now he's the Cat King," said Jens Símun. "Move."

"Why are you doing this?" Jonathan took a few steps toward Jens Símun. Some of the boys used the opportunity to get in a hit, and stones bounced around Jonathan's feet.

"We always do this," said Jens Símun. "It's traditional." He emphasized the last word with a grin. Then he threw another stone.

Jonathan retreated to the sidelines. From out of the barrel came a deep yowl, which only spurred the boys to throw more and larger stones. Jonathan went into the Dahls' house to get assistance.

But the men were out fishing. "It's such good weather," said Maria. "What's wrong?"

"They're killing Tróndur—in a barrel." Jonathan put his hands up to his face. "It's terrible."

"Sit down," said Maria, pushing him into a chair.

"I tried to get them to stop. I couldn't."

Maria brought him a cup of tea. "Drink that."

"Can't we stop it?" Jonathan looked up at her.

Maria sat down at the table with him. "So, so, so," she said. She folded her hands and looked at Jonathan. "Now listen," she said. "This is an old custom—we don't really believe in it anymore, but the children still like to do it. People always did this at Shrovetide. They'd take an old cat and call him the King, and then they'd kill him. They thought that all the bad things they'd done, and the bad luck, would go with the Cat King, you see. It would clean away the bad luck. So it really isn't a terrible thing." She stood up. "Anyhow, it's only the children. We don't think that way anymore." She smiled at Jonathan, as if she was sure this explanation would make him feel better.

"A scapegoat," Jonathan said to himself in English. Maria looked puzzled. "I've heard of this," he told her. "But"—he was growing agitated again—"people don't do this anymore! This is something people haven't done for centuries!"

Maria went over to her stove. "We do it," she said.

Jonathan could tell he'd insulted her. "Maria—" He didn't know what to say. "I mean—well, it's a very old custom. I'm surprised, I guess. I'm surprised anybody still does it."

"I told you we didn't believe it." Maria's voice was even and expressionless. Jonathan couldn't see her face.

"Then why—" He stopped; no use asking. But she could tell him one thing: "How does the cat die? After all, the stones don't hit it because it's in the barrel."

Maria turned around and put her hand on her chest,

then made a fist. "Heart stops," she said, and went back to cooking.

"Oh," said Jonathan.

For the first time in many months, Jonathan missed Cambridge. Wanting to be somewhere other than the Faroes was not the same as wanting to be home; he'd spent plenty of time wishing for Copenhagen or Paris or anyplace with a decent climate and a better diet. But now he wished he were home—specifically, in Widener Library, where thousands of feet pursuing knowledge had worn a groove in the marble floors and where he could assuage his uneasiness by reading about scapegoats rather than by turning on the radio to drown out the noise of Tróndur's death.

Tróndur must have been in possession of all nine lives when he was put into the barrel, for he took a long time to die. His yowling persisted even after sunset, which occurred these days at the normal hour of five o'clock. Sitting in his twilit kitchen with the BBC chatting through the static and the stones thudding against the barrel, Jonathan tried to calm himself with logic. Guy Fawkes burnt in effigy was a scapegoat, kids at Halloween put on masks to drive out evil spirits, Jesus was the ultimate scapegoat, even spring cleaning—Jonathan gave up on this line of thought. Listing parallels didn't quell his agitation. Then he tried to be pleased that the Faroes had offered up to him such raw proof of their primitive nature: the anthropology department was going to have to eat its collective hat over this! But at the moment he didn't give a damn about the anthropology department, though he was pretty sure they'd be impressed. He wasn't impressed, he was shaken.

He kept coming back to an image from his first year in graduate school. He'd taken a course in taboo that relied heavily on Leviticus, one of the few codifications of the forbidden not written by an anthropologist. The lists of impermissible clothing, marriages, and food had stupefied him, and it was in the context of this boredom that the goat had struck him so forcibly. "And Aaron shall cast lots upon the two goats; one lot for the Lord, and the other lot for the scapegoat." The scene had risen before him in perfect detail, and he saw it again now: the rude, mud-brick altar, the hot wind blowing sand, the two goats with their white bellies and nervous tails, the string dipped in blood tied around the scapegoat's neck by the priest's strong brown hands. Then the animal pushed out into the desert, balking, bleating, flinging up sand with its unwilling hooves. Jonathan had identified with that goat.

Sitting in his steamy kitchen, he found his sympathies had shifted. He no longer saw himself in such a sentimental, pitying light—and therein lay his unease. For if he was not the sacrifice, he was necessarily the one with the knife.

A Visit

The boat that bore Daniela was still a speck out on the ocean when Jonathan ambled down to the dock. He'd spent a slow afternoon listening to Scottish ship-to-shore radio, which tended to run along these lines: "So." "Aye." "You know the cow died." "Aye." "So." He was tired of the

taciturn north. Last night Heðin had stayed away, though
for once Jonathan was eager to talk about Daniela. But
Heðin had wanted precisely to avoid that conversation, just
as Sigurd, instead of chatting, had kept his head in the
potato bin while Jonathan bought out the store. Weather,
history, and village gossip were the only fit topics for talk
in their book; an anxious or excited heart was not something
to be discussed. Grumbling about this to himself only made
Jonathan more nervous about Daniela. She was Faroese too,
and, despite Paris, she was no more forthcoming than his
neighbors in Skopun.

He looked out to where the *Másin* shone white against
waves that were green on the crests and purple in the
depths. The boat's kittiwake escort was visible now, a chat-
tering halo announcing the estimated time of arrival. Practice on the few boats about during the chill, dull winter
had paid off, and he was now able to calculate distance at
sea—or rather to know it, for there was no formula. It was
a sort of natural magic, like reading the clouds, which in
these past months of rain he'd also been able to do.

Now the sun was out, and he could no more foretell
the weather than he could predict the course of Daniela's
visit. The *Másin* cut her engines in preparation for the slow
journey through the maze of jetties. In the silence he could
hear the kittiwakes' thin piping cries as they turned back
to sea in search of another vessel.

Jonathan decided to buy some halibut. Being occupied
at the moment Daniela arrived appealed to him. At the least,
he wanted to have evidence of a practical reason for being
on the dock. And so it was with a fish dangling from each
hand that he moved through the crowd to find her.

She was standing beside the boat with her small,
square bag between her feet, looking like any Faroese girl
on a visit: gray overcoat, city shoes, face pale from seasickness. When she saw him, her cheeks turned pink. "Hello,"
she said, "I'm here."

She was so pretty, with her fair hair braided around her head and her brass buttons marching down her chest, that he regretted the fish for preventing him from embracing her, which might possibly have seemed natural at this moment. But as they stood looking at each other the moment passed, leaving them silent and awkward.

"Was the trip rough?"

"Did you get a haircut?"

They had spoken at the same time. If Jonathan's hands had been free he would have tried to amend his awful haircut. "I was going to mention it," he mumbled.

"You look different," she said. "You look more—Faroese."

"Were you seasick?" He didn't want to pursue how he looked.

"Yes. I haven't been on a boat for a while. But now I'm fine."

"I got us some good dinner." He lifted the fish for her to admire.

"Oh, that's nice," she said. "You know, we buy fish in stores now in Tórshavn." She shook her head. "I sound like Eyvindur."

"How is Eyvindur?"

She picked up her bag without answering. Then she said, "Okay," which might have referred to Eyvindur but seemed more likely as an indication that it was time to leave the dock.

They walked uphill in a silence that at first seemed companionable, then made Jonathan uneasy. His head was full of unsaid words: descriptions of who lived in what house—but why would she want to know? offers of activities for the afternoon—take a walk, have a *temun*, jump right into bed; the final offer stopped him from mentioning the others. By the time they arrived at his door he was thoroughly confused. Everything she did or didn't do seemed to reverberate with meaning—but he couldn't understand *what* it meant. Now, for instance, she was putting her suitcase in the hall; did that mean she too wanted to postpone the assignment of bedrooms? And how about the fact that she was taking off her shoes and leaving them next to the suitcase? Good Faroese manners or an invitation to further disrobing? Had she said nothing on the walk because everything was understood, or was she waiting for him to clear things up, or, worse, was she bored?

Jonathan flopped the halibut into the sink and Daniela sat down at the table. Keeping his back to her, he began to clean the fish.

"Shall we have a *temun*?"

He stopped mid-scrape and turned around. "My hands are all fishy."

"I'll do it." She put the kettle on the electric ring and went straight to the crockery cupboard.

Jonathan watched as she opened the cutlery drawer, took the teapot from the cabinet next to the sink, found bread, butter, and jam and put them on the wooden board that he kept at the end of the counter. "How do you know where everything is?"

"All Faroese kitchens are the same."

"One of these drawers is filled with hundred-year-old eggs. The first day I was here I opened it, looking for a spoon, and I got so depressed I had to go out for a walk."

Daniela looked up from the teapot. "Last drawer on the left?"

"Does everyone in the Faroes keep petrified eggs in the last drawer on the left?"

She smiled. "No. But everyone keeps things they don't know what to do with in that drawer." She peeped into the kettle to see if the water was boiling. "I'm sure even in America that drawer has strange things in it."

"They don't smell bad," said Jonathan. "I expected they would."

"When you're done with the fish, there's hot water to wash your hands."

He turned around to look at her, a woman who had hot water ready for him. She was setting the table, her clear profile poised above the teacups. Months ago, during his bout of fantasy, he'd imagined her doing homey things like this. In his fantasies she'd been beautiful; she was not as beautiful as he'd made her, but she was here. He sliced off the last fillet. "I'm done," he said. Would she bring him the water?

But her domesticity did not extend that far. "Good. The tea's done too."

Jonathan got himself his water and cleaned his hands in the yellow plastic bowl that, on washdays, he used for soaking his socks. Stealing another look at Daniela, he saw her struggling to pour the tea without losing the lid of the teapot—a near-hopeless effort. "It doesn't stay on," he told her, embarrassed for all the cracked, mended, worn-out items in his house. This kitchen, with its dusty curtains and warped linoleum, was not a romantic setting; his bedroom, where the bowlegged bedsteads hunched against a wall decorated with a map of Nowhere drawn in mildew, was no better. "I'm afraid everything here is slightly broken."

"It reminds me of my grandmother's house in Saksun. That's where I grew up, you know."

"I thought you'd grown up in Tórshavn."

"Tórshavn is no place for children." She put two spoons heaped high with sugar in her tea.

"What about Eyvindur's children?"

"Mmmm," she said. "Eyvindur always does things his own way."

"So," said Jonathan. He didn't know where to go next. "You grew up in Saksun?"

"Yes. My father went to the *Løgting* when Marius and

I were still quite young, and we grew up in Saksun at my mother's mother's house. Have you been there? It's very beautiful."

Jonathan shook his head. "I haven't traveled much."

"We could look out over the whole Atlantic there— no islands to the west of us." She sipped her tea dreamily.

"We can do that here too." Jonathan broke into her dream. "We can take a walk to the Troll's Head—" He scrambled to his feet.

"I want to eat something first."

Jonathan dropped back into his chair. He had no appetite, and now that he had the idea of taking a walk, he was eager to go before the light failed.

"We could go tomorrow," she said. She took a big bite of bread and butter.

"It might rain."

She shook her head. "It won't. We can take a picnic."

"Fine," said Jonathan. That took care of tomorrow, but this afternoon and tonight loomed ahead of them. He was so overwhelmed by nervousness at her presence that he disregarded it and put his head into his hands and sighed.

"Are you troubled?"

He looked up. She was chewing and smiling. Her old-fashioned syntax made him smile too. "I'm tired," he lied. He decided to pull himself together. "Tell me where you learned to speak English so well."

"In Denmark."

"You went to university there?" She nodded. She was as tightfisted as ever with personal information. "You don't like to talk about yourself, do you?" he asked.

They were both surprised by his boldness: she blushed, he lowered his eyes. Then, feeling he had nothing to lose, he persisted. "Why? Why are you like that?"

"I don't know."

"I don't believe you." Jonathan poured himself another

cup of tea. He felt manly and capable all of a sudden, and he remembered that he had once kissed her. That fact had been buried in the heap of wishes and worries he'd piled on the image of her, but he'd done it—he could recall the texture of her skin, the dark doorway where they'd stood pressed together. He looked at her until she looked up at him. "I don't believe you," he said again.

"It's so complicated."

He waited. Something in her voice made him think she would tell him.

She drew a breath. "I'm a hybrid," she said. "We talked about it that night." She sighed. "The only people who are content here are people who have never left. Once you've been somewhere else, life here doesn't quite make sense. It's all so hard." She gave him a wan smile. "It's all slightly broken."

"I think it works the other way too."

"What do you mean?"

"Once you've been here, life elsewhere doesn't make sense. I had a long talk about this with Wooley: you know, the other anthropologist. Both of us had a secret plan to stay—to never go home."

"Jim was here?" Daniela's face brightened.

Jonathan winced. They were lovers, obviously. The perfidy of Wooley! The question of Daniela's psychology disappeared under Jonathan's horrible need to know about her relations with Wooley. "He was here in November. I haven't seen him since. Have you?" He thought this rather well done.

"Oh, yes," she said, cheerfully. "He's living in Tórshavn now. So I see him all the time."

Jonathan was astounded. "Living in Tórshavn?"

"He's working at the Folklore Institute with Marius. He comes for dinner after work."

"Every night?" It was more than he could bear.

"No, not every night." Daniela looked puzzled. "Often. You know," she went on, "it's odd that he's never mentioned his visit to you."

Jonathan nodded dully. He didn't think it was odd at all. Adding to his misery were memories of bragging about Daniela to Wooley. Oh, God, what had he said? Whatever it was, Wooley several nights a week had the opportunity to gloat. Jonathan put his head back in his hands.

Talking about Wooley seemed to have enlivened Daniela, and she bustled about, clearing the table and washing the dishes while Jonathan stared into his teacup. When she was finished, she sat down in the chair beside him rather than the one across the table, where she'd been before. She was close enough for him to sense the warmth of her body and to see the fair, delicate hair on her arms, moist from washing.

"So you like it here? Will you stay?"

"How can I?" Jonathan straightened out of his slump and looked away from her. "How can I?" he repeated. This time his tone was less rhetorical, and he looked back at her as if perhaps she could tell him how. It struck him that they had a depressing effect on each other. Their similarities, which he'd noticed that evening at Eyvindur's, were not comforting. This probably explained Wooley.

"People do change their lives. You said that to me, remember?"

"I didn't believe it anymore than you do right now." Jonathan spoke sharply. Neither of them was a candidate for change; it took a character like Wooley's to make external rearrangements.

"Why did you say it, then?" She sounded hurt. "I did believe it. I thought about it often."

"You're kidding."

She frowned. "No. You just appeared in my life for an evening and said that—it had a strong effect on me. You were a voice from another world."

"I'm sorry." And he managed to sound apologetic. What he felt, though, was pleased: he'd made an impression on her.

"You shouldn't be sorry. You helped me."

Jonathan spoke before he could stop himself. "Helped you to change your life with another, more appealing American?"

Daniela stared at him. "What are you talking about?"

"Wooley. I'm talking about Wooley—Jim, as you call him." He shook his head. "You really didn't have to come all the way over to Skopun to tell me about it."

"Oh," said Daniela. "Oh." She covered her mouth, but her laugh slipped out. "I would never—" The laugh broke through again.

"You wouldn't?" He reached for her arm and held it around the elbow.

"No," she said. She dropped her arm to the table, eluding Jonathan's grip.

It then occurred to him that she might be dismissing more than Wooley.

If Daniela noticed Jonathan's retreat behind a wall of politeness, she gave no sign. She was delighted by his ministrations—perfectly done halibut, a Belgian butter cookie with her coffee—and she was talkative, praising his cooking, exclaiming over the coziness of the kitchen as night fell, offering up tales of life in Saksun and asking if such things happened also in Skopun. Jonathan's brief answers were accompanied by strained smiles. Each time she returned one of these—and she had a lovely smile, shy and a little lopsided—he marveled at her stupidity or her cruelty, he couldn't tell which.

But he knew she wasn't stupid, and she wasn't saying cruel things, so after a while Jonathan had to conclude that he'd finally learned to sulk without being obvious. A poorly timed achievement: it would have been useful with Wooley;

it was counterproductive tonight. Not only did he have to broach the topic of his dismissibility with no prompting from her, he had to plunge into it without the fanfare of a "mood," which might at least have laid a groundwork for her sympathy.

Well, then, nothing for it but to be bold. He took a deep breath, inflating himself for his next move. He wasn't sure what it would be.

"Is there more coffee?" Daniela asked. "I'm a little chilly."

"I could warm you up," said Jonathan.

In the total silence that followed, the clatter of the door was remarkably loud. Then two familiar bangs, as Heðin knocked his clogs off in the hall and strode into the kitchen.

"So, so, so," he said.

"So, so, so," said Jonathan.

Heðin walked over to Daniela. "Heðin Dahl," he announced, and extended his large, coarse hand.

Daniela put her tiny, bitten-down fingers in his palm briefly.

"Daniela," Jonathan told Heðin. "Smith."

"What did you have for dinner?" Heðin asked, settling into a chair.

This had been one of Eyvindur's complaints—people wanting to know what you had for dinner. Jonathan glanced at Daniela to see if she remembered it too, but she was looking quizzically at Heðin. "We had halibut," said Jonathan.

"It was very good." Daniela recited this as if it were a formula.

Heðin nodded. "Yes, fish in the villages is very good."

Jonathan hoped Heðin wasn't going to start on a Life in the Village routine.

But that was just what Heðin had in mind. "You can't get fish like that in Tórshavn anymore."

"Daniela said so herself," Jonathan broke in. "Didn't you?"

Daniela nodded and looked, for a moment, at Jonathan.

"My next-door neighbor," he told her in English. "He comes over almost every night."

"Hah, you speak English together." Heðin turned to Daniela. "You've lived in America?"

"No."

"Hah," said Heðin. He was playing his part to the hilt. He tipped his chair back and put his hands behind his head, frankly staring at Daniela. "So." He let the chair bang down again and leaned on the table. "Where did you learn it then?"

"Down There." Daniela waved her fingers toward the south to indicate the low, loathsome kingdom of Denmark.

"I've never been there." Although Heðin spoke with pride, Jonathan heard a note of self-pity in his voice.

"Don't go," said Daniela. She looked at Jonathan again.

"Some coffee?" Jonathan figured it was time to move Heðin on to the next stage of his visit.

"I have something better." Heðin pulled a half bottle of aquavit out of his back pocket and placed it in front of Daniela. Then he flashed her one of his best wacky grins. "For you," he said, flourishing his hand.

Daniela blushed with what looked like pleasure, and Jonathan flushed with what he knew was jealousy—of Heðin's forceful charm that came so easily and was so effective. But before he had time to get worked up, Heðin kicked his foot under the table and winked at him.

"Now we'll all get stinking drunk," he said.

Jonathan was touched. Heðin was trying to smooth the path of love for him. And though it was a crude method, it had probably worked well many times—with girls who weren't Daniela. Jonathan leaned toward her and, in English, asked, "Do you want to get drunk?"

She shrugged, "I'll have a drink."

Jonathan took three glasses from the cupboard and gave them to Heðin, who poured rather modest shots and pushed them across the table. He raised his glass and declaimed, "To the Faroes!"

So they all drank to the Faroes.

"Now," said Heðin, refilling the glasses, "we'll drink to America."

"The land of the free," said Jonathan. The aquavit had started burning in his veins already.

"Why do you say that?" asked Heðin, a little combative. He downed his shot.

"We call it that. It's a tradition."

"We're free here too," Heðin objected. "We'll drink to the Faroes again." He poured a third round.

As he raised his glass, Jonathan was moved to improve on the toast. "To the Faroes, the gem of the ocean." This went over well. Both Daniela and Heðin smiled. Jonathan had a moment of uneasiness at stealing this line of praise from his country, but it seemed more fitting for an island nation. One could hardly call a landmass as big as North America a *gem*.

"Now you make a toast," Heðin told Daniela.

Daniela looked into her glass. Then she looked at Jonathan. "To our host," she said, in English.

"What did she say?" Heðin listed toward Jonathan.

"To me," Jonathan answered, grinning. He drank; maybe all was not lost. He immediately refilled his glass and raised it to Daniela: "To our visitor."

"What did you say?" Heðin sounded irritated.

"To her, we're drinking to her now."

Heðin enthusiastically drank to Daniela.

"You're not mad at me?" Jonathan asked her.

"What did you say?"

Jonathan didn't answer. Daniela shook her head.

"No more toasts," Heðin said.

Jonathan was willing to go along with that. Five shots of aquavit in half an hour was a pace he couldn't maintain. Heðin could, though; his arm snaked along the table in search of the bottle, which was beside him. "Where is it?" he mumbled.

Daniela put it in his hand.

"You are very kind and very beautiful," he said, enunciating each word carefully.

She began to giggle.

"Don't laugh! It's true. Isn't it true, Jonathan?"

Jonathan nodded. "Completely true," he said, in English.

Daniela stopped giggling.

"What did you say?" Heðin refilled his glass. "Doesn't matter," he said, "I don't need to know." He spent a minute trying to screw the cap on the bottle, then gave up. "I don't need to do that," he told them.

Jonathan realized he was staring at Daniela. He tried to shift his gaze, but there was nowhere else worth looking; his eyes kept snapping back to her face. "You are beautiful," he heard himself say.

She smiled at him.

All the aquavit in Jonathan's body rushed into his head at that smile, and his blood crashed in his ears.

"Talking goddamned English," Heðin muttered. He straightened his back. "Jonathan."

"Yes?" Jonathan slowly turned his head away from Daniela.

"Who do you think discovered your goddamned country?" Without waiting for an answer, he said, "The Faroese, that's who."

"Oh?" Though Jonathan knew this wasn't true, he wasn't surprised to hear Heðin say it.

"Erik the Red."

"Heðin," Jonathan protested, "Erik the Red wasn't Faroese."

"It wasn't him anyhow," Heðin growled.

"Leif Eriksson," Daniela put in. "That's who you mean."

"He wasn't Faroese either." Jonathan resumed staring at Daniela.

"I happen to know that seventeen men on his crew were Faroese."

"Seventeen?" Jonathan was amused by this number.

Heðin moved his glass around, then admitted, "Well, twelve, anyhow. We discovered Russia too," he went on, but he didn't sound as authoritative as before.

Daniela spoke up. "Now really, you can't say that."

"We went there! We went there!"

"Why are we arguing?" Jonathan asked. "Vikings went everywhere."

"Vikings," said Daniela, "but not Faroese." She shook her head. "Faroese never went anywhere," she said to Jonathan in their private language, English. "At least in Denmark they have Hans Christian Andersen to brag about. It's sad."

"It's not a fairy tale," Heðin said. "We went there." He was getting sulky.

"She didn't say it was a fairy tale," Jonathan reassured him. He smiled at Daniela, but she didn't smile back. She looked a bit sulky herself. Was it drink that made the Faroese sad and quarrelsome, or did drink just reveal their true nature—which was sad and quarrelsome to begin with? Drink tonight was making him elated, but that probably had to do with Daniela's presence. He closed his eyes and imagined her in his arms, her slight, warm body breathing against him. He opened his eyes and looked at her again. Then he looked at Heðin and wondered when he was going home.

"Have to finish this." Heðin picked up the aquavit.

"We don't have to," Jonathan said. "I don't want any more."

"It's not worth saving." Heðin raised the bottle to his bloodshot eyes. It held more than an inch of liquor, enough to make all of them regret drinking it.

"We always have to finish the bottle," Daniela told Jonathan in English. "Haven't you learned that yet?"

Heðin slammed the bottle on the table. "No more English!" He poured himself and Daniela another shot. "When I come to visit you in America, Jonathan, then we'll speak English."

Heðin in America was unimaginable. Jonathan tried to picture him strolling along brick sidewalks under maples and oaks in fiery autumn plumage, eating spaghetti and meatballs in an underfurnished graduate-student apartment: he failed. The little image of Heðin in these scenes kept floating away, rising off the ground or the chair and drifting into the ether, bound, presumably, for the Faroes.

From this he concluded that Heðin would never come to America, and that therefore each sodden evening spent with him was precious. His crazy grin, his Norse chest-beating, his useful courting advice—if he managed somehow to transport them across the ocean, what good would they be there? Jonathan suddenly remembered how as a child in Maine he'd once found a rock where starfish lived: rosy ones, dark throbbing blue ones, striped and speckled ones glistening in the waves. Laboriously he'd peeled their fierce arms off the granite and taken them home. By sunset they had turned the color of bones on a beach and were stiff and smelly. He got sad thinking of it and, leaning toward Heðin, said, in unconscious imitation of Daniela, "Don't come to visit."

Heðin glared at him. "You think I'll embarrass you with your friends?"

"No, no, no." Jonathan grabbed Heðin's hand, which lay open on the table: rough, hard skin, warm and strong, yet limp from drunkenness. "I think it would make you unhappy."

Heðin snorted. "Are you unhappy here?" His hand came to life and returned Jonathan's grip. "Hah!" He lifted Jonathan's hand up in the air. "You are happy here."

"It's not the same," said Daniela.

"You haven't been there," Heðin said. He put Jonathan's hand back on the table. "She hasn't been there," he repeated.

"But she's right. It's easier to be happy in the Faroes."

Heðin's expression softened; he looked like a man in love listening to someone praise his girl, and he nodded agreement with Jonathan. Then, with the quick and mysterious changes of mood aquavit can produce, he clenched his teeth and banged the table. "I get so sick of this place!" He closed his eyes. "I want to see the world." He opened his eyes and said, with perfect sobriety, "I'll never do it, I know that."

This made Jonathan sad again; in fact, he didn't know which was sadder: Heðin denatured and confused in America, or Heðin trapped in the Faroes. And if he was sad, Daniela, he noticed, was miserable, brooding over her empty glass with tears in the corners of her eyes. "What is it?" he asked, putting his hand on her shoulder. She didn't respond.

Heðin stood up. "So, so, so." He lost his balance and landed back in the chair. "Hmmm," he said, and tried again. This time he succeeded. "I reckon so," he mumbled. Without bothering to wait for Jonathan's *so, so, so,* he lurched into the hall, put on his clogs, and smashed out the door and down the stairs. He was making a lot of noise, and when he reappeared in the kitchen after a minute, Jonathan figured he was too mixed up to know what he was doing.

Heðin had something to say, though. "There's a full moon," he announced. He gave Jonathan a comically obvious wink and left for good.

Was the moon going to assure him Daniela's favors? Jonathan doubted whether anything could, at this point. She looked awfully glum. Maybe now that they were alone, she would tell him what was bothering her. The trouble was, he didn't want to know. He also didn't want to embark on the business of cajoling, listening, comforting—a kind of foreplay, but not the kind he was in the mood for. Couldn't he just skip it? After all, he was drunk and so was she: they could dispense with the formalities.

So Jonathan said, "Still cold?"

"You know, I am more like him than I am like you."

This was a surprising response to a pass. He mulled it over and decided that she had moved the game back to square one: cajoling. He sighed. It was almost midnight. Would they arrive at comforting, with its promise of physical contact, before they both fell asleep? Not if they didn't get going. "You are?"

She nodded.

They'd have to move faster than that. "What do you mean, exactly?"

"I don't know if it's the weather or . . ." Daniela trailed off.

"Or?" Jonathan prompted.

"A racial trait." She was still drifting.

"I don't understand." He made his voice as stern as he could. "You'll have to be more specific."

"It's as if we're ignoring the rest of the world. People stick to the old ways, but it's"—she paused—"it's *conscious*. It isn't simple. We know there's another way to live, but we can't change. And we can't forget about it, either. And we don't leave. So we're all depressed and unsatisfied." She looked worn out after what was, for her, a long speech.

Jonathan found this irritating—mostly because it was such a slow seduction method, but also because everything she said struck at him as right and yet he had opposite feelings about the Faroes: it was the prospect of leaving that

made him depressed and unsatisfied. "Daniela," he said,
"Have you ever considered that there might be good reasons
for staying here?"

"For you," she said. "They wouldn't be good reasons
for me."

"What do you want?" He was exasperated. "Chinese
restaurants? Department stores? Noise? Don't you understand—all that is addictive. I can't imagine living without
it, not for my whole life. I need it. Why do you want to
do that to yourself?"

"You think I'm not like that?"

He looked at her and knew that she wasn't. "You're
toying with it, just the way I toy with staying here. I'm
not going to stay and you're not going to leave, and neither
of us wants to admit it. We want to be romantic and
thwarted. At least Heðin's honest. And I think—" He had
to stop for a minute, because he was actually going to say
what he thought. "I think you're getting a better deal."

"Of course you think that. If you didn't, you wouldn't
have the problem."

He was taken aback. She was not as drunk as he'd
thought, or perhaps he was more drunk. "Good point," he
said. Now what?

"What do you like so much about this place?"

How could he answer? Why, for that matter, should
he? There was no answer that didn't reduce his experience
to sentimentality or mystify things that, unspoken, were
clear. Maybe not so clear to her. She was sitting at his
elbow with her face turned toward him and her chin
propped on her hand, waiting for clarification.

Jonathan slid his hand under hers so that her cheek
was in his palm. The whole curve of her jawbone fit into
his hand, and he had the sensation of holding someone's
life. Her pulse beat under his index finger, swift and steady.
His own pulse seemed to have stopped, and his breathing
too, as if his body was shocked into stasis by contact with

hers. Her eyes widened; before she could protest or even collect herself into any reaction, he kissed her.

He'd meant to kiss her once, to make a statement of his intentions and gauge her response, but her skin was so fragrant and smooth that he couldn't stop. Her ear, her nose, her taut rosy eyelid, her determined chin with its dab of soft flesh at the end—he kissed them all and then started again. Each time she tried to speak he kissed her mouth to prevent the words. What could she possibly say that was more important than this? But she was bent on saying something, and while he was burying his face in her neck, she did.

"Just for tonight."

He pulled away from her. The space between them seemed enormous now that he had bridged it once.

"I mean, this visit and that's all," she went on. "Okay?"

"Why?" he said without thinking. Then her meaning began to sink in. "Why just this visit? What are you talking about? No, it's not okay. How could it be okay?"

She shook her head. "I didn't want to have a conversation about it. I'm just trying to be fair."

"Fair!" Her elbows, her breasts hiding under her sweater, the notches of her spine that were visible as she bent toward him: he hadn't kissed any of them, and what was fair about that?

"I don't want us to make each other unhappy. This way there won't be any disappointment."

Whose disappointment was she talking about, though, hers or his? Instead of asking, he spat out, "Where did you learn this sort of thing, Paris?"

"Don't be angry." She reached for his hand.

He looked at her wrist, which he'd thought fragile and pitiable that night at Eyvindur's. "It's so calculated. Suppose we want to keep seeing each other?"

"Maybe you're right," she said. "Maybe it's best we don't go to bed together."

He was amazed. In less than five minutes they had begun and destroyed a love affair. And he couldn't blame her alone. If he hadn't questioned her rules, they'd be upstairs instead of stymied at the table. Heðin wouldn't get himself into this situation—and if somehow he did, he'd get out of it: one quick lunge ought to do it. Jonathan made a verbal lunge. "You're just scared. You have to know how it's going to end before you begin."

"You're the one who's scared," Daniela retorted. "You have to pretend there isn't going to be an end."

"If you didn't arrange everything, there might not be." His voice was rising. "Why bother to start?"

"I can think of some reasons." She took hold of his forearm and then slid her hand up toward his elbow.

He shivered. He was about to capitulate—but how had everything switched, so that she was the seducer and he the reluctant object? As her hand crept under his shirt sleeve and stroked the inside of his arm, he looked into her eyes where a miniature Jonathan looked back at him, still hoping for assurances. He wasn't going to get any. All he could get was the comfort of flesh and distraction from his disappointment. He pulled Daniela roughly into his arms. Her body was his compensation for her unreachable heart, and he wanted it.

"Okay," he said, looking down at her face that was pale with desire. "Let's go upstairs."

Jonathan dreamed all night of Daniela, thereby multiplying his pleasure at waking beside her. They were crammed together in his single bed; she clasped most of the eiderdown in her arms, a soft substitute for him. Her braids, which they hadn't troubled to undo the night before, had fallen out of their pins and bands and lay in lazy curves on the pillow. In his dreams she had been on the move—walking ahead of him, leaving a room as he entered; he was relieved to see her settled down in sleep.

She was a composed sleeper: no noises or flailing about. She was lying on her back, so he could look his fill at her face. Her face, though, was nearly familiar to him and still not quite beautiful. He tugged at the eiderdown: what he really wanted to see was her body, which he knew only by taste and touch. She kept a firm hold on the puff and frowned when he pulled. He managed to expose one breast. Her nipple was pale pink and very small, though her breast was a nice size. As if aware of being observed, the nipple curled even tighter into itself. Jonathan felt shamed for spying on it; he covered her up again. But he was restless. He pushed his knee against her side, hoping she'd move around and reveal some other part of herself. She didn't do anything except sigh.

He looked at the ceiling; he looked at the clock (eight-thirty); he looked at the other bed, where their clothes were tangled together as if they too had spent the night making love. He wished she'd wake up. He put his leg over her belly.

Daniela opened her eyes.

"Good morning." He pressed a little closer.

"Early." She tried to move away from him, but there was no space in the bed.

"You just rest, I'll do everything," he said, and immediately began to.

"Mmmm," she said. She was moving around underneath him. This encouraged him, and carried away by passion, he pushed right into her. "Stop it," she said.

But it was too late to stop. He felt her jaw clenched beside his cheek and her arms stiff under his as he shot through to the end of desire.

When he lifted his head a few minutes later, she would not meet his eyes.

"Daniela."

She turned away.

"I thought you wanted to."

"I said to stop." She was still turned away.

"I thought you wanted to," he said again.

"Never mind." She moved as if to get out from under him.

He clamped his legs around her hips. "Wait. Can't we talk?"

"There's nothing to talk about!" She was angry. "You always want to talk about everything, and you don't understand anything."

"What don't I understand?" She didn't answer. "Didn't you like it last night either?" He rested his forehead on her collarbone. "I thought that was nice, last night," he said softly.

"It was nice." She put her hand on the back of his neck. "We don't have to talk about it." She patted his head.

Was she patronizing him? He moved his head so he could see her. She was staring off into space. She ought to be staring into his eyes.

"I'm going to get up," she announced.

He let her go.

But out on the headland, where they sat on a boulder eating their picnic in pale new sunshine, he started questioning her again.

"Why did you say I don't understand anything?"

To his surprise, she answered him. "I don't think you know what the point of making love is."

Jonathan choked on a mouthful of bread and cheese; the world went into a brief eclipse as he lost his breath. He'd never heard this complaint before—but then, he hadn't probed his other lovers for complaints. A few had said they wanted more of his time and attention. He'd taken that to mean they were pleased with what they'd got, otherwise why want more? She must still be angry because of the morning. "I'm sorry I jumped you this morning."

"It was the same last night."

"It was *not* the same last night. You wanted me—I know you did."

"Of course I did. I'm not talking about that." Daniela shook her head. "You see, you don't understand."

He glared at her. "You'd better explain it to me, then."

"It's not something to explain." She lowered her eyes and then looked at him almost flirtatiously. "You have to show."

"So show me." He edged a little closer to her, excited despite himself.

"I think some other girl will have to do it."

Jonathan dropped his chin onto his chest. He had just about reached his limit. There was no pleasing Daniela, because there was no knowing what she wanted—in bed or out of it. And from her last comment he figured they wouldn't be in bed again. He appeared to have botched the whole business, though he'd been trying as hard as he could to do everything her way. She had a lot of nerve, accusing him of selfishness. He stood up. He didn't feel like sitting next to her. He almost wished she wasn't there.

"I could go home this afternoon," she offered in a low voice.

"That's a good idea." He didn't turn around. He could hear her wrapping the cheese in its waxed paper. Out over the ocean the sun's rays were short and bright: not yet one o'clock. The boat left at three.

"Jonathan?" Her tone was tentative.

"Yeah." He braced himself for a new accusation.

"It wasn't really right, what I said."

"Oh?" He turned around.

"It's that I felt alone." She paused. "As if you didn't want me in particular."

"Well, whose fault is that?" He was tired. "You made such a fuss about no future and just this visit. What do you expect me to do?"

"You could be *with* me. Then you'd have more to remember."

"That's just a fancy way of saying more to lose."

"Maybe losses are wealth," said Daniela.

Jonathan stared out to sea. Was he the sum of his losses, soon to be increased a hundredfold when this landscape no longer met his eyes? He turned back to look into her eyes and was surprised to see the glaze of desire on them. He moved a step closer, and she stood up. For a moment she was standing in his arms, then they were falling onto the cool cushion of grass, their green, cloud-canopied bed.

Swamped, flushed, speechless, they lay in the hollow their bodies had bruised in the tundra. They had bruised each other too. The marks of his teeth were on her shoulder, and there was a thin, raised scratch on his thigh. They hadn't really undressed. His calves were tangled in his trousers; her arm was trapped by the neck of her blouse. He lifted her up a little and pulled the material back into place. She flapped her hand in the direction of his pants but couldn't reach them.

"Doesn't matter," he said. Nothing mattered except lying there watching the sun drift across the sky and cast pearly shadows on her skin. But it wasn't warm enough to lie still for long, and goose bumps were appearing on her arms.

"You're cold." He draped his sweater over her like a blanket.

"Aren't you?"

"I'm pretending I'm not."

She laughed. "You are often pretending you don't feel something."

If she'd said this at breakfast, he would have been insulted. Now he said, "You're right, I'm cold."

She sat up and began pulling her clothes back together.

"The day is much longer already," she said, looking out to sea. "It's almost spring."

A chill went through him; it really wasn't warm. "Not yet," he said, rubbing his arms to get the blood going.

The walk between the cliffs and the village, which had been interminable on the way out, went by much too quickly on the return. It seemed to Jonathan that the simplicity of the landscape had simplified things between them. He looked at Daniela. She looked happy, swinging her arms and tramping along in his borrowed boots stuffed with a pair of his socks. He liked knowing she was wearing some of his clothes, though this morning, when he'd lent them to her, he'd thought her impractical for bringing only city shoes. He could see them, her warped black pumps, waiting in the hall beside his clogs, as if she lived there too.

They crested the last hill and the harbor came into view. Half a mile out, the *Másin* chugged away from Skopun with the afternoon mail and without Daniela. She would put on her shoes and board the boat, but not today, not yet.

Past Perfect

Warm winds blowing up from the Indies had moistened the tundra and made it soft and green again. Mosses shaped like stars edged every rock. New lambs, fluff balls who could barely stand, dotted the outfields, where wild orchids were coming into bloom. The puffins were cleaning their burrows in the cliffs; the skuas were scouting the grass for nesting spots. Each day leaped further into light—fifteen, twenty minutes longer than the day before. Only the brightest stars were still visible; they were leaving, slipping away to their summer pastures, and it was time for Jonathan to leave as well.

The complexities of departure were daunting, and for a while they screened him from the fact of it. He had a lot of stuff for a fellow who'd lost his luggage. Books, the eiderdown and its heavy striped cover, some sturdy blue mugs that had caught his eye in Sigurd's store (an improvement over the cracked flowered teacups in his kitchen), high rubber boots, all those extravagant sweaters, his slicker, his two-pound picture book of Faroese views: added to his clothes, this made a heap that would never fit into a suitcase.

So Jens Símun was building him a box. It was as long as a coffin, but wider, and made of new, sweet-smelling pine. The resin and the pale curled shavings brought a whiff of home to Jonathan when he went to check on its progress, which he did four times. This was no slapped-together item; if it had been a house it would have stood for centuries. Jens Símun labored over the dovetailed corners, the recessed handles, the inner lip that kept the lid secure, with the reverence of one who works with rare material. Wood: the malachite and chalcedony of the Faroes. Jonathan thought of the green mineral pillars in the palaces of the czars, and also of how many lengths of lumber once used as bookshelves he'd discarded because they were a little warped.

The day the box was finished Jens Símun carried it over balanced on his head and placed it on Jonathan's kitchen table, where it needed only a candle to complete its funerary likeness. Jonathan himself would do nicely for the corpse; the sight of the box made him ill.

"You can put everything you have in there," Jens Símun assured him.

That was just the trouble. Jonathan broke out in a

light sweat that made his back clammy and his head hollow. Looking around the room to avoid the box, he noticed the radio: it would never fit; he was reprieved from leaving— for as long as it took to build a bigger box. Wordlessly, he pointed at it.

Jens Símun scowled. He seized the radio, wrapped it in a dish towel, and jammed it sideways into the bottom. "Hah! Perfect." He could not resist congratulating himself on his craftsmanship. "That's a fine box you've got there."

"I reckon so," said Jonathan.

Jonathan and the box had different itineraries. It was to be sent by mail boat to Tórshavn, but there their paths diverged. Petur had a cousin-in-law who knew a man who worked on an Icelandic boat that fished off Newfoundland and delivered its haul to Gloucester, thirty miles north of Boston. For two bottles of aquavit, this boat would carry Jonathan's box across the ocean. The bottles had already been sent over to Tórshavn. Now it was the box's turn— for the boat was due to leave the Faroes in three days. Not so Jonathan, who planned a week beyond that to wind up his affairs and had yet to book his plane.

He'd laid in a first-class *temun* for Jens Símun: cake, cheese, jam, and the white loaf known locally as Vienna bread, which was used only for company. Jens Símun was pleased but didn't hesitate to charge Jonathan a good many kroner for his work. The wood alone cost as much as a handmade sweater. Jonathan wondered what Jens Símun would have charged to build him a new bed, for instance. Far less, he imagined. It was because the box was for export. Whatever stayed in the village was community property, even if it lived in a specific house. Jonathan was sending a portion of Skopun's capital—labor and wood—to another world. Such profligacy had its price.

His own capital—five notebooks filled with kinship charts, village anecdotes, recipes for killing and cooking whale, puffin, guillemot, directions to the best egg-

gathering sites—was not going to be entrusted to the hold
of an Icelandic trawler. The small bag he'd bought the week
he'd arrived held, barely, two changes of clothing and all
the notebooks. With a toothbrush and comb in the pocket
of his old tweed jacket, he'd be all set to travel—to Tórshavn, to Reykjavík, to Logan Airport.

Jonathan spent an evening packing his things and enlisted Heðin's help carrying the box down to the dock in
the morning. Jens Símun had painted what he thought was
a sufficient address on the lid: JONATHAN BRAND, AMERICA.
Jonathan wished it were so easy. He borrowed a black
crayon from the foreman of the fish factory and added: HOLD
FOR PICKUP IN GLOUCESTER. Then he had to give elaborate
instructions to the ticket taker on the *Másin:* This box is
going onto the trawler *Sagafjord*, which should be in the
harbor tomorrow, and then it will go with them to
America—here Heðin interrupted.

"Vestmanna Jákup, you know with the black hat; he'll
get it."

"So I'll just leave it up by the harbormaster's?"

Jonathan began to protest, but Heðin nodded to the
ticket taker.

"What do you think will happen to it?" Heðin asked
Jonathan. "Everybody will know it's going onto the *Sagafjord*, because of the address, you see." He grinned. "You
worry too much."

"Some things never change," said Jonathan, grinning
back.

He was lonely in his house without the radio and his
own bedding. The ancient eiderdown from the other bed
was just a sack of feathers with no quilting to organize their
distribution; he spent much of his first night under it in
battle. No matter how vigorously he kicked the bottom to
move the stuffing up toward his chest, within half an hour
it had all sunk down to his feet again. He gave up trying
to sleep and pulled the chair over to the window.

The evening star had set hours before, and the partial moon was faint against the never-dark, now-brightening sky. Great schools of mackerel clouds tinted pink on their bellies arched over the water. A rooster warned of sunrise.

He was looking at light he would never see again. The ocean that was a dark reflecting pool, the earth polished by new grass to a silver surface, the latitude, all bent light and beamed it sideways, condensed it into a new substance in which every house, electrical pole, and rock on the streets of Skopun seemed the essence of house, pole, and rock, absolutes planted in more than three dimensions. Jonathan had seen this happen before and he knew it was a trick, an effect of northern dawn; he could even tell himself it was done with mirrors, since it was a consequence of reflection. At the same time he was convinced: here at the top of the world reality was visible, and he was looking at it.

In the morning, reality took the form of worry about his plane ticket. He'd delayed making reservations not only to postpone leaving but to avoid Daniela. With one part-time assistant, she constituted the Icelandair office; he couldn't get around talking to her and, eventually, seeing her. Though he'd chafed under her prohibitions the first week after she'd left, he'd come to find them comforting. She was right: he wasn't disappointed, because the time they'd spent together had been sweet and they had no opportunity to make things go wrong. He wasn't sure things would go wrong, but he preferred idealizing the past to pursuing the future. He knew he was doing this. Knowing made him only more uneasy about seeing her.

Daniela, though, sounded delighted to hear his voice. "How *are* you?" she asked. "It's been such a long time."

Jonathan shut the door of Sigurd and Jón Hendrik's parlor for some privacy. "Well, fine, I guess. I'm leaving."

"I've been thinking of you."

"I've been thinking of you too." This wasn't exactly

true. He'd been rerunning erotic scenes at night and otherwise stifling the whole experience.

"You should have called."

Jonathan made a face at the phone. "I thought we'd agreed not to."

Daniela giggled. "I suppose you're right. But a phone call would have been nice."

Maybe he wasn't meant to take her rules seriously, but at this moment he was glad he had.

"So," said Daniela. "Do you want to make your reservations?"

"Yes."

"The same as before, through Reykjavík?" She was all business now.

"Is there an alternative?"

"You could go to Bergen and then to Copenhagen and back to America from there. There's no direct flight from Norway." She was rustling paper. "Icelandair is cheaper."

"Copenhagen," said Jonathan. The imperial capital, fabled for sandwiches and pornography. "No." He had an urge to see something other than Scandinavia. "How about Scotland? I heard there was a boat."

More rustling. "I think it's been discontinued. I can't find the schedule. Nobody ever used it." Jonathan said nothing. "So, I'll book you through Iceland?"

"Okay." His heart was beginning to sink.

"What day do you want to go?"

"Next week." He had to clear his throat. "Sometime next week. You pick a day."

"Let's see, it would have to be Tuesday or Thursday."

"Thursday." Jonathan had to stop talking about it. "Thursday's fine. I'll see you."

"Jonathan!"

"What?"

"You have to pick up the ticket at least a day before."

"I know," he said, and hung up.

Nothing left now but to pray for bad weather. And what a splendid spring they were having! Jón Hendrik, fumbling around in the kitchen reheating a horrible fish-and-potato stew for Sigurd's lunch, couldn't stop talking about how fine the weather was—and would continue, from all signs.

"The fulmar babies are so fat," he crowed. "That means a calm spring."

"Terrific," Jonathan mumbled under his breath in English.

"Stay for lunch?" Jón Hendrik flapped his wooden spoon at the table.

"I have too much to do."

"I reckon so." Jón Hendrik chewed on his teeth. "I reckon you are happy to be going back to your homeland."

Jonathan said the obligatory "I reckon so" and high-tailed it out of the kitchen before Jón Hendrik could depress him further.

In truth, he had absolutely nothing to do: nothing to pack, nothing to send, nothing to arrange. The Dahls were fishing and would be out overnight. Little Jens Símun had been over to invite him for dinner tomorrow. Until then Jonathan was on his own, with no radio, no book, and no desire to see anybody.

Not quite. There was somebody he wanted to see, though he embarrassed himself just thinking of it: the *huldumaður*, the ghost shepherd of the outfields. If he existed, Jonathan would have to keep a balance between disbelief, which would surely prevent sighting him, and eagerness, which might scare him off. So he told himself that his mission was a fact-finding one, simply to determine the *huldumaður*'s habits and habitat.

With bread and cheese in one pocket of his jacket and an old pickle bottle full of water in the other, he set out. He stopped at Sigurd's for a chocolate bar, just like the old days. Since he'd sent off the box, everything was like the old days, he realized, when he'd been shipwrecked on this island with no possessions or attachments. Jonathan liked the way this thought made him feel, which was sad and also impressed him with how life was as artful as a novel in its circularity and patterns. As he dreamily handled the chocolate bars stacked on the counter and gave himself up to a wave of premature nostalgia for the entire year, Sigurd ruined his mood by snapping, "Which one are you going to buy? Or are you buying all of them?"

"Oh." Jonathan picked a dark chocolate with hazelnuts and tried to put the others back in a stack.

"Never mind." Sigurd pushed his hands out of the way and began to stack the bars himself. "You don't know how to do it," he grumbled.

Hoping to make amends, Jonathan said, "I'm going out for a walk."

Sigurd snorted, as if to say, Who cares?, and put the finishing touches on his tower of chocolate.

"Just like I used to do," Jonathan went on, enchanted again by the spell of regret he'd woven around himself. We come into this world with nothing, and we leave it the same way, he was repeating in his head, building to a crescendo of self-pity.

"Pah," said Sigurd. "Haven't you got better things to do?"

"I'm leaving in less than a week."

"So." Sigurd crossed his arms on his chest. "And the house. Is that going to clean itself?" He shook his head. "And your friends. Are you going to bother saying good-bye?"

"I haven't left yet," Jonathan said.

"You could have eaten lunch with us." Sigurd turned away from the counter and rummaged in a box.

Jonathan blushed. "I'm sorry. You and Jón Hendrik must come to eat dinner with me tonight."

Sigurd shook his head again. "You come for lunch with us," he insisted, "tomorrow."

"Thanks," Jonathan said. "I will." He headed out the door.

"That's one kroner fifty for the chocolate," Sigurd called.

The fields were in full glory, dense grass teeming with blossoms, fat sheep strolling everywhere, a handsome cow or two guarding a calf, birds thick as rain in the sky. All the animals were bleating and lowing and screeching to each other for the sheer pleasure of it. Jonathan wondered why he'd ever thought this landscape was stark and empty. He must have been depressed or blind. It was junglelike in its profusion. Right here—he kneeled to examine the ground— were three kinds of orchid, a miniature clover, a fern that grew below the grass, something that trailed purple flowers like tiny sweetpea, the track of a sheep, and a puffin feather, white tipped with black.

But it was a little too busy for the *huldumaður*. People still came here to tend a patch of potatoes or catch birds or check on the growth of lambs. His haunts were farther out, where the cliffs were steeper and fewer humans ventured.

Jonathan stood on a big rock and surveyed the landscape, which repeated itself in water-rimmed fingers of green and gray in all directions. The big rookeries were to the northwest; he decided to walk southeast. He sat down on the rock long enough to eat half his lunch, then set out.

After an hour or so he had a sense of crossing a border: rougher, longer grass grew here, unclipped by sheep; the smaller birds—puffins and guillemots—had been supplanted by skuas, whose tawny, flecked bodies hovered above him, casting shadows bigger than his own. Like eagles, they rode updrafts effortlessly, just lying on the air waiting for something to happen on the ground. As Jonathan was the only thing happening, he felt edgy. He would have found these birds menacing even if he'd never been attacked by one, and the memory of those clammy feet on his shoulder made it hard for him to relax. Each time a skua's wings hissed above him, he ducked, though he soon realized that this movement only piqued their curiosity and provoked them to swoop closer for a better look.

The ground ended abruptly at the top of a rise, dropping straight down hundreds of feet to gnashing gnarled waves. It was a heart-stopping cliff face, and he had to sit down and hold on to a tuft of grass to regain his equilibrium. Twenty feet away, a skua standing on a rock eyed him. Jonathan ignored it and took his chocolate out of his pocket. The foil flashed in the sun as he unwrapped it, and before he finished opening it, the skua skittered over and snatched it right out of his hands.

"Hey!" Jonathan yelled.

It took off for some secret place where it could eat undisturbed, gliding above the tundra with the chocolate clenched in its tough, mean beak.

"Goddamn it," said Jonathan. "Goddamn it."

But there was really nothing he could do about it. He finished his bread and cheese, thinking all the while of the hazelnuts in the chocolate and how he'd rather be eating them. He drank his water, and on an impulse threw the bottle over the cliff. It plummeted in silence for a good three seconds, then exploded on the rocks below. He moved back from the edge, unnerved again.

Everything was inauspicious. He felt chilly and tense, and had the urge to go home immediately. The *huldumaður* wasn't going to turn up. The truth was, Jonathan didn't want him to turn up. As he set his course back for the village, he wondered if perhaps fear wasn't the emotion most likely to conjure the *huldumaður*. This gave him the shivers, and he started to move at a good clip over the tussocks and stones. The clouds skidding across the sky made patches of light and dark on the land, which out of the corner of his eye looked to Jonathan like ghost armies perched waiting for him on every hill.

Soon enough he crossed that invisible yet palpable border between unknown and known. Puffins croaked in welcome, and some sheep looked up from grazing and nodded to themselves, or him, as if to say, He's back. Jonathan slowed down a little, then came to a halt. And without exactly deciding to, he turned around and faced into the other world.

It didn't look different from where he stood. Maybe the sky was more mottled and changeable over there, maybe the rocks were larger and more jagged, but then again, maybe not. Whatever it was, the animals were aware of it: the sheep simply didn't cross over, as if acknowledging a fence. But the very air must be fenced as well, otherwise how explain the murres, terns, herring gulls who could go anywhere, and didn't go there?

He couldn't explain it. He took a few steps forward, inserting himself momentarily back into mystery. Was it a hum? What was it? What made him sure that he was not supposed to be there, and yet lured him in?

As he stood alert and watchful, he felt the atmosphere retreating like a tide ebbing at his feet, beckoning and teasing him: Here, here, just another step, come closer. But he knew that was a false promise. He would drown in it; he'd been gasping for breath in it not ten minutes before. It was neither livable nor comprehensible, and it was right there in front of him, defying him to make sense of it.

Jonathan stepped back. "Okay," he said, to the empty grass rolling away from him. This was an admission of defeat and at the same time a salute to whatever was lurking out there. Something was out there, whether it was a *huldumaður* or an eerie miasma engendered by wilderness or a potpourri of his own anxieties strewn over the landscape. It didn't matter which, Jonathan thought as he walked the familiar path home. Its identity was nothing, its existence everything, a proof that anything was possible, that even he could be saved.

Surfeited with goodbyes, Jonathan stood on the deck of the *Másin* with his little bag slung over his shoulder, wishing the boat would leave. His last days had been a whirl of *temun*s and dinners. People he'd never visited, or even talked to, had snagged him on the street or burst into his kitchen with invitations. He'd seen more of private life in this one week than in a year, and he'd more than once considered staying on—just till September, well, maybe six weeks— to take advantage of his improved position. Musing himself through yet another long and brilliant summer was one way of easing the pangs of departure; even while doing it he felt himself detaching.

The night before he left was reserved for the Dahl family, including Sigurd, Jón Hendrik, and Jens Símun and his children. By then Jonathan was stunned with the amount of food and talk he'd ingested, and he sensed that his emotions weren't up to the occasion. Their genuine sorrow at losing him didn't quite penetrate, nor did it stir his also genuine gratitude and affection. Everything had already begun to look microscopic, telescoped, sealed in the past. And though Petur and Sigurd did their best to make Jonathan the centerpiece of the evening and turn the conversation to his future, his ignorance on the subject equaled theirs, and soon they were discussing how many lambs they expected to slaughter come fall.

Harvests of lambs, of cod and halibut, would there be *grind*, would there be storms, would the *Løgting* finally outlaw Danish in the schools, how about Lisabet *hjá* Jens Símun, absent and pregnant yet again, would she ever settle on a husband? The talk was familiar and at the same time fantastical, and Jonathan went home early, pleading exhaustion and his by-now well-worn "things to do."

It was Heðin who managed, momentarily, to break

through. He was drinking coffee in the kitchen when Jonathan came downstairs in the morning.

"I didn't want to miss you. If you're leaving on the morning boat."

"I am," Jonathan mumbled. "Well, maybe not." Then he imagined a whole afternoon spent on a new round of goodbyes. "I am."

"Have some coffee."

Jonathan drank and began to wake up.

"So, so, so," Heðin said. "Jonathan. You will come back for my wedding next year. Okay?"

"I'll try," said Jonathan.

Heðin cocked his head. "You won't come." He sounded more surprised than hurt.

"Probably not." Jonathan's eyes filled up as soon as he'd said this. He bent his head so Heðin wouldn't see, but a tear plopped into his coffee.

Heðin put his hand on Jonathan's arm. "It's okay," he said. "I'll think of you."

At this Jonathan's control slipped, and he put his hands over his face.

Heðin stood up. "Come on. You'd better go now." He rinsed the coffee cups. Then he pulled Jonathan out of his chair. "We had a good time, eh?" he said.

Jonathan wiped his face with his shirt sleeve and nodded.

Heðin was tactful enough to pretend he was busy and bustled off, leaving Jonathan to go down to the dock alone.

Now the engines were revving and heaving below his feet. In a matter of minutes he would be gone. He gripped the railing with both hands until his knuckles whitened and watched life in Skopun go on without him, boats unloading, old codgers gossiping, the fish factory foreman directing the stacking of crates of cod, the clouds dancing above the village in the blue untroubled sky of June, and saw all this shrink behind him as he put the first five miles of ocean between himself and the past.

The ticket taker, who was not from Skopun, said, "Going over to Tórshavn for a few days?"

Jonathan decided to nod.

"Good weather." Then peering at him, "You're the American, aren't you?"

"Yes." This was not the ticket taker who'd been in charge of the box but the other one, who'd yelled at Jonathan for standing on deck in a storm.

"So how do you like the Faroes?" He smiled in anticipation of Jonathan's praise.

How many times had he heard this question, accompanied by the same smug smile? Realizing he would never hear it again, Jonathan gave the best answer he could. "This is a beautiful country."

The ticket taker raised his bushy eyebrows. "Beautiful! This is the most beautiful country in the world!" He stepped over to the railing and swept his hand across the view, offering it to Jonathan. "We have everything," he said. "Am I right?"

"Absolutely right," said Jonathan.

At the Hotel Hafnia he hung his change of clothes in the closet and took a shower, washing off months of Skopun. Now to get the plane ticket and call Eyvindur. But first he had to debate whether to give Daniela the present he had for her. It was the watercolor set, never used, uncovered in his bureau drawer when he was packing. Would she find it insulting? She probably painted in oil, when she painted. It was such a nice little set, though; he wondered why he'd never used it, then why he'd thought he would. An escape from anthropology, bought back when it seemed he'd never penetrate village life. He would give it to her, he decided.

The phone on his bedside table rang and Jonathan

jumped. He stared at it; he hadn't answered a ringing phone
for a year. He grabbed it before it could ring again.

"Hah. Aha. What do you say to sheep's head? I bet
you haven't had *that*. It's Eyvindur," he added, quite un-
necessarily.

"I was about to call you. How did you know I was here?"

"In a town the size of a thimble? In a country as big
as a teacup? How could I not know you are here?"

"I'm leaving on Thursday."

"I know that too," Eyvindur yelped. "I know *everything*
about you. I know you are coming to dinner tomorrow night
to eat sheep's head." He paused. "I think you won't like it.
But Anna will make some fish too."

"I'd love to come."

"Bring your fiancée."

"Eyvindur, I don't think—"

He was off the line already, as usual.

At the Icelandair office Daniela was efficient and distant in her ugly uniform. Jonathan could hardly believe that
they'd ever romped around together. He didn't feel able to
give her the present.

"Would you like to have dinner with me tonight?" he
asked. He didn't really want to.

"I can't, thank you." She looked into his eyes for a
moment. "I could have a *temun* with you after work."

Much better. But why couldn't she have dinner? Jonathan scolded himself; it didn't matter anymore. "Fine," he
said, "I'll see you at the Hafnia."

She was prompt, appearing in the dining room precisely at five. Eager to get it over with, Jonathan shoved
the watercolor set onto her plate immediately. "This is for
you," he said. "A goodbye present."

Daniela smiled and reached into her pocketbook. "I
have something for you too." She pushed a soft little package
toward him.

He was taken aback, and saddened to know that if he

hadn't found the watercolors, he wouldn't have thought to give her anything. "You're so sweet," he said wonderingly.

"Open it."

It was a pair of mittens, in intricate patterns of black and brown.

"I made them," she said. "I know it's cold in Boston."

"Oh, Daniela." Jonathan felt himself choking up.

She was busy admiring her present and didn't notice. "This is perfect, Jonathan. You don't know how nice this is. I can go out to paint in the evenings. It's so easy with watercolors. And I've been silly, I wouldn't get myself any."

So they'd finally managed to make each other happy, he thought. It seemed pretty simple. And she rounded out his happiness by saying, "I don't think I'll come tomorrow night. You would like to say goodbye to Eyvindur alone, wouldn't you?"

To which he nodded. And had the good grace to add, "I like saying goodbye to you alone also."

"Jonathan—"

Whatever she was going to say, he didn't want to hear it; he could already hear it anyhow: *Do you think you'll come back?* He stood up abruptly, shaking the cups in their saucers. She followed his lead, and in the small, empty lobby they embraced for the last time, a polite hug without the slightest undertone of desire. He felt ashamed for his coolness, and as soon as she slipped out of his arms he wanted her back to do it right. She was opening the door; he grabbed her around the waist.

"Let's have a better goodbye," he said, and kissed her till they both were out of breath.

"I must go," she said, disentangling herself, straightening her hair.

"Yes."

"I really must." She stood looking at him. "Oh—" she stepped toward the door again, "Farewell, Jonathan."

*   *   *

A free evening: as always in Tórshavn, Jonathan fretted at the lack of bars. A bar would be the perfect place to spend his last night alone, getting sentimental with a bunch of tipsy strangers. But there would be bars aplenty soon enough, and forty kinds of shampoo and too many people— he pushed all that out of his mind. He would go buy himself a murder mystery for the plane and then take a stroll around the harbor.

He was in luck. The stationery store had received a new shipment, and there were two Agatha Christies he hadn't read. He bought them both; after all, he had a long trip ahead. As he put them in his pocket he thought how odd it was that by Friday he would be back in Cambridge, where there was a bookstore on every corner, stacked to the ceiling with things he hadn't read. He felt queasy imagining it. Was it all necessary, the shampoo, the books, the six varieties of oranges—more than that, was it even true? Were his memories of lavish choice accurate?

Jonathan walked in a daze down to the harbor. He wished now he'd booked a passage alongside his box. Two weeks at sea seemed like a good way to adjust to the change he was about to undergo. The fact that Boston was barely twenty-four hours away from this—the wooden boats with their Viking prows, the sod-roofed shacks along the shore, and all the wild enormous landscape of sky and sea—was unbelievable. Maybe it wasn't true either. He sat down with his legs dangling off the pier and looked across the fjord to the shadowy mass of Sandoy, his island home.

He waited there for a swell of emotion that never came. He expected to feel regret, to indulge finally the tears he'd had to hide in front of Heðin and Daniela, while the gulls keened a requiem for his loss. Instead he watched the light change over the water and smelled the fishy, oily, seaweedy air, content to sit swinging his feet until he was tired enough to go back to the hotel.

In the dining room the next morning, making his way
through a stale piece of Danish pastry, Jonathan saw a tall
fellow dressed in khaki and with Hush Puppies on his feet
ambling along the self-service breakfast line. Something
about him was familiar—with a shock he realized it was
Bart, his old pal from the Army, the Air Force, the CIA,
or wherever he was from. He jumped up to greet him.

"Hey, Bart!"

The man turned around. He wasn't Bart. Jonathan
backed away.

"Sorry," Jonathan said, in Faroese. "I thought you
were someone else."

The man squinted. "You speak English?"

Jonathan laughed. "I'm American. Are you?"

A nod. "I would never have picked you for an American."

"I've been here for a while." Jonathan wondered if that
explained anything. "Well, my name's Jonathan." He extended his hand.

The man squinted at his hand for a moment, then took
it. "Ridgely," he said.

"Is that your first name or your last name?"

Ridgely stacked a couple of pastries on his plate and
didn't answer.

Undeterred, Jonathan asked, "Are you here to look at
the system?"

Ridgely shot him a black look and shook his head.

"Oh, come on. Everybody knows about it."

"Sloppy," said Ridgely. "Bad security."

"So, anyhow," Jonathan floundered, "do you know
Bart? Who was here last year."

"He's moved on." Ridgely bobbed his head at the
ceiling.

"Fired?"

"Permanently laid off." A mean smile flitted across
Ridgely's face. "Dead, you might say."

Jonathan was confused, as he suspected he was meant to be. "Is he actually dead?"

Ridgely wasn't telling.

Poor old Bart, with his terrible cough and his lax sense of security. Jonathan tried one more time, in honor of Bart's memory. "He looked pretty sick when he was here."

"Should've," said Ridgely. "Godforsaken place."

Jonathan couldn't tell if these two comments were connected, or if Bart had deserved to look sick on his own account. He remembered how free Bart had been with information and hoped he'd managed to die without help from the Company.

"Why are you here?" Ridgely asked.

"I'm leaving tomorrow."

"You said you've been here a while. How long?"

Jonathan giggled nervously; he was being interrogated. "About a year." He felt himself grinning, trying to make friends with Ridgely.

"What are you doing here?" He was as persistent as a fly.

"I'm an anthropologist. I'm doing research."

"Hunh?" Ridgely squinted again. "What's that? An anthro-whazzis."

"It's nothing, Ridgely," Jonathan said, suddenly released from the spell of Ridgely's interest. "It's just someone who lives in foreign countries. I've been living in a cement house with no hot water and no vegetables for a year and now I'm going home. It's got nothing to do with anything you care about."

"Don't be so sure," said Ridgely. Then he ambled off on his long legs to a table in the corner and began gnawing on his breakfast.

Jonathan had to laugh. If there was one thing he was sure of, it was the irrelevance of his hard-won knowledge to anybody in America, and the notion of the military taking an interest in the recipe for blood sausage or the length of rope needed to haul in a struggling whale was particularly ridiculous. As he resumed his attack on his half-eaten pastry, he doubted that his expertise would seem any more exciting to the anthropology department. Pummeling it into a shape that would make sense to them was going to be a difficult task. He shook his head, thinking of Ridgely, of Harvard, of the whole revved-up modern world that fed on facts, that moved ever forward, constantly kicking over the traces of the past. Those who couldn't keep the pace just fell behind. Whereas here, where life was circular, anybody could get the hang of things after a little while.

As he had the night before, Jonathan waited for misery to wash over him at this thought and was again surprised when it didn't. He couldn't seem to work himself up about anything. The comfort he'd found in the repetitiveness of Faroese life, his inevitable return to God-knows-what in Cambridge: these were simply the conditions of his life. No point getting into a stew over it.

He glanced at Ridgely in the corner, still bent over breakfast. Jonathan scooted out of the dining room. He wanted to get Eyvindur a wonderful present, and he knew that could take most of the day.

In the end, he spent the entire day on it with no success. The options were limited: a sweater, a picture book about the Faroes, various kinds of frozen birds—in short, stuff that, if Eyvindur didn't have, he'd never wanted in the first place. It would be better to send him something from America anyhow, Jonathan had decided, and mulling over exotic American offerings as he walked, he tramped for the last time up the hill to Eyvindur's house.

Eyvindur had shaved his beard.

"It was a disguise," he told Jonathan, who preferred him with it and must have shown this by his expression. "I was proposing myself as the artist, you see. It had to go."

"What does Anna think?"

"She misses the tickles." Eyvindur winked, grinned, writhed his naked face into a leer. "And the babies! They didn't know who I was. They hid from me."

"I wouldn't have recognized you," Jonathan said.

"Yes. Now I have a new disguise—the real me."

Jonathan laughed. "Eyvindur, you say the damnedest things."

"What are damnedests?" Without waiting for Jonathan to answer, he said, "You don't look like yourself either."

"Who do I look like?"

"Me!" Eyvindur slapped him on the back several times. "Jonathan, I missed having our important conversations. I'm glad to see you."

"Me too."

"Now for dinner we have the most specially peculiar Faroese thing—even more entirely typical than whale. Well, maybe not. First you have to burn off the hair with a candle, but you missed that part, because it's been boiling at least two hours already." He leaned close to Jonathan. "Do you want to try?"

"Do I have a choice?"

"No." He took Jonathan by the arm and led him into the kitchen, where Anna was enveloped in clouds of steam smelling of boiled shoe. "Look," said Eyvindur, lifting the lid of the huge pot on the stove.

Jonathan looked. Bobbing around in the pot was the head of a sheep, complete with eyes, ears, and teeth, though its color was a pinkened gray unseen on any known species of animal. Jonathan's gorge rose; he hastily backed away from his dinner.

"I don't know about this, Eyvindur."

Anna said, "I told you he wouldn't like it."

"The point isn't to like it." Eyvindur dropped the lid back with a clatter. "The point is to experience it."

"I can make you a little bread and herring," Anna

whispered. "I've got a nice fresh herring in there." She pointed at the refrigerator.

"Jonathan," Eyvindur cajoled, "your last chance to eat real Faroese food."

"I'll try," said Jonathan.

But when the head arrived at the table on a platter, an ovine John the Baptist martyred for the greed of the world, Jonathan thought perhaps he would not try. This, finally, made him truly sad. Life was just eating and dying, eating and dying, and he felt the burden of instinct, from which none could break free. The futility of all earthly effort—in the end you ate or were eaten, and that was all there was to say.

Eyvindur stuck a spoon into the sheep's eye and gouged out the orb. "There's a good piece of fat back here," he said.

Jonathan burst into tears.

Eyvindur let go of his spoon with its piece of fat and scrambled out of his chair to Jonathan's side. "You are unhappy because you are sorry for the sheep?" Jonathan shook his head. "Ah," said Eyvindur. "I understand. You are unhappy because in America you will never eat real food like this."

And although he didn't think he would miss boiled sheep's head in America, Jonathan knew that essentially Eyvindur was right. "Yes," he said, and he stopped needing to cry. "That's it, Eyvindur."

"Well, eat it now. Here, eat this piece of fat, eat some brain, eat up everything you can of the Faroes."

Banked back into the wind, winding in and out of clouds, the plane was struggling to break the tug of earth, churning its propellers in thinner and thinner air. First the landing strip, then the island, filled Jonathan's window. Soon, he knew, the entire archipelago would be a map briefly dis-

played on that small screen. But poised in the moment
before it all was reduced to an illustration, a topography
only hinted at by light and shadow, he felt the hills, bays,
and fjords with their wave-embroidered outlines, the very
rise and fall of the fields, in the rise and fall of his pulse.
And his footsteps on that country—though they went
round and round in circles—were each precious, each tread
known to him and, annealed by memory, visible at this and
greater distances.

About the Author

Susanna Kaysen lives in Cambridge, Massachusetts.